Precious
Little
Devils

EILEEN SHAPIRO

PAGE PUBLISHING, INC.
New York, NY

First originally published by Page Publishing, Inc. 2016

ISBN 978-1-68348-127-0 (pbk)
ISBN 978-1-68348-128-7 (digital)

Printed in the United States of America

Prologue

He awoke to the sterile odor of antiseptic and a severe pain that penetrated his very being. His piercing blue eyes, confused and frightened, carefully opened for the first time in three months, but only for a moment. The intense pain forced them shut once again, delaying his entrance back into consciousness.

"Tristan, Tristan, please try and wake up," a small, balding Indian doctor with a calming, melodic voice insisted. Gently leaning over him, the doctor tapped his cheek. "Tristan, Tristan . . ." Slowly and cautiously, his eyes reopened. This time, despite the agony consuming his body, they remained open. His mind, although slightly tainted by the medication, cried out to explore what had happened to him, where he was, and more importantly, what was to become of him.

Three months prior to his awakening, the doctor had decided to put Tristan into a medically induced coma until his soul could learn to withstand the hurt.

Chapter 1

The Selection

"Mon, pick your band already, Tristan," Jamison coaxed with his pro-nounced Jamaican accent. "We have all been sequestered inside this room for three days and nights now." Tristan ignored his plea and continued to focus on the video before him.

Tristan Bondage, accompanied by four other once-upon-a-time platinum recording artists, plus a young producer, had been assigned to a large office located in the heart of New York City. The room offered its inhabitants a large oval table, marble in design, adorned with several plush chairs for them to sit. Above the table loomed a seventy-two-inch flat-screen television suspended in thin air. The walls inside the room were painted a pale sage. Looking at the walls made Tristan slightly uneasy as it reminded him of the green walls inside the hospital, where he was forced to call home for nearly six months. Although it had been close to a year since his release, his pain still lived on as a constant reminder of what had happened.

Several minutes had gone by when Tristan turned to Jamison, who was still awaiting a response. "I'm not going to pick just to pick. This is a big decision and I'm not going to rush into it because you want to go home." Jamison sighed and slapped both fists onto the marble table out of frustration.

Jamison Brown was a popular reggae/rock crossover artist in the early 1980s whose songs reached the top of the charts. He was a small, slender black man who possessed an unusually heavy Jamaican accent. His face appeared kind, and he had an overly animated smile. His skin was smooth, and the only clue to the fact that he was fifty-nine years old was the long, gray dreads that framed his face and reached below his shoulders.

Adjacent to Jamison sat used to be superstar Billy Blaze, whose fame during the late 1980s was nothing short of epic. Dressed in a long black cape covered in rhinestones, he sat quietly biting the end of a pen. Although he stood only 5'6" tall in boots, his bleached white liberty spikes on top of his head allowed him at least another two inches. He owned intense navy blue eyes and a permanent snarl fixed upon his lips. He had a deep, sexy voice, and when he spoke, one could detect a hint of a proper British accent that had been tamed long ago via life in Los Angeles. On his next birthday, he would become fifty-eight years old.

Hailing from South Africa, the handsome Devin Liam enjoyed both a music career as well as several acting roles in televisions and movies. He stood over six feet tall and boasted a thin but muscular physique. With his boyish face and charming smile, at age fifty-five, he was still considered hot by his fans. He had long thick silky brown hair and elusive olive green eyes. The dimples on each side of his mouth were deep and pronounced when he laughed, and his teeth were florescent white. He wore tight jeans with a button-down shirt left half-opened, allowing the soft brown hair on his chest to be exposed.

The only female in the room, Delilah Carnes, was born and raised in Brooklyn. She started as a lead singer in an all-girl band. In 1987, she went solo and released a provocative video which lifted her to a superstar status.

Delilah was a petite woman with a large attitude to match her large blue eyes, and her large, full breasts. She had long, over-highlighted blond hair that fell down below her waist. Years of tanning had damaged her skin and caused her to look every bit of her fifty-seven years. She spoke with an extreme Brooklyn accent, but when she opened her mouth to sing, her unique, natural vibrato made her sound like a broken angel.

Delilah positioned herself in front of one of the windows in the office overlooking Central Park. With coffee in hand and tension upon her sunbaked face, she turned to Adonis, the young producer who was sitting at the head of the table, and whined, "All of us have chosen our bands, can you tell me why we are still forced to remain here while Mr. I Can't Make Up My Mind chooses his?"

Adonis turned to Delilah and glared at her, trying to control his annoyance. "This way, you can start to understand what your competitors are about and begin to strategize early in the game. Please try and exercise a little patience, Delilah," he insisted. Delilah rolled her eyes and took a sip of her coffee.

The producer of *So You Wanna Be a Rock Star*, Adonis Hartly, was barely thirty-two years old but was already well-known in the industry as creative and innovative. He dressed in a gray pin-striped suit, which accentuated his tall, thin, and perfect body. Mr. Perfect, as he became lovingly known as, had the looks and stature of a living Ken Doll. His dark brown hair was cut, styled, and perfectly quaffed. His brown eyes sparkled every time he spoke. Adonis was especially excited and proud about this production since he was also slated to host it live on national television.

Once again, Jamison turned to Tristan and said, "We are all very tired. You have viewed well over three thousand videos and performances. Don't any of them strike you, mon—"

Delilah, still sitting on the windowsill, grasped the chance to turn the knife in the wound and mumbled under her breath, "This is ridiculous." Tristan, having viewed her remark as a personal insult, swiftly turned his head away from the TV screen and faced Delilah. He glanced at her silently, just long enough to show his disdain at her rudeness.

Billy Blaze, who had been sitting patiently, rose from his chair. He walked to the front of the room, where Adonis sat, and stretched. He then exclaimed, "Listen, all, I don't know about you, but it's been a long, long time since I've been a shining star, center stage! I've almost forgotten what a spotlight looks like. Let's get real—we have all been chosen for this project by the grace of God. Face it, we have all been selected because of who we were then, not because of what we are now. Personally, I need to see all the bands right from the beginning so I can see what I'm up against. This is our chance to make it back into the limelight, back into the media, the public eye . . . and it's our last chance. Tristan, dude, take your time."

Tristan smiled and gave Billy the thumbs-up. Tristan's smile was contagious. His lips were thick and shaped perfectly; they had a natural pink tinge that any drag queen would have been proud to call their own. His starburst blue eyes could catch the attention of anyone standing across a crowded room. His head was laced with long locks of beautiful light-brown curls, which were somewhat messy and tangled. His skin was void of imperfection, and at fifty-six years old, he appeared untarnished by age.

Noticeably thin, Tristan stood 5'10" tall, but his unique style of costume compensated for his small frame. Wearing a long maroon velvet jacket complete with tails and a silver shirt, he looked like Prince Charming on acid. Below his attire was a body filled with a lifetime of tattoos, now ravished from his ordeal.

In 1984, he was inducted into a well-known punk rock band and became an overnight success. He became known for his award-winning videos and his use of special effects during his concerts. During this time period, the words *sex* and *Tristan Bondage* had become synonymous. Presently, along with his mysterious demeanor and heavy cockney accent, he still reeked of sex.

Feeling that he should echo Billy's motivational words of wisdom, Tristan stood up from his seat, paused the video he was watching, and very quietly began to address the others. "To my fellow ex–rock stars, myself included, I have this to say, I have not done a concert in roughly fifteen years. We have all been blessed with this marvelous opportunity. Adonis and the gods behind him have invited us to take part in this innovative musical, competitive reality show. We have the privilege of selecting our own groups to mentor, to coach to the win. Using our own experiences, we have the potential to create legends, a new super group, at the least, America's new rock idols. The possibilities are endless."

Devin Liam stood as well, eager to jump on the bandwagon, and stated, "This can be bigger than *Idol*, more intense than *The*

Voice, and more popular than *Glee.* The rock groups that we personally have selected to become our own have a chance to win a recording contract and a concert tour, and if our group wins, guess who gets to lead that tour . . . That's right . . . One of us. There is so much at stake here, not to mention the money we're getting paid to do this." Devin turned to Jamison, whose head was still wrapped in his arms on the table, and asked, "What have you accomplished in the last fifteen years, bro?"

Jamison slowly lifted his head off the table and lamented, "I occasionally perform at reggae legend concerts, I occasionally do a rock festival here and there, I occasionally—" Devin interrupted him in midsentence.

"Key word—*occasionally.*" Devin then addressed Delilah and asked, "And you, princess? Where have you been for the past fifteen years?" Taken off guard, Delilah struggled to come up with an answer.

Before she could even begin to speak, Billy whispered on the top of his lungs, "She hasn't been to the Botox clinic." He chuckled to himself.

Delilah instantly turned to Billy in a rage. "Nice, Billy, you nasty little prick," she yelled angrily.

Adonis quickly interjected, "Hey, hey, come on, people. The competition hasn't begun yet, save the rivalry. We are all tired and cranky, but there's no reason to be cruel. Let's try and be nice to one another, okay?"

Pleasantly astonished at Billy's evil remark but at the same time fighting desperately to suppress the urge to laugh out loud, Tristan refocused on the video above his head. Devin was shocked at Billy's remark as well and silently prayed for someone to break the ice before he burst out laughing.

Finally, after what seemed a lifetime, Adonis turned to Devin and inquired as to *his* whereabouts recently. Devin told of his marriage and then his divorce and admitted, "I've been running about like a lost soul, doing a concert here and there, and just hoping for something like this to manifest itself."

Turning to Billy, Adonis asked, "And you?"

Billy smiled and said, "I've been getting Botox."

"Smartass," Delilah commented.

Realizing that he would be called upon to confess his goings on of the last fifteen years, Tristan became terribly uncomfortable. Focusing upon the video at hand became impossible. Tristan paused the screen once again and decided to get it over with and speak up.

"Nine months ago, I woke up in a hospital bed, not knowing whether I would ever recover. I promised myself and God that, if I lived, I would greatly appreciate life and anything good that came my way. I was ecstatic when Adonis asked me to do the show. I felt a revival of my self-worth, which had been nonexistent for the last fifteen years. I was as excited as a child visiting the circus for the very first time. I'm telling all of you here and now, putting you all on notice, beware, because I am going to do everything in my power to win—everything! That being said, I feel that it doesn't matter what I did or didn't do for the past fifteen years, it only matters what I'm going to do now!" Tristan turned his attention back to the video he was watching while the rest of the room was plunged into an awkward silence.

Hours seemed to have passed by, when suddenly Tristan began to stand up in slow motion. He leaned forward toward the TV screen. A huge grin appeared on his face as he pointed to the video with his index finger and yelled, "Bingo!" The room applauded.

Adonis paused the video and asked Tristan, "Are you sure?"

"Yes," he answered, "I'm sure," and then added, "How hauntingly beautiful the lead singer is. I love their energy. They are very different."

Billy laughed and said, "Different! You can say that again, their guitarist is a drag queen."

Tristan, still smiling, replied, "Love that about him."

Adonis stood and said, "It's a wrap."

* * *

Precious Little Devils, the last band to painstakingly be chosen, were an unusual bunch of creatures, composed of four talented and creative, young, handsome gay boys. The exception was the gorgeous

lead singer, Brooklyn Michaels. All were unknowingly abc
embark on the journey sure to change their lives forever.

Sitting Indian style on her living room couch, Brooklyn was
deliciously enjoying her Keurig-made Starbucks blend mixed with
an Almond Joy creamer. She was mentally choosing a costume for
tonight's gig at Stars by picturing in her mind every outfit hanging
in her closet. The Devils played at Club Stars, a large gay nightclub
located in Sayville, every Friday night. It was one of the few gay clubs
remaining on Long Island.

Brooklyn decided that upon finishing her coffee, she would
select some fashion for the evening. In the meantime, she picked
up the TV remote and switched on the weather channel. It was only
9:00 a.m. so calling one of her fellow band members for advice on
what to wear was totally out of the question since the boys never
woke before eleven.

As she finished the last drop of her Starbucks, her cell phone
resting on the arm of the couch began to sing "Airplanes" by BOB,
signaling her that she was receiving a phone call. *Strange,* she thought,
who would be calling at this ungodly hour in the morning? As she went
to answer it, she noticed that it had been a 212 area code, which
would indicate a Manhattan caller. Her first thought was that it was
someone calling in reference to a NY City gig. She was excited and
answered the phone cautiously. "Hello?"

The voice on the other side of the phone was bright and perky,
"Hi! Have I reached Brooklyn Michaels from Precious Little Devils?"
the voice inquired.

"This is she," Brooklyn answered.

Speaking very quickly, the woman introduced herself, "This is
Katie Thomson from the new reality show *So You Wanna Be a Rock
Star,* how are you today?"

Brooklyn's heart automatically began to dance inside her chest.
She reached the TV remote and silenced the weather channel, then
replied to the woman, "In shock."

The woman laughed and went on to say, "Well, you have been
selected as one of the bands to compete on the show!"

"No way!" Brooklyn managed to say before the woman continued, "Can you be in Manhattan by nine thirty Monday morning? All the information, such as the address, the details, what you need to bring, and pretty much all your instructions have been e-mailed to you and the other band members."

"We'll be there," Brooklyn said, still in a state of shock.

"If you have any questions, you can e-mail them to me, okay?" the woman offered. Before hanging up, Brooklyn remembered her manners and thanked the woman profusely.

Scrambling to collect herself, Brooklyn immediately dialed Dazzel Diamond, the group's lead guitarist and token drag queen, while grabbing her laptop to see the e-mail. "Please, answer, Mary," Brooklyn prayed out loud. Mary was a nickname the band used for one another; as a matter of fact, Mary is a nickname the entire gay community adopted for one another. Dazzel's voice message began to play and Brooklyn hung up. She immediately redialed the number—voice mail again. Feeling the excitement of the morning, as well as the frustration of reaching voice mail each time she tried to dial, Brooklyn vowed to give it one more chance. She wanted Dazzel to know first, because she would be the one most excited by the news. On the fifth attempt at reaching her, a sleepy, incoherent voice, which could have been construed as a man or woman, answered.

Brooklyn began speaking into the phone using a high-pitched tone, "Wake up, wake up!" Alarmed by the manner in which Brooklyn spoke, Dazzel was startled into a more conscious state.

"What's wrong, are you all right?" Dazzel asked. Brooklyn began to spill out the information quickly and haphazardly, making her barely understandable. Dazzel interrupted, "Gurrrlll, speak English, I can't understand what it is you're trying to say."

Brooklyn managed to calm herself down to say, "The video we sent to that show . . . We're going to be on television . . . go check your e-mail—now!" A loud, shrill scream emanated from the other side of the phone, causing Brooklyn to hold the phone away from her ear.

"OMG! I can't believe it," an overly excited Dazzel continued, "I'm gonna pass out. I'm hyperventilating." Brooklyn rolled her eyes and told her to breathe into a paper bag. She replied, "I can't, I haven't brushed my teeth yet and I don't want to smell my own breath." Dazzel added, "This is large . . . larger than life."

Brooklyn had been pacing around the living room. She pretty much had finished with Dazzel and was now looking forward to waking the next band member and reporting the news. "Listen," she said to Dazzel, "you call Garrett and let him reach Colin . . . I'll text Damian." Dazzel screamed into the phone one last time and hung up.

Dazzel, a.k.a. Johnny when he's himself, was blessed with a tiny frame and large hips. As a boy he resembled Curious George with a shaved head, light brown skin tone, deep brown eyes, and thick, full lips. As a girl, she was magnificent. She painted her face flawlessly, and with her array of wigs, she was glamorous. She designed her own costumes and wore nine-inch heels to match each one. She had a spunky, vivacious personality, both in and out of drag; however, when in drag, she also possessed a catty sarcasm and quick sense of humor that any drag queen would be proud of. He had an answer for anything. For his twenty-seven years of life, he had been through a lot, but it made him wise beyond his years.

"Please, call me ASAP - Urgent," Brooklyn texted to Damian as he never answered his phone. Text was his preferred means of communication. To Brooklyn's surprise, almost as soon as the text was sent, her phone began to sing. As she relayed the awesome news about the show, she took it down a few steps and lowered her tone and excitement.

Damian's response was "That's amazing," spoken in his usual monotone voice, with his usual attitude of I'll-never-admit-to-having-any-emotions.

Keyboard player for the Devils, Damian Sixt was a very tall, large-boned, and a largely outspoken redhead. In the gay world, he was referred to as a ginger, a popular thing to be on the dating scene. His very red hair was worn in either a braid or ponytail; however, his hair was shaved on each side of that braid or ponytail. He had a thin red mustache and manicured goatee, and his face was equipped with dimples, a tiny nose, and thin, perfectly shaped lips. He was in charge of arranging most of the Devils' music but had an extreme passion for Broadway tunes. He maintained a pleasant smile, which he inherited from his mom, as well as the right to be gay, inherited from his dad, who had discovered his own homosexuality very late in life. Damian rented an apartment in the city and worked in the television industry by day. Looking at him, one would take him for a go with the flow kind of person, but after closer examination, one would discover inwardly that he was riddled with conflict.

Colin Gerod, at age thirty-two, the oldest Devil and the most logical, was extremely handsome. Having jet-black hair and sky-blue eyes, he stood 5'105" with a muscular stature. There was nothing to identify him as being gay, and most of the time he was quiet and well-mannered. He played the bass guitar and helped Damian arrange music, as well as doing backup vocals. He stayed to himself more so than any of the others as he seemed to own a deep, dark secret he wished no one to discover.

The drummer, Garrett M. Jones, was quite the little Devil. In the world of gay, he was considered a twink, which can be better defined as a thin, young, good-looking boy. He was funny in an outspoken kind of fashion and made fun of everyone. He was a trickster, and often played jokes on the other members of the band. He might not have been the sharpest tool in the shed, and he often lacked tact, but he feared nothing and would brazenly ask questions that the rest would never dare.

Garrett lived with his grandmother and small niece since his lesbian mother deserted him and his brother to pursue an alternative relationship after the passing of his dad. His light brown hair was fashionably styled and his constant tan showed off his blue eyes and the sparkling whiteness of his teeth. He had a caring heart with a good set of ethics, standing up for what was fair.

Brooklyn was truly a free spirit, connecting with all but committing to none. She was blessed with natural beauty, an abundance of talent, and a true artistry. At twenty-five years old, she was already an accomplished composer and guitarist. She also wrote for a prestigious gay magazine. She loved everything about gay and vowed to return as a gay man in her next life. Most importantly, she could sing.

She had an angelic voice that conquered all pitches and tones. Her voice was magical.

Brooklyn's long, blond, silky hair hung down past the middle of her back, extenuating her turquoise eyes and full pink lips. Although she had a tiny frame, she had the right amount of curves in all the right places.

Her warm, outgoing personality devoured all who knew her and consumed all those she would meet. Like everyone else, Brooklyn longed for fame and fortune. What she would end up with after the contest would be so much more than she could have ever imagined.

* * *

Early Monday morning, the Devils set out to Manhattan to begin their exciting adventure; however, at 5:00 a.m., no one felt adventurous. They had all been awake most of the night, selecting outfits and primping for their big day. Damian, having slept over Brooklyn's house, was now mandated to drive; after all, he was familiar with the city. The ride was conducted nearly in silence, partly because of the Devils' apprehension and partly due to the fact that they were tired.

They were to meet in an old theater located in the heart of the East Village. They were asked to check in at a desk in the middle of the lobby, and promptly escorted into the theater proper. It seemed noisy and disorganized as a lot of the other competitors had arrived before them. They made their way up to the front and huddled together in the third row. Brooklyn whispered to Damian, "Should we make friends?"

Damian responded, "I don't do friends."

Garrett asked, "Do we know who picked us?"

Brooklyn shook her head no. Dazzel, in a loud voice, asked, "Why are we whispering? I hope he's hot."

"Shhhh," whispered Brooklyn, "get your mind out of your bed." They all agreed and laughed.

Adonis, the young producer, took the stage and tapped on his mic to grab the attention of the audience. As it squealed, the auditorium grew silent.

With a huge smile, Adonis began his opening remarks. "You have been chosen because you fit our needs and because you all have talent. Each one of the coaches personally selected you with the highest hopes of winning this competition. Now, before I continue, filming will begin three weeks after rehearsals. You will be working seven days a week with long and stressful hours. The show will air for twelve weeks and the winner leaves with a recording contract, a world concert tour, and a television concert introducing you to the universe. Your coaches will enjoy the glory of the win, the prestige that comes with winning, and a large sum of money, and since some of them haven't worked in years, they will be fighting to win. Is there anyone here that cannot commit to the time required?" Adonis paused and looked throughout the theater. When no one raised their hands, he continued to speak. "Okay then, your judges will be various celebrities associated with the music industry and entertainment field. They will be looking for talent, creativity, originality, and most importantly, improvement. The sooner you get acquainted with your mentor, the sooner you begin to work with and trust your coach, the better your chances of winning will become. Each of your coaches has enjoyed fame during the 1980s," Adonis's voice grew louder, more animated and more excited. "The 1980s were the best years of rock and roll." The audience applauded as Adonis moved closer to the edge of the stage. "Let's do it!" he yelled, the audience applauded again. "When I call the name of your band, please stand so that your competitors can get a look at you . . .

"Band number one, Rising Tides, please stand." A young, all-boy band rose as Adonis continued. "You will be assigned to studio number one. Your coach is the infamous Billy Blaze.

"Band number two, City Girls." Five sexy girls stood in the front row. "An all-girls band," Adonis commented and continued. "Studio two will be your assignment and Delilah Carnes will be your mentor.

"Now, band number three, Blood Red Orange, stand please." Four handsome boys and one female lead singer apprehensively rose. "You will be rehearsing in studio number three with your master Devin Liam.

"Band number four, Sin-cerely Yours, guess which studio you're in. You will be learning from reggae artist Jamison Brown, now stand up and let's see who you are." Seven members stood together holding hands, and Adonis continued, "Last of all, Precious Little Devils, reveal yourselves." The Devils stood as the others gave them a once over. "Good luck to you in studio five with your rebellious punk rocker, Tristan Bondage," Adonis concluded. The entire audience cheered, including the Devils.

Garrett whispered, "Who?"

Colin answered, "He had a lot of cool videos and an interesting genre of music."

Dazzel interjected, "Who cares? This is so awesome already!"

"But who the hell is he?" Garrett asked again.

Brooklyn smiled to herself. "My mom was in love with him in the 1980s. He was hot, really sexy."

Dazzel's ears perked up. "Hot, did you say?"

"And straight," Brooklyn added. Dazzel took her cell phone out in order to Google him, but Damian beat her to it. He stood holding a picture of Tristan Bondage and passed it to Dazzel and Brooklyn. "He is still incredibly sexy," admitted Brooklyn.

"I'd like to kiss me some of that," Dazzel said, licking her lips.

Adonis hit the mic once more. "In a few minutes, we will be walking next door to the studios so you can meet your mentors. In the meantime, go introduce yourselves to one another." The Devils walked about meeting the others. Brooklyn made it her personal mission to meet everyone possible.

The entire group followed Adonis to a big building two doors down from the theater. It was an old building with class and texture. It was laced with gargoyles and faded brick.

The theater parade marched quickly into the ancient hallways as the weather was brisk for early fall. Some piled into the large, old-fashioned gated service elevator, while the others climbed the cement staircase two flights up. It didn't really matter, however, because they all wound up in the same place—on the third floor in the center of a tremendous hallway. The tall red doors circled around the hallway were numbered in black one through five.

Adonis wished each band the best of luck and proceeded to walk back to the service elevator. He walked into it, closed the gate, and was gone. Damian turned to the Devils and demanded, "Let's go meet our mentor." He led the way into studio number five and they followed.

The studio was large. As they entered, they couldn't help but notice the high skylight in the middle of the room, bleaching them with sunlight as they walked past it. In the back of the studio was an engineering room with a sound proof recording sub-studio. The main room contained several couches, two chairs, several guitars leaning against a wall, a white piano, and their mentor, Tristan Bondage, perched inside a wheelchair. Although the Devils attempted to hide their shock and ignore the fact that their coach was sitting in a wheelchair, it was quite a surprise.

As the band grew closer to Tristan, he stood up from his chair to meet them and they all breathed a sigh of relief. Tristan took a step forward and shook Damian's hand, then Garrett's, and finally Colin's. Relief encompassed the Devils as Tristan actually walked toward Dazzel. When Dazzel extended her hand to shake, Tristan kissed it instead. This absolutely thrilled Dazzel. Tristan then reached for Brooklyn's tiny hand. He slowly pressed his lips against it and held it for quite some time. He looked directly into her eyes as he was mesmerized by her beauty. Garrett, feeling this to be very awkward, broke the silence with a chuckle and Tristan released her hand. Tristan requested that everyone take a seat and then returned to his own wheeled seat.

"Welcome to studio five," he said with his heavy cockney accent. "My name is Tristan Bondage. I'm from London, as you probably have noticed." Smiling, Tristan continued to address the Devils. "For those of you who aren't familiar with my music, please become so, as your first challenge will be to perform one of my songs. We have only three weeks to get to know one another and to develop a sense of trust toward each other. We will be meeting seven days a week and working twelve hours a day. Each category will become more and more challenging and personal.

"I am hoping that your video is a true rendition of your talent. I'll be looking to you for commitment, dedication, hard work, and especially drive. Keep in mind nothing matters as much as winning. There is much at stake here, and I plan to stop at nothing to win. This is my last chance at being in the spotlight and possibly your only chance. Any questions?"

Garrett bravely raised his hand as if he were back in school and blurted out the question that the rest of the Devils were dying to ask. "What's with the wheelchair?"

Tristan responded, "I am recovering from an accident. However, do not mistake my wheelchair for weakness." They all laughed.

Next, Dazzel asked, "What if we suck?"

"You're out," Tristan answered. "Here's the deal. After the third week, the first band will be eliminated—that's sent home, the end. After the fifth week, another group will have to leave. When week number seven rolls around, a third group is finished." Tristan paused, and then went on to say, "Then, it gets interesting. The last two remaining stay till the end, both vying to personally win the hearts of the judges and of America. I want the world to become enthralled with my Precious Little Devils. Now, Brooklyn, let's see if you can really sing." Tristan handed her a guitar, and she nervously began to play.

Can we pretend that airplanes in the night sky
are like shooting stars?
I could really use a wish right now, a wish right now,
a wish right now.
Can we pretend that airplanes in the night sky
are like shooting stars?
I could really—

Tristan rudely interrupted her song, "Okay, that's enough. I'll see you all tomorrow morning, nine sharp. Oh, and since you are all from Long Island, we will find a venue local to where you live for rehearsals. I am also located on Long Island." Tristan then rolled his wheelchair out of the room. No one dared to speak until they heard the gate on the elevator close.

Shocked, Brooklyn, nearly in tears, wondered, "Was it my breath?"

Dazzel, also in shock, added, "We were just dismissed."

Almost laughing, Garrett commented, "How rude."

Colin turned to Brooklyn and reassuringly said, "You did nothing wrong. Your voice is beautiful."

"I think he's a weirdo," exclaimed Damian. He added, "Well, we're done here for the day. Let's go play in the city."

Colin reminded the group, "We have to familiarize ourselves with this dude's songs."

Brooklyn rolled her eyes. "I don't want to think about him until tomorrow."

After a quick lunch in the village, the band took refuge in Damian's city apartment. It was small but cozy. They started listening to Tristan's songs on YouTube and watching his videos. His songs were musically annoying to the boys; however, Brooklyn enjoyed them—secretly.

They listened to his music for an hour, but it became torturous to the Devils, and they gave up. The boys decided to visit one of the drag bars for a few hours, but Brooklyn stayed at the apartment and continued reviewing Tristan's songs. She thought about Tristan, and as rude as he was toward her, she felt a connection to him. For some ungodly reason, she couldn't erase him from her thoughts until finally she drifted off to sleep. Then all of a sudden, it was morning.

* * *

The boys scurried to get ready and the once neat little apartment was now ravished. Dazzel, still exhausted from the night's affair, decided to go back to the studio as Johnny, although there was still some hint of mascara caked upon his lashes. Damian and Colin, completely hung over, pretended to be wide awake and ready. Garrett's head felt twelve times its normal size. Brooklyn, though well rested, was nervous and uneasy about returning to studio five.

Garrett stared at Dazzel, now Johnny, and asked, "What's with you, run out of makeup?"

She shook her head as they entered the studio and she commented, "Well, here we go again."

As they walked through the big red studio door, Colin whispered, "Let's try and behave. This guy is all full of seriousness, and I don't want to blow the only chance we might ever have to be famous." He looked at Brooklyn and sensed her uneasiness. He asked her if she was all right. She nodded, but it wasn't a very convincing yes.

Johnny grabbed her arm and said, "Gurrrl, don't let him ruin that I'm-better-than-anyone-else-in-this-competition attitude. You own this, Mary."

"Good morning, little Devils. So did you choose one of my songs?" Tristan asked directly. Their spokesman, Damian, explained to Tristan that they had spent the entire night listening to his music but had not selected a song.

Johnny whispered under his breath, "Oh my, this is not going to go well." Brooklyn shushed him.

Tristan, feeling that they were straying from the truth somewhat, looked at Johnny and exclaimed, "The transformation is amazing, and I won't be kissing your hand today." Johnny smiled. Tristan's comment was merely an attempt to break the ice in a room riddled with tension.

Tristan handed Colin a CD and pointed to the engineering room. "Why don't you guys go in there and *really* listen to my music? See if you can choose a song. Brooklyn, you can stay here so we can try and get to know one another."

Garrett took the CD from Colin and commented, "Looks pretty thin." Colin shrugged and turned and headed for the room. He turned back to look at Brooklyn, who had the look of terror in her eyes. He asked her if she would be okay. She nodded, but once again it was a very unconvincing yes.

Tristan, insulted by Colin's inquiry to Brooklyn, responded to Colin by saying, "I'm not going to bite her, she'll be fine." Tristan handed her a guitar and asked her to play a song.

She looked at him and sarcastically asked, "Do you want a whole song or just a few bars?" Without waiting for his answer, she began playing "Burn" by Ellie Goulding. It was a strong song and a perfect way to show off her range and her voice. Tristan turned from her and pretended to do some menial task. The fact that he seemed to be ignoring her made her sing with confidence and determination.

We, we don't have to worry 'bout nothing,
'Cause we got the fire, and we're burning one hell of a something.
They, they gonna see us from outer space, outer space,
Light it up, like we're the stars of the human race, human race . . .

By the time she made it to the chorus, Tristan could not help but turn his full attention to her. Her performance became nothing short of amazing.

'Cause we got the fire, fire, fire,
Yeah, we got the fire, fire, fire,
And we gonna let it burn, burn, burn, burn . . .

He sat, mesmerized by her song and awed by her beauty and innocence. When the song ended, neither of them spoke for a long time. Brooklyn waited patiently for some kind of comment from Tristan, while Tristan prayed for the right thing to say to her. Finally, he just blurted out, "With my help, you could be epic." Brooklyn took that as a compliment and sighed a sigh of relief.

Brooklyn positioned herself on the floor sitting, of course, Indian style. Tristan rose up from his wheelchair and moved to a couch directly across from the area in which Brooklyn was sitting. "So who makes your musical decisions?" he asked.

Brooklyn replied, "We all discuss, but Damian and Colin do most of the arrangements. Johnny and I write the music and Garrett just entertains us."

He then asked, "Do you all do vocals?"

Brooklyn sat and thought about that answer. "Well, the boys can all do backups. Garrett and Damian can rap. Damian loves to do vocals, but he can't stay in key to save his life. Oh, and Dazzel can lip sync."

Tristan smiled and inquired, "How did an innocent little straight girl become involved with . . . with . . ."

"All these homos?" Brooklyn finished his question for him. "I'm a fag hag, a fruit fly, and proud of it. I love gay men . . . working with them, playing with them, they're creative, sensitive, fun, and hot. I plan on being a drag queen in my next life. I love drag. It's larger than life."

"Should I be jealous?" Tristan asked jokingly.

"Only if you're straight." He then told Brooklyn that he loved her energy. Both Tristan and Brooklyn were happy from the sheer enjoyment of conducting a normal conversation with one another. Unfortunately, the fact that they had been civil to one another would be very short-lived.

Tristan turned his attention to the engineering room and noticed the Devils laughing and obviously distracted from their task at hand.

"I don't think they're concentrating on my music from the look of things," he commented.

"Maybe they're laughing at your music," Brooklyn replied.

Tristan smiled and said, "If you don't make it with music, maybe you could consider a career in comedy."

Sarcastically, Brooklyn replied, "Funny."

Tristan was staring at the Devils and shaking his head. "Before last night, or today, have any of you even heard my music? Be honest."

Brooklyn smiled and answered, "Honestly, when I was a child, my mom was a Tristan Bondage groupie. She took me to several of your concerts. I don't remember them, I was really young, but I do remember her listening to your CDs." Tristan smiled. He was almost excited that Brooklyn had been familiar with his songs, at least for some portion of her life. He thought that maybe she might even like some of his songs.

He looked at her and questioned, "Well? What do you think?"

Brooklyn laughed. "This is going to be a rough challenge."

Tristan laughed at her answer. "Wow," he said, "that bad, huh?"

"Actually, I think your music is the work of a genius. Unfortunately, the Devils aren't geniuses—myself included."

Satisfied with Brooklyn's opinion of his music, he suggested that she head toward the engineering room and select another Devil for him to become acquainted with. He probably should have enjoyed her company a little longer as it would be the last time they would be free of conflict from one another for weeks to come.

Tristan spoke with and tested the talent of each of the Devils separately. As he finished the last member, the moon could be seen from the skylight up above. Tristan was tired and feeling shooting pains in his legs. He grew pale and knew that it was time to say good night.

As the Devils prepared to leave the studio, Tristan announced that rehearsals would be taking place from here on in at a small studio in a land called Sayville, located on the south shore of Long Island, not too far from Brooklyn's cottage. The Devils were thrilled.

Tristan yelled after them as they left, "I expect that by tomorrow you will have selected a Tristan Bondage original. If not, I will choose it for you."

The days to follow would be anything less than calm. Frightened by his approaching feelings toward Brooklyn, Tristan would become more rude and sarcastic toward her in hopes of masking his true emotions for Brooklyn. He would have to portray nothing less than professionalism and be strict and demanding in order to hide what he was beginning to feel.

Chapter 2

Violated by the Truth

"No, no, no!" screamed Tristan. "That's not how the song goes. You just don't get it," he raged on. The band stopped playing mid-song. Dazzel kicked off her heels, causing her to shrink seven inches instantly.

Loudly, she yelled at the furious Mr. Bondage, "We've been at this for two days now, maybe it's just not the right song for her." She pointed at Brooklyn.

Tristan bellowed, "Maybe it's just not the right singer for the song."

Surprisingly calm, Brooklyn walked up to Tristan and stood face to face with him. She handed him her mic and said, "Okay, Mr. Bitch, show me how it's done." He accepted the mic hesitantly and stared at it. He knew he could sing the song. After all it belonged to him. He wrote it and he'd performed it—fifteen years ago. He wasn't sure, however, that his legs could withstand the pressure of being upright for the length of the song. He feared he would succumb to the pain that was sure to manifest itself.

Until now, he had managed to keep his past to himself and disguise the pain from Brooklyn and the Devils. He certainly had no desire to appear vulnerable. He thought that if his secret was violated by the truth, the Devils might feel sorry for him, and pity wasn't an option. He didn't wish to expose his weakness as he felt his affliction would put the Devils at a disadvantage. As a mentor, Tristan needed and demanded respect in order to coach his team to the highest level. But who would respect someone weak and chained to a wheelchair? It was his job as a coach to lend confidence to his group, but how could someone disabled instill confidence in anyone?

Tristan continued to look at the mic as if he had seen it for the first time. The band waited in silence for his next move as Tristan pondered his challenge. Finally he said to himself out loud, "Why not, fuck it, let's go." The band looked at one another and shrugged. "Let's go, Damian," he said and counted down. "Four, three, two, one . . ." and the Devils began to play his song. For a second, Tristan hesitated as the memories of twenty years ago came flooding back to him. He felt as though he was preparing for a concert, like old times so long ago. He sang his song with his heart, leaving Brooklyn in awe. Listening to him sing, the Devils realized he was truly an entertainer. Watching him perform his song encouraged the Devils more than Tristan deemed it possible.

When it came to the instrumental portion of the song, he motioned for Brooklyn to stand at his side. He borrowed Dazzel's microphone and handed it to Brooklyn. He whispered, "Sing with me, love." They began to sing together, and it was magical. The two felt a connection as their voices became one, their harmony came natural. They sounded like angels singing in a choir together. Tristan knew that Brooklyn felt their connection and when the song ended, he smiled and said to her, "Music will do that to you." She felt what he meant. Tristan remained standing long after the song ended. Strangely enough he hadn't noticed the pain.

* * *

The emotional day had finally come to an end. Exhausted, the Devils couldn't wait to leave the studio and relax at home, in a bar, at dinner, anywhere that wasn't here. Cordially, Brooklyn asked Tristan what his plans for the evening were. She had felt that after their heartfelt duet she earned the right to be friendly. She thought it was polite conversation to inquire as to where he would be going for dinner. He looked at her, smiled, and told her, "Don't you worry about it."

Taken back by his smug answer, she just glared at him. Her feelings were hurt by his nasty answer, and for a moment, Brooklyn felt a pang of jealousy not knowing his whereabouts. Then, quickly, she recovered and decided, rather than jealousy, it was annoyance at his rudeness that she felt, especially when she was trying to be civil.

* * *

Using a sparkling silver cane, Tristan made his way into a small, intimate cafe in the town of Sayville. His cane matched his look—sexy and mysterious rather than handicapped and afflicted. He walked over to a table in the corner of the room where a tall, handsome rocker type stood and hugged him briefly.

Terence was Tristan's physical therapist as well as his very close friend. He had been his only friend through his long hospital stay, visiting him each day as both medical personnel and as a buddy. Terence was most probably the reason that Tristan was now able to walk. He knew the real Tristan, the warm, kind, and brave person he hid so well from the Devils.

Tall, muscular, and also hailing from England, Terence had long dark-brown hair and dark-brown eyes. He had a thin mustache and warm smile. Recently, he had gone through a messy divorce that he claimed, if it wasn't for Tristan supporting him emotionally, he might have killed himself. Although the two saw each other nearly every day for Tristan's therapy, they enjoyed socializing as well.

The two ordered a bottle of wine and some appetizers and enjoyed some small talk. "So how are your pupils?" Terence inquired.

Tristan smiled and rolled his eyes. "My pupils, as you call them, are good, really good. They are good enough to teach me a thing or two." He remembered the day's events in his mind. "The hardest part of this whole thing is staying professional. I find myself wishing desperately to join in on their camaraderie, and Brooklyn, the lead singer, she has my heart. She's just amazing . . . beautiful and talented . . . I fantasize about what I would do for her if she were mine. I long to write songs about her and shower her with expensive gifts. Instead, I just yell at her like a tyrant."

Terence looked at him and laughed. "Why?" he asked.

A look of sadness came upon Tristan's face as he answered, "I have to protect myself from her. I might do something stupid, like fall in love."

"Wow," Terence said. "It sounds like it might already be too late for that. Why not go for it, even you deserve to be happy." The two laughed, "Well?" Terence asked again.

Tristan, sadly smiling, shook his head. "I'm more than double her age, I'm half-crippled and always in pain. She's young and beautiful and truly a free spirit. I have nothing good to offer her. Besides, I've known her for such a short time."

Terence insisted, "Haven't you ever heard of love at first sight?"

Tristan laughed. "More like love at first fight."

"Tristan," said Terence, "you are an amazing person, kind, generous, brave, and still considered one of the sexiest men on Earth. I'm sure no woman would throw you out of their bed. Besides, you are a famous rock star. Doesn't she know who you are?"

Tristan laughed and replied, "She knows who I was."

* * *

Meanwhile in another corner of the Earth (Queens, New York, to be exact), Billy Blaze and his group, Rising Tides, were having a blast. He mentored his band through laughter and good times. Each night after rehearsals, he would take the Tides out for dinner to discuss and laugh about the funny parts of the day. The Rising Tides were a young band. All were good-looking and slightly inexperienced musically. Billy recognized the opportunity to mold them into what he thought they should be in order to win the competition. Perhaps his strategy would work for him, but regardless and in the meantime, he and his band were having fun. The five members of the group were young; as a matter of fact, their lead singer was still finishing his senior year of high school. They were lovingly nicknamed the baby boy band by others, and although mere babies, they were talented enough and would prove to be worthy contenders.

City Girls, the only all-girls band, consisted of five members, twenty-five to twenty-nine. Their vocals were strong; r instrumental ability was weak. What they lacked in musical talent, they made up for in seductive appearance. Delilah Carnes counted on their presence to keep them in the competition.

Jamison Brown's Sin-cerely Yours had a special sound. Their strength lay in the rap. Consisting of three Jamaican females and four Hispanic males, their style resembled that of rhythm and blues with a Latino twist. The seven members of Sin-cerely adored their mentor. Jamison was kind, low-key, and relaxed—perhaps a little too relaxed to clinch the win.

Blood Red Orange would quickly become the favorites as their coach, Devin Liam, was by far the most popular mentor. Like the Devils, the lead singer was female and the rest of the band were male. Like the Devils, the lead singer was vivacious and strong on vocals. Unlike the Devils, Blood Red loved their mentor. Each day they were excited to arrive at rehearsals in their studio, which remained in New York City.

* * *

When the Devils entered the studio the next morning, they were pleased and temporarily relieved to find Tristan not yet present. Brooklyn smiled and announced hopefully, "Maybe he's dead."

Colin laughed and asked her, "Ready to be yelled at and insulted again?"

"Funny," Brooklyn answered. "Why don't any of you guys get yelled at or insulted?" she questioned.

Garrett, laughing as well, responded, "You're special."

"Maybe he just hates women," Damian said with conviction.

Dazzel rejected Damian's comment and said, "Nope, he doesn't hate women, just the opposite. He's in love with Brooklyn."

"Oh yeah, I can tell by his rudeness." Brooklyn laughed.

Still laughing, Garrett teasingly added, "Maybe you like him too. After all, how did you put it?—'he's incredibly sexy.'"

Brooklyn rolled her eyes. "Enough, Mary." Their laughter and camaraderie swiftly came to a halt as Tristan entered the room.

"So sorry I'm late," Tristan said apologetically. Without even a smile he announced, "We will be taking a road trip today. We have been rehearsing for over a week now and the producers have decided that it's time to check out our competitors, and it's time for our producers to check us out. There is a white van waiting for us outside to transport us to a venue close to your hearts. The producers have borrowed Stars, your venue, so you should have some semblance of comfort. Now let's go." The Devils walked out to the van and piled inside. They left the passenger side available for Tristan; no one really wanted to sit next to him anyway.

When they arrived, they paraded into Stars with a feeling of confidence that marched along with them. Stars was a large four-thousand-square-foot nightclub equipped with a granite bar, a large stage, a DJ booth, sound system, and techno lighting system. The club came alive each weekend with strobes, lights, music, and hundreds of gay kids of all ages safely able to dance the night away. However, by day, it was just a space.

When all the bands and mentors had made it to Stars, Adonis ran on stage, all pumped up, bright-eyed, and animated. "Bands, mentors, it's time to meet your matches. Today, we borrowed the venue belonging to Precious Little Devils. However, at the end of next week, Blood Red Orange will be our hosts. Therefore, for now, Blood Red, come take the stage and show us what you've got!" Adonis demanded.

One by one, the Blood Red members climbed onto the stage. They took their places by their instruments of choice and prepared to rock the stage with one of Devin Liam's biggest hits. Their performance was flawless and applauded by all, including Adonis.

As they exited the stage to make room for City Girls, the next band up, Brooklyn noticed that their performances were being videoed. After hearing Blood Red's perfect performance and realizing how important their song really was, she became nervous and apprehensive. Tristan's eyes never left Brooklyn for a second. He sensed her uneasiness and sat down next to her; however, Tristan wasn't the only one noticing her. The handsome Billy Blaze moved from the opposite side of the room over to Brooklyn and sat on her other side. "Hey, little girl. Don't be so nervous," Billy said to her. Brooklyn smiled. He extended his hand and nobly introduced himself. Brooklyn shook his hand and told him her name. Tristan was annoyed. He watched on as

Billy continued to flirt with *his* lead singer and put her at ease. Deep in his heart, Tristan wished he could put his arms around Brooklyn and hold her close instead of observing Billy put the moves on her. Logically, he realized he would have to come up with something very wise in order to comfort her instead of just sitting there and letting Billy take over.

Suddenly, without warning, Billy put his arms around Brooklyn and hugged her. It was all Tristan could do not to choke him. Luckily, his band was called to the stage and he felt inclined to direct their performance. After all, he was their coach. Tristan moved closer to Brooklyn and put his arm around her. She was now more nervous than ever, but not because of the pending performance. Tristan whispered in her ear, "Just pretend we're singing it together, like we did last night." Brooklyn could only nod. Inwardly, she noticed the tenderness in Tristan's voice as he advised and comforted her. He rubbed her shoulder with his hand. Strangely enough, Brooklyn enjoyed his touch. She actually felt chills going up and down her spine.

City Girls and Sin-cerely Yours were less than mediocre. Brooklyn was convinced that neither group at this point of the competition would pose much of a threat. Rising Tides were good. Garrett made his way over to Brooklyn and commented, "Look at all those cute little boys."

Brooklyn replied, "Yes, Garrett. All these cute little straight boys." The Tides left the stage content with their performance. Adonis summoned the Devils to the stage.

As Brooklyn left her seat to take the stage, Tristan took her hand in his and said, "Brooklyn, this is your stage and it's a Friday night. All your little gay fans are standing around you as they do each week." He winked at her, still holding her hand, and said, "You own this, now go kill it." Tristan might have been mean, but he was a good coach, and his motivation at the last minute was magical.

The Devils delivered. They too were flawless on stage. Brooklyn performed Tristan's song with the magic of the night before when they sang it together. She had followed Tristan's advice and pretended she was singing along with him for her Friday-night fans. Tristan was proud of his Devils and extra happy with Brooklyn's effort. From the corner of her eye, Brooklyn saw Tristan smiling as he applauded. As she left the stage, she expected some words of encouragement from Tristan, perhaps even a compliment, but when she passed him, he was silent.

The lead singer from Blood Red Orange greeted Brooklyn and told her what a great job she did. "We are scared of you guys!" she added.

"Thank you," Brooklyn said, "and we are scared of you guys as well."

The lead singer from Blood Red was a tall pretty brunette named Joy. Joy asked Brooklyn how she liked working with the rebellious Tristan Bondage. Brooklyn looked over at Tristan, who, although just saved her life, hadn't even congratulated her on her magnificent showmanship. Her answer to Joy was, "I hate him."

Surprised and taken back by her answer, she said, "Really? That's too bad. We love Devin."

"You're lucky. Tristan is mean."

Joy, trying to be positive, asked, "Well, are you learning anything?"

Brooklyn snapped, "Yes, how to hate music."

Joy laughed and added, "Well, you certainly couldn't tell from your performance."

Brooklyn had the urge to hug Joy, so she did and said, "Thank you, I really appreciate that."

"Brooklyn," Tristan called and motioned for her to come over to him.

"Coming!" she yelled. She said good-bye to Joy and walked over to Tristan to see what kind of criticism her mentor would offer. Tristan looked at Brooklyn, who stood before him.

She was still hoping for some words of encouragement, but instead Tristan commented, "Fraternizing with the enemy?"

Now totally angered by his lack of praise, she answered, "The 'enemy' was telling me what a great job I did, unlike my coach. You know, every so often, a person likes to be appreciated, even by the 'enemy.'" She turned to walk away from him, still furious.

Tristan grabbed her arm, realizing that he had been a jerk, and said, "Look, you were spectacular."

Unfortunately, it was too little too late. She glared at him, freed herself from his grip, and walked away. Standing and observing Tristan, Dazzel said, "If looks could kill." Tristan looked at the queen as she continued, "You better repent."

He looked at the queen and said, "And the war rages on."

As Brooklyn prepared to leave the club, Billy walked over to her and asked, "So what did you think of the other bands, beautiful?"

Tristan came up behind Brooklyn and, as he looked straight into Billy's eyes, said, "My team doesn't comment on the other competitors." Tristan turned to Brooklyn and demanded she head toward the van along with the rest of the Devils. Damian innocently asked if it was cool to wish the others good luck. Tristan glared at him and responded, "We're done here, let's go.

Dazzel whispered to Brooklyn, imitating Tristan's British accent, "By golly, love, I think he's jealous!" They both laughed uncontrollably as they entered the white van.

On the ride back to the studio, Dazzel and Brooklyn's laughter became contagious to everyone, except Tristan. He remained stone-faced and silent until their return to the studio.

Knowing they had done well during their performance and still recovering from their laughter, they began happily packing up to leave, assuming the day had ended. "Where do you all think you are going?" barked Tristan.

Dazzel answered pleadingly, "Tristan, it's been a long day, it's Friday and we have to go back to Stars and play tonight, so we all just thought we were finished for the day."

Tristan, sarcastically mocking her words, replied, "Oh, we were amazing today, I thought we were finished! That attitude will win nothing!" he added.

Brooklyn, puzzled, asked Tristan, "Why are you so angry? I sort of thought today was a small victory."

"A victory!" Tristan exploded. "A victory!" he repeated. "The competition hasn't even begun yet. Yes, you were good today, but you were also lucky."

Brooklyn, trying to control her temper but not quite accomplishing that task, stood up and looked directly at Tristan, hands on hips. "We were amazing today," she said angrily. "And you're conceited on top of everything. That attitude is not going to help us win, so get over it."

Brooklyn exploded, "Listen, you," yelling boldly at Tristan, "Blood Red and the Tides might be as good as us or better, while the other two bands clearly suck. However, they're all having fun, enjoying the experience, while we're stuck here with a nasty dick."

The Devils sat silent and in shock while they tried to digest the fact that Brooklyn just spoke to their coach that way. They were secretly proud of her but dared not to speak. No one said a word for what seemed like a lifetime. Finally, feeling like the dick Brooklyn had accused him of being, Tristan told everyone to go. "Just go," he said, and they ran out of there without looking back.

The club with all its excitement and life proved a worthy escape from the tension of the studio just hours before. As Brooklyn entered the bar, she felt a sense of exhilaration. The music was pumped up loud, the lights flickered colorfully, and the familiar faces of the patrons and employees were a welcome sight. As the time drew closer to their first set, Damian had to pull Brooklyn away from the DJ and the other employees as well as the four hundred followers who came to see the Devils. Brooklyn loved the role of social butterfly, but the time had come for her to take the stage. The fans seemed especially receptive to the Devils tonight. It seemed as though, through Tristan's guidance, the band had already improved enough for the patrons to notice a marked difference in their performance. Tristan might have been a dick, but he was a wonderful and successful teacher.

As Tristan entered Stars, he thought how different the venue appeared from this afternoon. It was full of life and excitement. He found a seat at the bar and watched Brooklyn as she sang her heart out. He came with the intent of apologizing to Brooklyn and the Devils for his rude behavior today but instead sat quietly alone, suffering from the mental anguish he had brought upon himself.

Through the flashing strobes and smoke from the fog machine, Brooklyn caught a glimpse of Tristan at the bar from the corner of her eye. Her heart stopped for a moment as she tapped Dazzel to inform her that Tristan was present in the room. Dazzel rolled her eyes and said, "Why in the world is he invading our space?"

Brooklyn said matter-of-factly, "He's probably doing his homework and checking us out."

"No," Dazzel reported, "he probably feels guilty."

When the set ended, Brooklyn made her way over to where Tristan sat miserably. She stood in front of him and said nothing. Tristan stood and smiled at her slightly. He touched her face and at that moment she came to the realization that he was a human being. Although feeling that her sentiments of the day were correct, she said to him, "Hey, I'm sorry I called you a dick."

He brushed her hair out of her face and said, "I can't stop thinking about you."

He looked sad, and Brooklyn thought she saw a hint of a tear in his eye. "What's your deal?" Brooklyn asked. "What are you really about?" she echoed.

He shrugged his shoulders, and before he could answer, Garrett grabbed her for it was time to do their second set.

When the last song of the set had ended, Brooklyn searched the club for Tristan. She had the desire to finish the conversation they had started. She searched through the crowd but to no avail. Tristan had fled the club, taking with him a sadness that physically drew pain from his heart. Brooklyn was sad as well for she felt a connection between them that she just couldn't shake.

* * *

The following week flew by, and the Devils were on their game. Tristan never let up for a second. He concentrated on the music, their showmanship, and song arrangements. He was driven. It seemed to take his mind off his feelings for Brooklyn slightly. Although their conflicts still raged on, they seemed to become a little less dramatic, almost as if it were the calm before the storm.

Several days before the show was about to go live, Adonis had the bands gather together one final time, once again choosing Stars as their venue. They had all met and rehearsed in other venues several times; however, this would be the last before the show. Spirits were high and the bands were both nervous and excited. The bands had all formed some type of bond with one another, but unfortunately for Tristan, Billy Blaze still continued his attempt to bond with Brooklyn in very provocative way.

While Brooklyn awaited her turn on stage, she felt two hands begin to massage her shoulders. Without turning around, she shut her eyes and prayed that by some miracle it was Tristan. Logically, she felt it wasn't, and when she finally peeked at her masseur and found it to be Billy, one couldn't help but read the disappointment on her face. Billy bent over and whispered in her ear, "So I figured I'd give you a massage to calm your nerves."

She thanked him and replied, "But I'm not nervous."

"Should I take that as a 'Go away, Billy'?" he asked. Brooklyn simply smiled. He kissed her on the cheek and told her he'd catch her later, while Tristan observed the transaction, his eyes never straying.

Tristan was physically in pain. Under stress, the pain in his legs always grew worse than usual. Assuming that what he saw transpire between Billy and Brooklyn was a romantic interlude, he began to feel saddened. The sadness hurt worse than the physical pain and he wondered how he'd get through the rest of the day. He took some medication, which would relieve his physical pain, but was left with the hurt he felt inside.

After the rehearsal, they all piled back into the white van, which transported them to their destination back to the studio. Once inside, Tristan, with no prior warning, grew mean to the Devils, taking his bitterness out on the innocent boys. He began to criticize them relentlessly from the way they dressed to their ability to play music and sing. The band sat in silence, dumbfounded by Tristan's sudden slander and outbursts. When the studio was in sight, Brooklyn began to feel uneasy. He had not yelled at her in the van, but she knew it was coming. She feared the worst . . . and she was on target, as the worst was about to begin.

The Devils quietly walked into the studio and even more quietly sat on the couches, all fearing what Tristan would do next. Tristan walked to his wheelchair and sat down in it. He closed his eyes for a moment. When he opened them, they were filled with rage.

"This is not a high school battle of the bands," he announced. As he continued, his voice grew louder and louder. Turning his entire attention to Brooklyn, the tyrant was now exploding with rage. "Almost three weeks have elapsed and I see very little improvement in your vocal ability. You are the lead singer and supposed to be carrying the others. Instead, you get your cues from them. Three weeks of intense practice and you just don't get it."

Horrified at his cruelty, Brooklyn felt warm tears well up in her eyes, but she forcefully held them back. She was determined not to satisfy Tristan by allowing him to see her cry. All full of justice, Damian came to her defense. "With all due respect, Brooklyn is an amazing vocalist. Maybe you can't find the improvement you're searching for because she's already near perfect."

Stealing the courage to speak from Damian, Garrett chimed in and said, "The only thing I can make out of the madness is perhaps you consider this some kind of motivational therapy. Well, let me tell you, it's not working and you need to go to therapy yourself."

Tristan stood up from his chair and walked directly over to Brooklyn. "So your fan club disagrees with me. Why don't you take your admirers and leave? All of you. Just go home, now."

Dazzel raised one eyebrow and stated, "Oh no, not another dismissal." She had declined to comment thus far because, in her infinite wisdom, she knew exactly what was going on. She had watched Tristan as he watched Billy and Brooklyn. She sensed his anger was a direct reaction to what Tristan thought he had observed.

As the boys began to collect their belongings, Damian turned to Tristan with an anger the Devils had never known him to be capable of having. "You hide inside your golden chariot and demand perfection from someone who you goddamn already know is near perfect. You criticize and belittle us as you hold court, playing judge and jury, dismissing us at will." Damian's fists were clenched and the others grabbed him before someone got punched.

Colin yelled, "Let's go, Damian, it's not worth the fight." It took him and the other boys to pull Damian out of the studio, leaving Brooklyn alone to defend herself.

Tristan retreated to his wheelchair and sat down once again. He looked up at Brooklyn, who hadn't moved from her spot, and asked, "Why are you still here?"

She stood and walked over to Tristan and said, still hurt and angry, "Damian is correct. You use that wheelchair as a weapon to derive sympathy as you clearly don't need to be in it. You're supposed to teach us artistry, but we're learning how cruel you are instead. I was so excited when the Devils were chosen. I was even more excited when I learned that you selected us and that we would get to work with you, learn from you. Now all I look forward to is the stomach-ache I get each day as I enter the studio.

"You know, I actually do feel sorry for you, but not because of the fact you're in a wheelchair. You're so self-centered that you never even took the time to really know us. You don't know that Dazzel was in the *New York Times* at age two because her biological parents abused her until she nearly died. You don't know that she cares for her adopted mom, who is eighty years old and has been paralyzed for ten years due to a stroke, and the only thing Dazzel asks for is for her mom to see her perform in drag, which will never happen. You also don't know that she's HIV-positive.

"Poor Garrett was raised by his grandmother after his dad died because his mom abandoned him and his brother to pursue an alternative lifestyle with her lesbian lover. You know nothing about how Damian was thrown out of his house at age fifteen because his gay father couldn't cope with the fact that he was gay. He lived on the streets until his dad realized his own homosexuality and finally accepted him years later. You don't know that Colin was bullied in school so much that he almost took his own life. And you know nothing about me.

"You asked me why I hang out with gay men. Well, perhaps it's because they suffer catastrophic issues and still arise victorious. They deal with their problems, overcome them, whereas you straight boys cry over a hangnail."

Tristan blatantly interrupted her and asked, "By straight men, do you mean like Billy Blaze?"

Furious, Brooklyn turned her back to Tristan to try and collect her thoughts before she really went off.

"Billy Blaze," she yelled. "Is that what this whole thing is actually about?"

Tristan, feeling quite embarrassed, wished with all his heart that he had never mentioned Billy's name. Since it was too late to take it back, he would be forced to live with the fact that he admitted jealousy, an emotion he wasn't proud of but couldn't hide.

"Let me tell you something, jerk," Brooklyn said angrily as she spun back around to once again face Tristan. "When Billy came up behind me and started rubbing my back, I was hoping beyond hope that the impossible happened, that it was you. When I turned around and saw it was Billy, I cringed. My whole fantasy came crashing down and my hopes destroyed. I pretty much told him to get lost."

Despite all the emotions circling around their hearts, Tristan felt joy and relief that she didn't like Billy, and Brooklyn was thrilled at the fact that he was truly jealous.

It might have been an opportune moment for Tristan to confess his deep, dark secret to Brooklyn. He thought about it, however, she was so mad at him he decided against it. Sensing that the next move was his, he got up from his chair and put his hands gently on Brooklyn's shoulders. He looked directly into her eyes as he was searching for something to say without appearing vulnerable. Finally, he gave into his heart, "Brooklyn, the truth is that you are the most beautiful and talented creature I have ever laid eyes on. I'm hard on you because I'm an asshole, but also because I want you to win this. I want you to learn what I know, what I spent so many years learning the hard way. I can teach you so much, but the one thing I can't teach anyone is artistry. People are just born with that gift and you have it, I can only show you how to use it.

"As for my situation . . . well, I'm afraid it's a little more than a hangnail. I was in an accident nine months before I was asked to do the show. I'm still trying to recover. I'm in a pretty good amount of pain every day of my life, so hence the wheelchair.

"All the coaches grabbed this opportunity in hopes of stealing one last moment in the spotlight. Brooklyn, you have become my spotlight, and it's not about me winning anymore. I want you to win. However, you're missing the most important component: drive." He gripped her shoulders tighter and spoke louder, "Why aren't you driven?" All of a sudden he tightened the grip on her shoulders and shook her like a rag doll while yelling at the top of his lungs, "You have no drive!"

He then pulled her close up against his own body and held her tightly. His eyes were closed; his heart was racing. All the love and longing he felt for her at that moment transcended from his soul into her very being.

Brooklyn closed her eyes and melted into his arms. She hugged him back so tightly that for a moment she had forgotten how to breathe. Suddenly she panicked and became terrified of her own feelings toward Tristan and pulled away. She gently pushed him away and exclaimed, "Don't you think I want to win?" Still frightened by what she thought she felt for him, she screamed, "Winning means everything to me and the Devils, but I can't live with the pressure you impose and the drama you cause. I feel like you're using me and the band to conquer your own personal demons and that just doesn't work for me. I'm done. I quit." Near hysteria, with tears rolling down her mascara streaked face, she cried, "I quit, I quit." Tristan reached out to her to try and wipe her tears, but she backed away and ran outside into her car.

Tristan slowly sat down in his wheelchair in disbelief of what had just taken place. He knew he had to stop her, even if it meant confessing his whole story to her. He jumped from the chair and started to run after her, but just at that moment, a sharp, devastating pain shot through his legs and back. It was so agonizing that he fell to the floor and hit his head against the wooden corner of the couch. He lay there unconscious in a pool of blood.

Brooklyn started her car and took a second to calm down and think. Her own words "I'm done, I quit" seemed surrealistic to her. She couldn't believe those words left her mouth, nor could she believe the way she had just behaved. She turned the engine off, wiped her face, and went back inside.

She found Tristan lying face down, lifeless on the cold tiled floor. There was blood everywhere. She gasped and fumbled for her phone to dial 911. As she waited for the emergency operator to answer, she called to Tristan. She touched his back to see if he were breathing as she blurted out the address to the operator, who repeatedly asked her to remain calm. "OMG," she said out loud, "what have I done?" She called to Tristan repeatedly until the paramedics rushed in. She took his hand as the first responders gentled lifted Tristan into the ambulance.

Chapter 3

The Truce

Brooklyn paced back and forth on the tiled floor of the waiting room in the emergency room, while the Devils made themselves at home on the chairs strategically placed. She didn't remember calling the Devils, yet they were all there. Damian, attempting to ease the tension of the circumstances, asked, "Do you think we should start packing?"

Dazzel laughed. "I wouldn't be so hasty. You know, I believe he's in love with her, and furthermore, from the way she's wearing out the tiles, she might even love him back."

Brooklyn snapped, "Don't be stupid, we hate each other, that's why this happened."

Dazzel asked, "So then, why are you here?"

Brooklyn replied, "I need to know that I didn't kill him."

Garrett, still angry at Tristan, said, "He deserves this, you're a free spirit and he's confused your thinking and your confidence, not to mention your emotions."

Colin added, "Look at you, you're devastated."

Brooklyn continued to pace. She had never recalled feeling such guilt in her life. "Can you all please just be quiet?" she begged.

The room Tristan was in was only steps away from the waiting room. His door was closed. However, several nurses and what appeared to be a doctor walked in and out of the room at various times. Their faces were blank and void of emotion or information, and Brooklyn hadn't the courage to challenge their knowledge and ask them the status of Tristan's condition. She couldn't help but wonder why there weren't more doctors inside his room with an injury as serious as she thought his was.

From around a corner appeared a man wearing a leather jacket. It was Terence, Tristan's good friend and physical therapist. He walked directly over to Brooklyn and introduced himself. He extended his hand to her, and just to confirm it was her, he asked, "Brooklyn, right?"

Confused, she asked, "How do you know who I am?"

He replied, "Tristan speaks of you often. So what happened exactly?"

With tears streaming down her face, she confessed, "It's my fault. We had an argument and I told him I was done with him and the show. I left in a huff and ran outside to my car. I realized that I was being dramatic and emotional and went back inside to apologize and found him near death on the floor."

Terence put his arm around her in an effort to comfort her. She asked him if he could go into Tristan's room and see if he were still alive. Terence couldn't help but laugh. "He's alive all right. He called me from his cell, that's how I know he's here. He's been through a lot worse, believe me."

Brooklyn questioned Terence, "His accident?"

Still laughing, he replied, "Accident? Is that what he's calling it?" Terence continued, "Okay, well, when he had his 'accident' the doctors told him they doubted if he'd ever be able to walk again. Actually, it was a miracle that he survived. He was in the hospital for many long months and in agony most of the time. He still gets a taste of that pain every day of his life."

Dazzel interjected, "Is that why he's so mean?"

Terence, his long hair in way of his face, questioned, "Mean? I've heard him described in many strange ways: rebellious, arrogant, brilliant, but mean isn't one of them. Tristan is a gentle soul, very generous, kind, and a great friend."

"Oh, really?" Dazzel laughed sarcastically. "Then why does he spend his spare time thinking about new ways to torture her?" She said as she pointed to Brooklyn.

"Are you sure you're talking about the Tristan inside that room?" Damian asked, bewildered.

Just then, as they were conversing, a tall Indian doctor came out of Tristan's room. He came up to Terence and slapped him on the back gently. "Hello, Dr. Powell." Terence said. "How's he doing?"

Dr. Powell shrugged his shoulders. "He's in a lot of pain, but he'll be fine." Dr. Powell then turned to the Devils and asked, "Which one of you is Brooklyn?"

Brooklyn volunteered, "I am."

Smiling, the doctor introduced himself quickly, then stated, "He is asking to see you."

Dazzel held her hand to her heart and said jokingly, "Oh shit, he's gonna press charges." Garrett laughed as Brooklyn shot him a dirty look.

Brooklyn asked Dr. Powell, "Is he going to be all right?"

"Yes, yes," he answered, "just go right inside and see for yourself," Dr. Powell suggested as he pointed toward the door.

In a soft voice, Brooklyn said, "I think I'll pass, I'm probably the last person on Earth he *really* wants to see."

Puzzled at her decision, the doctor insisted, "No, on the contrary, he was quite insistent upon seeing you."

As tears began to fall once again, she said, "Please, just tell him I'm so sorry." And she turned and started walking away.

Terence walked after he and grabbed her arm. He asked her to come out to the hallway so he could speak to her privately. Terence, feeling slightly awkward, said, "Hey, I know we've just met, but through Tristan, I feel like we're friends. I'm taking a big risk by violating a confidence, but I just know both of you will eventually thank me. Tristan was not in an ordinary accident as he apparently would like you to believe. He was attacked and beaten for hours. I am not only his friend but his physical therapist as well. I can tell you that he has gone through more than any one human could stand. Part of the pain he still experiences is due to stress and tension. I'm telling you this because I care about him. Please just go in there and see what he has to say. Just give him a chance to make this right." Terence pulled his cell phone out of his coat pocket. "Look, he's lying in a hospital bed in pain, yet he sent me this text." He showed Brooklyn the text on his phone. "He's not the master of text, but in essence he wrote, *Terry, I fucked up. Please convince Brooklyn to come and talk to me. Need to say sorry.*" Brooklyn looked sadly at Terence as he made one last effort to convince her to go and speak to Tristan. "Please, just hear what he has to say."

Brooklyn nodded yes and slowly walked back into the waiting room. She informed the Devils that they should go home and get some sleep. Dazzel was curled up on one of the chairs already and offered to wait.

Shyly and apprehensively, Brooklyn stepped into the room. Tristan was lying upright with an IV in his right arm, a small bandage on his head, and very obviously in a lot of pain. Propped up on several pillows, he smiled as Brooklyn entered the room. She stood by the doorway, feeling very uneasy seeing him so vulnerable and in pain, which he no longer chose to hide from her. Sensing her uneasiness, he held out his hand to her. "I wasn't sure you would come, but I'm glad you did. Come closer," he said, trying to be funny. Brooklyn slowly walked to his bedside and instinctively took his hand and held it inside hers.

"I don't know where to start," he said as he winced in pain. "I never meant to hurt you the way I did. I'm so sorry I was so cruel. My behavior is inexcusable." The pain made it difficult for him to speak but he had to go on. "I don't deserve it, but please give me another chance. You don't have to forgive me, although I hope you will in time, but please, just give me a chance to make it up to you . . . please . . . ," he begged. Tristan lay back, exhausted from the effort.

Brooklyn felt so guilty seeing Tristan lying there, so hurt, so pale, and so fragile. A tear rolled down her cheek and then another tear. She touched his head ever so gently. "Does it hurt?" she asked.

Tristan noticed her tears. He painstakingly sat up and with his free hand wiped her tears away. "Please don't cry," he begged. "Those tears hurt me more than my head," he disclosed as he smiled at her.

"I never meant for anything like this to happen," she said quietly.

"Shhh," he whispered, "I'm an idiot. I panicked when you said those words, I quit. I was scared that I'd never see you again. I don't think I could have dealt with the fate of never seeing you again. So how about it, love? One more chance?" he asked again, barely able to speak.

Brooklyn touched his hair and then his face and nodded and added, "I should be the one asking for forgiveness." He squeezed her hand, then brought it up to his lips and kissed it.

Just then, Dr. Powell entered the room with Terence. Tristan managed to announce, "Terence, this is Brooklyn."

Terence laughed. "Yes, I figured that out."

"Terence, have you come to take me home?" Tristan asked, knowing full well that his pain was nearly unbearable and he wouldn't be leaving tonight.

Dr. Powell interjected, looking at Tristan, "Are you able to stand up, Tristan?" Tristan just smiled. Dr. Powell smiled back and said, "Then I guess you will remain here until you can."

Terence smiled also and said to Tristan, "I'll pick you up in the morning. Rest well, it seems you're in good hands." And he looked at Brooklyn.

Brooklyn hugged Terence. "It was nice meeting you, and thank you."

Terence hugged her back. "It was my pleasure, and thank you." Terence left the room. Dr. Powell wrote on Tristan's chart and then informed him that he would be giving him something for the pain. Tristan agreed. He had wanted his head to be clear when he talked to Brooklyn and had refused to take anything for pain until they spoke. Dr. Powell said good night to Brooklyn and told Tristan he'd check on him later. A nurse came in and added something to his IV. Within moments his pain had eased.

Tristan, still holding Brooklyn's hand, said, "You must be exhausted after all those emotions thrown at you today. It's okay if you want to go home and get some sleep."

Brooklyn felt strangely compelled to stay with him. "If it's okay, I want to stay here with you," she said.

Once again, Tristan kissed her hand as he held it, and replied, "I would love it if you did."

Brooklyn touched his hair. She began to play with it. Her touch made him relax. Between the morphine he'd been given and Brooklyn's soft touch, his eyes slowly began to close. Mentally he tried hard to stay awake and cherish these moments with Brooklyn. Physically it became impossible for him to continue to remain awake. Brooklyn felt his hand slip out of hers and she knew he had fallen asleep.

Brooklyn continued to stroke his hair. As she sat by his side and watched him sleep, so many thoughts unraveled in her head. There was a certain sweetness about him. She thought back a few hours to the feelings she had when he hugged her at the studio. The feeling that frightened her, causing her to push him away and lash out at him. She remembered the connection they both felt when they sang together, and finally she remembered the way she hoped Tristan, instead of Billy, was massaging her shoulders during the rehearsals.

Suddenly, Tristan awoke. He was pale and his body trembled with pain. Before his eyes fully opened, he called out to Brooklyn. She took his hand once again and reassured him, "I'm right here."

He managed to say, "I'm glad you didn't leave me."

This guy was really sick, and Brooklyn began to get frightened. "What can I do?" she asked him.

"Nothing," he said, "I just have to ride it out," he whispered.

"Do you want me to call someone?" she asked.

He shook his head no as he tried to sit up. "Just . . . just hold me, put your arms around me, just for a minute," he pleaded. Brooklyn quickly moved onto his bed and hugged him. He rested his head on her shoulder as she gently rubbed her hand up and down his back, hoping to comfort him.

Just then, a nurse entered the room and put some more medication into his IV bottle. A minute or two later he stopped trembling as the pain attempted to leave his body. Tristan wished that she would hold him like that forever and made no attempt to leave her embrace. Brooklyn did not move either. After a time, she could tell he fell asleep again. It wasn't until then that she quietly maneuvered him back onto his pillow.

The nurse reentered the room shortly after the episode and whispered to Brooklyn, "You should go home and get some sleep, it's nearly 3:00 a.m."

"But what if he wakes up again?" Brooklyn asked concerned.

The nurse replied, "Not a chance." As she got off the bed the nurse, sensing her apprehension, added, "He'll be fine in the morning. He always is."

Brooklyn echoed her words, "He always is?"

"He's a regular here," the nurse replied.

"A regular?" Brooklyn repeated.

"Yes," said the nurse, "he's here at least once a month, poor guy has pain management issues," the nurse added.

"Listen," the nurse offered, "I'll tell him I threw you out when he wakes up." Brooklyn bent down and gently kissed his forehead, and then left to collect Dazzel, who was still sleeping in the waiting room.

"Dazzel, wake up, Mary. It's time to go home," Brooklyn whispered.

"What time is it?" Dazzel asked half-conscious.

"Never mind, let's just go before the sun comes up," said Brooklyn.

"What went on in there all night?" Dazzel inquired.

"He's really kind of sweet, nothing like that monster he pretends to be," Brooklyn proclaimed.

Dazzel jumped up from the chair and clapped her hands together, "I knew it. I knew the moment he kissed my hand that very first day we met him that he was a good person."

That morning when Tristan awoke, his very first thought was of the guardian angel who held his hand and kept watch over him through the night, giving him strength.

* * *

At 4:00 p.m. that same day, the rain was pouring down cold and hard. It was an icy rain that was beating down upon Brooklyn's skylight in her cottage. A chill caused her to light the electric fireplace in the living room.

Knowing that there would be no rehearsal today, Brooklyn was hell-bent on spending the day just relaxing and thinking. Earlier, she had enjoyed a scolding hot shower and out of habit applied makeup and blow-dried her hair. After all one never knew what Devil might appear at the doorstep. She slipped on a plain white V-neck tee that barely covered her tiny panties. Her hair was trapped in a high pony-tail, leaving wisps of extra hair flowing freely.

She sat down on her pink leather couch with a cup of hot tea and stared at the rain. The rain was comforting to Brooklyn; however, if she was forced to go out in it, that would have been a completely different story. There hadn't been any news on Tristan today, and as the rain fell, Brooklyn wrestled with the urge to dial his cell phone. She smiled to herself as she thought about him and hoped he was doing better.

* * *

Her small cottage was located in Sayville on the south shore of Eastern Long Island, only minutes from the studio they rehearsed at. An unusually long walkway led up to the front door from the country road the cottage was on. The door opened to the living room with its pink couch and love seat, its gas-driven fireplace, and its eclectic decor. Beyond the living room was a kitchen, tiny but adequate enough for the Devils to come over and cook dinner on a regular basis. There was a small guest room and a bathroom right off the living room. Only a few steps from the living room was the huge and luxurious master suite, with its Jacuzzi shower, walk-in closet, and magnificent French doors leading to the backyard. The enormous French doors overlooked a lake and a large woodsy area. At first glance, you might think it was Pandora, the moon where *Avatar* took place.

* * *

Brooklyn had finally come to grips with the fact that she cared for Tristan much more than she wanted to admit. She needed to know that he was all right and she knew he would appreciate a call from her. Just as she took a breath and gained enough courage to call Tristan, she noticed a shiny black car drive up in front of her cottage. Her first instinct was to run into her closet and get dressed. Once in the bedroom she looked in the mirror and decided she wouldn't have time to choose a costume and change, and after all she wasn't naked.

She waited in the bedroom for the doorbell to ring until finally she decided whoever had parked in front of her house wasn't coming to visit her. It was already becoming dark outside, so she took the time to light a scented candle and put it on the dresser. She walked back into the living room when at last the doorbell finally sounded. Brooklyn peeked out the window and saw the black car still parked outside. She opened the door slightly. "Tristan!" she exclaimed, very surprised as she opened the remainder of the door. Shocked that Tristan was standing in her doorway, she just stood and looked at him, forgetting to ask him to come in. He was holding a very expensive bottle of champagne and wearing a silver cane and a big smile. He was soaked from head to toe by the freezing rain. He stood at the door, still smiling as he offered her the bottle of champagne.

"I just wanted to thank you for saving my life last night," he said.

"After I almost took your life," Brooklyn answered. Catching herself and finally realizing he was still standing in the rain, she pulled him inside. "OMG, come in," she offered.

Tristan handed her the champagne. She accepted the bottle as they both stood inside the doorway feeling an excited awkwardness. Brooklyn, in her infinite wisdom, broke the ice. "You're soaked."

He gently answered, "You have a very long driveway and I walk very slow."

Tristan was shivering, but he wasn't sure if it was because of the cold or because he was as nervous as a kid on his first date. Seeing him shivering, Brooklyn collected herself and her manners and offered to take his wet leather jacket. She hung it on the antique coat rack near the door. "Come sit by the fire," Brooklyn insisted.

"I don't want to drench your furniture," he said considerately.

"It's okay," she said, "you're freezing. Come here and sit down," she insisted as she took his hand and guided him over to the pink couch.

Still holding the champagne in her hand, she glanced at it and noticed the label. "Nice," she commented and added, "but you didn't have to do that, thank you. Hey, listen, I have Garrett's clean sweats inside the guest room. Why don't you change into them? You're going to stay and drink this with me, aren't you?" she asked.

Shyly he answered, "I can? I mean, I'd love to."

Brooklyn put the champagne down on the counter and ran into the guest room to get Tristan some dry clothes. While she was gone, Tristan put the bottle of champagne in her fridge. Brooklyn found a pair of gray sweats that appeared to be the right fit for Tristan. She rushed back to the living room and found him searching for champagne glasses. Brooklyn held up the dry clothes and summoned Tristan. "Come here," she said. He moved toward Brooklyn. "Come closer," she said. Brooklyn put the dry clothes down besides Tristan. She decided to help him change, at least his shirt, but as she started to unbutton his shirt, Tristan took her hands in his. He held them for a moment and asked where the bathroom was. She pointed to it, thinking that it's a little strange to choose the bathroom over her. She shrugged it off, thinking maybe his underwear was dirty, and laughed to herself. She continued the quest for the champagne glasses.

While Tristan was changing in the bathroom, she opened the bottle of champagne and poured out two glasses in crystal flukes as the Dom Pérignon he brought definitely called for crystal. Moments later he came out of the bathroom holding his wet clothes. Brooklyn took them from him and put them in her tiny dryer hidden in the hallway inside the guise of a closet. She then handed Tristan the crystal fluke filled with champagne. They cheered each other and took a sip.

Brooklyn sat on the couch and motioned for Tristan to sit beside her. He sat down next to her, a little farther than she'd have liked, however. She leaned over to him and touched his head where the bandage lies. "Does it still hurt?" Brooklyn asked.

"Nah," he said, "just a hangnail." Brooklyn's face turned red remembering of how she implied his afflictions were comparable to a hangnail.

"Sorry about that, I didn't know what the real deal was," she admitted. Tristan told her not to worry, there was no way for her to know, and then thought to himself, *Just wait until she knows the whole truth.*

Tristan enjoyed watching her smile, but he had a purpose in coming to her little cottage besides thanking her. After the way he treated her and because of the way he felt about her, she deserved to know his secret, she deserved to know the truth, and Tristan longed to get it over with before he lost the courage to tell her.

Brooklyn had moved closer to Tristan slowly, so that he might not notice her boldness. He touched a rouge piece of her hair that had fallen out of her ponytail and began to speak in almost a whisper. "Brooklyn, besides wanting to see you and wanting to thank you, I came here to share something with you . . . a secret. My secret. You need to know the real truth about . . ." He hesitated, so Brooklyn filled in the blank.

"Your accident?" she asked.

"Yes," he admitted.

She didn't want to rat on Terence, who was so nice to her last night, but on the other hand she didn't want to lie either, so she simply admitted to Tristan, "I think I already know."

"Terence?" Tristan asked.

She nodded yes and added, "But if you need to confirm . . . ," she offered.

"It's hard for me to even think about it. Those who know only know because they lived through it with me. The rest of the world believes it was just an ordinary car accident."

Brooklyn put her hand on his face and caressed his cheek. "If you're uncomfortable talking about it, it's okay, you don't have to."

He looked deep into her eyes. "I hate living a lie, and I especially don't wish to keep secrets from you." Tristan held her face with both his hands. He took his finger and touched her lips to the tip of it. "I need to tell you what happened. I've never told anyone before, so just bear with me while I fumble for the words . . ." He couldn't even manage to finish the sentence. How could he confess the horror he'd lived through?

Brooklyn saw the pain that seemed to come from his soul as he attempted to begin. She feared what he was going to tell her and what her reaction to it would be. Tristan took a deep breath. He put his empty glass of champagne down and went over to the fridge. He grabbed the bottle of champagne and brought it to the coffee table where his empty glass sat waiting for a refill. He poured some in Brooklyn's half-full glass and then refilled his own. He put the bottle down, took a sip from his glass, and started to tell his story.

"I was leaving my flat in London that night. It was cold and raining like tonight. It was late and I can't even recall where I was going. Out of nowhere, three men wearing ski masks grabbed me dragged me into some desolate alleyway. I was told they took my wallet and I can't recall if I resisted or not. One of them punched me in the stomach and I went down. They started kicking me." Tristan stood and walked to the window. He continued telling his story as though he was mentally reliving it in a voice devoid of emotion. It was almost as if he were in a catatonic state. "First they broke my ribs. I heard them crack as they continued to kick me. I covered my face instinctively. At that point, I felt more fear than pain until they took a metal pipe and broke my legs in several places. The pain was enormous and at that moment I prayed that they would just kill me. I kept fading in and out of some surrealistic, painful reality, but I didn't lost consciousness completely. Then I felt them rip my shirt off and with a jagged edged broken beer bottle they cut my chest. The cuts were deep and massive, and after many plastic surgeries they still remain." Tristan fell to his knees and covered his face with his hands. Brooklyn ran over and tried to comfort him, but he didn't seem to realize she was there as he continued. "After they cut me, I lost consciousness and woke up in a hospital three months later. After eleven operations on my legs, I still experience some pain. Sometimes a lot of pain, each and every day. I also have horrible nightmares very frequently." Tristan grew pale and silent. He was trembling and tears streamed down his cheeks.

Brooklyn kneeled down next to him and took his hands in hers. She began to tell him softly that he was safe now and that it was over. He didn't respond. He just stared at the rain outside the window. "Tristan," she called, "Trist—" Finally he turned to her and put his head on her shoulder. Brooklyn put her arms around him and once again told him he was safe now. Tristan picked his head up and Brooklyn released him form her embrace. He went on to explain to Brooklyn that the scars on his chest were hideous, hence he changed in the bathroom.

Brooklyn admired his courage for living through the experience and for admitting to her what had happened. "Now you know it all," Tristan said. "It was harder than I thought reliving that mess," he continued. Brooklyn started stroking his hair. He looked at her and asked, "Can you do me a favor?"

"Of course." Brooklyn smiled.

"Can you put your arms around me again for a minute?" Tristan asked.

Brooklyn replied, "I would love to." And she held him once again.

When Brooklyn finally let go of him, she stood up and took his hand so that he would follow. She led him back to the couch, but this time she made sure they were sitting very close to one another. Tristan felt relieved, but he wasn't finished yet. He still needed to explain his horrible behavior these past weeks.

Tristan took her face in his hands and said, "Brooklyn, I am so sorry for the cruel way I treated you and the Devils."

Brooklyn interrupted him and said, "Hey, we did that last night, we can move on now." She smiled.

Tristan went on all the same. "In my stupid, warped mind, I thought, if I was mean to you, you would hate me. If you hated me, it would erase all the chances of you having any other kind of feelings for me as I have for you. You can't tell someone how much you love them while you're sick and in pain. I have nothing good to offer you. You're beautiful and free and you don't deserve to be tied down to someone twice your age, half-crippled and always in pain."

With Tristan still touching her face, she bent over and kissed him seductively on the lips. He kissed her back. They began to kiss relentlessly, both in awe of each other's kisses. A feeling of warmth and excitement entrapped her entire body as an electricity the likes of which he had never felt before encompassed his. Brooklyn whispered in between kisses, "I've never been kissed like that before."

Tristan replied, "My god, neither have I." They continued to kiss profusely.

"Tristan, make love to me," Brooklyn begged.

Tristan kissed her one last time and replied, "Baby, I would love that more than anything, but I'm not sure I can."

She giggled and said, "I'll be gentle, I promise." And she kissed him again. He pulled away suddenly. He never wanted her to see those grotesque scars on his chest. It seemed as though he really had no choice but to show her. After all he promised her the truth.

"Okay, love. Let's see if you still want me now." Tristan pulled the sweatshirt he was wearing over his head, exposing his ugly, massive scars. Brooklyn gasped and covered her mouth with her hand. He tried quickly to pull the shirt back down. Brooklyn pushed his hands away and lifted the shirt off. She gently touched the scars and then pressed her lips against them. With tears rolling down her cheeks, she said to him, "How that must have hurt you."

"It doesn't anymore," he replied. She kissed the scars again. He lifted her face away from his chest and wiped her tears away with his finger. "Don't cry, love," he said. "Those tears hurt more than any pain I've ever had." At that moment, Brooklyn realized that she was in love with him. He kissed her again and again. Finally, Brooklyn coaxed him into the bedroom.

* * *

All traces of daylight were gone and the cold rain had transformed itself into bright, sparkling white snow. Her bedroom was illuminated by the single candle she had lit earlier. The flame from the candle danced inside the reflection of the mirror on the dresser, causing a seductive glow. They stood at the foot of the bed as their shadows danced to the candle's flame.

With his finger, Tristan traced the lines of her chin and then her nose and finally her lips. She looked into his eyes and thought how sexy he was. Underneath the scars he had a perfect body. His tattooed body was muscular from all the physical therapy, and his face blessed with perfect features, making him appear extremely handsome.

Tristan playfully kissed her forehead, the tip of her nose, and her neck. His hands rubbed her shoulders. He slowly lifted her tee over her head. Brooklyn pulled off the rubber band that held her hair prisoner on top of her head, leaving her silky blond hair falling all around her body. Tristan stared at her. "Your beauty is distracting," he said.

The punk rocker had not made love to anyone in a long while, but his vast experience in the art of lovemaking was overwhelming. He was a master. With his left hand, he reached behind her and effortlessly unfastened her bra. He touched the sides of her breasts, carefully and purposefully. His hands ventured downward inside her panties. His touch filled her body with a warmth she'd never felt before. Tristan smiled at her and then kissed her with a passion she'd never known. She put her arms around him and her body melted up against his. They fell onto the soft, warm bed and soon lay entangled inside one another. Both of their bodies trembled with uncontrollable lust and passion.

She lay on the pillow while he laid over her at her side. When it was over, not one of them moved for an ageless amount of time. He was still touching her face and softly kissing her neck and forehead. Still in awe of his style of making love, she admitted, "No one has ever made love to me like that, so sweet, so passionate, so—" He interrupted her with a soft sweet kiss on the lips.

"I love you, Brooklyn," he confessed. "I love you with all my heart and soul." She sat up slowly and kissed him with every emotion she possessed in her heart but wouldn't commit to out loud.

Then, all at once, without any warning, she jumped up, wiggled off the bed, opened the French doors leading out to the snowy white wonderland, and ran through them, leaving Tristan dumbfounded and bewildered. Without hesitation, he ventured after her thinking out loud, "She's crazy." She hid behind a tree. He called to her, "Brooklyn, where are you, love?" She peered her head out from behind the huge tree.

"Isn't it so beautiful?" she said, referring to the snow.

"You're so beautiful," he yelled back, "but you're crazy."

Laughing, she answered, "Uh-huh!"

He chased her round and round the enormous tree, finally capturing her using his arms. He trapped her against the tree, blocking her from any chance of escape. He kissed her and said, "You realize we're going to be arrested for indecent exposure if anyone sees us . . . or freeze to death."

"How romantic," she answered playfully and kissed him back, then swiftly ducked under his arm and ran again. Strangely, neither of them seemed to notice the cold.

"Seriously," As he ran after her, as fast as his affliction would allow, in an attempt to recapture her. She ran from tree to tree. Tristan followed close behind until finally he was able to overcome her. He grabbed her and pulled her into his arms and held her. Out of breath, he exclaimed, "Don't make me pick you up and carry you in because I probably can't." Thinking that he might just be crazy enough to attempt just that and hurt himself, she took his hand and led him back inside. He noticed that she was shivering slightly. Tristan grabbed the throw at the edge of the bed and wrapped it around her. He held her close, hoping the warmth of his cold body along with the blanket would keep her cozy and safe. He dried her naked body gently, ignoring his own wet and frozen self. She moved even closer to him and began kissing him. He felt his desire for her rise once again in his heart and in every part of his body. The blanket previously covering her had fallen to the floor. "Come on," Tristan whispered as he led her back onto the bed. Their bodies once again became one while he deliciously continued to kiss her.

* * *

As the night faded into the dawn, Tristan climbed silently out of bed, knowing he had a date with Terence for his physical therapy in the early morning hours. He dressed in the sweats he'd borrowed and left his own clothes in the dryer as an excuse to return. He took a small red box out of his coat pocket and placed it on her night table next to the bed with a note that simply said, "I love you." Then he was gone.

Shortly after he left, Brooklyn awoke with a smile on her face and the memories of last night. She turned to hug Tristan but his side of the bed was empty. She called out to him. When he didn't answer, she instinctively jumped out of bed and searched for any trace of his presence. Although he was gone, she enjoyed the mystery of his disappearance.

She ran to the bathroom to brush her teeth. Then it hit her— did he take his clothes out of the dryer? She was hoping that he had left them so she could hold them hostage until his return. They were still there and she breathed a sigh of relief. Now he'd have to return.

Brooklyn glanced at her bed. She decided to change the sheets and pillowcases. She was already excited at the possibility of Tristan spending another night with her. It was then that she spotted the tiny red velvet box and love note beside her bed. She would have been thrilled to have received just the "I love you" note alone, but there was a gift as well. She was overwhelmed. She sat on her bed and carefully opened the tiny box. She couldn't help but gasp as her eyes widened in amazement. There in the box sat a pair of extremely large, glittering diamond earrings. They sparkled in the sunlight that now encompassed the entire bedroom. She sat, stunned, just holding the box containing the expensive gift. Finally, she carefully inserted them into her ears and ran to the bathroom mirror to see how they looked. *This guy is crazy,* she thought to herself.

She continued to stare at them in the mirror for another moment and then impulsively decided to get dressed and arrive at the studio before the other Devils. She hoped he'd be there early so she could properly thank him for the gift, the note, and last night. She took the note and slipped it inside her jewelry box along with her other precious keepsakes she had collected throughout her life.

* * *

In the meanwhile, Tristan was enjoying his physical therapy session more than he ever had. Although he hadn't much sleep, his adrenaline kept him wide awake. He spent the hour confessing to Terence the events of the evening like a silly schoolgirl telling of her first date. When the session was over, he showered, changed, and headed directly to the studio very pumped to see Brooklyn.

He was there as Brooklyn entered the studio, just as she suspected and hoped for. Surprised and elated to see her there so early, he greeted her with "Good morning, love, you're here so early."

"I'm becoming driven," she answered and laughed. He raced over to her and kissed her long and hard.

Brooklyn licked her lips with her tongue and kissed him back slow but softly fearing any further passion might arouse the lustful passion of last night. Brooklyn changed the subject and showed him the earrings he gave her. "They're so beautiful," she said. "You didn't have to do that."

"Shhh," Tristan pressed his finger against her lips and said, "I wanted to, and they look so pretty on you."

Just as they were about to kiss again, Tristan noticed out of the corner of his eye the boys arriving. They had pulled up in front of the studio and would be walking inside within moments, interrupting their temporary paradise. Tristan quickly asked Brooklyn, "Hey, do you care if the Devils know how much I love you?"

Thinking to herself, *Believe me, they already know, especially Dazzel.* She nodded and answered, "I can't wait for them to find out."

Smiling, Tristan said, "Good, because they are about to find out." And he took her in his arms and kissed her seductively.

Just at that moment, in walked the Devils. They stopped dead in their speechless tracks. Their mouths dropped. Stunned, they politely waited and watched for their kiss to be over. Dazzel bravely broke the ice and asked, "Hey, did you two get married or something?" Tristan winked at Dazzel as he released Brooklyn from his arms.

Still stunned, Colin realized that they had not seen or heard from Tristan since that night at the hospital. Out of concern, Colin asked Tristan, "Hey, man, how are you feeling? Are you all right?"

Before he could respond, Dazzel jumped in, "Look at him, he's obviously better than all right." She then turned her attention to Brooklyn and demanded, "Guuuurrrl, you better tell us everything." Brooklyn smiled and turned red. "Everything," Dazzel reiterated.

Tristan smiled warmly at Brooklyn and touched her chin with one of his fingers. He then grabbed a regular chair, turned it backward, sat down, and began addressing the Devils, "I feel as though I'm standing before Brooklyn's brothers, oh—and sister," he added, referring to Dazzel, "and asking for your blessings." The boys all laughed at Tristan's ice breaking humor as he continued, "I'm not very good at apologizing, but you guys certainly deserve one. I'm truly sorry for my inexcusable behavior. I hope that in time you all might find it in your hearts to forgive me."

Dazzel rushed in and offered, "If you give us some of whatever you gave Brooklyn, we might." The band laughed uncontrollably at Dazzel's suggestions and it became Tristan's turn to become beet red.

Recovering, Tristan continued, "Seriously, though, some months before all this started, I was beat up pretty badly. I won't go into details, but I don't mind if you get those details from Brooklyn. Anyway, because of my affliction, I became very vulnerable and weak-minded. I thought, if you guys sensed that you would have less respect for me as a mentor and I guess as a man, I was cruel and harsh to all of you, and in doing so, I wound up losing your respect anyway. I promise, though, if you just trust in me and give me the chance, I will be doing everything in my power to gain it back. I want this experience, win or lose, to be fun for you. I want it to be the best experience you've ever had, or will have, in your cute little young lives." Tristan, having finished his speech, put his head in his hands for a second, then looked up and smiled. The Devils couldn't help but applaud his efforts. As they all clapped, Brooklyn looked at him with pride as she knew what he had just done was difficult for him.

Tristan went on to explain the events of the next few days. "We have two more days before the show begins. The producers have rented a portion of a luxurious hotel in Manhattan where we will be staying during the duration of the show. We will be in the city from Sunday night to Thursday night. For the next thirteen weeks, we will be rehearsing on Long Island. Friday, Saturday, and Sunday, for each challenge. Keep in mind, the shows are live. There will be rehearsals for the show on Monday. The remainder of the week we will be shooting videos and doing interviews and all the other fun stuff that comes with being a star. With that out of the way, let's go make some music."

* * *

The Devils worked extra hard this day. Tristan's heartfelt speech motivated them to care again and renewed their excitement in the project. By 9:30 p.m., the remastered Tristan Bondage original song was rapped. Breaking only for pizza, the bands energy levels had faded. Tristan, having little sleep the night before, was spent. However, it was a Friday night and the club called to them as the show must go on as they say. The gig started at eleven thirty, which left little time to go home, get dressed, and get to Stars. There would be no power nap. However, the Devils would certainly make a little time to learn the details of what happened between Tristan and Brooklyn.

The Devils packed up and began to leave, but not before reminding Brooklyn that they yearned to know every detail. One by one, they said to her, "Mary, we gotta talk," using that or a similar phrase. When they were gone, Tristan remained sitting on the couch, which was the only thing keeping him upright for the last hour of rehearsal. Brooklyn sat down next to him. Tristan lay back and pulled her on top of him, wrapping his arms around her, kissing the top of her head, holding her like that made him happy beyond imagination, but he felt a twinge of pain in his legs and knew he needed to get up to take some medication to ease the pain before it got any worse.

Brooklyn felt Tristan's body stiffen. She picked her head up to look at him and noticed he had grown pale. She kissed his lips, then asked him if he was okay. Tristan sighed. "I'm just tired, love," he whispered. "I need to go take some pain medication."

"Where is it, I'll get it for you," she offered. He pointed to his jacket. She found a vial of large white tablets and showed it to him. He nodded and she brought him one with a glass of water.

"Come here and kiss me, please," he begged. She obeyed, but he sensed she was nervous about the fact that he was in pain. He offered, "Don't be frightened. I'm okay, you're just sensitive toward me because you love me," he said playfully.

"I never said that," she said back jokingly.

"But you will," he said with conviction.

"You're arrogant," she added, laughing.

"And conceited," he added. They both laughed.

Time was passing and Brooklyn knew she'd have to leave to go home and get ready for tonight. She didn't want to leave him though. Just then, Tristan suggested that the hour was growing late. "I don't want to leave you," she told him.

"Hey, I'm okay," he told her. "I promise," he added reassuringly.

"No, it's not that, I just want to be with you longer," she admitted.

Elated that she wanted his company, he volunteered, "I'll come to the club with you and hang out."

"No," she insisted, "you've had no sleep whatsoever and—" she interrupted her own thought. "Hey, why not come home with me and sleep there? I'll wake you when I get home from the club." Tristan loved that idea and they left for the cottage together.

* * *

Once at Stars, Brooklyn couldn't wait to return to the cottage. It was all she thought about during the gig. She was overtired yet exhilarated at the prospect of Tristan sleeping beside her tonight. She thought how sweet it was for him to offer to hang with her at the club even though he was exhausted. Little did she realize he had no desire to be without her either. Her mind drifted to the memory of last night and the way he had made love to her, and when the last set ended, she ran home. She was filled with excitement at seeing him.

Brooklyn carefully and quietly unlocked the door of the cottage, brushed her teeth, and showered in the bathroom of the living room and then slid into bed where Tristan lay peacefully sleeping. She felt guilty disturbing him, but she had promised. She rested her head gently upon his chest. Instinctively, his arms reached around her. While still asleep, he whispered, "I love you." Brooklyn, being past exhaustion, fell asleep almost immediately, feeling safe and warm inside his caress.

The morning sunlight crept into the bedroom, bringing forth warmth and an overwhelming desire for each other. Still wrapped inside his arms, Brooklyn felt his fingers touch her buttocks and then the inside of her thighs. She felt him aroused against her body. She pressed her body softly against his, but she couldn't seem to get close enough. Tristan kissed the inside of her ear and whispered, "Good morning, my love." He continued to gently touch the inside of her thighs until his own passion became impossible to control. They made love with an intense longing for one another, then continued to hold each other in silence. Both were afraid to end the magic. Tristan, still in a state of disbelief that anything could feel that wonderful, whispered to Brooklyn, "I love you so much it hurts."

She thought to herself, *This man who was such a monster just a few days ago had magically transformed into a tender and loving creature.* Still, the words *I love you* remained beneath her heart and stuck in the back of her throat, never making it past her lips.

* * *

It was 6:00 a.m. This would be the last rehearsal day before they left for Manhattan tomorrow. The two attempted to become ready to leave for the studio. Brooklyn gave Tristan a brand-new extra toothbrush as well as his clothes that were still held hostage in the dryer. In exchange, she imprisoned his clothes from yesterday. Silly as it seemed, as long as there were clothes in the dryer, they both felt there was an excuse to return.

Tristan turned the shower on and stepped inside. It was not long before Brooklyn followed. She stood behind him as the warm water rushed downward. She pressed her body against his while he pretended to ignore her. This made her even more determined to arouse him once again. She reached her hands around Tristan's front with a bar of soap and began to lather his nipples, all the way down past his other body parts until he could no longer resist her aggressiveness. He turned around to her and took her face in his hands. She looked into his bright blue eyes and thought how incredibly sexy he was with the bead of water glistening upon his face. She saw in him what she thought Jesus would have looked like. Tristan kissed her, urging her tiny body into the corner of the shower.

* * *

Brooklyn finished drying her hair and sat down by her vanity to paint. Tristan sat beside her and applied eyeliner and mascara to his own eyes. Being so used to Dazzel painting next to her, she barely noticed Tristan as he shared her makeup space.

The Devils arrived at the cottage loudly banging on the door. "It's opened." Brooklyn yelled. They found the two just finishing their makeup. Both had applied a different flavored lip gloss. The two decided to mix and match them by kissing each other's lips.

Once again, surprised to find Tristan there so early and assuming that he had spent the night, Dazzel asked, "Are you sure you two aren't married?"

They arrived at the studio, Starbucks in hand. They worked hard until the evening approached. Tristan was musically brilliant. He taught the band so much in such a short time. He gently guided and motivated the band to a level they had never been able to reach or even believe they were capable of reaching. By the time the moon could be seen through the window, the Devils were musically ready for national TV. The band then dispersed, all heading off to their separate homes to pack and get some decent sleep before their city adventure began. Damian went home with Garrett since his belongings were already at his apartment in the city. Tristan hadn't seen his own home in days. He needed to pack and arrange for Terence to come into the city along with them so he could continue his physical therapy on location. Saying good night to Brooklyn proved to be harder than he imagined. "How am I going to be able to sleep tonight without you in my arms?" he asked Brooklyn. He had actual tears in his eyes.

Feeling sadness herself, Brooklyn tried to comfort him. "It's just for a few hours, we'll be together in the morning." Tristan insisted upon walking her to the cottage door, but she rejected his offer. "No," she said, "it's cold and dark and I'm just going to run up the walk way. You stay here and watch until I get in," she offered. "Besides, if you walk me to the door, I'm going to insist you come in and then I'm afraid that I won't let you go."

Tristan smiled, happy to realize that she would miss him too. "That's because you love me," he said jokingly.

"I never said that," she answered. She turned and kissed him one last time, hoping to remember the taste of his lips and she was gone.

Chapter 4

Love, Lust, and the Show Must Go On

The Devils were first to arrive at the exquisite Manhattan hotel. They were immediately consumed by a slew of photographers, reporters, and television media. A vast array of flashes continued to go off while microphones were shoved under their noses. Hundreds of Tristan's fans chanted his name and applauded his arrival from behind barricades. All were hoping to get a glimpse, and perhaps a picture, of the legendary rock idol.

All the hype was created by the producers and publicists involved with the series as a promotional tool for the upcoming debut of the show. The Devils were neither warned nor prepared for such extravagant and overwhelming confusion. Tristan placed his arm securely around Brooklyn, his hand on Dazzel's shoulder, and protectively guided them through the enormous lobby to the front desk. They stopped only for pictures while the Devils followed very close behind. Tristan turned around to the mesmerized Devils and advised them to just keep smiling and enjoy the chaos.

Once safely in front of the check-in desk, Tristan released his hold on Brooklyn and Dazzel and turned to face the cameras. Adonis, who was nearby, appeared and handed Tristan a mic. His fans exploded with admiration as he greeted everyone and told of his excitement to be part of the show. The cheering and applause grew louder as Tristan introduced the Devils to the TV cameras and the world.

When the check in was successfully completed, Tristan resumed his prior position with his arm tightly draped around Brooklyn and his hand planted firmly upon the shoulder of Queen Dazzel. He made a bold attempt to maneuver the Devils in the direction of the elevators. Dazzel, quite impressed by the huge number of Tristan's fans, commented, "Wow, some people actually know and love you."

Laughing, Damian suggested, "Clearly the producers must have spent a fortune hiring all those extras to pretend they loved you!"

Tristan rolled his eyes and announced, "As long as Brooklyn loves me."

Brooklyn interrupted, "I never said that."

Tristan assuredly said, "But you will."

Just then, Billy Blaze and Rising Tides made their entrance and the attention was diverted to them. Tristan took advantage of that and escaped with his band inside of the ornate elevators. Safely inside, Tristan took Brooklyn in his arms. "I've been waiting to hold you like this all day. I missed you terribly last night," Tristan admitted.

Dazzel glared at the two of them and said, "How could you possibly have missed her when you called her every five minutes?" Tristan ignored Dazzel's remark and continued to hold Brooklyn in his arms until the elevator stopped on the forty-first floor.

Tristan walked Dazzel and Brooklyn to their room, which they had been assigned to share. This was a happy choice for both of them as they were already accustomed to sharing their wardrobe and makeup. Their luggage had arrived before they did and stood there waiting to be allowed to enter their room. Tristan whispered to Brooklyn as she began to unpack, "Do you want to come upstairs with me for a minute?" Brooklyn nodded enthusiastically. She turned to Dazzel and told her she'd be back soon.

Unconvinced, Dazzel handed her a makeup case and said, "Take this just in case soon becomes later."

Tristan grabbed one of Brooklyn's costumes placed on top of her suitcase, and turned to Dazzel. "This is in case later turns into much later." They exited the room and closed the door. As they headed toward the elevator, Dazzel opened the door and reminded them that they were scheduled to be picked up in two hours to record their life story videos to be used on the show. Tristan yelled back, "She'll be ready!"

Alone in the elevator, Tristan pulled Brooklyn close and confessed, "Last night was rough without you." Brooklyn hugged him and admitted that she missed him as well. This time the elevator stopped at the penthouse. Tristan took her hand and led her to one of the penthouse suites and opened the door with his key card.

His suite offered a breathtaking view of New York City. The king-sized bed rested against a wall, which, if followed, led to a master bath with a Jacuzzi and doorless shower. It had a wide flat-screen TV, two recliners facing the window, a walk-in closet, two dressers, and a balcony at the window. "It's so beautiful," Brooklyn commented.

"You're so beautiful," Tristan answered and handed her the extra key card to his room. She stood holding it, not sure what to say.

Tristan smiled and said, "Just consider us roomies." Brooklyn walked over to Tristan and put her arms around him. He lifted her chin and kissed her on the lips, then took her by the hand and directed her onto the king-sized bed.

Slowly she began to unbutton his shirt and then his pants. He could barely wait to hold her. His entire body trembled with anticipation. He removed her shirt and then her bra. He began caressing and kissing her breasts as she melted into his arms. Finally, he climbed on top of her naked body and they made love to each other as if it were the first time.

An hour had passed and he knew Brooklyn needed to get ready to film the video, which would become part of the show. He also needed to coach the band and direct them as to what should be said on the video. "I could hold you here in my arms forever, love," Tristan whispered, "but we have to get ready now." Brooklyn playfully continued stroking his hair and kissing his lips with short, quick kisses. Realizing it was the only way either of them had the slightest chance of becoming ready on time, he literally dressed her and led her back downstairs, along with her makeup bag to the door of her room. Before she entered, he kissed her hand and said, "It's going to become a little hectic later, but I'd be honored if you would join me for dinner this evening."

She loved when he used his proper British etiquette and answered, "I'll live for it." Just as he began to kiss her one last time, the door to her room opened and an arm reached out and grabbed Brooklyn's shoulder, then pulled her into the room.

The door closed once she was in, and Dazzel yelled, "You're going to cause her to be late, now go away."

"I love you," Tristan yelled through the door, laughing.

Dazzel answered back, "I didn't know you cared." She quickly reopened the door and stuck only her head out of the room. All Tristan could see was her wigless head, long fake eyelashes, and her big bloodred lips puckering up to kiss him. He pretended to be horrified and screamed running down the hallway.

One hour later, the Devils were picked up and transported to the set where their life story videos would be filmed. It had been decided that Dazzel would be Johnny for the first half of the video; however, the second portion of it would star Dazzel Diamond. In between the two parts of the Dazzel/Johnny video, Brooklyn would be shooting hers, giving Dazzel time to transform back into Johnny for the first half of his video. They would be shooting the second half of Dazzel's video first since it took less time for Dazzel to become Johnny than Johnny to become Dazzel.

The mentors were all invited to watch the videos in progress. Tristan was present but chose to remain hidden, feeling that his presence might make the Devils self-conscious.

Dazzel began the drag portion of their video with a cartwheel and a split. She borrowed one of Tristan's songs for the background music, which surprised and touched him greatly. She described the birth of Dazzel Diamond, and some of her more humorous experiences as a drag queen. Tristan was impressed with her impulsive wittiness and her funny sarcasm.

Johnny's video would prove to be one of the most emotional, dramatic, and turbulent films made. He sat as a boy in front of the camera, immersed in sadness as he spoke of his childhood. He told of his birth mother's addiction to heroine and how her boyfriend beat him so badly at age two that he was taken away. He showed newspaper clippings, which he carried with him always, of his abuse, as if he felt no one would believe it really happened without proof. With pride, he spoke about how his adoptive parents took him in and raised him as one of their own.

Tearfully, he shared the wish that they would one day be able to watch him perform in drag, although he knew that was impossible. At eighty years of age, his mom was paralyzed and bedridden, requiring constant care due to a stroke she suffered six years prior.

His sad story had a surprise ending to it, with Johnny proclaiming to the world that he was HIV-positive. He hadn't planned to make that public knowledge, but somehow in the drama of the moment, it slipped out. Tristan grew emotional at Johnny's video and vowed to himself to be kinder to him.

Brooklyn felt surprisingly at ease in front of the camera. She was spunky, animated, and well spoken. Her childhood was far from dramatic, so she focused upon her experiences with the band and her fight for gay rights. That is until one of the interviewer's voice came out of nowhere and asked if the rumor that she and her mentor Tristan Bondage were in love was true.

"Scandalous," she answered jokingly as her eyes widened and sparkled. Tristan held his breath in anticipation for the rest of the answer, as did everyone in the room. She calmly announced, "I speak for myself as well as the other Devils," and she thought all the while how anyone could know about Tristan and herself already. "We had a real rocky beginning, but we all have grown to love Tristan very much." Tristan was proud of Brooklyn's instant and perfect answer. He thought it to be nothing shy of genius.

One by one, the rest of the band recorded their videos, each professing their dramatic tales. Garrett was next. He talked about the death of his dad and how his mom abandoned him and his brother to enjoy an alternative lifestyle with her lesbian lover, leaving his grandmother to raise them, while Damian confessed how rough his teenage years were due to his father being unable to accept him as gay until he himself came out at age forty-five. Damian was forced onto the streets, surviving by selling his body and his soul to stay alive. Lastly, Colin explained how he was severely bullied as a kid, causing him to attempt to take his own life. He went on to say how music had saved him. When the shoot had been completed, Tristan came out of hiding and applauded the Devils for a job very well done. Surprised to see him, the band all began to speak at once, forcing Tristan to order a group hug. Before they left to return to the hotel, Tristan whispered to Brooklyn that she was amazing and that he would pick her up for dinner at eight. She blew him a silent kiss and told him she would be ready. Tristan was a video master and remained behind to help edit the films.

Promptly at eight, Tristan knocked on Brooklyn's hotel room door. When the door opened, Tristan was astonished. He never expected to see the sight before him. Brooklyn stood in the door-way wearing a sexy black low-cut dress. Her hair was fashioned in an up do, her makeup flawless and sophisticated. She mimicked a 1930s starlit. It was several seconds before he was able to speak. He got down on one knee and kissed her hand as if she were a princess. "My god, you're so beautiful," he finally whispered. He stood up and offered her his arm. She slipped her arm through his and they walked through the lobby like proper British royalty out to the white limo that Tristan hired. As he helped her into the limo, he said, "I wish to show you romance and to make every night of your life special."

Tristan entered the limo wearing a sparkling silver jacket, with tails, of course. He had on silver pants as well, with blue high-top sneakers and a shirt the same color as the high-tops. While they sat in the backseat of the limo, Tristan couldn't take his eyes off her. She leaned over to him and asked, "Aren't you going to kiss me? You're wearing as much lipstick as I am." She laughed. Without a word he leaned forward and kissed her gently. Then he touched her face as if he couldn't believe she was real and that she was actually with him.

"Love, turn to the window, please," he suddenly ordered. Brooklyn turned and looked out of the window figuring there was something special he wished for her to see. Tristan pulled something out of his pocket and placed it around her neck. Then he leaned over and kissed the back of her neck. His kiss sent chills down her spine as she touched the magnificent black and white diamond necklace fastened around her. She looked down at it and gasped.

"Tristan, are you crazy? OMG, it's the most beautiful thing I have ever seen." She turned, hugged him, and whispered, "Except for you."

The luxurious glass-enclosed restaurant was on the rooftop of an exclusive hotel. One could view all of Manhattan from one's table, which was adorned with fresh cut roses and expensive candles. When they were seated, Tristan ordered a bottle of Santa Margherita Pinot Grigio with Brooklyn's consent and then took her hand and held it in both of his from across the table. Brooklyn thanked him obsessively for the necklace while Tristan just stared at her beauty.

"Your answer today at the video shoot was brilliant," he commented.

"How did they know about us?" she questioned.

Tristan laughed and said, "I told them!" She looked at him completely stunned as he continued to explain. "I didn't want them to find out and disqualify us, so I simply told them. Adonis decided that if we agreed to allow our relationship to become part of the show's drama, it could be an asset to the ratings. I wanted Adonis to know the truth. Brooklyn, I want the entire world to know the truth," he said proudly. Tristan waited to see what her reaction would be.

"I love being with you," she said, "and I want everyone to know," she proclaimed. Relieved and happy, he lifted her hand that he was still holding up to his lips and kissed it.

Just then, two women, fans of Tristan, ran up to their table. Apologetic for disturbing them, they asked him for an autograph and begged him to allow them to take a picture with him using their cell phones. He politely agreed to all the above, and then they were gone. Embarrassed, Tristan tried to apologize. Brooklyn exclaimed, "I love that."

Tristan smiled and said, "Just wait until it starts happening to you."

As dinner arrived, Tristan insisted that Brooklyn tell him everything about herself. "Everything?" she asked. He nodded. "Well," she started, "I was born in Brooklyn, moved to Long Island at age three.

I have two older brothers who play guitar and sing as well. My parents always supported our musical desires and dragged me to Tristan Bondage concerts as a baby. Oh, and you already know, I love gay men."

"That's it?" he said. "I poured my heart out to you the other night and that's all I get?" he asked.

"Yep," she said. "That's all you need for now, the rest you will figure out as time passes," she mysteriously announced.

"Okay then, is there anything else you want to know about me?" he asked unquizzically.

"Nope," she said, "I Googled you."

"Jesus," he said and rolled his eyes.

Brooklyn began, "You were born in London. In the mid-1980s, you rose to fame with your first hit single as a lead singer in a punk rock band. You've been married several times, you're considered a video master and musical genius in the industry and were voted the sexiest man on earth," she finished.

"Wow." He laughed. They seemed to laugh a lot together.

"I do have one question," Brooklyn admitted.

"What's that, love?" Tristan asked.

"Are you sleeping with me tonight?" she wondered.

Tristan laughed at her aggressiveness and answered, "Do you want me to?"

"Yes," she said, "very much so. I don't know exactly what's happening between us, but I have no intention of questioning it or stopping it," she continued.

Tristan looked at her seriously and explained, "It's called falling in love. I love you and you love me."

She laughed and said, "I never said that."

He answered, "You will."

Still laughing, she admitted, "I admire your arrogance and I think you're incredibly sexy," she said seductively.

"Thank you," he said, "I can't wait to hold you in my arms."

She smiled at him and said, "I'm ready whenever you are." Tristan paid the check and they headed for the limo.

On the return trip to the hotel, Tristan sat in the corner of the backseat of the limo while Brooklyn sat leaning up against him with her legs up on the seat. Tristan rubbed his hand up and down her leg and then, not being able to resist, his hand went under her sexy short black dress. After that, it was a miracle that they made it to the hotel without making love. Brooklyn turned around and climbed onto Tristan's lap, straddling his body and facing him. She pushed her body close to his and began kissing him. Both of his hands immediately found themselves underneath her dress, pulling it way up. He felt himself losing control of his passion like a naughty teenager at a drive in movie theater. "My god," he whispered, "look at what you've driven me to do." Brooklyn laughed at him, as the limo pulled up to the hotel. Tristan shook his head in disbelief of his own behavior and then fixed Brooklyn's dress. Unnerved by his own behavior and still quite aroused, Tristan rushed through the lobby with his arm around Brooklyn. She insisted upon stopping at her own room first to collect her makeup, a toothbrush, and a costume for tomorrow.

Brooklyn opened the door slowly, in case Dazzel was sleeping or doing something else, but she was absent. There was no sign of her and Brooklyn decided to lock her out. Tristan laughed and agreed as he pulled Brooklyn over to the bed. They began to kiss ferociously. Just then there as a knock on the door. "Damn," Tristan said. Brooklyn ran and opened the door. Dazzel ran past her, jumped into the bed where Tristan lay, and planted a big, wet kiss on his lips. "Ugh," he said and wiped the kiss right off. They all sat there laughing until tears filled their eyes and their stomachs began to hurt.

After the laughter, Tristan grabbed Brooklyn and began to kiss her again. "Go get a room!" Dazzel said and added, "Your own room." They began to laugh some more as Brooklyn grabbed her paraphernalia and Tristan's hand. She closed the door behind them and headed for the elevator.

The door to Tristan's room hadn't fully closed yet when he was already holding Brooklyn in his arms and unzipping her dress. Her dress fell to the floor as she ripped the clip out of her up do, allowing her hair to fall. Tristan threw his jacket on the floor while Brooklyn opened his pants. He quickly unbuttoned his own shirt and took it off. Finally, they both stood naked in front of one another. Tristan grabbed her with an urgency she hadn't seen in him before, and she loved it.

He picked her up and carried her across the room and onto the bed. He was more aggressive than he'd ever been as both their bodies trembled with desire. Tristan climbed on top of her. He hadn't remembered ever feeling this aroused in his life. Once inside her, his passion screamed to a climax.

Brooklyn awoke to the sound of her cell phone alarm blaring. Once again she searched for Tristan, and once again he had disappeared. However, the room was filled with hundreds of red roses.

* * *

The set was busy. Everyone seemed to be running in different directions, hoping to make their own separate issues become solved. Adonis greeted each band as they arrived and gave them a personal tour of the dressing rooms, wardrobes, makeups, the green room, and the actual set, where they would be performing live in just a few short hours. The mentors had all arrived with their groups, except Tristan, who was nowhere to be found. Brooklyn hoped that he was all right.

Blocking seemed to be very important as they worked on that portion of the show for what felt like hours until everyone knew their places on the stage and how to reach them. As the day grew shorter, the Devils became more and more anxious. Lighting was experimented with, and sound checks were completed. A brief rehearsal was done, and an order of group performances was selected. Just as the Devils were about to start panicking, Tristan graced the set with his presence.

Through the hustle and bustle of confusion going on, on the set, Dazzel yelled to Tristan across the room, "Nice of you to show up." Tristan merely winked at her.

Brooklyn, most relieved to see him, mouthed the words, "The roses are amazing." He blew her a kiss back.

The Devils, as well as the other groups, were ushered into wardrobe and then makeup. Forty-five minutes before the show was to begin, Adonis gathered the bands and mentors together and presented them with an amazing pep talk. He then introduced them to their judges.

Judge number one was Jeffrey Dawn, one of the top concert promoters in the world. The second judge was Michelle Rice, a sexy MTV DJ, and judge number three was Austin Rivera, an icon from the 1980s who knew all the coaches well. After the introduction Adonis directed each group into a green room to await the opening of the show as well as their fate!

The Devils sat in silence, one more frightened than the other. Tristan empathized with their apprehensiveness and whispered, "Listen, guys, use that nervous energy to your benefit. You're only performing a song, something you've done a thousand times before."

"But not in front of billions of people," reminded Damian.

Tristan continued, "I want you to pretend you're at Stars on a Friday night. I promise all of you, once you start to play, after the first eight bars of music, the nervousness you're feeling will magically transform itself into power. You will sound strong and have control of the stage. I promise."

Brooklyn looked at Tristan, almost in tears, and asked, "Promise?"

He took her hand and kissed it reassuringly and said, "I wouldn't ever lie to you."

Suddenly they heard someone yell, "Quiet on the set!" The countdown to the shows beginning started. "Lights, camera, action." The time had approached.

The set darkened. Spotlights were moving in a thousand different directions, filling the stage. The theme song of the series began to play and the large, live audience that filled the auditorium began to applaud. A random, booming voice from nowhere began speaking, "Welcome, America, to the new hit series *So You Wanna Be a Rock Star*, where *you* get to choose the first ever rock star super group." The audience clapped wildly. "Let's welcome our host, Adonis Hartly!" The applause grew louder.

Adonis entered the stage by way of a lighted red carpet placed in the center of the set. It appeared as though he were descending from the heavens. He offered an opening speech explaining the premise of the show and announced that the groups were competing for. He then explained how the voting would be accomplished in order for all of America to be included in the selection of the winner. Lastly, he introduced the judges, who all said a few words and made their way down to a big judges' desk in front of the audience, facing the stage. It was then time for a commercial break. When the sponsors were finished, it would be time to show America the groups and coaches that they would be expected to fall in love with during the next twelve weeks.

As the commercial came to an end, Tristan had a brilliant idea. "Huddle, guys," he ordered. "This is how you're going to make your grand entrance. When I introduce you . . ." He whispered the details to the Devils and announced, "Okay, guys, it's show time!"

The group wore outfits resembling Tristan's band from the 1980s. They all had black sequined jackets, with tails of course, high silver boots with pink laces, tightly fitted black pants, and pink and silver tank tops. The Devils would be announced last, and they would be last to perform, probably because they were last to be selected.

As their huddle finished, Adonis announced the first group. "And now, America, it's time to meet the bands and their coaches. One of these groups will be our future winners. First give it up for mentor Jamison Brown, the legendary reggae sensation." Adonis handed the mic to Jamison as the crowd clapped.

"Thank you, judges and America," Jamison began. "It gives me great pleasure to introduce you to Sin-cerely Yours." The band came out holding hands and bowed to the judges. The audience applauded and they took a step back to join their coach.

Next Adonis introduced "the talented and animated Billy Blaze, one of the most popular rockers of the 1980s!" The audience cheered with delight as Billy took the mic from Adonis.

"Here for your love and approval, meet my young and talented Rising Tides." The baby boy band made their entrance wearing jeans and T-shirts bearing the name of their band. They waved and took a step back.

Delila Carnes was next to come onto the stage. She introduced her band as the only all-girls band. Brooklyn looked at the Devils, thought to herself, *That's what she thinks,* and laughed to herself. City Girls came out on stage wearing sexy jumpsuits, each a different color. They held their hands up presenting to the audience the victory sign and then it was their turn to step back with their mentor. The band did receive whistles and applause.

"Now," Adonis announced, "one of the hottest rock stars of the 1980s, Devin Liam." The audience went wild. Obviously Devin still had it going. He shyly took center stage as well as the mic from Adonis. It was several seconds before the audience allowed him to speak.

"Settle down, America," he started. The audience loved him and began to applaud uncontrollably again. Clearly Devin and his band would become the favorites thanks to Devin's popularity. Finally, Devin was able to introduce his band. "My band, Blood Red Orange, the group you, America, will fall in love with." Blood Red came out wearing orange and red jacket, pants, and ties, except the lead singer, Joy, who wore a matching formal gown. They too held hands and waved to the audience as they continued to applaud loudly.

In moments it would be the Devils' turn to take the stage—and take the stage they would! Their entrance was unrehearsed and chancy at best. However, if it was carried out successfully, America would never forget it!

"Last of all," Adonis announced, "one of the sexiest men in the world, the rebellious punk rocker, Tristan Bondage." The audience cheered for Tristan but were not quite as loud as when Devin was announced. Tristan's applause was a close second. He waited for the audience to quiet down and then introduced his Devils proudly.

"America, I have truly fallen in love, and I know when you get to know these guys, you will too. Here are my Precious Little Devils!"

The Devils took the stage with the gayest display of showmanship ever to grace the stage of any reality show thus far. Damian, Garrett, and Colin walked out together holding hands, while Dazzel sat on top of Colin's shoulders and Brooklyn was perched on top of Damian's. Without notice or warning Brooklyn and Dazzel landed a backward somersault, timed exactly in sync. Then they grabbed the hands of the person carrying them and slipped between their legs to the front. If that were not enough, they completed their endeavor with Brooklyn and Dazzel crisscrossing each other on the front of the stage with a cartwheel and ending in a split.

The judges, the audience, and even the cameramen gave them a wild standing ovation. Adonis yelled above the audience's rioting screams, "That was an accomplished display of acrobatics! Give it up, America, for all these amazing artists. When we return, we'll be hearing from Sin-cerely Yours!"

The Devils couldn't contain themselves. They were elated until Adonis ran backstage and began to yell at Tristan in front of the group. "Tristan, are you out of your mind? That was risky. I shudder to think what the outcome would have been if one of them fell. Let me remind you that this is a live show." Brooklyn attempted to interrupt Adonis and take the blame.

Instead, Tristan apologized to Adonis. "I'm very sorry, I don't know what I was thinking."

Adonis looked at Tristan and continued to rant. "Don't ever let anything like this happen again. No more surprises." And he stormed off but not before congratulating the Devils on winning round one in his opinion.

Tristan literally pushed the Devils into the green room and shut the door. "Are you guys crazy? You could have killed yourselves!" Tristan angrily whispered. Tristan had suggested that the boys carry Brooklyn and Dazzel on their shoulders for their introduction; the acrobatics was Dazzel's idea. Tristan accepted the blame for their antics in order to protect the Devils. He continued ranting. "If any of you got dropped we would have looked like assholes in front of the entire world!"

"Relax," Dazzel interrupted, "we begin our Friday night gig with that little act of acrobatics or one similar. We have been doing it that way for the past five years. I always use cartwheels and splits when I perform drag. I was a gymnast and I taught Brooklyn everything I know. If you had taken the time to watch us at Stars on Friday for more than the second that you did, you might have known that."

Tristan thought for a second and then smiled. "Okay, you got me. However, one of you could have been hurt or made a fool of. It was dangerous to attempt that on national TV—and live, no less." Tristan stood looking and their guilty faces and then added, "But you guys were superb, like magic and I'm sure they will play that little act of yours over and over again through the entire show when they recap. I'm very angry at all of you, but at the same time, so proud. Good luck on your performance. I love you all!"

Brooklyn ran into Tristan's arms and said, "Thank you." She was relieved that he wasn't really angry, especially at her.

When the commercial ended, Sin-cerely Yours had already been placed on stage. Before each group's attempt at performing the rec-reated song made famous by their coach, a video of an actual performance of their mentor singing the song would be shown, making this week's challenge more entertaining.

Sin-cerely Yours performed Jamison Brown's song just as he had done it and the judge's comments reflected just that. After the commercial, Billy Blaze's band took center stage. They were decent, but nowhere near as exciting as the video of Billy Blaze that played before they performed. City Girls were the least impressive. They chose a slow song, and although their vocals were on spot, the song itself was boring. Delilah Carnes's video had also been boring.

As Devin Liam's video began, the crowd roared with admiration. Blood Red Orange had a stellar performance. It was flawless, creative, and inspirational. The judges complimented them over and over again until it was time for another commercial.

The Devils anxiously awaited their turn behind stage. Right before they were to go on, Tristan put his arm around Brooklyn and whispered, "Remember when we sang the song together?" She nodded.

He continued to whisper in her ear, "When you sing it, pretend we are singing it together. Listen for my voice and my harmony in your head. I'll be right there with you, and remember that I love you." She smiled, but she was still nervous.

As Tristan's video played, Dazzel commented, "Boy, he was hot!"

Brooklyn also commented, "He still is!" Tristan's video was awesome. He was familiar with artistry and showmanship, and he knew, back in the 1980s, how to make a crowd dance.

When the video ended, the crowd roared and the Precious Little Devils were about to make their debut in front of millions. Brooklyn shined. Their performance was flawless, animated, and sexy. The judges remarked how well their delivery was and how creative their rendition of Tristan's song was. Judge number three, the 1980s icon Austin Rivera, commented, "I might have chosen a different song. However, if memory serves me, all of Mr. Bondage's songs were quite difficult."

Adonis used the last moments of the show to remind everyone to vote for their favorite group and that in two weeks the first elimination would take place. The Devils had survived their first television performance and, for the most part, with flying colors. Tristan summoned the band back to his hotel room for some talk and a late buffet.

Once locked safely away in Tristan's suite, he told the Devils how amazing they were and how proud he was of them. He also warned them that, if they wanted to beat Blood Red, they'd have to step up their game a bit more. He reminded them that Devin was the most popular, making his band an instant favorite.

Colin spotted Tristan's guitar propped up against the closet in the corner of the room. He grabbed it and began to play "Demons" by Imagine Dragons. Brooklyn started to sing it. Tristan decided to sing it with her. Together their voices were filled with a seductive harmony. The Devils listened in awe and applauded when they had finished. There was a magic created when the two of them sang together; there was no mistaking that fact!

The guitar was passed around half the night. They took turns singing and playing. Tristan loved this night! He loved the music, the friendship, the laughter, and Brooklyn's unadmitted love for him. It grew late and the Devils decided it was time to go to their respective rooms and rest for tomorrow. One by one, they planted a wet kiss upon Tristan's lips, and one by one he methodically wiped it off as soon as he received them. Brooklyn laughed the entire time.

When they had all left, Tristan said, "Thanks for coming to my defense!" She was still laughing as she gave him a very unconvincing sorry. Tristan lay back on the pillow and admitted to Brooklyn, "Tonight was a good time." He remarked, "You were amazing today. You're a very special little girl."

She laughed at him once again, began kissing his lips ever so deliciously, and said, "I'm not such a little girl."

Tristan touched her face and whispered, "You're very precious to me." She joined him on the pillow and kissed him deeply, noticing that he didn't seem to be responding in his usual let's-make-love way. She noticed he was pale and when she touched his cheek, she realized he was in a cold sweat.

"Hey, Tris, what's wrong baby?" she asked. Straining to hide the fact that he was in agony, he told her that he hadn't taken any pain medication today. She immediately ran to his jacket and grabbed the bottle of pills she had given him before. She took a single one out and handed it to him with a glass of wine from their buffet dinner. He moaned as he sat up to take it, trying to hide the fact that he was in pain seemed pointless now. "What can I do?" she asked, becoming frightened.

"Come here," he asked of her. "Just put your arms around me and don't be nervous. The medicine will work soon and the pain will stop." She obeyed his request and put her arms around him for what seemed an eternity while he struggled to hide the actual amount of agony he was in. He began to tremble and Brooklyn tightened her arms around him. She kept remembering what the nurse had said in the hospital, referring to him as a regular. While he struggled to control his pain, Brooklyn struggled not to call 911.

Tristan finally began to relax; the severe pain began to subside. He reassured her, "It's okay now, the pain is starting to go away." Brooklyn relaxed her grip as she felt a great sense of relief. "I'm sorry, love," Tristan said. "This pain situation makes life a little bit tough, so don't give up on me, okay?"

"Don't talk crazy," she answered. "I've never been happier with anyone, you jerk!"

Tristan smiled. "Do you mean that?" he asked.

"Yes," she admitted.

"I just want to love you—that's all." Tristan confessed.

"You are very sweet." she volunteered.

"That's because you love me," he joked.

"I never said that," she joked back.

"But you will," he said and kissed her on the top of her forehead.

Brooklyn laid her head on top of his chest. He began stroking her hair and moving his hand up and down her back in hopes of making her relax. She was exhausted from today's events and within moments she was fast asleep. Tristan continued stroking her hair. He watched her sleep for a long time and thought to himself how lucky he was to have her beside him. He thought about her day and night. To say he was obsessed with her would be an understatement. Tristan had conquered many other relationships in his lifetime and he knew with all the variables against him, being age, his medical condition, and the pressure of the reality show making this relationship work wouldn't be easy. From experience he knew love just wasn't enough. He decided to change his mind-set and focus upon the positive things they had going. He knew spoiling her would never be an issue. They had common interests in music and songs. They were magnificent in bed together and he loved her very deeply, enough for the two of them. Satisfied that he could take on the challenge of their relationship, he drifted off to sleep with his arms surrounding her.

* * *

The set was a breeze on Tuesday compared to yesterday. The Devils were able to enjoy their moments on stage as it was a performance-free event. Yesterday's performances and introduction were recapped and next week's challenge was announced. The bands were sentenced to performing a song from Broadway and a song from a movie. Damian and Dazzel loved that challenge; however, the only Broadway song Brooklyn ever sang was during karaoke, when Damian forced her to.

The remainder of the week was spent learning numbers with the other bands for the purpose of a show opener and a show filler. More personal videos were shot of the bands in order for America to become more familiar with each and every one of the band members, in the hopes that America would form an attachment with their favorite competitor.

The nights in the city after the show were filled with fancy restaurants, romantic interludes, excitement, and laughter. On Wednesday, Dazzel was commissioned to perform in drag at one of the larger gay bars on the west side. Off they all went to support her—the Devils, Tristan, a videographer from the show, Devin Liam, Blood Red, and Billy Blaze. Once on stage, Dazzel dragged her heart out. She did back flips, cartwheels, splits, and lip syncing all at once. The videographer recorded it all. The crowd welcomed her style of drag and requested a second number. The DJ downloaded another song for her and the audience cheered.

The Devils loved the gay city bars and after a time disappeared into the crowd with high hopes of finding love and lust. Devin and Blood Red would be leaving to visit another bar, but not before Devin joined the queens on stage to do a number. Devin jumped at the chance to perform, unlike Tristan, who declined. Tristan did make a short appearance on the stage to promote the show and the Devils. Billy Blaze was also asked to do a song, but he was on his way to becoming extremely intoxicated and bowed off. Brooklyn was asked by Dazzel to perform "Telephone" by Gaga as a duet, and the audience loved it.

Brooklyn felt at home in a gay bar more so than any straight club she'd ever been at. She mingled, made new friends, and had various short reunions with the Fire Island crowd. Although she periodically ran to Tristan, who stationed himself on a bar stool, and gave him a quick kiss here and there, she was pulled in a million different directions by the patrons of the club. It was as though she were a gay magnet.

Tristan adored watching her having such a good time as she committed social intercourse. Finally, after hours of being social, Brooklyn returned to Tristan and suggested they leave. "What about the boys?" Tristan asked, truly concerned.

"I haven't seen them in hours. I don't even know if they are still here," Brooklyn admitted. "They'll find their way back," she said with confidence, knowing exactly what gay boys do when let lose in the city.

"Were you bored to death?" Brooklyn asked Tristan.

He answered, "Not at all. I was smiling the whole time just watching you. Besides, I was hanging with my drunk buddy over here." He pointed to Billy. The drunk rock star turned to Brooklyn and put his arms around her. Normally, Tristan would have been horrified at his aggressiveness toward the woman he loved, but under the circumstances, he let it slide. Tristan got him a cab and ordered it back to the hotel, while he and Brooklyn hailed a different taxi for their trip back.

* * *

The session on set ended early the next day, thankfully, since half the bands and their mentors suffered from severe hangovers. Tristan offered to take Brooklyn to dinner; however, they decided together that the more responsible thing to do would be to leave the city and start practicing for next week's challenge. They had to be amazing by Monday and they only had four days to become so.

The ride home had become a vehicle for discussion as to their choices of selections for their Broadway and movie performances. The ultimate decision was Tristan's, but he was wise and knew that the Devils best knew what they were capable of doing better than anyone. Brooklyn suggested "I Can Hear the Bells" from the show *Hairspray*. She was most familiar with that song because the drag queens chose it often. Tristan was unimpressed by the level of difficulty of that song and told Brooklyn to let it stay a drag number. Garret wanted to do something from *Rocky Horror* but Tristan shot that down also, thinking everyone would be expecting someone to do Rocky. "One Song Glory" from *Rent* was Damian's choice. Tristan thought it too sad and emotional to perform; however, a medley of *Rent* songs might be appropriate coming from an almost all-gay group. The dramatic aspect could be advantageous and the difficulty level would be appreciated by the judges. They all agreed that a medley would also be different and unexpected.

Next, a song from a movie needed to be chosen. Tristan already had a song in mind ever since the challenge had been announced. "I think you should do 'Let it Go' from *Frozen*. The difficulty factor is there, and every mother's child loves it," Tristan explained.

Brooklyn rolled her eyes. "My voice isn't that good," she admitted. "When you do a song with that kind of magnitude, you have to be unmistakably fabulous," Brooklyn rationalized.

"Yes, but I think you can pull it off. We will dress you up as Elsa, we'll make it snow, and the boys can dress as Olaf. We can add some special effects to the performance and I'll coach you until you get it right," Tristan said reassuringly. "Besides, where's that confidence, missy?' he asked Brooklyn.

"It's too hard," she said.

"Will you try it for me?" Tristan asked.

"Fine," she said, "I'll try it."

Tristan lured the Devils directly to the studio, stopping briefly at each of their residences so they could drop their luggage off and pick up their transportation home from the studio. He promised to buy them dinner. The band was excited to start working on the Broadway challenge and would have gone to the studio even without the promise of food.

Damian began working on an arrangement for the *Rent* medley with Colin, while Dazzel and Garrett looked up the words and music to *Frozen*. Tristan picked his guitar up and within moments figured the music out to "Let It Go" on his own. Brooklyn wasn't as lucky. The first time she sang it, she could reach the high notes, but her performance was pitchy and uneven. She looked at Tristan and said, "Okay, I tried it, now pick a different song."

Tristan calmly walked over to Brooklyn and kissed her frowning forehead. "That was a noble attempt," he said. "It's going to take a little work, but I know you can get it, now let's try again." Brooklyn sighed.

By the end of the evening, both Tristan and Brooklyn were exhausted from the effort. Tristan's patience was dwindling as he felt Brooklyn was purposely not trying her hardest. He began to raise his voice too. "Brooklyn, you're not really trying!"

She yelled back at him, "I am trying!"

"You're not following the way I told you to," Tristan insisted.

"You're just being annoying," she said angrily to Tristan.

"Well, we're staying here until you attempt to get it right," he scolded.

Dazzel couldn't resist putting her two cents in. "Trouble in paradise?" she asked.

Tristan ignored her remark and continued to yell at Brooklyn, "Just try and focus a little on what I'm saying to you."

With that Brooklyn lost it and screamed at him, "OMG, this is like déjà vu. It's like five weeks ago when we hated each other."

Somehow hurt by that remark, Tristan went over to Brooklyn and put his arms around her stiff and angry little body.

He put his forehead against hers and whispered, "We never hated each other. You know it and I know it. We both felt a deep connection from the start. I love you, baby." Brooklyn's body relaxed and Tristan put his arms around her. He continued to hold her as he dismissed the band for the evening.

Brooklyn already felt guilty for yelling at Tristan and for hurting him with her mean comment. She hugged him tightly and asked, "Can you come home with me tonight?"

"I was hoping you'd ask, and I would love to more than anything else in the world right now," he said, still hurting slightly from her remark, being the sensitive person that he was.

Brooklyn brushed a lock of his hair out of his eyes and said, "I'm sorry I said that to you. I know we never hated each other. I was just being mean and angry," she confessed.

"I deserved it," he admitted "for insisting that you sing that stupid song. It's okay if you want to do another instead."

"No, I'll do the song," she said. "I'll embrace the challenge," she decided.

Tristan released his grip on her and sat down on the coach. "Come here," he summoned. She climbed on top of him, straddling his lap, placing one knee on one side of him and the other knee on the other side, being careful not to actually sit on his lap, fearing she might hurt him accidentally. She pressed her chest up against his chest and her lips up against his lips.

Their physical desire for one another quickly grew out of control. He pulled her body even closer to his and urged her downward until she was actually sitting on his lap. She felt him become aroused through their clothes. Without getting up, he gently laid her down onto the couch and pressed his own body on top of hers. Their clothes began to come off until they were naked. He slowly and gently found his way inside her. Their climax was exciting yet tender and romantic.

When they were finished making love, Tristan ran to the closet and found a black velvet cape to cover their nakedness. He locked the studio door in case one of the band members were to return. He shut the lights except for a small light near the bathroom and rejoined Brooklyn on the couch. She lay there with her head upon his chest and began to drift into that dream like state that happens right before sleep becomes real. "Come on, love," Tristan coaxed, "before we wind up here for the night without a toothbrush."

Just then, before they even had the time to get dressed, there was a knock on the door. "I forgot my music to 'Let it Go,'" Dazzel's voice bellowed from the other side of the door.

Tristan yelled, "We're indisposed, use your key." Faster than the speed of light, her key came out and Dazzel unlocked the door and was inside.

"Just in time," Dazzel exclaimed joyously.

Brooklyn answered seductively on purpose, "No, actually you're too late."

"So apparently you two made up," Dazzel commented.

Brooklyn explained, "That wasn't really a fight. However, if this was our way of making up, I would fight with him every day of my life."

"I'm so jealous," Dazzel admitted.

"You should be," Brooklyn insisted. With that Dazzel grabbed her music, pretending to be mad and she was gone.

"Let's go home," Brooklyn suggested. They climbed into separate cars but arrived at the cottage simultaneously. Tristan lit a fire once inside and Brooklyn turned on the shower. He quickly joined her and then dried Brooklyn and himself both in the same towel. She changed into a tiny pink nightgown and he put on his underpants that he had left in the dryer before they left for the city. He went to sit by the fire, and shortly thereafter Brooklyn joined him. She sat close beside him and began to brush her wet hair.

He touched her face and exclaimed, "God, I love you!" And then he playfully added, "And you love me."

"I never said that," she reminded him.

"But you will," he reminded her. He took the hairbrush out of her hand and began to brush her long blond we hair until it was knot-free. She jumped on top of him and began kissing him in between her words. "Tris, before at the studio"—*kiss*—"that was crazy"—*kiss*.

"And wonderful," he added as he kissed her back.

"Trist," she called as she suddenly rolled off him and got her guitar from the edge of the fireplace where it lived. "Play 'Let It Go,'" she asked as she handed him the guitar. He began to play it and she began to sing it. He began to sing some harmony with her and together they sounded amazing.

"That was near flawless," he commented.

"Because we sang it together," she suggested. "I think we need to cancel Stars tomorrow and rehearse this some more," she thought.

"No." Tristan jumped up suddenly. "You're going to perform it there tomorrow night," he said.

"Really?" she questioned. Then she had an amazing idea. "Tristan, do a song with me at Stars tomorrow, please, please, please?" she begged.

He laughed. "Settle down, girl. I haven't been on a stage performing in a very, very, very long time." Changing the subject purposely, he said, "Let's go to bed."

* * *

Just before dawn, Brooklyn awoke to Tristan, tossing and turning and talking in his sleep. "Stop, please stop, that hurts . . . no, no, no!" he yelled.

She shook him gently and called to him. "Tristan wake up baby, wake up . . . you're safe, you're safe." Tristan jumped up suddenly. He was drenched in sweat and shaking uncontrollably. Brooklyn put her arms around him. "It's just a bad dream, it's over now," she said to him soothingly.

He put his face in his hands and then lifted his head and said, "I'm sorry, love." He apologized again and again for waking her.

"It's okay," she told him over and over again.

But it wasn't really okay. This was no ordinary nightmare. He was greatly affected by it. "Do you want to talk about it?" she asked.

"I'm okay now," he lied, trying to talk himself into calming down. "Go back to sleep," he told her.

"Hey, like that's really going to happen now," she responded. "Talk to me, Tristan," she insisted.

Tristan put his face inside his hands once again. When he lifted his head back up again, he stared into the darkness.

"Remember when you accused me of chasing my own demons? Well, you were right. They haunt me all the time. They come in the form of these recurring nightmares. I'm scared all the time, wherever I go. I'm scared of the pain . . . scared of the dreams . . . scared of the future, and now, after tonight, I'm mostly scared of losing you." Brooklyn took his hand, placing it lovingly upon her own face, and reassured him that wasn't going to happen anytime soon.

"There is something else I'm scared of, and you really need to know what it is. I'm scared of the stage. I know I can never perform on stage again, ever," he sadly admitted. "The dream goes like this, it's identical each and every time. I'm on stage, ready to start a concert, but then I can't even speak. I try to sing, but the words won't come out. A gripping fear comes over me, and then everything goes black in the dream. Somehow I'm back in that dark alley, scared and in so much pain. I feel them ripping my shirt off and cutting my chest. Then I wake up like this, shaking and half-delusional."

Brooklyn sat there speechless, not knowing what to say to comfort him. She wiped the tears away that were falling from his eyes. "Now you know my darkest secrets." He admitted. Trying to add a bit of humor to a dark situation, Tristan added, "If Barbara Walters ever interviews you and asks about me, you might not want to let on about the stage fright."

Brooklyn hugged him. "You know I would give anything to see you live on stage," she told him, attempting to be encouraging.

"I would die to give you anything you wanted," he said and added, "but I don't think I will ever be able to give you that. I'm sorry, love."

"For you never to perform on stage would be worse than a crime with your amazing talent. You are an artist of epic quality, but I'll respect that for now," she added. "I'll let you make it up to me in bed." He laughed finally and hugged her, feeling a great sense of relief having told her of his dilemma.

He then went on to say, "When I woke up in the hospital, there was so much pain, so much fear. The doctors said I would never walk again, if I lived. I wanted to die. In fact I prayed for death, but now, I thank God every day that I survived. You see, life has all of a sudden become very precious, and that's because of you."

The first light of dawn appeared through the French doors and Tristan suddenly asked, "What time is it?"

Brooklyn looked at her cell phone. "It's 4:30 a.m."

"I have to go now," he announced. Brooklyn laughed, thinking he was joking, until he began to dress.

"You're serious?" she said in disbelief.

"I have to, love, go back to sleep," he ordered.

"Seriously?" she said half-laughing. Tristan sat back down on the bed and took her disbelieving face in his hands.

"I have to go to physical therapy. I go almost every day. It's bad if I miss it."

"I wish you could stay a little longer," she said.

"So do I, but I can't, love. Now go back to sleep and I'll see you in a few hours." He kissed her and was gone.

* * *

Brooklyn sat there dumbfounded for a second, and then dialed the phone. A voice half-asleep on the other end answered, "Hello?"

"Dazzel, are you sleeping?" Brooklyn asked, knowing full well she was.

"Really?" answered Dazzel.

Brooklyn begged urgently, "Can you come over. Now?"

Dazzel asked, half-annoyed, "Now?"

"Yes, now," Brooklyn pleaded.

"Are you okay, what's the matter?" Dazzel asked, now almost fully awake.

"I have to talk to someone," Brooklyn informed her.

Dazzel asked, "Well, why does it have to be me at this time of night?"

"Please?" Brooklyn begged.

Finally Dazzel agreed, "Okay, okay, you sound desperate, and just for your own personal knowledge, I'm not painted."

Twenty minutes later, Johnny knocked on her door carrying a dress and a makeup bag full of Dazzel. "Now what's wrong? And it better be good."

"Tristan just left," Brooklyn stated.

"Now?" Johnny asked. "Did you guys fight again?"

"No, no, nothing like that, he went to physical therapy," she said.

Johnny asked, "And you don't believe him?"

Brooklyn laughed. "Of course I believe him. It's not that . . . it's just . . . that . . . well, I don't know what the hell I'm getting myself into."

"Speak, girl," Johnny demanded.

"I'm falling in love with a man twice my age."

"But very sexy," Johnny interrupted.

"Yes," Brooklyn said, "he's very sexy, but that's the least of the issue. He needs care. He's always in pain and tries to hide it from me and the rest of the world. He has terrible nightmares, he leaves our bed before dawn, and I think he doesn't trust that I'll continue to be with him because of all these issues."

Johnny suggested, "So then talk to him, just tell him there's too much drama and it's not going to work out. Tell him you just want to be close friends with benefits!"

"I can't," Brooklyn said. "I think I'm in love with him. He's so sweet, so romantic. He is so talented, so brave . . . and so incredibly sexy as you pointed out before. I've never had anyone make love to me the way he does—never. It's almost as if I'm addicted to his lovemaking!"

Johnny then said, "Well, that's it, it's just lust you're in love with . . . Does he have a big . . ."

"Stop it, you size queen!" Brooklyn laughed.

Out of curiosity Johnny asked, "Has he told you he loves you?"

"Yes," Brooklyn admitted. "He tells me constantly, in words, actions, with romance."

"Have you professed your undying love for him yet?" Johnny wondered.

"No." Brooklyn said.

Johnny, who was sitting on the couch painting his face and well on his way to becoming Dazzel, thought for a moment. "Maybe the fact that he's in pain and needs you makes you love him more?"

"No," Brooklyn said, "I feel bad that he's in pain, but he tries never to admit to me just how much he's hurting. Sometimes I wish he would tell me how much pain he's in, other times I wish he'd never told me he was in pain at all."

"Well then," Johnny suggested, "talk to him."

"And tell him what? To please stop being in pain in front of me?" Brooklyn said sarcastically.

"Listen, gurrll," Johnny began, "you can't have it both ways. You have to take the good stuff with the bad. The man is outrageously sexy, he showers you with expensive diamonds that sparkle so much they are blinding, he takes you to extravagant restaurants, he apparently loves you more than you deserve to be loved, he's considerate enough to hide his suffering from you so that you're not stressed, he's brave as you say, and he's addicted you to sex. What could be better? But most importantly, he believes in you. Mary, if that's not enough for you, then you are really a spoiled brat. I would give the wig off my head for a man like that. Hey, is this really the same monster we met a few weeks ago?" Johnny asked.

Brooklyn smiled to herself and said, "Yes, that's him. That devil has become my savior. He's becoming very special to me."

Playing devil's advocate Johnny pointed out, "Well, he's old."

"But he's hot!" Brooklyn answered. "He has so much to give, and I feel like he's giving it all to me."

Johnny continued to play advocate. "Well, you two are way too entranced with each other, considering you only met a minute ago."

Brooklyn announced with conviction, "I'm sure I could spend the rest of forever with him."

Johnny, who had now completely transformed into Dazzel, stood up and decided, "Clearly this has been settled then." Brooklyn, at ease with her decision, agreed. Dazzel then yelled, "Well then, why did you make me come here, at the crack of dawn, half-asleep, unbedazzled, and uncoffeed?!"

Brooklyn hugged Dazzel. "I love you, Dazzel."

Dazzel laughed. "You should."

* * *

Brooklyn and Dazzel arrived at the studio very, very early, both carrying a delicious Starbucks coffee. Neither one of them had anything else to do at 6:00 a.m. anyway. They practiced "Let It Go" for over an hour until Tristan walked through the studio door. He was smiling his contagious smile and happy to see that his girls were so driven. "My ladies," he said enthusiastically and with the heaviest cocky accent he could conger up. He walked over to Dazzel and kissed her on her forehead, then proceeded to wipe his lips off in plain sight of her. He then took Brooklyn's hand and led her into the bathroom, closed the door behind them, and kissed her lips with the emotions of his entire heart. "Hey," Tristan said, "are you mad at me for leaving?"

"Very," she said as she passionately kissed him back.

"Do you still love me?" he asked.

"I never said that," she answered.

"You will," he answered back, and winked at her. Then he pulled a little scarlet box from his pocket and explained, "Here's a little something for putting up with me last night and for being so sweet to me."

"Tris, baby, you cannot keep doing that."

"It makes me very happy to buy you beautiful things, love. Now open it, see if you like it," he said. Brooklyn hugged him and opened the box where a shiny diamond bracelet sat just waiting to be worn upon her delicate wrist. Tristan placed it on her wrist and she hugged him and told him how much she loved it. Just then there was a knock on the bathroom door, with Dazzel standing on the other end of the knock.

"I have to pee, I drank coffee, you know!" Tristan opened the door but made no attempt to vacate the premises. The two stood there hugging. "Really!" Dazzel announced. Her eyes fell toward Brooklyn's new bracelet. She gasped. "You have to be kidding me, where's mine?" she asked jealously.

Tristan smiled and said, "You're not my girlfriend."

Dazzel retorted, "You know I would be if you let me."

Hearing those words, Tristan referring to her as his girlfriend, made Brooklyn happy. He had told her a million times that he loved her, but calling her a girlfriend sort of gave her a place in time. On the other hand those words connoted some form of belonging as well as commitment. She thought to herself, *This is starting to get real!*

The night brought them to Stars, all the Devils plus one. Tristan had promised to attend their gig since it was his suggestion that they perform "Let It Go." Their first set was filled with acrobatics. Tristan, realizing how well they performed their tricks, decided to incorporate those splits, backflips, and cartwheels into their TV acts. He sat in a corner of the club, quietly trying to remain inconspicuous while thoroughly enjoying the show. Before their first set ended, Damian announced that they had a little surprise for someone. "Hit it!" he yelled, and the Devils began a medley of Tristan's hits. He felt tears well up in his eyes and felt a new appreciation for the band he so painstakingly chose and had grown so close to.

"Please, welcome our fearless leader, Tristan Bondage!" Damian announced. Surprised, Tristan came to the stage.

Garrett took the mic and asked, "Tristan, can you please tell these homos how to vote for us?"

Tristan took the mic and shyly explained the voting process to the patrons. A large crowd formed around the stage and applauded wildly for Tristan. As he left the stage, he was bombarded with autograph and photo requests, which he gracefully accommodated.

Between the club kids all over Tristan and the kids who demanded Brooklyn's sole attention, the two didn't even get a chance to steal a kiss from one another. The second set went down without a hitch. They began it with the *Rent* medley. Not wanting anyone to take away their gay cards, the kids applauded loudly for Broadway.

Before the last number of the set Brooklyn announced, "Tristan, I'm gonna attempt to do this song next, but I'm scared. So can you come up here and give me a kiss?" Tristan ran to the stage and kissed her long and hard while most of the kids cheered for their happiness. The remainder made comments referring to the fact that Tristan was a breeder. She began to sing "Let it Go." Tristan loved her performance. She hit each and every high note perfectly and felt the song. He waited for her by the stage so he could tell her and the others how amazing they were, before the kids whisked them away to Gayland.

He took her in his arms as she left the stage. She told Tristan to go home to the cottage and get some sleep. He declined, telling her he wanted to stay. He also told her that she and the boys really delivered and he was proud of them.

Garrett, who was already half in the bag, cried out, "Shots, everyone!" They went to the bar while shots of fireball had already been lined up for them. By the end of the last set, Brooklyn was buzzed and playful. Tristan enjoyed watching her. She flirted brazenly with Tristan as he wondered to himself if it were really fair of him to be loving her like he did. Did she deserve a life with someone so much older than herself, someone who had an affliction and was in pain half the time as he was? He vowed right there and then to give her the best life he could, filled with dreams that only come true. He would devote his life to making her happy. He certainly loved her enough.

* * *

When Monday rolled around, the Devils were confident and well-versed in their song and music. They were prepared thanks to Tristan's leadership. Dressed in *Rent*-appropriate outfits, they performed their medley flawlessly. The judge's comments were favorable and void of criticism.

Backstage, Brooklyn dressed for their second number. Wardrobe and makeup prepared her to resemble Elsa from *Frozen*. She had on a shimmering white and blue gown, which sparkled.

Blood Red Orange was to perform just before the Devils. They choose "Circle of Life" from *The Lion King*. They were all dressed in cute little lion cub suits. The audience and judges couldn't help but fall in love with them. Their song was rich in tone and music. The entire auditorium applauded wildly. Brooklyn knew that this would be a difficult act to follow.

As Brooklyn prepared to take the stage, Tristan held his breath. The Devils were all dressed as the cute little snowman Olaf. Dazzel was dressed as Olaf in drag, with a wig and eyelashes. The music began and Brooklyn began to sing. By the first chorus Brooklyn owned the stage, and by the second chorus, the snow began to fall. Brooklyn knew about the falling snow, but what she didn't know was that, each time she pointed to something or raised her hands, an illusion would appear. The illusions were clips from the movie. One couldn't help falling in love with the Devils and Brooklyn. The illusions were magical. She didn't know how they got there, but she knew Tristan had a hand in it.

Chapter 5

Hero

The first elimination was scheduled to take place next week. Relatively certain it wasn't going to be them, the Precious Little Devils set out to select songs for next week's challenge. The first of the two-part challenge was choosing a song which best describes the band. For the Devils, that was a no brainer. "I Am What I Am" from *La Caux aux Folles* was no doubt the most relevant selection. They knew the song well since they performed it nearly every Friday night at the club. Accepted as a sort of gay pride anthem, Tristan would have to agree that. "I Am What I Am" was not only the best choice but the only choice. A video of the Devils just being playfully gay would run as the song was performed, along with some tribute clips of those famous gay men who passed, such as Liberace and Rock Hudson.

The second portion of the challenge would prove a bit more difficult. The groups had to pick someone or something that they absolutely idolized and dedicate a song to them or it. The selection of the idol would be difficult in itself, especially for Dazzel, who idolized herself. It was Garrett who finally came up with a scathingly brilliant idea.

"Why not dedicate a song to Tristan?" Garrett decided. "After all, he has taught us so much in such a short time." Brooklyn, of course, was in love with the idea; however, she had to inform the band that Tristan would never allow that.

"Why does he have to know? Why can't we surprise him?" wondered Damian.

"We already got yelled at for creating a surprise, rather, Tristan did," Dazzel reminded them.

"Okay, it's risky, but here's a way we can do it," Colin offered. "We inform makeup, wardrobe, and Adonis of our intention. If we can get Adonis as an ally to our scheme, the rest will be easy."

Damian, excited by the element of risk and surprise, had a plan. "Here's the deal, we allow Tristan to select a random idol that we all agree to and a random song to go with it. We learn it, rehearse it, and lead him to believe we love it. In the meanwhile, we rehearse the song we're dedicating to him at Stars." Brooklyn thought this idea was pretty solid, except for the fact that they hadn't chosen a song or taken into consideration the fact that they would have to ditch Tristan in order to practice it.

Tristan would certainly be surprised and honored but only if the performance was amazing. Once again the Devils would attempt to bring down the house with the element of surprise. It would be a dangerous proposition hiding this from Tristan, and actually hiding from Tristan himself would be even more risky, especially for Brooklyn. However, the band felt that, after everything he had been through and the effort and kindness he now showed them, he deserved it.

Colin was slated to take care of the rehearsal meetings, which of course would be Stars. The club was closed by day and didn't open for business until 10:00 p.m. This would give the Devils time to rehearse after they rehearsed the fake song at the studio during the day. If Tristan should get suspicious as to Brooklyn's whereabouts and happened to show up at Stars, the band would lie and say they were trying out a new sound system or something to that effect.

Damian would be in charge of contacting wardrobe, makeup, set designers, musical directors, and cameramen. He would also meet with the shows videographer in hopes of creating a video with Tristan in mind. Some of Tristan's old videos would work.

Brooklyn would have to contact Adonis and convince him to go along with their scheme and perhaps even help them. She would also have to find a way to ditch Tristan. She decided Terence would be a noble way to separate herself from Tristan. He wouldn't suspect anything if Terence asked him to dinner, and it wouldn't be hurtful to Tristan because Brooklyn wouldn't have to make up an excuse not to see him.

Garrett would be in charge of urging Tristan to invent a hero for them and he would also have to be in charge of finding Terence's phone number. He would have to steal it from Tristan's phone while Brooklyn diverted his attention elsewhere.

Dazzel was needed to fill in the blanks. Her job was the hardest because she, besides Terence asking Tristan to have dinner, would be the fill in for the three more nights of rehearsal that had to be accounted for. She knew Tristan was on Brooklyn like the rain, and it would be hard to share Brooklyn's time without him suspecting something. She decided she would tell Tristan that Brooklyn had to accompany her to a doctor's appointment or, if that didn't work, perhaps a shopping spree would.

Everything was set to work. The Devils each had a responsibility and a job to do. The only thing left was to select a song for Brooklyn to dedicate to Tristan. Brooklyn suggested "Holding On for a Hero." They all knew it, they had done at the club, and besides, Tristan was truly Brooklyn's hero. The song was unanimously agreed upon.

Brooklyn called Adonis and skillfully explained their devious plan. The young producer loved the idea and even volunteered to help them in every way possible. He thought it a way to set the stage for the Brooklyn/Tristan romance scandal that he had planned for later in the series. Now it was time to go to the studio and meet Tristan to discuss and implement this week's challenge.

It was already Thursday afternoon. Once again, the white van had dropped the Devils at their cars and Tristan at the studio. When they entered the studio after kissing Brooklyn and admitting to her that she was missed, for the hour they were apart, he complimented the Devils on the past week's performance. His only worry was that "Let It Go" was so flawless and perfect that it would be hard to top it.

Tristan loved their selection "I Am What I Am" and agreed to it immediately. He felt that pulling the gay card would endear most of the audience to the band. Now all they had left to do was select an idol. "Any suggestions?" Tristan asked. They all sat there with blank faces until Dazzel named a slew of drag queens she loved. Tristan diplomatically explained to her that it wouldn't be advantageous to the show since all of America was not familiar with those queens. Garrett mentioned the Beatles. Tristan decided the Beatles would not be believable as an idol to a bunch of twenty-year-olds.

"Would it be too gay if we chose Marilyn Monroe?" Damian wondered.

"Most definitely," Tristan answered, "but only because you're already doing a gay song, and we don't need to shove gay down America's throats all in one shot. Garrett?" Tristan asked, "Who's your favorite recording artist?"

Garrett thought and then answered "Melissa Etheridge!"

"Next," Tristan said. "Brooklyn, yours?" Tristan asked.

She answered, "Tristan Bondage."

"Come on, you guys, we need a believable nongay idol!"

"America!" Brooklyn called out. "A medley of 'Star-Spangled Banner,' 'My Country, 'Tis of Thee,' and 'America the Beautiful.'"

"Not bad," Tristan said. The others in the band glared evilly at her as these were hard songs to master and created more work for them when they already had too much pressure to conquer. Brooklyn simply figured that Tristan wouldn't suspect anything with such an out-of-the-box suggestion.

It was time for their devilish plan to be seriously jolted into action. They would all be spending the next couple of days dodging Tristan. This would be one of the most difficult tasks Brooklyn ever could imagine mostly because of the guilt of lying to him alone. After rehearsal ended, Brooklyn told Tristan that she had promised Dazzel she would accompany her to a doctor's appointment. Feeling guilty about the lie and wanting to selfishly see Tristan later, she asked him if he wanted to hang out at the cottage or meet her there later. He told her he'd be waiting.

Tristan put his cell phone down on the piano, exposed to the world. Seeing this, Brooklyn took advantage of his carelessness and randomly dragged him into the bathroom. She began kissing him seductively. Amused at her impulsive affection, he asked, "What did I do to deserve all these delicious kisses?"

Brooklyn answered him with yet another kiss and said, "Nothing, I just feel like I'm going to miss you for the next few hours."

"Not as much as I'm going to miss you, shawty," he admitted. Then he gave her his credit card and told her to take Dazzel out to dinner.

"Are you trying to ditch me?" she asked, trying to cover up her own deceit.

"Not at all, I'm going to take a power nap—I'm old, remember?"

She hugged him tightly and said, "But so sexy." She kissed him one more time and then exited the bathroom, knowing that it had been more than enough time for Garrett to steal Terence's phone number from his carelessly exposed cell phone as he had already text her the number she required.

The Devils rushed to Stars and began rehearsing "Hero." Thanks to Adonis, their secret had developed into a well-planned surprise. On Monday, before the Devils would be dedicating their song, Adonis would summon Tristan to help him out with some false dilemma. The Devils would run to wardrobe and each dress in a different superhero costume. Brooklyn, in a free-flowing sky-blue dress, would come out on stage and announce their tribute to Tristan. She would then run off the stage to an orchestra pit just below the set. The introduction to "Hero" was a two-minute instrumental that would give her time to reach her destination. She would stand upon a pedestal that would be raised to stage level just as her vocals began. Throughout the song, the pedestal, with her still on it, would be finally raised into the heavens. A wind machine would be in full force and effect, causing her dress and her silky blond hair to blow gracefully. As the end of the song approached, she'd be lowered back to stage level. Dazzel, who'd be attached to strings from the ceiling, would fly through the air as Wonder Woman. Someone would dress Tristan halfway through the song in a knight-in-shining-armor costume in hopes that he could be convinced to walk up to the stage right before the song ended and rescue her from her heroless plight. It was perfectly theatrical, full of romance and honor.

Brooklyn walked into the cottage quietly, hoping to find Tristan asleep. It was later than she'd hoped to get home. She and Dazzel had made up a dinner story complete with every detail, including the amount of cocktails they ordered and the conversations they factiously enjoyed.

"Hey, baby." she heard Tristan call from the bedroom. She ran into the bedroom and jumped on the bed where Tristan lay. She began kissing him ferociously, praying inside that he wouldn't question the lateness of the hour. "Wow, what a greeting, you really must have missed me," Tristan said, kissing her back. "I knew you loved me," he said with excitement.

"I never said that," she whispered.

"Damn," he said, "you will."

"You're arrogant," she said as she continued to kiss him.

"Yes, and conceited," he said in between kisses. Tristan put his arms around her and asked if everything was all right with Dazzel.

"Yep, perfect, like you," she answered.

"Come here, you little devil," he playfully said as he pulled her even closer. "I love you so much," Tristan said, smiling his contagious smile.

"Are you going to keep talking or are you going to make love to me?" she asked seductively.

"I think you're trying to take advantage of me," he whispered.

"I am," she admitted.

"Okay, then, I surrender," he said and kissed her deeply.

* * *

After rehearsal at the studio the next day, Tristan informed Brooklyn that Terence had asked him to go to dinner. "Cool," Brooklyn said.

"Will you come with us?" he asked. Brooklyn became flustered, not knowing how to decline. She didn't want him to get suspicious, nor did she want to hurt his feelings.

Luckily, Damian stepped in and said, "We have to be at Stars early tonight. They installed a new sound system and the DJ needs to do an early sound check."

Brooklyn jumped on Damian's deception. "Tris, you go ahead. Why don't you bring Terence to the club after?" she suggested.

"Are you sure, love? I can tell him another time," Tristan volunteered.

"No, no don't be silly. Will you come to Stars after?" she asked, hoping he'd say yes.

"You know I will," he answered.

"Come on, Brooklyn, go home and change, there won't be time to do it later," Damian insisted.

"Go on, love, I'll see you soon," Tristan said as he kissed her quickly.

"Have fun and say hello to Terence. Make him come to the club," Brooklyn insisted as Damian shoved her out the door.

"That was a close one," Brooklyn said to the Devils.

"Too close," Garrett agreed. "Tomorrow and on Sunday it will be hard to ditch him," Brooklyn said apprehensively. "You're going to have to start an argument with him, Brooklyn," Colin decided.

"No, I can't do that. He's way too sensitive. I just can't hurt him like that," she said.

"Well then, Dazzel's going to have to fake an illness or a lovers' quarrel," Damian thought.

"I'm not sick, and everyone knows very well that I don't have a lover," Dazzel said, annoyed that the responsibility all of a sudden fell on her.

Just then, Brooklyn received a text from Tristan: "I miss you already, don't make plans for tomorrow night, I have a surprise."

She texted him back, "I miss you too, and I love surprises."

"Now what?" Brooklyn asked as she informed the band of her text. Damian thought a moment, then decided that his surprise, if it were late, could work in their favor. "How so?" Brooklyn asked.

"Text him back and ask him what time he plans to have plans with you. Maybe it will become a late surprise. You could dress for your little rendezvous at Stars and meet him at the cottage."

"I'm not going to ask him now, I'll try and find out later."

The band rehearsed "Hero" until it was time for Stars to open. Brooklyn warned the DJ of their lie about the sound system and went back into the drag room to get dressed for the show.

Just as the band had finished their first number, Brooklyn noticed Tristan and Terence walking into the club. Brooklyn called out to Tristan from the stage as the spotlight flew through the audience and landed upon Tristan. "Hey, baby!" Brooklyn announced on the mic. Brooklyn threw him a kiss and he pretended to catch it. The audience clapped and the Devils completed their set.

During the intermission, Brooklyn ran to Tristan. She greeted Terence with a big hug and kiss. "Don't I get one too?" Tristan asked. Brooklyn turned to Tristan and put her arms around him.

"Did you guys have fun?" she asked.

"Yes," Tristan said, "but it would have been more fun if you were there."

Changing the subject, Brooklyn asked, "So what's the surprise?"

"If I told you what it was, it wouldn't be a surprise now, would it?" he said, teasing her. "You just be ready and at the cottage at eight thirty," Tristan ordered. Relieved that the surprise now at least had a time, she kissed him and said okay. That would give them some rehearsal time, she thought to herself.

* * *

Tristan allowed the Devils to leave the studio early that next day. He reminded Brooklyn to be ready by eight thirty sharp and to dress warm and festive. He also suggested that she bring a change of clothes and her makeup. Assuming the surprise included a sleepover, she happily agreed. Brooklyn kissed Tristan on the lips and off to Stars she went. The Devils rehearsed until seven, when they unanimously voted to end early. This gave Brooklyn enough time to get ready for her surprise while the boys had enough time to decide how to make the rest of Saturday night count.

Brooklyn chose a sparkling red sweater and black jeans with dazzling red boots as the evening's attire. She draped a dyed red fox coat around her shoulders and packed a small overnight bag, topped with all accessories and necessities. Promptly at eight thirty, her doorbell chimed. She ran to the door expecting to see Tristan, but instead there stood a man wearing a pink tuxedo and top hat waiting to escort her to her clandestine destination. He bowed, took her overnight bag, and led her to a pink limousine. She adored the mystery and intrigue and could only just imagine where her surprise journey would take her. After a forty-five-minute drive through dark, winding country roads, the limousine finally stopped.

There, in front of her disbelieving eyes, stood a flamboyant carnival, enriched with a heritage of enchanting sounds and exuberant lights. Brightly dressed juggling clowns, effervescent fire eaters, and brave sword swallowers, as well as a festive carousel and explosively lit Ferris wheel, decorated the lawn of a tremendous house reminiscent of the *Great Gatsby* mansion. The handsome ringmaster greeted the limo, and Brooklyn saw it was Tristan. She stepped out of the limo, holding on to Tristan's hand, and stood staring in disbelief at the fantasy that he had created for her.

It was cold outside, but she didn't feel the weather. Instead, she felt warmth and an amazing amount of love for this innocent, childlike romantic who had generated such a magical world for her. Tristan felt it was time she saw his lavish home on the water and wished her to always associate it with joyful memories as he hoped beyond all hope that she would live in it one day for the rest of their lives.

Brooklyn thought to herself that the Devils would never believe this spectacular display and wished with all her heart that they could see it. Suddenly, the front door of the mansion opened and out came her beloved Devils, laughing hysterically and yelling "Surprise!" as they began to enjoy the carnival along with Brooklyn and Tristan.

The carnival would last but another hour and then all the little carnival creatures would then pack up and leave without a trace of evidence that there ever was a carnival present. Hopefully all the Devils would follow suit. Tristan longed for time alone with Brooklyn. He felt robbed of precious time he should have spent with her but didn't.

Tristan made sure that Brooklyn made her grand entrance into his home via red carpet. Embraced by a dramatic entry, which led into the grand interior, were stylish columns and arches repeated through the home. It had a Hollywood influence with a flair for intricate details inside and out. The water element of the backyard added an interactive dimension to its design, creating a sense of movement and connection with the environment. Past the foyer sculptured ceiling treatments provided a sense of separation between the grand ballroom and formal dining area. A wet bar and butler's pantry ensured easy entertaining for any event. The gourmet kitchen overlooked the breakfast area. The lower level contained a media room and sound-proof recording studio, both separated by a heated Olympic-sized pool and hot tub.

Double doors led to the master wing, a secluded retreat with individual baths, two walk-in closets, a flat-screen TV framed inside the wall, a large round bed centering the room, a circular step in shower, and a spa tub overlooking a secret garden. Attached to the master was an enormous balcony overlooking the beach and the Long Island Sound. Three guest rooms were sequestered into private spaces, each having its own bath area. An elevator had been specially implanted into the house after Tristan returned from his stay at the London hospital since the Hollywood staircase would present too much of a challenge for him to conquer.

After giving Brooklyn a tour of his home, he escorted her up to the master wing and onto the balcony. He stood behind her, holding her around the waist and kissing the back of her neck as she marveled at the breathtaking view of the sound. Flabbergasted might have been an understatement as to the way Brooklyn was feeling after the carnival, the mansion, and the water's radiance. She stared at the moon dancing upon the water, realizing that she had never been so pleasantly overwhelmed in her life. Absorbed in the fantasy and the romance created by Tristan, she nearly confessed her love for him, but at the last minute the words "I love you" remained on her tongue, unsaid.

After some time, Tristan led Brooklyn back inside the master and took her coat like a proper English gentleman. Brooklyn, who had been speechless since the onset, finally whispered to Tristan, "I loved my surprise, more than you will ever be able to imagine, and your home is enchanting."

Tristan took her face in his two hands and kissed her, completely ignoring her praise and whispered back to her, "I've missed you."

Making love with Tristan was pure ecstasy, especially tonight upon the big round bed. When it was over, neither of them moved. They remained as one, pressed up against each other, entwined inside each other's caress. Finally, Tristan attempted to get up. Brooklyn pulled him back and whispered, "Please don't leave." He fell back down onto the fluffy pillows and kissed her forehead.

"I'll be back in a moment," Tristan assured her. He jumped off the bed and took something from one of the dresser draws. Back into bed he went, handing Brooklyn a golden box. She sat up Indian style and opened the box. In it was a golden key attached to a champagne diamond key ring. "It's the key to the house. Use it whenever you want for whatever you want," Tristan explained.

"I thought it was the key to your heart," Brooklyn joked.

"You already have that," Tristan admitted and leaned over to kiss her. "I want you to live here with me." Tristan suddenly got the courage to ask. He saw her body immediately grow tense, and he then added, "It doesn't have to be right now, whenever you're ready to. No pressure intended." Brooklyn thought to herself, *This is one step below a marriage proposal*, but strangely enough it seemed okay.

Tristan certainly did not wish to take the free out of the sprit, and he knew she required space to navigate, but he just couldn't help wishing she would hurry up and become ready to live with him. He loved her so much and the mansion was lonely. Realizing that she had never even told him she loved him, he knew from the bottom of his soul that she did. Still it would be nice to hear.

Brooklyn held the key to her heart and said thank you to Tristan. Sensing his disappointment, she told him she would keep it close to her heart always. Brooklyn put it back into the gold box and rested it upon the night table next to the bed. Without warning she pushed Tristan down onto the bed and pinned his arms above his head with her two tiny arms and trapped his body in between her legs as she kneeled on each side of his body. He didn't resist. "Okay, you got me," he said, laughing.

She leaned down, kissed him, and demanded, "Tell me what I have to do to make you love me always."

Deeply elated that she asked him that special question, which he considered close enough to an "I love you," he answered, "I love you more than I love my own life, just in case you haven't noticed. I'll never stop loving you," Tristan promised. Then with one swift motion he freed himself from her bondage and exchanged places with her. "Now what, my love?" he said.

Laughing, she demanded, "Come down here and kiss me!" Tristan gladly followed her command.

The second time was always more intense, deeper, and longer. As they lay in each other's arms, Tristan asked her if she were hungry. She told him no and echoed the same question to him. "No," he said and then asked, "Do you want to go swimming?"

"Come on," Tristan urged. He took her hand and led her naked to the heated pool. Tristan jumped in and then held his hands out for her. She jumped into his arms. They laughed, they splashed each other, and they hugged and giggled like children the entire time. Tristan then scooped Brooklyn into his arms and carried her to the hot tub.

Laughing, Brooklyn scolded, "You shouldn't be carrying me!"

"Shhh," he insisted, "you're light as a feather."

For a change, Tristan woke up next to Brooklyn. He skipped physical therapy, not wanting to leave her alone in a strange house, actually not wanting to leave her at all. It was a magical night filled with fantasy and romance for both, but dawn approached quickly. "I wish this night never had to end," she professed.

"It doesn't have to, you know," he reminded her.

* * *

They all arrived at the studio at the same time, the Devils in their cars and Brooklyn and Tristan in the pink limo. Tristan brought a little red velvet box with him, but instead of giving it to Brooklyn, he walked over to Dazzel and handed it to her. "This is for your help with the orchestration of the carnival last night, and even more so for leaving with the rest of the boys as you promised," he announced.

Inside was a large ornate crystal necklace, a true piece of drag jewelry. Dazzel jumped up and kissed Tristan on the lips, holding his neck so he couldn't break free. When she finally let go he wiped his mouth and announced, "Look at what I've become reduced to, accepting kisses from drag queens!" The Devils laughed until they couldn't laugh anymore. "Baby, will you still kiss me after that?" Tristan asked jokingly.

"Not until you rinse your mouth," Brooklyn joked back.

"You little bitch!" Dazzel teased Brooklyn.

Rehearsal went well, that is, until Dazzel informed Tristan that she was making Brooklyn go with her to see her mom after rehearsal. "Do you mind if I spend some time with her?" he asked Dazzel.

"OMG, you spent the night together, now it's my turn," Dazzel answered.

Brooklyn touched Tristan's face and whispered, "I'll meet you right after."

"For a late dinner?" he asked.

"For anything you want," she answered.

"At the cottage?" asked Tristan.

"Yes," she continued to whisper and then kissed him dramatically.

As the weekend came to a close, Brooklyn and the band were exhausted from the pressure of dodging Tristan, not to mention double rehearsals. At least the lies and deceit would come to an end. "I hope he's worth all this," announced Colin as they left Stars, having just finished their final rehearsal.

"He's worth this and so much more," Brooklyn said. Dazzel drove Brooklyn to the cottage where Tristan was waiting anxious to see her.

* * *

The white van carried Tristan and the Devils back to Manhattan. Still exhausted, the Devils slept the entire ride. Brooklyn sat up against Tristan as he held her. She thought about the eventful weekend but especially her carnival fantasy. She whispered to Tristan, "I'm not giving up the cottage in case one of us gets mad at each other and needs a place to think."

"What did you just say?" Tristan, overjoyed, turned her around to face him.

"I said okay, I'll move in with you."

"Are you sure?" he asked as tears of joy rolled down his cheeks.

"I'm sure," she said, smiling. Tristan hugged her tightly. "Any man that went through all that trouble to give me such a magical fantasy that I will remember for the rest of my life has got to be okay."

"Well, love, you just gave me my fantasy!" Tristan said as he hugged her. She wiped his tears away. "You see you do love me," he said still filled with tears.

"I never said that still," she said, kissing him.

"But you will, I promise," he said.

As promised, Adonis asked Tristan to help him with an emergency just before the Devils were to enter the stage. Tristan returned as the Devils took the stage wearing superhero costumes instead of American flags. To his dismay, he gasped and mouthed the words the words to himself. "What the fuck?" It was too late to change anything, so he held his breath and prayed. He was one second short of having a genuine panic attack. Brooklyn had taken the stage in her dazzling, flowing sky-blue dress and began her tribute speech.

"When it came to choosing an idol for this week's challenge, the Precious Little Devils unanimously decided upon someone we not only idolize but who we have grown to worship. For me personally, this man has become my guardian angel, my savior, and my soul mate. With America listening as our witness, we wish to dedicate our song to Tristan Bondage, my hero." She blew him a kiss, which he pretended to catch, and she ran off the stage to take her place in the pit below the stage that would ascend to the heavens of the set. Adonis took a seat next to Tristan in the front row where he noticed the tears streaming down his cheeks. Reminding him that this was live TV, he warned Tristan to try and control his emotions.

Brooklyn slowly started to rise from inside the bottom of the orchestra pit to the stage. When she became level with the stage she began to sing.

Where have all the good men gone?
And where are all the gods?
Where's the streetwise Hercules
to fight the rising odds?

By the time the chorus began, she and her pedestal had risen far above the stage. The wind machine blew her flowing dress and long blond hair in a sexy fashion.

I need a hero.
I'm holding out for a hero till the end of the night.
He's gotta be strong,
He's gotta be . . .

Midway through the song Adonis whispered to Tristan, "Come with me now." Tristan, although confused, followed Adonis beyond the stage. Standing there was a wardrobe engineer holding a knight in shining armor costume. "Hurry and put this on," Adonis insisted. As soon as Tristan viewed the armor, he immediately got it and slipped it on.

As Brooklyn sang the last refrain, Tristan walked on to the stage. He removed the steel helmet and bowed traditionally to Brooklyn. Although Dazzel had been flying all over the stage in her Wonder Woman costume, the audience's attention focused only upon the love so prevalent between the knight and his damsel. The audience cheered and stood up from their chairs as Tristan walked off into the sunset, arm and arm with his distressed damsel. The judges flew from their chairs, giving the Devils a standing ovation. The MTV DJ wiped the tears from her eyes as the two remaining judges remained astonished.

The audience was overwhelmed with admiration, causing Adonis to race onto the stage in an attempt to control their cheers and applause; however, his efforts to calm them failed. He quickly summoned Brooklyn back to the stage in hopes they would become silent at her return. His prediction was correct. The audience yearned to hear what she would say next. Adonis handed her the mic, hoping she would do well at the art of improvisation on live television. Flustered at first, she called Tristan back to the stage. "Where's my hero?" she announced. Tristan had taken off his armor and returned to the stage. The audience grew silent in anticipation of a dramatic yet romantic grand finale.

Upon his arrival onto the stage, he kissed Brooklyn and whispered thank you in her ear. The audience jumped out of their seats once again but silenced as Brooklyn began to speak. "As God and America as my witness, Tristan, I want you to know that I love you. I love you with all my heart and soul." Tristan hugged her, having difficulty keeping his emotions in check.

"She loves me!" he yelled victoriously to the audience as they cheered relentlessly. It was an emotional moment, truly heartfelt and unrehearsed, and the audience sensed that.

Adonis announced a commercial break—"We'll be back to this romantic chaos in a moment, don't go away"—as if anyone would dare to turn their televisions off.

"Great job," Adonis told Tristan and Brooklyn as they remained attached to one another in a romantic embrace. "You saved the day," he told Brooklyn and the Devils.

"That was an amazing bit of showmanship." Dazzel walked over to the two, and having just lost her wings, she stated, "Could you have chosen a more intimate moment to profess your undying love, in front of millions of people?"

"I don't care," Brooklyn announced. "I want the world to know!"

Damian snickered. "I think you have already accomplished that," he said sarcastically.

Tristan, still filled with tears of joy, whispered to Brooklyn, "I told you that you loved me."

"Yes, you did, and I do . . . very much," she confessed as she kissed the tears away from his cheeks.

"Okay, you two, dry those tears and get yourselves together. We return from break in three, two, one . . . ," Adonis said as he grabbed the mic from Brooklyn.

"Welcome back to *So You Wanna be a Rock Star: The Honeymoon Edition*," Adonis teased. "Tomorrow, sadly, is our first elimination, one of the bands and mentors will be leaving us. See you tomorrow 8:00 p.m. Eastern Time . . ."

* * *

Tristan was in his own happy little world on the ride back to the hotel. "Did you suspect anything?" Brooklyn asked, waking him up from inside his thoughts.

"No," he said. "How impossible was it to try and get rid of me?" he asked, knowing now that even the dinner with Terence had been contrived.

"Very," she admitted. "But mostly because I really would have rather been with you," she added.

Tristan leaned toward her and took her face in his hands, holding it so that he could look her straight in the eyes, and asked jokingly, "So tell me, do you really love me, or was that just a producer's play to raise the ratings?"

She laughed. "The truth?" she asked.

"The truth," he echoed.

"When I discovered that you were our mentor, I was ecstatic. I thought you were the sexiest man I'd ever seen. As mean as you were originally, I sensed sweetness inside of you and I was in love with that right from day one," she confessed. Tristan put his forehead against hers and then lightly kissed her face and finally her lips.

Still looking at her eye-to-eye, he asked, "Why was it so hard for you to tell me that you loved me?"

She looked into his deep blue eyes and said, "It's like the song by Ashanti: 'Every time we get so close, I feel like love will lose us both.'"

He took his own finger and kissed it and then placed it upon her lips and said, "I don't mind being lost in love."

Brooklyn tried to explain, "It's not about being lost in love but rather losing our own identities. It's irrelevant now because I just love you. I decided to embrace it and start a whole new canvas."

Back at Tristan's grand suite hotel room, the two showered in silence and in awe of one another. Both physically and emotionally exhausted, they lay under the comforter, softly kissing. Tristan began mildly caressing each and every part of her body. He was physically gentle as he made love to her, but she could feel him impassioned with sentiment and emotion.

* * *

Today was the first elimination. Who would be going home? Surely it wouldn't be Blood Red Orange or the Devils. Yet both bands were nervous just in case, by some strange twist of fate, America voted them away. Damian, starving for some reassurance, asked Tristan if he thought that there was a chance of the Devils being eliminated. Tristan smiled and said with confidence, "We got this one, next time could be different, but no way will we be leaving today. Relax and enjoy the show!"

The random announcer with the booming voice introduced Adonis, who took center stage. "Good evening America, and welcome to our first elimination night. By the end of this evening, only four bands will remain. Please join me on the stage, Blood Red Orange and Devin Liam." They came out on stage and Adonis, through flashbacks, recapped the last three weeks of their performances while the audience wildly applauded. "Drum roll, please," Adonis demanded. The drums rolled and Adonis announced, "Blood Red Orange, you are safe!" They breathed a sigh of relief and returned backstage. Brooklyn hugged and congratulated the lead singer and Tristan shook Devin's hand.

Next, Adonis commanded Billy Blaze and Rising Tides to step up to the stage. After their recap and the drum roll, Adonis announced the fact that they too were safe. "You get to keep on rockin'," Adonis said.

Adonis then had the last three bands join him center stage, Precious Little Devils and Tristan, Sin-cerely Yours and Jamison, and Delilah and City Girls. He began by recapping the historic performance of the Devils. He ordered the drum roll and announced, "Precious Little Devils, congratulations, join the others backstage, you are safe!" Adonis announced a commercial break and said, "When we return, we will be saying adios to one of these bands. Stay tuned!"

Happily, Tristan group hugged his band and said, "Well, we made the first cut."

Damian asked him, "Who do you think will be going home?"

Dazzel answered for Tristan, "Who cares? We're not."

Tristan interjected, "Don't be so cocky, missy. I can judge from the applause, we still aren't the favorites."

When the commercial had ended, Adonis proclaimed, "City Girls, Sin-cerely, one of you will continue, the other will be singing the blues all the way home. First, let's recap. Judges"—Adonis turned to focus on their table—"before I decree the band who will be eliminated, is there anything you wish to say?" He called on judge number one first, the world's most famous promoter.

"I feel it's going to be sad to see either one of them leave. It's too early in the competition to see what they really have to offer," said the judge.

Then Austin, the 1980s icon, spoke, "Quite frankly, I think the winner of this competition is already backstage. Whichever one of these groups remain, they better step it up if they hope to stay longer."

Backstage, the Devils waited to see the outcome. Garrett commented, "Ugh, this is killing me, just say who's staying already."

Damian, trying to calm Garrett's curiosity, said, "Relax, we will know soon enough."

"Are you guys still watching this?" Dazzel asked. "Who cares who leaves as long as it's not us!" she added.

"I want the City Girls to stay, they are fun to hang with," Garrett admitted.

"What's your prediction, fearless leader?" asked Colin.

Tristan smiled and said, "City Girls are leaving." He then took Brooklyn's hand and pulled her outside the green room. "Listen, love, I have to go back to the hotel for a while," he advised.

"Are you all right?" she asked.

"Of course," he said.

"But I should go with you."

"No, I'm okay, that's why I'm leaving now." He kissed her, but she could tell by his kiss that he was in pain.

"I'm going with you," she insisted.

"No, you're gonna need to go back on for the finale. I'll wait for you in the room. Come back to the hotel when you're finished, and don't worry, please, love," he declared. But she was worried. She watched him leave. He was pale and he was limping, holding tightly to his cane. She sensed a feeling of dread in the pit of her stomach as she believed he was hiding just how much pain he was in. She immediately phoned Terence and informed him of Tristan's condition. Terence reassured her that he would meet him in the lobby.

Feeling slightly relieved, she turned her attention to the drum roll that Adonis demanded. "The group that will be going home is . . ." Thirty seconds of silence filled the room. "City Girls, I'm sorry." Sin-cerely breathed a sigh of relief and exited the stage, while City Girls did a final number.

Dazzel applauded. "Good riddance, those girls needed serious help with their makeup anyway," she said. Garrett and Colin were saddened by the decision, and Brooklyn was just preoccupied with Tristan.

As soon as the show was finished, Brooklyn told Adonis that Tristan wasn't feeling well. He insisted she leave right away to be with him. She thanked him and grabbed a taxi. Terence had texted her while she was in transit. The text read, "Tris wanted me to tell you he was okay, but he's not. Come as soon as you can." She texted him back that she was almost at the hotel.

Brooklyn ran directly to Tristan's room, and used her key card to open the door. "Hey," Terrence said. "He's in agony. He keeps fading in and out. Go over to him and see if you can coerce him into consciousness so I can find out the last medication he took and how much." She ran over to the bed and called to him. She took his hand and held it in hers. She called to him again. This time he squeezed her hand. She lay down next to him and kissed his face. He opened his eyes and squeezed her hand again.

Terence whispered to Tristan, "When was your last medication?"

Tristan whispered back, struggling to speak, "Not since this afternoon." Tristan moaned in pain while Terrence prepared a syringe and proceeded to administer it to him.

"Let's see if it helps. Otherwise he's going to need to go to the hospital," Terence decided.

"What is it?" Brooklyn asked.

"It's morphine," Terence said as he injected it intravenously into Tristan's vein.

Brooklyn's eyes opened in horror. She was frightened. She remained calm for Tristan's sake. Still holding his hand, she whispered, "Please be all right, please." Brooklyn started to cry softly.

Tristan squeezed her hand again. "Don't cry, love." He took her hand and slowly pulled it to his lips and kissed it. He opened his eyes and pulled her hand to against his face. "Come closer," Tristan asked Brooklyn. She went back to lie beside him, kissing his face and stroking his hair. Terence felt his pulse. He noticed that he began to breathe easier.

"He's going to be okay," Terence told Brooklyn.

"The pain is starting to go away," Tristan said, still struggling to speak. Terence sat on the bed next to the two of them.

"Tristan?" he asked. "Do you want to go to the hospital?" Tristan painfully attempted to sit up, so Terence helped him.

"No," Tristan insisted. "I'm okay now. Thank you both," Tristan said. He turned to Brooklyn and gently said, "I'm sorry I scared you. I'll make it up to both of you. Let's go to dinner," he suggested. Neither one of them answered. "Well?" he asked. "Are you both mad at me?" he asked innocently.

Terence laughed. "First of all, it's 1:00 a.m., and secondly, I just gave you a giant shot of morphine, and you need to stay in bed and try and relax."

Tristan looked at Brooklyn. "I'm sorry you had to see that, love," he said, concerned.

"It's okay, I'm just glad you're okay," she said, relieved.

"I'll teach you how to give him these shots, just in case," Terence offered. "He only gets that when he's, well, like he was tonight." Terence took his pulse again. He looked into Tristan's eyes and said, "You'll live. We might not, but you will."

Tristan bent down and kissed Brooklyn's forehead. "I'm sorry, you two," he said. Terence felt bad for Tristan. He certainly didn't deserve this torture.

"Why don't the two of you get some rest?" Terence suggested.

"Hey, how did you know to meet me in the lobby?" Tristan asked as Terrence opened the door to leave.

"Ask your girlfriend."

Brooklyn thought to herself, *How am I going to be able to take care of this guy? He needs real medical attention. I'll just have to love him double time.* She watched him painfully walk to the bathroom and then watched his agonizing walk back to the bed. "You're still in so much pain," she stated.

"I'm just dazed from all that morphine," he tried to convince her.

"Not buying that," she said.

"Okay, then, just come here and hold me in your arms, and I know the pain will go away," he begged. Brooklyn did just that until he fell asleep. He woke up once during the night. Brooklyn tightened her grip around him and asked him if he were all right. He smiled and asked, "So you really love me that much, huh?"

"More than you realize," she said. "Now go back to sleep."

"I'm sorry to put you through this nonsense," he apologized.

"I'm so sorry you're in pain and that I don't know how to make your pain go away," she said sadly.

"Shhh," he whispered. "You make living in pain wonderful. I've never been so happy in my entire life," he proclaimed.

Brooklyn kissed him. "Me too," she confessed. Eventually, they both drifted off to sleep.

* * *

Tristan woke to a knock on the door. He let Terence inside, who immediately asked him how he felt. Tristan motioned to Terence with his finger upon his lips. "Shhh, Brooklyn's still asleep," he whispered.

"Sorry," he said. Remembering his initial question, Tristan reassured Terence that he felt fine, although perhaps a bit shaky from the morphine. Just then Brooklyn awoke, said a quick hello to Terrence, and hit the shower and the toothbrush. Wearing only a tee and panties, she announced that she was running downstairs to her room to get ready for the day's activities on the set. As she left, she quickly kissed Tristan and ran down the hallway to the elevator. Terence shook his head and asked Tristan, "Are you going to allow her to run through the hotel half-naked?"

Tristan laughed. "She does whatever she wants to do. Besides, look how cute she looks." They watched her as she caught the elevator and then they shut the door. Tristan thanked Terence over and over again for coming last night and saving his life. Terence explained that, if it wasn't for Brooklyn calling him and alerting him to the situation, he probably would have landed in the hospital or worse.

Tristan thanked Terence again nevertheless and jumped into the shower. He then ran down to the lobby to meet the Devils. They all jumped into the limo with the Tides and Billy and journeyed to the set. When they arrived on the set, the bands and coaches received an invitation by the producers to play among New York City's famous attractions and points of interest, for the purpose of filming a video for one of the show's segments. Their tour would include a visit to the Empire State Building, a ferry ride to the Statue of Liberty, and a walk through Central Park. When the day switched to night, they would be dining at one of New York's prestigious restaurants and then a walk through Times Square and Broadway would follow. Finally there would be a visit to the East Village, where they would relax at several nightclubs and bars, including Stonewall, the oldest gay bar in the city.

In between the day and evening activities, they would all get a two-hour hiatus, where they would be able to return to the hotel to regroup and change accordingly for the nights adventures. In Dazzel's case, she would be filmed as Johnny by day and then transform into Dazzel by night.

The weather was seasonably cool for the time of year, but it was bright and sunny. The visit to the Empire State Building proved to be exciting and humorous. The Devils all lifted Johnny up and threatened to throw him off the top. The cameraman was able to film a stolen kiss between Tristan and Brooklyn from the back of the ferry carrying them to Ellis Island. The Statue of Liberty just happened to be part of the background. Finally, they all piled into the horse and buggies at Central Park and pretended to race one another through the park. The videographers were satisfied with the days filming, especially when Johnny and Brooklyn did cartwheels on the grasses and lawns inside the park.

The day's activities proved to be hectic and exhausting, and the trip back to the hotel was welcomed by all. Tristan ordered the Devils to rest before dressing for the evening. Concerned for Tristan and the effect that running around all day might have had, she followed him to his room and made sure he rested in bed. He assured her in his heaviest cockney accent that he was "holding up famously."

Jamison and Devin decided to coach their bands and rehearse segments for the evening portion of the video. This would eventually work against them, as Adonis didn't want the filming to appear contrived. Billy's Tides used their hotel time to play video games, while their coach retired to his room and relaxed with several glasses of wine. This left him quite buzzed even before the night's festivities began.

The cameramen followed the group as they traipse through the city from one location to the next. They captured the excitement of Times Square, the blazing lights from Broadway, the camaraderie of the bands mingling as one, and the special glances of love between Tristan and Brooklyn. They filmed Dazzel in her glory at Stonewall, where queens ruled, and they caught Billy becoming more and more intoxicated as the night passed.

At the end of the day, Adonis would be pleased with the culmination of the videographer and cameraman's efforts. Once the cameras were silenced, Jamison, Devin, their bands, and Rising Tides returned to the hotel, while the Devils, Tristan, and Billy Blaze remained at Stonewall. Tristan observed Brooklyn having a fabulous time with all the queens she knew from Fire Island, where she summered with Cherry Grove's finest. Dazzel was having a blast as she was offered a chance to do a guest spot in the most famous gay bar. Billy stayed on for the soul purpose of having just one more.

As Dazzel began her number, a huge crowd formed around the small stage to watch. Brooklyn stood behind the crowd, conversing with the queens, when all of a sudden the drunk Billy Blaze appeared and wrapped his arm around her. Brooklyn, realizing how drunk he was, simply made an attempt to move away from him. Out of the corner of his eye, Tristan observed the annoying Billy, following Brooklyn as she tried to keep him out of her space.

His jealousy of Billy had long since ceased; however, he started to make his way toward Brooklyn in case she needed assistance. Then, all of a sudden, without warning, Billy cornered Brooklyn against a wall and pinned her to it, trying to kiss her. Tristan saw red and pushed his way through the crowd to Brooklyn's rescue. Knowing that Billy was drunk and not wishing to cause a scene, Tristan tried diplomatically to convince Billy to release Brooklyn. She was proud of Tristan and the way he tried to handle the situation and relieved that Tristan didn't just try to hit Billy and be done with it.

Tristan was able to coerce Billy to release Brooklyn, and when she became free, he quickly handed her over to Garrett for safekeeping and started to walk away. The out-of-control Billy Blaze turned to Tristan and grabbed him, landing one single punch to the corner of his mouth, forcefully sending him flying across the room and to the floor against another wall. Brooklyn saw a single drop of blood trickling from Tristan's mouth and lost it. She wildly freed herself from Garrett and ran toward Billy with all the anger and adrenaline she possessed from the depths of her soul. Just as she reached Billy and was able to give him one swift kick, Garrett and Damian picked her up and carried her out of Billy's reach as she kicked and protested. Dazzel then appeared behind Billy and began hitting him with her high heel. She too was swiftly carried away by a bystander in the crowd.

Brooklyn made a second attempt to attack Billy as soon as her feet were allowed to touch the ground. Garrett grabbed her once again and reminded her that Tristan was lying there, probably hurt. "You better go over there and make sure he's okay." Without a second thought, Brooklyn ran to Tristan, who was still perched up against the wall. Colin sat there, guarding his attempts to get up and fight with Billy. He knew any retaliation would not end well. Even drunk, Billy was stronger and healthier than Tristan and therefore no match for him. Besides, someone had already called the police, and along with the police, the press would follow.

Brooklyn, now hysterical, hugged Tristan. "I'm okay," he reassured her over and over again. "It's just that he"—pointing to Colin—"won't let me get up . . . shhh," Tristan said trying to calm her down. "Listen, we have to get out of here quickly. Please, Brooklyn, you need to stay calm for me. The last thing we need now is bad press," he calmly explained to Brooklyn, who immediately calmed herself. Colin helped Tristan to his feet and readied the two for their great escape. Damian escorted Brooklyn through a side door with Tristan behind. The rest of the Devils followed as Dazzel still held her heel in her hand and waved to fans as Colin pushed her inside the limo.

Brooklyn wet a napkin inside the limo and wiped the blood that still trickled from Tristan's mouth. He smiled at her and said, almost laughing, "Please promise me that you will never get that angry at me, Tiger." He referred to her vicious attack on Billy. Colin kept staring at Tristan. To him, he looked pale and like he might have been hurt more than he was willing to admit. Colin secretly convinced the limo driver to stop at the emergency room at NYU Medical Center. Once there, Tristan refused to leave the limo. "I swear to you all, I'm okay," he said.

Colin told him that he didn't look okay and said, "Why don't you just let them check to make sure?"

Brooklyn, using her tears as a weapon to manipulate Tristan's decision, cried, "Please, Tristan, go for me." Unwilling to deny her request or to deny her anything for that matter, he went inside.

He was released after only an hour but was exhausted and very sore. "Let's go back to the cottage," he requested. "Please," he begged. "We can stop at the hotel and collect what we need and still be home before dawn." Brooklyn agreed and thanked him for being so brave and for stopping inside the hospital.

They both slept all the way home. Brooklyn made Tristan lay down on her lap while she stroked his hair and held his hand. When they arrived in front of the cottage, Tristan was so stiff he could barely stand up. The limousine driver helped him out of the car and to the front door. Tristan thanked the driver and handed him a $200 tip.

Brooklyn ran to the bathroom, brushed her teeth, and turned the shower on, hoping that the warmth and steam of the water might sooth Tristan's aching body. Although he could barely stand, the water looked inviting. Once inside, Brooklyn propped him against the corner of the wall so she could help him balance as she practically had to hold him up. She disguised the fact that he could hardly stand and the fact that she was his main support by hugging him as he leaned against the shower wall. She inspected the sight of wound where he was punched, and miraculously it wasn't swollen. After the shower, Tristan nearly fell into the bed and Brooklyn rushed to join him. Before they fell asleep, she texted the other Devils to let them know they were home and that Tristan was okay. She informed them that she was going to let Tristan sleep in, so they would be arriving at the studio late, to start without them.

She then turned toward Tristan, who instantly put his arms securely around her. She kissed his chest and then the corner of his mouth where he'd been hurt, and then reached up and put her arms around him. She held him as if he were more precious to her than ever before. She placed her head below his chin and told him that he really was her hero.

Tristan closed his eyes and began thinking to himself, *Do I really have the right to love her so much? If the Devils hadn't been there tonight, Brooklyn might have been hurt.* He realized that he wasn't even capable of defending her the way a man should. He thought himself selfish for wanting and needing her so desperately. Catching him so lost in thought, she kissed his lips, which distracted his thinking and brought him back to the bedroom.

"Hey, are you okay?" she asked. He told her he was fine, just preoccupied with the repercussions that tonight would cause when Adonis got wind of what had happened. Brooklyn jokingly asked if that were the reason that he hadn't told her that he loved her since they left the bar.

He turned to her, kissed her deeply, and said, "I will never stop loving you, always remember that." They both drifted off to sleep embracing one another.

Chapter 6

Still Victorious

Brooklyn was up early. As she watched Tristan asleep next to her, she fought the urge to wake him. He seemed peaceful, so she quietly showered, dressed, and ran to Starbucks, deciding if he wasn't up by the time she reappeared, she'd wake him.

By the time she returned, Tristan had already showered. He greeted her as she opened the door with a huge, passionate kiss. She greeted him with a huge Starbucks latte, both equally delicious, both equally desirable. Brooklyn was relieved to see Tristan walking around the cottage seemingly pain-free and decided to take advantage of it.

As Tristan sat down on the couch, trying to enjoy his coffee, Brooklyn quietly lurked behind him, then began to kiss the back of his neck and bite his earlobe ever so gently. It took him only seconds to feel his desire for her grow. His wanting her overshadowed thoughts of his own inadequacy that he experienced last night. He leaned back to kiss her. Brooklyn climbed over the back of the couch and made herself comfortable upon his lap. He caressed her face with his hands and then wrapped his arms around her, gently lifting her so that her lips met his. Once in his arms, her addiction to Tristan took over everything and her body seemed to melt into his.

Tristan might not have gotten points for his ability to bar brawl, but he knew how to make love. He was well-versed in the art of music, fantasy, and especially love. He did things to Brooklyn's young body that sent her to places that she never wanted to return from. The way he touched her, the way he kissed her. They never made it back to the bedroom.

* * *

The Devils sat waiting at the studio for Tristan and Brooklyn to arrive. As soon as the two entered together, Tristan's phone began to summon him. It was Adonis. The band listened as Tristan partially admitted blame for the bar fight. "Look, Adonis"—they listened as Tristan spoke—"I wasn't going to stand by and allow that drunk idiot to fall all over her. He was wasted and sloppy he might have hurt her . . . Yes . . . I understand . . . Adonis, I'm sure he said he was too drunk to remember. He probably was, I'm sure." Tristan spoke nothing for the next five minutes, apparently being scolded by Adonis and harshly. "I'm sorry," he finally said. "No, there will be no tension on my behalf. I realize he was drunk and didn't know what he was doing. The Devils were not at fault whatsoever. If anything, they were smart enough to get us out before the press came." Then yet another pause. "I'm sorry," he said once more and then pressed the End button on his phone. All at once, the Devils protested the phone call and the fact that Tristan was treated so harshly. "Settle down, settle down," Tristan insisted. "It's over."

Colin jumped up and asked, "Well, what did he say to you?"

Tristan smiled. "He said I was still as rebellious as I was back in the 1980s."

Still smiling, Tristan yelled "Okay—song for the challenge, yell 'em at me!" he playfully demanded. Brooklyn insisted upon singing the Dolly Parton rendition of "I Will Always Love You." "Good," Tristan said. "Done. Now, which of you can rap?" he asked. The Devils had no volunteers. "Okay then, which of you is going to spend every waking hour of the next four days learning how to rap?" he asked. "Look," he said, "I pretty much realize that we're going to wind up giving this one to Jamison, so let's just try and have fun with it," Tristan suggested.

* * *

If I should stay
Well, I would only be in your way
And so I'll go, and yet I know
That I'll think of you each step of my way
And I will always love you
I will always love you

Brooklyn sang her heart out, and when she had finished, America cried. Adonis applauded as he joined the Devils on stage along with their mentor.

"Judges, what do you think?" asked Adonis.

The first judge stood. "Spot on, I feel like crying."

The next judge chimed in, "Are you sure you don't want to switch to country?"

The last judge commented, "I believed you. Now, who were you singing that to?"

Tristan took the mic from Adonis and said, "Love, please tell me you weren't singing that to me." The audience roared.

Unfortunately, their rendition of rap was not received as well. The judges' comments were less favorable. Judge number two stood and said, "It was a decent attempt. However, I'd love to hear you repeat the first performance."

The Devils sat watching the remainder of the show from a TV monitor backstage. Adonis saw Brooklyn sitting in the green room. Still annoyed at the bar incident, he decided to speak with her and summoned her into his private office. He offered her a seat and then began to speak calmly. "Let me teach you a little something about television and reality shows. The more you give a producer what he wants, the longer you get to stay on the show. Reality shows aren't real. They are totally produced. The Devils are one of the top contenders for the win, and I would hate to see the Devils leave prematurely. What happened at the bar the other night was inexcusable. Tristan continues to be rebellious. However, you are a beautiful distraction for him. Sometimes I feel like his emotions are clouded by his actions, and he tends to forget what's expected of him as a TV personality. That's disappointing. I was hoping that since he doesn't seem to want to deny you anything, perhaps you might guide him next time if another less than desirable situation arises."

Brooklyn was furious. "Do you know what actually happened the other night?" she asked angrily.

"No, not exactly," Adonis admitted. "Billy claimed he remembered nothing from that night. Sources informed me that the Devils and their mentor wound up sneaking out a side door and Tristan wound up in the hospital."

Slowly, Brooklyn curbed her anger and began to explain the factual account of the other night. Adonis interrupted her as he had to go onto the stage but warned her not to leave the office, that he would return momentarily. When he returned, he asked her, "Why didn't Tristan explain this to me? He should have just come out with the truth." Brooklyn told him that it seemed like from the sound of the phone call that he really didn't give Tristan much of a chance to say anything.

She went on to say, "I know you are aware of Tristan's medical history. He's strong and brave when it comes to music and playing the 'I'm sorry' game, but physically he's very fragile. He took the fall because he didn't want the stress of knowing he got anyone in trouble, including Billy. And just for your information, the acrobatics at the beginning, when we were introduced to the world, was my fault. He knew nothing about our little surprise. It was totally the Devils' doing, yet he took the blame to protect us."

Just then there was a knock on the door. "Come forward," Adonis yelled. It was Tristan. An awkward silence filled the room. Adonis finally stood up and walked over to Tristan. He extended his hand toward Tristan and pat him on the back. "I owe you an apology," Adonis exclaimed.

"For what?" Tristan wondered.

Adonis answered, "For not having more faith in you." Brooklyn smiled. As they left, Adonis added, "Don't ever let this girl go." Brooklyn shrugged and walked back to the green room, leaving Tristan standing there perplexed.

* * *

Next week's challenge called for three original songs from each of the groups. Brooklyn was anxious for Tristan to hear some of her songs, so she decided to invade his privacy and head on up to his suite. She had spent the night with him there but left to get dressed in her own room. She knocked on his door, and assuming it was Brooklyn, he yelled, "Come in, love!" Tristan was sitting on the bed with his guitar, wearing glasses with large white frames. She thought him amazingly sexy and couldn't quite decide if she wanted to play for him or with him. He was writing some music down so she tried to peek over his shoulder. He covered the writings and informed her that it was a surprise.

"Fine," she said, pretending to be annoyed until he leaned over and kissed her. "So I wanted you to hear some Devil originals," she announced.

"I'd love to, let's see what you got," he said as he handed her the guitar.

In the silence of the night, when hearts are still
And kids are in their beds
All is calm but yet I hear the trembling hearts
And the living dead
All the men who thought their lives too difficult
Are lying in the street
Thinking life the beautiful has past them by
And dying ain't too sweet
Mourn for them, you must mourn the living dead
Cry a tear, you must cry a tear, I said
Just because you have all the things you need doesn't mean
You can live the life you lead

Tristan sat, listening with a giant smile on his face. He actually loved the song and appreciated the subject matter and its contents. "Play another," he asked as the song ended.

Young man his fist clenched fast, soul hungry
Sees all, hears all, knows what is in

Old man, he was young once, he's been there
He knows bout shadows in the wind
First it's there, then it's gone, he looks high but it is low, and then
*   it hides again*
What good is playing hide and seek, I'm always it
I never win

Tristan stopped her as the song was about to finish and ordered, "Another, play another."

"You didn't like either one of those?" she asked.

"I did," he said. "Brooklyn, you can write. Why don't we collaborate and write a song together?" Tristan offered.

"Why, is that going to be a future challenge?" she asked half-kidding.

"I don't know, but even if we were to write a song for this challenge, it would be something different. I can bet that none of the others will do that." Brooklyn thought for a minute.

"No," she said, "our styles are way too different."

"I have many styles," he confessed.

She still refused. "Nope," she insisted.

"Listen," he said, "musicians are like gifted storytellers. Why won't you write a song with me?" he asked.

"I would feel inadequate," she admitted.

"You are a musical genius, you're so talented and creative."

"You're a rock god!" she professed.

Tristan laughed and said, "I am far from a rock god."

Brooklyn touched his face. "You're my rock god," she said lovingly.

Still smiling, Tristan said, "I love the admiration, but if you start to think of me as any kind of god, I'm afraid you're apt to be disappointed in me. I want you to love me for who I am, not who I was."

"Don't be silly, I barley know who you were." She laughed.

"Come here, love," Tristan requested. Brooklyn moved closer to Tristan on the bed. She knew she was going to get some kind of speech. He began speaking to her ever so gently. "I love you so much that sometimes it actually physically hurts my heart. This is so new to both of us and I don't want to blow it. You are on your way to becoming a star, and I will do everything I can to ensure you get there. I just keep thinking that, once you're there, will you still want or need someone like me? Let's face facts, you're young and so beautiful and about to become more famous than I ever was. Remember, I'm just regular. I haven't performed in years, nor do I intend to. I'm way older than you and I have physical issues. All I can offer you is my love and eventually I don't know if that will be enough."

Poor Tristan was merely trying to explain so sweetly that he was only just a man. He wanted her to realize that she was just as talented as he was. He wanted to instill more confidence in her, but Brooklyn misunderstood. She jumped off the bed suddenly and said, "Are you trying to imply that our love is that fragile?" Before he could even protest or explain, she added, "Why don't you believe in our love? Why don't you believe that I love you just as much as you love me?" And she slammed the door behind her.

Tristan sat on the bed alone and in a state of disbelief and panic. "Damn," he said to himself out loud. He tried to run after her, but by the time he snapped out of his state of shock, she was already gone. Brooklyn's elevator ride down to her room was thought provoking. She thought, *Why did I just do that to him? He suffers so much. Now here I am adding to it.* But her feelings were hurt too, not realizing that Tristan was really looking for assurance for his own insecurity rather than challenging their love as she assumed. She decided to let him think about it for a while besides she needed to calm down as well.

Tristan dressed and ran down to her room. He found only Dazzel there, painting. Tristan was very obviously upset. Dazzel stopped what she was doing and asked, "Lose something, like your girlfriend?"

"Brooklyn is really mad at me," he confessed. "I said something stupid as usual. She took it the wrong way. I have to find her," he said almost in tears. He covered his face with his hands.

Dazzel continued, "Brooklyn cannot be found unless she wants to be. Furthermore, if you give her some time, she will be hunting you down. Like a wild animal. I don't think you really know just how much she loves you."

"Thank you," Tristan said to Dazzel and then calmed down considerably.

"I'm almost finished," Dazzel said. "You can ride with us to the studio. I'm sure Brooklyn's already on her way."

On her way she was. She had taken a cab to the set. Brooklyn might not have portrayed the highest amount of confidence in her songwriting, but she was extremely confident that by now Tristan was freaking out. She continued to think about everything Tristan had said. She played it back and forth in her mind over and over again, like an old-fashioned tape recorder. Then it finally hit her. She began to see it from a different perspective and thought maybe he was having issues with his own self-confidence and self-image. Maybe he was merely reaching out for some encouragement from her. However, on the other hand, surely he was aware of how much she loved him. Brooklyn was confused. This was their first real unrelated to work fight.

Tristan and the Devils walked onto the set together while Brooklyn watched safely from behind stage. She looked deeply into Tristan's eyes, and it hurt her to see him so saddened. She thought him to be so handsome, like a prince or a model. *He is a perfect boyfriend,* she thought as she analyzed him form her hiding place. He was romantic, sweet, talented, and kind and gave her everything her heart desired and more. He denied her nothing. He was brave and smart and made love to her like no other. She thought for a second what would life be like without him and felt tears run down her own cheeks. Brooklyn realized for the first time that he meant everything to her. She already was convinced that she loved him more than any other, but now she realized that she also appreciated him as well.

Should she just run into his arms or play it cool and see what his next move would be? As she stood deep in thought, Dazzel reached behind her and tapped her on the back of her head. "He's a mess, you know," she informed Brooklyn. "Whatever he said to you, he didn't mean it the way you thought he did," Dazzel added.

"I know that now," she confessed. "Okay." Brooklyn decided she'd already carried this nonsense way too far. She set out to find him and let him know everything was fine. He was gone. Unbeknownst to Brooklyn, he had gone back to the hotel, broken and disheartened. He didn't think he could spend a day on the set knowing Brooklyn was so angry with him.

This would prove to be the longest day on the set ever for Brooklyn. She felt a sickening feeling in the pit of her stomach the entire day. When the day finally ended, she darted into a taxi and raced back to the hotel to find Tristan. The ride back seemed endless. A dreadful fear came over her. What if he took the day off to reevaluate their entire relationship? What if he had come to the conclusion that it was too drama-filled and that the mental anguish wasn't worth it? What if he was trying to find a kind way to leave her, with his little speech before? *What have I done?* she thought. A panic raced through her entire body.

As the cab landed at the hotel, she ran out and directly up to Tristan's suite. "Please let him be there," she prayed out loud. Once standing in front of his room, she raised her hand to knock on his door and froze. She thought, *What if he tells me to go away?* Deciding not to give him that option, she reached into her bag for the key card he had given her. She was nervous. *Please don't let him break up with me*, she thought; this time she prayed silently.

She entered his room ever so quietly. The room was dark, except for a small candle flame burning on the windowsill. Tristan sat in a chair by that very same window, staring outside and praying the exact same prayer as Brooklyn.

He turned to her and then stood. Within less than a second, they both rushed toward each other, tears streaming down both of their faces. She fell into his arms and he held her tight. They began to apologize profusely. Tristan whispered in her ear, "I don't think I can ever live without you."

She softly whispered back, "You don't ever have to, because I don't think I can either." When they both had sufficiently calmed down enough to talk, she asked him why he left the set. He explained that he didn't think he'd be able to concentrate, and seeing her so angry with him would hurt too much. He sat by the window most of the day trying to figure out a way to make this okay again. He attempted to explain what he was trying to convey this morning, but she put her finger on his lips and said, "Shhh, I get it," and then kissed him. She confessed to him that today made her realize that, no matter what the future would hold, she could never leave him. He would have to be the one leaving and she hoped with all her heart that would never come to pass.

He reassured her that she was safe. He would never be able to leave her and that she had become his whole life, his reason for living. They made a pact that, should they fight again, breaking up with one another would never be an issue. However, in the back of Tristan's mind still loomed the belief that she was too young and free to spend the rest of her life with a half-crippled older man. Somehow he would have to resolve that issue in his own way.

Having survived their first non-work-related fight caused them to become even closer. That same evening Tristan took Brooklyn to an adorable, cozy cafe in the West Village. He had offered to take her to one of the finest eateries in Manhattan and then out on the town, but she declined. She explained that, although she loved and appreciated all the fantasy he created for her, tonight she only wanted him.

They spoke very little during dinner, but they held hands and touched. They looked into each other's eyes as if they had fallen in love all over again. When they returned to the hotel, they made love as though their romance just began and it was the first time. They remained locked inside each other the entire night, him holding her as if he were afraid if he let go she'd be gone.

When morning arrived, they showered together and got dressed. Brooklyn was about to return to her own room to collect the rest of her clothes for the day from her room, when they heard a loud, obnoxious knock at the door, accompanied by an even more obnoxious voice, "Are you two still alive?" it yelled. "No one killed each other did they?" it continued. "Let me in! Open this door!"

Brooklyn giggled. Tristan shushed her. "Maybe it will go away."

"Come on, you guys, do I have to call hotel security?"

"You better let her in," suggested Brooklyn.

"Fine," Tristan said as he released the lock but still wouldn't open the door. Dazzel came barging in, holding her heart for dramatic effect.

"Oh, so you're both okay, thank God. I brought you clothes and makeup, in case you were still living."

"Thank you, Dazzel," Tristan said as he answered for Brooklyn.

"That's not a proper way to thank me," Dazzel insisted and then dived on top of Tristan, forcing him down upon the bed. She then lunged at him and kissed Tristan smack on the lips.

"Ugh, gross!" he said, wiping his lips furiously. Brooklyn ducked into the bathroom to change into the clothes Dazzel brought her. Tristan pleaded, "Don't leave me alone with her, please, love."

"You're all mine!" Dazzel yelled, filled with glee. Brooklyn ran out of the bathroom to rescue Tristan. She informed Dazzel that she doesn't share, even with her sister. "Oh, really?" Dazzel said. "Well, you used to." Brooklyn turned red as she known that in the past that had been true.

The weekend was spent at Tristan's home, he and Brooklyn and all the Devils stayed over. They used Tristan's small recording studio to practice their originals. He felt that the songs should be recorded just in case since he wasn't sure they were copy written properly.

The Devils loved Tristan's home and made themselves very comfortable. As a matter of fact the only time they left was to play at Stars Friday night. Tristan welcomed the house full of noise as his home had been quiet way too long.

Saturday morning Tristan awoke to find Brooklyn gone. Instinctively he glanced out on the beach just as the sun came up and noticed her walking on the sand. She looked lovely with the wind blowing through her hair and the sun coming up behind her. Once again he couldn't help think what a free spirit she was. What would become of them? His medical situation wasn't improving. Brooklyn caught him watching her. "Come down!" she yelled. He ran downstairs and poured her a cup of Keurig coffee. He prepared it the way he knew she liked it and joined her. Thankful for the warm coffee she took Tristan's hand and walked along the shore. The wind was brisk but exhilarating. He stopped to hug her and noticed she was shivering. He convinced her to walk back to the house despite her protests.

The Devils were all sitting around the living room, hung over from the night at Stars. Garrett spotted Brooklyn and Tristan kissing before they entered the warmth of the house and said, "My stomach can't take that today, ugh."

Brooklyn yelled at the top of her lungs. "What's wrong? No one feels too good today. You all have headaches?" They all cringed, and Brooklyn laughed at their drunk affliction.

Then Tristan announced loudly, "Precious Little Devils, report to the studio in ten, we have a lot of work to cover." Garrett ran to the bathroom while Damian held his head and Brooklyn laughed.

* * *

Monday night arrived quickly. Tonight the bands would showcase their original songs while tomorrow would bring forth the second elimination. Another group would be leaving. The Devils were up first and to Tristan's delight. The judges loved their creativity and their magic, as judge number two phrased it. The other judges were positive and rewarding. However, Blood Red Orange did just as well.

Tuesday night would tell the tale. The Devils were nervous and there was no motivational speech that Tristan could think of to make them feel at ease. He summoned them to his suite Tuesday morning. He watched their nervous little faces as he began to speak. "I know there is nothing I can say to reassure you about tonight. I do not believe that we will be leaving. Not this time anyway. However, I'm going to do my best to change the subject in your minds."

"Huh?" Garrett asked.

"I'm going to give you something to do to get your minds off tonight," Tristan explained clearer.

Dazzel insisted, "There's nothing you can do to make us forget about tonight."

"Oh, really?" Tristan insisted. "How about this?" He reached into his pocket and took out on American Express credit card. He handed it to Brooklyn and said, "Go take your Devils on a shopping spree, but be back by 4:00 p.m.," Tristan said, smiling that handsome, contagious smile. The Devils cheered.

Dazzel literally screamed and Brooklyn just said, "Are you out of your mind?"

"Yes," he said, "totally."

"I'll meet you guys in the lobby shortly," Brooklyn announced, which was the Devils' cue to leave her alone with Tristan.

"Don't blow this shopping spree, Brooklyn," Dazzel warned.

"Close that door behind you," Brooklyn told Dazzel. "What are you doing Tristan?"

He laughed at her and said, "Don't let them go over $4,000 collectively. You can spend whatever you want. Go have fun, that's an order," Tristan insisted. She looked at Tristan and then at the card and said, "Trist, this has your name on it, it's your own personal credit card. I am not going to let you do this."

"It's my gift to all of you. Now why can't you just accept my gift?"

"Why don't you at least come with us and monitor the situation?" Brooklyn asked.

"I have to run over to the hospital for a while," he explained. "It's just routine monitoring, nothing earth-shattering."

"I want to go with you," Brooklyn said, all of a sudden worried.

"Hey, this is just routine stuff, like a checkup. I'm a big boy, I can do this myself. Besides I need you to hold my hand when it's a big deal. I promise I'll let you know when I need you to be strong for me. Right now I need you to babysit that card more than I need you to wait in a waiting room while I get a couple of x-rays," he insisted. "Now go, before you make me late. You're wasting precious shopping time." Brooklyn kissed Tristan apprehensively. "That's no way to kiss me when we're gonna be apart for hours," Tristan teased. He took her in his arms and kissed her in a manner that sent chills up and down her spine and then whispered, "Now go, I'll call you in a little while."

Although Brooklyn wasn't thrilled with the idea of him going to the hospital for anything, Tristan did seem happy and relaxed. He also seemed so excited about giving them his credit card, like a child getting a Christmas gift. She decided to go with it. He wasn't nervous, so chances are, he was telling her the truth. She ran down to the lobby and met the overly excited Devils. "Okay," she announced, "let's go shopping."

"Did Tristan give us a limit?" asked Dazzel.

"Just you have a limit," teased Brooklyn.

"Damn," Dazzel said.

"Don't worry, you're allowed to purchase more than one wig," Brooklyn added, still teasing her.

"Yay!" Dazzel exclaimed.

* * *

Tristan sat waiting for the doctor in his office so he could find out his test results. He sat very still, numb with fear, anticipating the worst. He hoped that he had been able to convince Brooklyn that this was merely a "routine checkup," even though he knew better. This visit was anything but routine. As the time passed, he became more and more concerned with his fate. He decided to phone Brooklyn before receiving any type of news that might prove to be disheartening. She answered his call immediately. "Hey," she said.

"Hi, love, how's the shopping going?" he asked, trying to sound positive and lighthearted.

"Your credit card is crying, but more important, is everything all right there?" she asked.

"I'm almost finished here, just waiting for the doctor to refill some prescription," he informed her.

Relieved, Brooklyn said, "Thank you, Trist, for the shopping spree. I miss you!"

Just then the doctor appeared. He stood in the doorway, glancing at Tristan's chart. "Hey, Brook, the doctor is here, I'll call you soon. Brooklyn, I love you." And he pressed End.

"Is that your girl?" asked the doctor.

"Yes," said Tristan, "how did you know she was my girl and not my wife?" Tristan joked.

"Because you said, I love you to her," the doctor said, teasing him back.

The Indian doctor walked behind his desk and sat in his chair. It seemed to take him forever to speak as he reviewed Tristan's chart. His silence was awkward and uncomfortable. Tristan began to fidget in his chair and finally not able to wait any longer he asked, "So what's the verdict?"

The doctor looked up from his chart and looked directly into Tristan's blue eyes. "Medicine is not an exact science," he began. "According to your medical history and the severity of your injuries, you should not be walking at all. The nerve damage to your legs was nothing less than catastrophic. You are a medical miracle. Now according to these latest test and x-ray results, I see no reason why you won't be able to continue to have somewhat of a normal life, for a time," the doctor said.

"For a time?" Tristan interrupted.

The doctor answered, "Eventually that nerve damage is going to catch up with you."

"How?" Tristan asked.

The doctor hesitated, then continued, "The nerves will finally die and paralysis will set in."

"When? How long?" Tristan asked in a monotone voice as though he were asking the questions in regards to someone else.

"Five, maybe ten years," the doctor answered. "I don't know exactly. However, the more physical therapy you have, the more stimulation, the longer the nerves might survive," he advised.

"How much of me will be paralyzed?" Tristan asked, his voice quivering and his eyes filled with tears.

"I think the paralysis will be limited to your legs, where most of the nerve damage is concentrated. You should still be able to go to the bathroom, make love, and perhaps even stand with the help of braces," the doctor said.

Devastated Tristan thought out loud, "How do I tell Brooklyn?"

"Are you asking my advice?" the Indian doctor inquired. Tristan nodded. "I think from knowing you, Tristan, you'll probably attempt to end your relationship with Brooklyn, fearing you will become a burden. I implore you not to! Do not deprive her and yourself of what could be years of living a normal life, filled with love or whatever life has in store for you. What is it they say? Love conquers all? Just be honest with her. Pick the right time and place to tell her, and above all, at least give her the choice," the wise doctor suggested.

"What if love isn't enough?" asked Tristan.

"Then you might need to reevaluate your relationship, but I think you need to have more faith in that girl's love," the doctor added.

"I will try," promised Tristan as he stood to leave. The doctor extended his hand and when Tristan shook it the doctor gave him a quick hug. His heart went out to Tristan.

Tristan left the hospital numb. He walked outside and took a breath as the cold air hit him in the face. He couldn't bear to live without Brooklyn, yet he couldn't bear to watch her sprit destroyed by caring for an invalid. He knew he would have to try his hardest to dismiss this from his mind at least until after the elimination tonight. The Devils needed a strong coach. They needed encouragement and strength. Besides the doctor's words echoing in his mind still did not seem real to him.

Tristan's phone began to vibrate with a call from Brooklyn. Still too upset to speak to her without letting on that something was wrong, he left the call unanswered. When it stopped vibrating, he took another long breath and decided to get his act together and call her back. He knew she would be worried not hearing from him. He looked down at the phone but wasn't clearly able to focus on the keypad. Thoughts kept flooding his mind, interfering with his rational thinking.

Just as Tristan finally had found the courage to call Brooklyn, he noticed a text from her. When he opened it, he read it to himself out loud, "Tris, I just wanted you to know that I am the luckiest girl in the world. I love you so much and I hope you will always believe in our love. Please let me know that you're okay." Tristan sat down on one of the marble steps of the hospital, put his hands over his face, and cried his eyes out. He was inconsolable, not that anyone in New York City would have stopped to try and console him. He finally lifted his head out of his hands and dried his eyes. He seemed to feel stronger after that cry and decided it was time to dial Brooklyn. "Tristan," she said warmly as she answered.

"Hey, love, I'm fine," he lied.

"Wanna meet us?" she offered.

He hesitated, then said, "It's already two o'clock, I'll meet you back at the hotel, okay?" he asked.

"Okay, you sexy thing," she said and they said good-bye. Tristan pressed End. His main goal was to return to the hotel, take a shower, and psych himself up into acting normal. He decided first to do a little shopping himself and ducked into one of the more prominent jewelry stores.

When the Devils returned, hands loaded with packages, Brooklyn stopped at her room with Dazzel and dropped off her store-bought goods. She phoned Tristan and told him she'd be right up. Tristan left the door open in anticipation of her arrival. She immediately ran into his arms and whispered, "I missed you." He held her close and tight. Almost too tight. She whispered, "You're squishing me."

He released her and said, "I'm sorry, I just love you so."

She kissed him and asked, "Do you swear that you're okay?"

"Do I look okay?" he asked her back as he kissed the tiny frown on her forehead.

"You look amazing," she said as her frown turned into a smile. She handed him his credit card and thanked him.

"What did you buy? I wanna see," he announced.

"I'll show you later," she said.

"I went shopping too, come here," he said. He took something out of his pocket and held it in his hand. He took her hand and dropped the item he held inside hers and closed her fingers around it. She opened her hand. Inside it was a white gold necklace rendered in the beloved shape of an elegant heart. She examined it, and to her astonishment, delicately written with inlaid white diamonds was "I believe in our love." On the flip side of the heart it was signed, "Forever yours, Tristan." Tears flowed onto her cheeks, and Tristan held her as she cried. "Sometimes I think that you're more sensitive than I am," he whispered. He wiped her tears, then took the heart inside her palm and fastened it around her neck.

Brooklyn looked down at it and touched the necklace with her fingers. "Thank you," she said, still very overwhelmed. "I love it, it means more to me than you'll ever know."

While she sat on the bed and stared at the pendant, Tristan put his arms around her from behind. He kissed the back of her neck and then moved his lips onto her shoulders. She sat paralyzed by the chills embracing the top half of her body, and the warmth down below. He coaxed her down onto the fluffy white pillows and gently touched her face with his fingers. He watched her small frame tremble as he slowly undressed her, one button at a time. He kissed her underneath her ears and underneath her chin. When he finally kissed her lips, she responded with a compelling and reckless desire. As they made love, she felt his strength on top of her. He entered her precious body slowly and tenderly. He made love to her as if every cherished moment counted. Still filled with emotion from his devastating discovery, he carefully disguised his sadness with his passion. He knew he would never have the courage or strength to let her go.

Just then, as if she could read his thoughts, she whispered, "Tell me that we'll always be together."

"I'm not going anywhere," he said, emphasizing the *I'm* as those words "give her the choice" echoed in his mind.

Growing slightly suspicious by the way he answered her request, she inquired, "Are you sure everything went all right today?"

Trying to avoid lying, he explained that her text made him realize just how much she really loved him and that he was finally believing it. Then as he left her body he asked her for a "forever hug." Momentarily forgetting that he completely changed the subject, by his touching remark and his appeal for a "forever hug," she settled down and buried her head in his chest with her arms around him. In the back of her mind the fact that he avoided a direct answer to her question would be revisited later.

Although Tristan would have literally continued that hug forever, it was getting late and the fact someone would be eliminated tonight loomed in the back of both their hearts and replaced their passion by fearful anticipation. "Come on, love, it's nearly show time," he reminded her.

"Just one more kiss," she pleaded, and he kissed her once more.

* * *

When Adonis was announced, there was dead silence on the set.

An uneasy feeling crept through the young hearts of all the band members. Brooklyn feared that, because of the bar incident, it might be the Devils farewell performance. "It's another sad night for one of our amazing groups, America," Adonis told the audience. "Who will leave us tonight?" he continued. I need all four remaining bands to join me on stage . . . and bring your coaches with you . . . Blood Red Orange and Devin Liam, Precious Little Devils and rebellious coach Tristan Bondage, Sin-cerely Yours and mentor Jamison Brown, and, Rising Tides, bring forward your mentor, Billy Blaze." The bands and mentors all made their way onto the stage, standing behind Adonis, who turned to face them. "After tonight there will only be three bands remaining. Your challenges will become longer and more difficult as well as more personal. In just a few moments we will announce the challenge for next week—see you after a word from our sponsors."

As the break ended, Adonis stepped back onto the center of the stage and the audience applauded. "Now as promised, I will announce next week's challenge . . . wait"—Adonis surprised the bands—"shall we allow one of the nervous groups some relief?" The audience applauded and cried "Yes!" from their seats. "Drum roll please," demanded Adonis. "Blood Red Orange, you can breathe a sigh of relief, you are safe." The band hugged each other and the mentors all congratulated Devin Liam. "Don't go away, Blood Red, here is your challenge. The other three, listen carefully because two of you as well as Blood Red will have to provide us with a professionally made music video." The audience applauded the challenge. "Wait," Adonis yelled through the mic, "it can be any type of song, but it must be currently on the charts and have a video by the artist already aired as well as the video you will be doing, Kamikaze Karaoke. The judges will give you a choice of five songs and you will get to select one. Then you will have twenty minutes to prepare a performance with the song you have chosen. Now after we come back from the commercial, we will announce the next band who will safely remain until week number seven." During the commercial Brooklyn whispered to Tristan, "Who's going home?" he answered. "Come here and give me a hug."

"Now I'm scared," Brooklyn said.

The break ended and Adonis asked for another drum roll. "The second band to remain on the show is . . . Billy Blaze and your Rising Tides," Adonis announced. Garrett whispered to Brooklyn, "Ugh, this is terrible, we're in the bottom two again." The audience cheered for the Rising Tides, who hugged each other profusely on the stage. Adonis called for yet another break and had the two "safe" contenders leave the stage. He instructed the Devils and Sin-cerely not to disperse but to remain exactly where they stood.

The audience was already applauding loudly as the show returned from the commercial. "Welcome back, America," Adonis said. "Judges, would you like to weigh in on this before we say goodbye to one of the two remaining bands?"

The first judge stood and said, "Both groups have come so far. It will be sad to see either one of them leave."

The second judge announced, "After last night's performance, I would like to see the Devils remain in the semifinals."

Judge number three simply said, "Good luck to both of you."

Adonis recouped his command of the stage. "Drum roll please, and make this a long one . . . The band that will return for the semifinals is . . . Precious Little Devils and coach Tristan Bondage. Jamison, we are truly sad to say good-bye to you and Sin-cerely Yours. The Devils hugged Jamison's band, and although sad at their departure, they were still very relieved that they themselves got to stay. Brooklyn ran to Tristan once the show had ended and said, "I guess we were forgiven." He knew exactly what she meant.

The band congratulated each other. A lot of hugs were exchanged until it was time to return to the hotel. Tristan suggested to Brooklyn that she invite whomever she wanted and loved to the mansion on Thursday night for a victory party while they were all still in a victorious status. Tristan figured it would raise the moral of the competitors and take his own mind off the doctor's catastrophic diagnosis. It would also perhaps create another fantasy for Brooklyn if it were done properly.

* * *

The setting for the party was as grand as "Gone with the Wind" only instead of horses and carriages pulling up in front of the plantation, there were fancy cars and impressive limos pulling up in front of Tristan's home, all greeted by Disney characters. As the guests entered the front door (escorted by either Mickey, Pluto, or Donald), both Tristan and Brooklyn were there to greet them. Surprisingly enough the brazen Billy Blaze came to attend the festivities. As he walked through the door, he approached Brooklyn first and kissed her hand. He then extended his hand to Tristan. He must have felt similar to Scarlet O'Hara shaking hands with Melanie after she seduced Ashly, her husband. "I'm sorry, man," he related to Tristan.

Tristan hugged him and said, "It's over, man, come on in." Brooklyn admired Tristan's ability to forgive. It was just another attribute she could add to the list of reasons why she loved him.

Inside the grand ballroom was a magnificent buffet that would make any wedding caterer jealous. The DJ was set up on the second-floor balcony above the ballroom. While silver and white balloons floated gracefully through the air, filling the room with celebration, a bubble machine was creating large, extravagant, iridescent bubbles, which soared through the crowd until they died.

Tristan's house was filled with music and laughter as the bubbles danced through the rooms for hours. After all the guests were comfortable, Brooklyn and Tristan dispersed and became the perfect host and hostess apart from one another. Sometime during the evening she noticed that Tristan seemed quiet and made it a point to walk over to him and ask him how he was holding up. "Are you having fun?" he asked her.

"I am," she responded.

"So am I," he said. She was satisfied with his answer and moved on to talk to Devin and then Terence, who had recently arrived.

When the clock approached midnight, the guests began to disappear and Cinderella kicked off her shoes and sat on the couch with Terence. She thanked him over and over again for convincing her to go into Tristan's hospital room that night. Terence listened but appeared preoccupied. "Brooklyn," he finally said, "Tristan seems quiet over there. I'm going to see how he's doing. I'll be right back." Terence knew all too well the telltale signs of Tristan's painful existence.

Terence made his way over to Tristan and told him that the party was amazing. Tristan turned to Terence and thanked him. "So how are you really doing?" Terence asked.

"I'm okay, there's a little discomfort here, but I'll get through this. Terence, I don't want Brooklyn to know."

Unfortunately Brooklyn had walked up to Dazzel, who was standing next to Tristan and heard Terence's conversation with the rock star. "Know what?" Brooklyn asked. "Know that you're in pain? Know that you don't trust me or our love enough to admit your pain because you think I'll love you less if I find out you're in pain? Do you think I'll run from the drama? Our love must be very fragile to you still," Brooklyn finished and headed for the French doors leading to the patio.

Dazzel, who was also privy to the conversation, rolled her eyes and said, "Oh boy, you're in trouble."

Tristan grabbed Dazzel's arm and asked, "What was that about, Dazzel?"

"Never mind," she said.

He tightened his grip around her arm and threatened, "You tell me right now or I will rip that wig right off your head and burn it in front of everyone."

Dazzel gasped. "All right, all right, don't get your feathers in a tizzy. Look, she loves you more than life itself, but she's tired of wondering how much pain you're actually in. It's stressful for her and no one needs any extra stress. She thinks you lie to her about your condition and your pain. She feels you're too proud to admit you need help. She feels you hide the truth from her because you think she'll leave you if she finds out how much pain you're in."

"How do you know this?" Tristan asked as he released his grasp on her arm.

"Honey, we're sisters, we talk, and it's time for both of you to talk," yelled Dazzel.

"Excuse me," Tristan said to all and grabbed his jacket for Brooklyn as he walked through the French doors to find her.

He didn't have to go far. She was standing on the patio, staring out at the sound. He came up behind her and slipped his jacket around her shoulders. He began to kiss the back of her neck. Brooklyn stood motionless as the waves from the sound gently touched the sand. "I guess I fucked up again," Tristan admitted. Brooklyn stood silent. Tristan grabbed hold of her and spun her around to face him. "Talk to me, Brooklyn," he asked briskly.

From down below the depths of her emotions, she let him have it without coming up for air. "I hate that you're in pain all the time, it's cruel, it's unfair, and the fact that you won't let me help you makes me so mad. Do you know what it's like wondering each time you hurt, if you're going to wind up in the hospital or worse? This is no way to live," Brooklyn said as tears welled up in her eyes.

"Baby, this is the rest of my life," he whispered softly.

"It hurts me to see you in pain," Brooklyn whispered back, "but it hurts even more to know that you don't trust me enough to be honest about your pain. The night Terence gave you that morphine injection, I thought you might have died. You push so hard and hide your pain so well, it builds up inside of you until it becomes danger-ous to you. You avoid my questions and never give me a direct answer. I feel like you're trying to protect me from some surreal truth. You've endured so much more than most humans could, and I admire your bravery. It's part of the reason I love you so much, but maybe if you confessed your agony, I could force you to relax or give you medicine and it might be okay," she finished.

Tristan took a breath. He was about to do the hardest thing he ever had to do in his life. He lifted Brooklyn's face with his fingers. He needed to have eye-to-eye contact with her in order to say what would come next. "Brooklyn," he whispered, "I will never be okay. According to the doctors, my pain is here to stay for the rest of my life. My condition will never get better than it is now and in fact it will worsen. On Tuesday at my routine checkup, I was informed that eventually I will become paralyzed perhaps within the next five to ten years. I am going to wind up in a wheelchair, Brooklyn, for the rest of my life. So please understand why I'm going to say this to you, even though it hurts so much more than any pain I've ever had," Tristan said courageously.

Brooklyn instinctively tried to hug Tristan, but he grabbed her hands and held them in his before her arms reached him. "Please, baby, listen to me," he pleaded. "I've been so selfish and delusional thinking that our lives together could be anything less than perfect and wonderful. Now that you know the real deal, and now that I've come to realize that it's not fair to hold you hostage to my heart, I need you to know that I love you enough to let you go, even though I pray with every ounce of my heart and soul that you'll chose to stay." Brooklyn felt her own heart sink. She felt emotional pain throughout her own body so intense that she was on the verge of panic.

Tristan desperately tried to hold back his own tears, but his lips were quivering and his heart was trembling. Brooklyn tried to speak, but Tristan put his finger over her lips. "Shhh," he said, "please, don't answer now. Search your soul first because this is a one-time offer. I will never have the courage to ask you again. My heart is breaking just thinking of the possibilities."

Brooklyn took her hand and touched his face in an attempt to comfort him, but he took her hand and shook his head. Barely being able to speak, he said to her, "You're freezing, please go inside now. I don't want you to see me lose it. Please," he begged. She removed his jacket from her shoulders, put it on his, and walked inside.

When he heard the French doors slam, Tristan broke down and cried. He cried more than he had ever cried in is life, even as a wounded child. He remained outside for a long time, crying until finally he used up all his tears. His emotions were drained. He was freezing, but he didn't care. He knew full well that, if she chose to leave him, he would never care about anything again. If she, by some miracle, chose to stay, he would spend his entire life making her happy in any way possible. He didn't wish her to stay out of pity, but with his heart so heavy, he wanted only to hold her in his arms and tell her that no matter what he would never stop loving her.

The house was dark and silent. His sadness was overwhelming, so much so that for a split second he was tempted to inject himself with a lethal dose of morphine just to end this pain. Tristan didn't wish to die though, but if she decided to leave him, he knew he would die inside. In his mind he was already trying to rationalize that, if she left, at least he would take comfort in the fact and she'd still be a free spirit and not burdened with a cripple. Tristan looked at the Hollywood staircase. He couldn't bear to climb those stairs up to his empty room, but he was exhausted. Finally he slowly ascended, climbing one step at a time while dreading the loneliness that would follow.

He had a responsibility to Brooklyn and the Devils. He had to try and force himself to shield the band from his emptiness and somehow create a video for this week's challenge. Still, it hurt so much.

As he reached the master wing, he heard what he could only describe as an angel singing through the closed door. As he opened it, he saw Brooklyn sitting in the middle of the bed, playing his guitar and singing ever so sweetly. He rushed over to the side of the bed and sunk to his knees. He took Brooklyn's hand and kissed it, then he held it to his face and began to cry, but these were tears of joy.

She smiled at him and put the guitar down next to her. Then very matter-of-factly she said, "Can you please stop trying to ditch me. I'm not leaving . . . ever," she added. "Oh, and can you please stop thinking that you're not worth my love?"

Tristan got up off his knees and climbed onto the bed. He put his arms around her and rested his heads on top of hers. "So you love me enough to stay with me even though I'm considerably older than you, always in pain, and an invalid?" he asked in between tears. "Baby, this is a tough decision to make so quickly," he added.

"There was never a decision to make," she answered. "It was very brave and noble of you to try and dump me for my own good. However, I think in your emotionally twisted heart you had to know that I wouldn't leave you."

"I thought it a fifty-fifty chance, but I had to give you the opportunity to bail, just so I could live with myself? Remember, though, this was a one-time offer and now it's expired," he reiterated.

"Okay, then, is this finished now? Are we okay? Can you start to accept the fact that I love you unconditionally and that I will always love you? Can you stop trying to hurt us both and eighty-six the drama. Oh, and one more thing, I'm going to live here now. I think you are a physical and emotional disaster and you need me. I love you for so many reasons, Trist, but mostly because of the way you love me. I know that no matter what life has to offer, you will always love me like that, and I'm not willing to let that go . . . ever," she announced. "One more thing," she added.

"What's that, love?" he asked feeling overjoyed.

"Can you take your clothes off and come here under the covers because you're freezing, and I want you to hold me in your arms now please," she ordered. Tristan gladly obeyed.

Once in each other's arms they heard a timid knock on the half-closed bedroom door. "Don't tell me," Tristan whispered.

A buzzed Dazzel, burst in the room and observed, "Oh, if it isn't Romeo and Juliet."

"Go away, Dazzel," Tristan insisted.

"I was just making sure the two of you were okay," she claimed.

"We've never been better." Tristan smiled.

Chapter 7

And Then There Were Two

The video was seductive, but sweet. It was sexy, yet innocent. It was technologically sophisticated and soulfully mastered. The video was a work of a genius and nothing short of a masterpiece. Anyone who'd ever seen one of Tristan's videos would not be surprised. He had the Midas touch when it came to creating a film.

He chose the song "All of Me" by John Legend. It was emotionally seductive, yet complicated enough to make a difference. It was a very romantic love story. Although primarily a boy song, Tristan felt that Brooklyn was convincing enough to rule it and that it would sit favorably among the judges.

He carefully scripted the video and then masterfully directed it. He dressed his star in a glittering Swarovski crystal encrusted bikini and filled his turquoise indoor pool with red and white thornless roses for Brooklyn to dive into. After her dive, he reversed the sequence back and forth so it seemed as though she were rising from the depths of the water many times to the words of the break: "My head's underwater, but I'm breathing fine."

At first, Tristan was at a loss as he tried to find Brooklyn a lover for the video. It had to be someone sexy and believable and someone he trusted not to fall for her in real life. He auditioned several actors for the role; however, their connections with Brooklyn did not seem believable enough for anyone to think they were completely in love.

The Devils and Brooklyn put their heads together and were able to uncover the perfect man for the role. Although they knew the actor would decline, Brooklyn would insist upon him and no one else. After all, he was the sexiest man she'd ever seen and she already loved him very much. Tristan refused at first, but despite his protests, the band and Brooklyn left him no choice. He finally agreed, partially because he hadn't the strength to deny Brooklyn anything and also because he couldn't stand the thought of another man kissing her.

By 6:00 a.m. on Sunday, the video in all its glory was completed, and it was one of Tristan's finest hours. Adonis had given them Sunday off, an extra day for creation of the video. The Devils were finished and exhausted, so when Tristan announced they would all be going out tonight, they actually protested. "Where?" Garrett asked.

"It's a surprise," Tristan replied.

The hours passed quickly and when evening finally rolled around, the band gathered in Tristan's grand ballroom, still tired but prepared to go wherever Tristan's surprise would take them.

"Ready?" Tristan asked as he held the door open for them to depart. The car ride began to seem all too familiar, and when it stopped in front of Stars, the Devils became confused.

"Really?" Damian said.

"It's karaoke night here," Garrett informed Tristan.

"Exactly," Tristan said. "What's the best way to prepare for Kamikaze Karaoke for the Monday challenge?" he asked. "Rehearsal!" he shouted and held the car door opened for them to exit.

The Devils wound up having fun singing for their lives. They were all kamikaze'd several times. Tristan watched as they laughed, sang some, made mistakes on others, but all owning up to the challenges the DJ bestowed upon them. Mark, the karaoke DJ, offered Tristan the mic finally, but he respectfully declined. Brooklyn walked over to him and pleaded, "Sing with me, please?"

"No, thank you, I'm good," Tristan said.

"Tris, this isn't exactly a concert hall, now sing a song with me," Brooklyn insisted.

"Fine," he agreed, once again too emotionally weak to deny her.

Brooklyn announced, "Tristan is going to do a song with me." The Devils and other karaoke patrons applauded and gathered around the stage to watch and listen. The DJ asked if he wanted to be kamikaze'd. Tristan laughed nervously and said no. "Try 'Demons' by Imagine Dragons." Tristan turned to Brooklyn and asked her if she knew the song. "The words are on the screen," she reminded him.

The DJs threw a mic to Tristan while Brooklyn already had custody of hers. As before, they began to sing together and their voices once again rang from the heavens. When the song ended, Tristan kissed Brooklyn seductively and those present in the club rose to their feet and applauded. Brooklyn knew that Tristan felt those words. They had become personal to him, and now to her as well.

* * *

The Devils enjoyed their group date at the club, but once again Monday night came rapidly and the show was about to begin. Adonis prepared to take his usual stance in the center of the stage. The random, booming voice announced the sparkling-eyed, animated show host, who ran to the stage, mic clutched in hand. "Good evening, America! Tonight, it's Kamikaze Karaoke, and let's get to it! May I have the remaining groups on stage please? Blood Red, Tides, and Precious Devils." The three marched up to Adonis. "Now, Mr. Billy Blaze, Devin Liam, and the rebellious Tristan Bondage, please join us!" The mentors rushed to join their bands and the young show host. "Which of you wants to go first?" Adonis asked, hoping for a volunteer. Tristan winked at the Devils, signaling them raise their hands. Brooklyn stepped out in front, raised her hand, and the Devils followed suit. "So the brave little Devils, choose one of our prestigious judges please."

They huddled for a second, and then Damian announced,

"We would like Austin, please."

"Austin, our 1980s icon, please hand Mr. Bondage your song selections."

Tristan examined Austin's choices. "Devils, I've chosen 'First Real Love' by Ashanti," Tristan decided. This was a great song for Brooklyn to show off her vocals, plus he knew Damian could do the rap. "Twenty minutes, Devils, head into our soundproof studio along with your coach and start rehearsing."

Twenty minutes later, the Devils emerged victorious, Brooklyn was impressive, and Damian had practiced the rap the night before at Stars coincidentally. "Judges," Adonis called, "Austin, why don't you weigh in first?"

Austin stood and said, "Tristan, I commend you on your choice. You really know your band." Each group completed their karaoke song while recaps of past shows were shown in between their performances. Then it was time to unveil the videos.

Rising Tides was the first to present their video. Their video was cute and entertaining, and the judges clapped to the music and sang along. Blood Red chose to do a history lesson to the song "Pompeii" by Bastille. The judges loved the musical arrangement but thought the video lacked creativity.

After the Devils video aired, the judges and the audience were silent as if they couldn't believe what they had just witnessed. Suddenly, all the judges stood at once and applauded. The audience followed with an overwhelming standing ovation. The first judge claimed that an entire movie should be filmed around the video. The next judge announced that the video just assured them a spot in the finals. The last judge, Austin, summoned both Tristan and Brooklyn to the judges' table. They walked there hand in hand. "So," he asked, "how do you both feel now that all of America has witnessed the two of you making love?" The audience roared with laughter.

"Proud," Tristan said, and the audience applauded again. The judge turned to Brooklyn and said, "Very touching, I hope you're going to take care of this video genius."

Tristan replied to his comment, live, in front of America, "She takes care of me in many wonderful ways and ways you can't even imagine." Once more, the audience rose to their feet and cheered.

* * *

Next week's challenge would be large. All three groups were slated to do a concert in a real concert hall, with a real audience, who would be purchasing real tickets to see them perform in person. There would be three different colored tickets, each representing a different band. The fans would buy the color tickets that represented their favorite group. The competitors would be judged by the amount of tickets representing them and of course by America and the judges. Devin and Billy would also be performing; however, Tristan declined, claiming his health issue would not allow him to. His excuse was accepted by everyone except Brooklyn, who knew the real truth.

Brooklyn went to Tristan to plead one last time for him to reconsider. She asked him gently to think about performing and he snapped at her, "Brooklyn, you know I can't do that, so please don't ask me to." Realizing he had overreacted the moment the words left his mouth, he ran and hugged her.

She hugged him back and made it clear, "If you ever decide that you want to conquer this crazy little fear of yours, I'm there for you. I won't ask again, I promise," she said.

"You're disappointed in me, aren't you?" he asked.

"No," she replied, "I'm just disappointed."

With the show's growing popularity, the concert became sold out. Tristan easily staged their acts. Because of their spectacular video, the Devils were the favorites this week, so they would be performing last at the concert. Tristan would fill their songs with special effects that would blow the audience away.

They would sing "Airplanes" by BOB. The room would be pitch-black, and then as they began to sing, beams of light would make it appear as if shooting stars were everywhere. Next they would use pyrotechnics to enhance the song "Burn" by Ellie Goulding. He would have Brooklyn wear a dress capable of burning as in *The Hunger Games* movie. For their final number they would be performing "It's Raining Men," a classic associated at times with the gay community. Tristan would hire a hundred go-go boys to descend from the ceiling of the auditorium onto the stage, all holding white umbrellas. The ensemble would be doing a well-choreographed dance number and then be unleashed into the audience, taking their dancing and bikini bottoms with them.

The Devils rehearsed furiously that entire week. Just learning the intricacies of the special effects Tristan mastered for them was a task. Finally the night arrived, and their hard work would prove valuable.

The coliseum seemed larger than life. The Devils, as were the others, were overwhelmed with both excitement and fear. Tristan, to his dismay and unbeknownst to him, would be forced to introduce his band upon the concert hall stage. Brooklyn watched his introduction from behind the stage. She was scared for him. Would he freeze like in his recurring nightmare? Tristan felt his legs grow weak with fear. He turned to look at Brooklyn, who mouthed the words, "I love you." Somehow this gave him courage. As he took the stage, the audience began to applaud widely. He still had a vast amount of fans who loved him. They didn't stop clapping and cheering for quite some time until Tristan said on the mic. "It's been a long time." His fans shrieked. "Thank you," he said as he became slightly more comfortable with the situation. "Good evening, everybody!" he said in his very English accent. "It is with my greatest and sincerest pleasure that I give to you my Precious Little Devils."

Brooklyn breathed a sigh of relief. "Good job," Brooklyn whispered as she took the stage and kissed him.

He whispered back, "Break a leg, I love you," and he returned backstage to watch.

Damian counted down to introduction, and the band began their first song, "Burn." "Yea we got the fire, fire, fire, and we're gonna burn, burn, burn . . ." The last *burn* provoked a shot of fire emanating from her wrists. The audience gasped. They roared as Brooklyn "burned" her way through the rest of the song, finally winding up in a ball of flames. The audience held on to their seats in fear and suspense. The stage grew dark as the ball of fire burned until there was only silence and blackness. This enabled Brooklyn to slip out of her burnt offerings and begin "Airplanes."

Through the darkened stage and arena flashes of light flew through the air, mimicking shooting stars. "Can we pretend that airplanes through the night sky are like shooting stars . . ." The stars filled the auditorium. Projected upon a huge screen was an airplane flying in the night sky, which exploded as the song ended in a burst of fireworks worthy of the bicentennial Fourth of July. No one in the audience remained seated.

The last song, "It's Raining Men," was the performance of the evening, perhaps even the century (at least in Tristan's eyes). As the go-go boys descended from the heavens and were carefully lowered to the stage the audience cheered in disbelief. Chaos broke out as the boys were let loose upon the unsuspecting crowd. They danced their way through the arena. Before the song ended, they rushed back on stage forming a pyramid. They lifted Brooklyn to the top of it, and their grand finale caused a ten-minute ovation.

* * *

"Welcome, America, to our last elimination before the winner is chosen," shouted the motivated Adonis through the mic. Brooklyn, Tristan, and the Devils sat quietly backstage, one more nervous than the next. Adonis recapped the highlights of last night's concert while the bands prayed. This could be anyone's game and each of the groups was aware of that.

"In a few short moments only two bands will remain in the completion. Now can I have the three remaining groups up on stage by my side, along with their coaches," Adonis yelled. "Devils to my right, Tides to my left, Blood Red behind me," Adonis instructed. "Drum roll please." The drums rolled for what seemed like hours until Adonis yelled, "Stop! Devils, you are an amazing group, coming in second in the ticket sales from last night. Let's revisit some Devil highlights from the first seven weeks." As their highlights played, both Brooklyn and Tristan were sure they were going to be eliminated. Tristan held on to Brooklyn's hand tightly. He bent down and whispered "I love you" to her. When the highlights finished, they figured so were the Devils. Then Adonis announced, "You are safe. You will be competing till the end in the finals. Congratulations, Devils!"

Tristan grabbed Brooklyn and kissed her as though they were in the bedroom right on live TV. The audience howled. Then they ran backstage and kissed again. "I thought for sure we were going home," the relieved Dazzel commented breathlessly.

"My heart can't take anymore," Tristan confessed jokingly, clutching his chest.

Brooklyn smiled at him and said, "You are my heart."

He replied, "Thank you from the bottom of my heart." Brooklyn thought Tristan looked a little pale, so she asked him if her were okay. He answered, "I've never been better, especially after my heart attack." They both laughed.

Who's going home?" asked Garrett.

"I would assume Billy since Devin's popularity continues to grow," answered Tristan. Shortly thereafter Adonis announced the demise of Billy Blaze and the Rising Tides as predicted by Tristan. The audience applauded for Blood Red but shed a tear for the Tides as they left the stage.

The two bands hugged and cried. They had grown very close. They wished each other good luck and hugged again. Billy walked over to Brooklyn. "I'm going to miss seeing you the most," he said sadly.

Tristan put his arm around Billy. "Okay, one last supervised kiss," he offered.

Billy hugged Brooklyn and said, "In a minute once you're tired of him"—he pointed to Tristan—"just look me up and I'll come running." And then he was gone.

Tristan just smiled and shook his head. "Tonight we celebrate," Tristan insisted.

"Our victory?" Brooklyn asked.

Tristan laughed. "And the passing of Billy Blaze," he added.

Brooklyn laughed and replied, "I never even liked him. I was too busy falling in love with you."

"Good choice," Tristan said with conviction.

"You're conceited," Brooklyn remarked.

"And arrogant," Tristan added.

Tristan and Brooklyn ducked into a taxi for the ride back to the hotel. Tristan wanted to be alone with Brooklyn. "Hey," Tristan asked, "do you wanna make out?"

Brooklyn responded, "Clearly." And she began kissing him.

By the time the cab pulled up to the hotel, they were practically making love. Somehow they made it up to the suite and made love with a wild frenzy. You would have thought that neither one had ever had sex in their lives. When they finished, Tristan insisted, "Get dressed, love, I'm going to take you somewhere fancy."

Brooklyn put her head on his chest. "Really, I thought this is how we would celebrate the victory, all night long."

Tristan protested, "You have to eat."

"Dial room service," she suggested. "I'm not sharing you tonight." She started kissing him all over again. He instantly "rose" to the occasion.

Brooklyn playfully licked his lips with her tongue, and then licked his earlobe, making sure to dodge his earing. She kissed his ear and then gravitated down the side of his neck and down his naked shoulder. She continued kissing his chest and licking his nipples until reaching his stomach, and then further below. Tristan was wild with passion. He was throbbing and he longed to be inside her. Soon the desire became a necessity and he whispered for her to come to him. He kissed her with every emotion he possessed as he slipped inside her.

* * *

Sometime during the edge of night, just before dawn, Tristan awoke. He tried gently to remove Brooklyn from on top of his chest without waking her but that proved futile. Half-asleep she asked him, "What's wrong, Tris, you having one of those dreams?"

"No," he replied and whispered, "I just need a little pain medication. Go back to sleep, princess," he insisted. Brooklyn suddenly became wide awake and offered to get him a pill and some water. "No, love," he answered, "I need something a little stronger. I'll be right back," he assured her.

"Okay, my little drug addict, I'll be waiting," she joked.

He kissed her forehead, raced for the bathroom, and closed the door. The next sound Brooklyn heard was a loud, horrifying thump. "Tristan," she yelled as she ran toward the bathroom. She found

Tristan lying on the floor unconscious, with a syringe filled with liquid next to him.

She called to him but received no response. She didn't know if he had taken his medication or perhaps even overdosed until she eyed the syringe by his side noticing it was full of whatever he had prepared it with. Immediately she summoned Terence and conveyed Tristan's present status to him. He instructed Brooklyn to put the phone on speaker as he was about to instruct her how to deal with the situation.

"Is he breathing?" Terence asked, half-serious.

"He's breathing," she told him.

"Okay, first hide the needle. The last thing we need is a syringe hanging around in case you should have to call an ambulance. Now wet a towel and wipe his face with it. See if that wakes him up."

Brooklyn followed his directions, but Tristan did not respond. "It's not working," she relayed to Terence.

"Okay," he said, hearing the panic in her voice, "calm yourself right now. He probably just waited too long to take that injection, and he probably passed out from the pain. Just try slapping his face gently and calling out to him. Just keep trying to wake him, otherwise you're going to have to call an ambulance. If you do get him to wake, you're going to have to give him that injection and I'll talk you through it."

Brooklyn tried and tried to wake Tristan, but he was out cold. In a panic she told Terence she was going to hang up and call 911. Just then Tristan started to stir. She took his hand and called to him. He tried to sit up, but he was in agony. He finally managed to sit up against the shower with Brooklyn's help. "Come sit next to me," he asked her, his voice quivering with pain. Very calmly and barely able to speak he whispered. "I'm going to teach you how to give me a shot of morphine. First you need to find the syringe," he explained. Brooklyn reached for it in the hiding place she reserved for it. The rubber safety was still fastened to the needle.

Terence, who was still on speaker phone and relieved that Tristan came out of it, interjected, "Tristan, relax, I'll explain it to her, you just watch her before you pass out again."

"Hi, Terence," Tristan said weakly.

Brooklyn did exactly what Terence told her to do. She found a tourniquet and fastened it on the upper portion of his arm. She checked the syringe for air bubbles and then searched for a vein that wasn't superficial. She injected the morphine into his veins like a professional and then waited with Tristan to see if his pain would subside. "Good job," Tristan said. He put his arm around her and laid his head upon her shoulder. "I'm so sorry I scared you like that," he told her. "Are you okay?" he asked her.

"No," she answered. He let go of his grip around Brooklyn and took her hand instead. "What can I do to make it better?" Brooklyn asked and he kissed her hand. Brooklyn touched his hair and attempted to inspect his head to make sure he hadn't hit it when he fell. "Did you hit your head when you passed out?" she finally asked him.

"No, I was already sitting down on the floor, trying to negotiate this injection. I didn't fall far." Tristan laughed. "I'm sorry, love," he said, echoing his last apology. "Are you mad at me?" he asked. The pain began to dull and his face began to become colorful again.

"Are you okay?" she asked.

"Almost," he answered.

"Then yes, I'm mad at you," she said, teasing him.

"I'm going to attempt to stand up," he suggested.

"No," she insisted, "just wait a few minutes more until you're stronger. I'll stay here with you," she suggested. "Tristan, did I do this to you?" she asked.

"What are you talking about?" He laughed.

"I mean all that lovemaking we did before. Was that what caused this?" she wondered.

"No, no, no silly. It's just how I roll. I woke up out of a deep sleep in pain. It just happens sometimes," he said. "You having second thoughts?" he asked nervously.

"Never," she insisted. "Not for one minute and don't even go there again. I love you and I'm not leaving, that's final," she said, still trying to pretend she was angry. "And furthermore, stop being a jerk," she added.

He kissed her hand again and said, "God, I love you."

"Tris, if I wasn't here, what would have happened to you?" she curiously suggested.

"Someone would have found me eventually, unconscious with a needle by my side and assumed I was a drug addict. They would have called the newspapers, I would have gotten some outrageously bad press and would have been forced to explain my story to the world and hope they believed it!"

"No, I mean physically. What would have happened?" she inquired.

"I would have come to at some point. Baby, this is not the first time this had happened," he explained. Brooklyn stood up. "Where are you going?" Tristan asked.

She replied, "Nowhere, I just thought I'd try and help you get back into bed."

"Come here," he said as he took her hand again and pulled her back down next to him. "I don't think I can make the attempt to get up yet," he said as he smiled.

"You're still in a lot of pain," Brooklyn asked, already knowing the answer to her question.

"I'm okay sitting here, but I think if I stand, I might pass out again," he explained.

"Anything I can do?" she asked.

"Just hold my hand for a while, okay?" he requested.

Brooklyn took his hand in both of hers and held it up to her own face. "How much pain are you in, and tell me the truth," she insisted.

"Enough . . . A lot," he admitted. Brooklyn just continued to hold his hand.

It seemed like hours that the two of them just sat on the bathroom floor, Tristan with his head on her shoulder, Brooklyn just holding his hand in hers. "Brooklyn, go to bed, love. I'm okay as long as I'm sitting here," he offered.

"I'm here for the duration," she insisted.

Tristan looked at her and smiled, "You make me smile," Tristan told her. "Do you know I smile every time I think about you, which is constantly? Through the worst pain, I'm still smiling and that's quite a miracle," he added. Brooklyn caressed his face, which was still at rest upon her shoulder. "How long have we been sitting here?" he asked.

"About an hour, hour and a half. Why?" she asked.

Tristan took a breath. He was again growing pale and his breathing was slightly labored. He was in more pain than he cared to admit, even to himself. He knew he'd have to let Brooklyn know, but he didn't wish to alarm her. He was desperately trying to avoid a visit to the hospital, but in his heart he realized a hospital stay was eminent.

"Brooklyn, come closer, I wanna tell you something," he said.

"If I come any closer to you, I will be sitting on your lap," she exclaimed. She moved slightly closer to him.

He lifted his head off her shoulder and held her face in his hands and attempted to explain his situation to her. "I need you to be really strong for me, okay?" She nodded. He continued, "I don't want you to be frightened, because it will be okay, I promise. This pain should have been gone or at least gotten better by now, but it's only getting worse. I think I need to go to the hospital, but we don't need the press, so . . . call the Devils and a cab. I need you to do it rather quickly." Just then there was a knock on the door.

"Trist, Brooklyn, it's me, Terence."

Brooklyn ran to let him in. "Your timing is absolutely impeccable. He needs to go to the hospital." He ran over to Tristan, who was almost out of his mind with pain but still trying it hide as much of it as he was able from Brooklyn.

"The Devils will be here in a second, I text them to help," Brooklyn informed Terence.

"Knock, knock."

"Come in, hurry," Brooklyn yelled.

"All right guys, he's in a lot of pain, so be very gentle," Terence demanded.

They lifted Tristan and helped him walk to the elevator as Brooklyn kept watch, making sure no one was peeking or in the elevator. No one was in the lobby at this hour, so they rushed Tristan out the door and into a taxi. Tristan's pain was so intense he began to lose consciousness. "Stay with us, Tristan," Terence ordered.

"I'm trying," Tristan said, fighting to stay conscious. "Where's Brooklyn?" Tristan asked.

She took his hand, "Right here, baby," she said. Once in the cab, Terence implored Brooklyn to continuously talk to him as he fought even harder not to pass out. "Tristan, look at me, baby, try and stay with us, don't let go," Brooklyn pleaded. Tristan was fading in and out of consciousness as Brooklyn tried to keep him awake.

"Tristan, look at me, baby. I want you to know that I love you so much. You're my heart," Brooklyn confessed as she held back her tears, knowing she had to remain strong for Tristan's sake.

Tristan looked at her and smiled. "You must really love me," he said, hardly able to focus on anything else but staying conscious. "Hey, look, I'm still smiling," he joked. Brooklyn leaned over and kissed him as Terence informed then they would soon reach the hospital.

"Hold it together dude, we're almost there," Terence told Tristan.

As the taxi pulled into NYU Medical Center, emergency, Terence jumped out and grabbed a wheelchair. They all helped Tristan out of the car and hurried into the building. Terence saw that Tristan was taken directly into a room as his breathing was rapid and pulse irregular. "You look concerned," Brooklyn said to Terence. He had no comment.

A young doctor stuck his head out of the room Tristan was assigned to. He looked around and then asked, "Who's Brooklyn?"

"I am," she said.

"Okay, do you want to come in here? He's asking for you," added the doctor.

She walked into the room and found Tristan sitting up, complete with an IV implanted in his arm and an oxygen cannula around his head. Brooklyn walked over to the bed and took Tristan's hand in hers. Tristan squeezed her hand and attempted a smile. A nurse administered some kind of medication into Tristan's IV, and moments later the color returned to his face and his breathing slowed to normal.

The young doctor announced that he'd be back shortly to check on Tristan and left, just as Terence took it upon himself to enter. He noticed a marked difference in Tristan's appearance and was relieved to see him better. "Now that you seem improved, can you tell me why you waited so long and caused all this drama? Maybe then you can begin to explain to Brooklyn why you scared the life out of her. Maybe she'll understand and forgive you, but maybe she won't," Terence scolded angrily.

"I don't know why, I just forgot, I didn't do it on purpose, Terence," the guilty Tristan confessed.

"You put your own life in danger, dude. For you to insist on going to the hospital you must have been in unimaginable pain," Terence said to him, still angry.

"Right. I'm sorry, you two, really sorry," he said sadly.

"What just happened here?" Brooklyn asked, perplexed.

"He needs to be on a regimented medication schedule so he can better manage his pain. Otherwise, *this* happens," Terence explained. He added, "If he doesn't take that medicine regularly, it builds up to the point where even morphine doesn't help. If the pain gets as bad as it did tonight, he runs the risk of going into shock or cardiac arrest." Terrence continued. "So now maybe you feel like explaining to Brooklyn why she had to sit on a bathroom floor all night, or why she was forced to learn how to inject IV needles, or why she so shaken that she's pale. And then maybe you can explain to me why she still loves you," Terence finished saying.

Brooklyn turned to Tristan, but before she could say anything, he admitted, "He's right. It's all true." He went on to say, "I'm sorry love, I didn't think of the consequences and I don't even know what else to say to you." His eyes filled with tears of regret and the remnants of pain. He took her hand and put it to his lips. Brooklyn figured that he had certainly suffered enough for his mistake and that she would wait to yell at him, if he ever let it happen again. Besides Terence had already guilted him enough for both of them. She sat down on the side of his bed and pressed his head against her breast. "We'll just have to try harder, together." He looked at Terence and asked, "Can you please get me out of here now?"

Terence asked, "Can you stand yet?"

Tristan replied, "I don't think so."

"Then you're not going anywhere," Terence insisted.

"Please" Tristan begged.

Terence shook his head. "I'll see what I can do." And he left the room.

"Can you forgive me?" Tristan asked Brooklyn.

"You've already been punished enough. There's nothing to forgive." Brooklyn kissed the top of his head.

"I love you," he said and she responded, "You better."

The young doctor came back into the room and tried to convince Tristan to stay for twenty-four hours. Tristan assured him that he was really all right and that he needed to leave. "I can't keep you here against your will. However, I do not recommend that you leave. I'm going to release you against my better judgment and under protest, you need to be off your feet for at least twenty-four hours and you must follow up with your regular doctor this week," the doctor literally ordered.

"Thank you," Tristan said to him. Brooklyn thanked him as well. As he left the room, Brooklyn told Tristan she was going to check on the Devils and that she'd be right back. Tristan smiled at her. Her intention wasn't to see the Devils. She ran after the young doctor in hopes of finding out if Tristan was really going to be okay.

"He's okay?" she asked the doctor. "Isn't he?"

"For now he seems okay. His vitals are stable and his spirit is good, but had he gotten here any later, I can't say what the outcome might have been," he said sternly. He added, "Take good care of him. He has a long road ahead, and I guarantee you, it's going to be full of potholes."

"Great," she mumbled under her breath.

Terence had returned to Tristan's room and was already getting him ready to leave. Brooklyn ran and informed the Devils to be ready to leave, then joined Terence and Tristan. Terence had Tristan sitting on the side of the bed with his feet dangling, not quite reaching the floor. Terence lowered the mechanical hospital bed so that his feet were planted on solid ground. "Okay," Terence said, "put your arm around me and Brooklyn and try to stand," he ordered Tristan, who obeyed. He was actually able to stand, but he was exhausted, high from the medication and slightly disorientated from the night's ordeal. Terence said to Brooklyn, "Just drop him in this wheelchair. He's not going to be able to walk out of here." Together Terence and Brooklyn maneuvered him into the chair.

"I think we should eighty-six the hotel and just go back to the island altogether," suggested Tristan.

"Yeah, at this time of day there is no way you're going through that lobby unnoticed, and you look scary," Terrence offered.

"True," Tristan agreed and then asked, "Are the Devils here?"

Terence sarcastically remarked, "Your little entourage is present and accounted for."

Tristan looked beat up, and fragile his eyes were glazed, his hair mattered, his face laced with exhaustion, as he painstakingly wheeled himself toward the Devils. As soon as they saw him, they gathered round and bombarded him with questions.

"Are you okay?"

"What happened?"

"What drug did you take?"

"Did you fall?"

The questions kept on coming. Tristan put his finger on his lips. "Shhh," he said as he began to address the curious little group, "I'm okay, I didn't take anything, I didn't fall. This just happens occasionally. It's a little souvenir while on the road to recovery from my ordeal. So here's the situation: We aren't going to chance returning to the hotel. As you have noticed, I'm not at my best. I thought we'd go back to my house and start rehearsing tomorrow for the next challenge. I've summoned the limo, but this has to be a unanimous decision," Tristan finished.

Dazzel clapped her hand in joy, "I choose the Gatsby mansion."

Garrett yelled, "I second it."

"Then Colin and Damian also agree," he said, smiling yet still knowing something wasn't right.

Tristan sat in the corner of the limo in the back with Brooklyn leaning up against him. He wrapped his arms around her and put his head on her shoulder. They stopped at the hotel to pick up whatever they needed for the weekend and the Devils "holiday" at the mansion. Once again, while the boys collected their belongings, Tristan asked her what was wrong. "I told you, I just love you, that's all," she said.

Tristan took a guess as to what was really wrong, and said to her, "I scared you tonight, didn't I?" he asked. Brooklyn buried her head in his chest and started to cry. "Shhh," he said. "Well, after what you've been through tonight, and you were so strong and brave for me, you deserve a good cry," he whispered to her. "I'm okay now, I promise," he said gently.

"But what about the next time? You could have died," she cried.

"Is that what this is all about?" he asked. "I will never let this happen again, love. I promise. We will do it together like you said. It's just that when I'm with you, the pain seems to vanish and I just forget that I'm even afflicted in the first place. And I thank you for that," he said dramatically. "I'll take my medication as I'm supposed to, I promise," he assured her.

Brooklyn was exhausted, both physically and emotionally. She put her arms around Tristan and laid her head on his chest and quickly fell asleep. Tristan was also almost catatonically exhausted; however, he didn't fall asleep on the ride home. He was strangely elated by Brooklyn's reaction to the night's events. If he ever doubted the fact that she loved him, tonight proved that those doubts were benign.

By the time the limo pulled up in front of the mansion, the Devils except Damian were fast asleep. Brooklyn was still asleep in the arms of Tristan. Terence had a brief nap but was fully awake by the time they approached the house. Tristan, who had been stroking her hair the entire ride home, whispered in Brooklyn's ear, "Wake up, beautiful, we're home." She awoke to Tristan's touch and his whisper and was somehow comforted by that.

The Devils piled out of the limo half-asleep, one by one. Brooklyn followed and then Tristan. He was no longer in much pain but very stiff from the long ride. Terence and Damian helped him out of the car and asked him if he were able to stand. "Yes, I think so," he said. Brooklyn ran ahead and opened the front door with her golden key that hung from her diamond keychain, while the boys walked toward the door.

"Hey, Brook, you wanna take a shower with me?" Tristan asked.

"Yes, I'd love to," she responded.

Tristan held on to the banister of the Hollywood staircase and started to climb the stairs slowly. Brooklyn took his other arm and put it around her own shoulder to guide him up to the second floor. He turned to look at her with admiration and kissed the top of her head. Once upstairs she made Tristan sit on the bed while she ran the shower.

The warmth of the shower felt good. Tristan took Brooklyn's two little feminine arms and held them with his hands and kissed her. "I just can't get enough of you," he whispered in her ear. He looked down and pointed at his penis and said to it, "You behave now."

Brooklyn laughed. "Not happening now, dude, that's how we got into this mess in the first place," she said.

"You're not going to be afraid to make love to me now, are you?" he asked.

"I'm more afraid not to," she said.

"That's a relief," he said as the warm water fell upon them both.

Tristan wrapped her up in a towel and held her close to him, unconcerned with his own wet body. When she was dry, he took the towel and dried himself. Brooklyn lay naked upon the big round bed when Tristan lay down next to her. She touched his face. "You must be so tired." She said to him. She instructed him to lie on his stomach and began to tenderly massage his back. Her touch relaxed him and aroused him at the same time, but finally his exhaustion won and he fell asleep.

It was four thirty in the afternoon by the time Tristan woke up. The sun was already setting on the beach and snow was in the air. For a second a gripping fear came over him as Brooklyn was absent. He remembered the sadness he saw in her eyes as she left the hospital. "Oh god, was she reconsidering this relationship?" crossed his mind for a split second until he looked out on the balcony and she waved to him. He threw her a kiss and she yelled out loud, "I love you, Tristan Bondage . . . Stay there, I'll be right there." At that moment he felt so close to her as if her were an empath, able to feel her very thoughts.

By the time she reached the master suite, the first glistening snow flurries were gracefully falling when she entered the bedroom. Tristan was at the door to greet her with a warm kiss upon her frozen lips. "You're supposed to be in bed resting, get back into that bed," she insisted.

"If you join me," he said. He took her coat and kissed her.

"Come here," he asked of her while he went to sit on the bed, taking her by the hand and guiding her on the bed with him. He lay down on the pillows and she along with him, still holding hands. "I wanna tell you something," Tristan announced.

"I'm listening," she said quietly.

"After last night's little crisis I realized, for the first time, without a shadow of doubt that you really loved me. I mean that you loved me forever, and it made me happier than I've ever been in my life. I sensed a truth to our love, and I knew at that moment that all insecurities vanished. I knew that we'd spend the rest of our lives together. I felt as if our souls touched each other's and fused into one."

"How romantic," she said, half-laughing at his revelation.

"You're making fun of me," he observed.

"No, not really," she said. "You're very sweet, and kind, and loving. You are what dreams are made of," she said as she kissed him gently on the lips.

He sat up and looked into her eyes and said, "Yet you seem sad."

"I'm not sad," she answered.

"You can deny it if you want, but you're better off telling me why so I can fix it. The truth will set you free," he joked.

Brooklyn sat up and looked directly into Tristan's eyes. "You're confusing sad with scared," she confessed. "Last night I realized something as well," she explained.

"Go on," he demanded.

"I realized that I can never, under any circumstances be without you in my life and that scared me. I didn't enjoy that feeling. It made me cry," she admitted.

"So what you're telling me is that it scares you to love me" he said, almost laughing at her confession.

"Now you're making fun of me," she said shyly.

"No, not really," he said, then added, "if you think for one moment you're going to separate from me emotionally. Well, you're not going to. I won't allow that," he said, still laughing. "It's too late for that, and I'm not going to allow you to 'unlove' me—just forget that," he continued.

"No, I could never 'unlove' you, silly. The point is, I love you too much, and I'm scared . . . scared of losing you . . . loosing you forever. Life is very fragile, especially your life . . . and I can't be without you. You have become my life, my heart, my soul and, Tristan, you could have died last night," she said as a single tear fell from her eye.

Tristan put his arms around her and hugged her close to him. Then he released her and with his hand held her chin so that they had eye-to-eye contact and he begun to explain, "Brooklyn, you can't stop loving me because you think I might die someday." He laughed. "Then you'd never be able to love anyone," he continued.

"I'll never stop loving you," she whispered.

"Listen, angel, I cannot allow you to pull away from me emotionally. I need you, so please don't ever leave me. Don't ever leave *us*, okay?" he asked, waiting and hoping for her to agree.

"Okay," she said, "but only if you promise to stay alive. Deal?"

"Deal," he answered. "Believe in me. I'll devote the rest of my life, however long that is, to making you happy if you give me the chance," he begged.

"You already make me happy, all the time," she admitted.

"Then just be happy . . . don't live with a cloud over your head. Just enjoy what we have together, and I promise I'll try not to die," he announced. She smiled at Tristan, relatively satisfied that he would be taking better care of himself from now on. "That's my girl." He smiled back.

Tristan eyed his guitar lying next to the bed and grabbed it. He told Brooklyn he loved her and began singing "I Won't Give Up" by Jason Mraz.

When I look into your eyes
It's like watching the night sky or a beautiful sunrise
There's so much they hold
And just like them old stars
I see that you've come so far, to be right where you are
How old is your soul
I won't give up on us
Even if the skies get rough
I'm giving you all my love
I'm still looking up
And when you're needing your space
To do some navigating
I'll be there patiently waiting
To see what you find
Cause even the stars they burn
Some even fall to the Earth
We've got a lot to learn
God knows we're worth it
I won't give up
I don't wanna be someone who walks away so easily
I'm here to stay and make the difference that I can make
Our differences they do a lot to teach us how to use
The tools and the gifts we got, yeah, we got a lot at stake
And in the end you're still my friend
At least we did intend for us to work
We didn't break we didn't burn
We had to learn how to bend without the world caving in
I had to learn what I've got and what I'm not, and who I am
I won't give up on us, even if the skies get rough
I'm giving you all my love
I'm still looking up, I'm still looking up
I won't give up God knows

God knows we've got a lot to learn
And knows we're worth it . . . I won't give up . . .

"That was beautiful, Tristan," Brooklyn said in a whisper.

"That's because you're so beautiful," he whispered back.

The snow was making its presence known on Long Island. From the balcony Tristan and Brooklyn watched the Devils playing in the snow. They were having a snowball fight—all of them against Dazzel. Tristan and Brooklyn couldn't help laughing uncontrollably at Dazzel being bombarded by balls of the cold, wet snow. Suddenly the Devils noticed the two standing on the balcony and changed their strategy and began throwing the snowballs at them instead. They ducked and ran inside the bedroom, still filled with laughter. They heard the Devils opening the French doors and entering the house full of noise, and their own brand of laughter.

"Let's go down, love, and play with them," Tristan asked hopefully.

"Okay, but take it slowly," Brooklyn cautioned. He was still shaky from last night's ordeal so he held on to the banister tightly as well as Brooklyn, who put her arm around him, as he challenged the steep staircase.

Damian greeted them holding a cocktail for both of them. "Are you two hungry? We made you guys dinner," Damian informed them.

"Starving," Tristan answered.

"That's another reason I love gay men, they can really cook," Brooklyn chimed.

The Devils prepared a gourmet, five-course dinner, including cocktails, various ethnic dishes, and desserts, all *Iron Chef*-worthy. "That was amazing, Devils," Tristan said genuinely.

Brooklyn offered to help clean up afterward but Damian insisted that she relax on the couch with Tristan, as she "had nails" and that she'd only be in the way. Relieved, Brooklyn headed toward the couch to be close to Tristan. Garrett followed her and stood in front of the two of them smiling.

"Can I help you, Garrett?" Tristan asked.

"He wants something," Brooklyn said, smiling.

"Come out with it," Tristan ordered.

Shyly Garrett asked, "Can we use your pool?"

"And your hot tub," added Dazzel.

"Amuse yourself any way you want. My—*our* house is yours," Tristan offered.

"What are you two going to do?" Garret asked, deciding whether or not to invite them.

"Really?" Dazzel said. "Why would you be asking two breeders their itinerary?" she added.

Tristan laughed and shook his head. "We were going to find some songs for Monday night's challenge, which by the way I was about to unveil to Brooklyn," Tristan exclaimed."

"Okay, you caught our attention," Colin insisted.

"Let's go sit beside Daddy," suggested Garrett.

Tristan rolled his eyes and mumbled "Daddy?" under his breath.

All at once the Devils were perched in front of the coach where Tristan sat. They all gathered on the floor beneath him waiting impatiently to hear this week's challenge.

Wishing to have a little British fun with the Devils, he began presenting the challenge in the most animated way he could think of. He sat up straight and tall and pretended he was Adonis as he removed an envelope from his pocket and proceeded to reveal its contents. He read the Devils the challenge as though he were in front of the TV cameras and a million people, only with a heavy cockney accident.

"Oh Jesus, when did Adonis become British?" Damian laughed.

"There will be two themes this evening. The first will be songs arising from a social consequence or protest. You will select three songs of protest or tributes, any genre, any time period, any artist. The second part of this week's challenge is my favorite of all—love songs. One depicting a new love, one heart-wrenching breakup song, and one 'couples reunited' song."

"Sounds like the two of you," Dazzel commented.

"And here is the best part of the challenge—your coaches get to select all the songs." Tristan stepped out of the Adonis character for a moment and said, "Guys, that means I get to pick them, in case that wasn't clear . . . Aren't you all going to applaud for me?" Tristan, a.k.a. Adonis, asked.

"That performance sucked," Dazzel expressed.

"Oh," Tristan said, faking his disappointment at his critics review.

"Speak for yourself," Brooklyn said, "I think you were marvelous" she added in an English accent put on purposely to imitate Tristan.

"You're prejudiced," Tristan said and kissed Brooklyn as though he were about to seduce her.

"Not in front of the children," commented Dazzel.

"Didn't you guys want to disappear and go swimming or something?" Tristan asked.

The Devils all got up and left one by one, all smirking.

Brooklyn proceeded to trap Tristan in the corner of the couch where he had been sitting, by positioning her legs on each side of his body and kissing him deeply. Tristan made no attempt to escape his captor, but instead put his arms around her forcing her downward on top of his own body. "Let's go upstairs," he whispered.

Brooklyn removed herself from on top of Tristan, took his hand, and anxiously led him upstairs, stopping only to kiss him along the way. Once upstairs Brooklyn lay upon the round bed, pulling Tristan on top of her. He took his finger and licked it with his tongue and then traced the outline of her lips, slowly and sensually. She lay still as Tristan moved beside her and touched her breasts over her shirt, and then under her shirt. He cthen handily opened her bra and softly held her breast and touched her nipple. Every nerve in her body tingled as he touched her. He gently lifted her to a sitting position and removed her shirt and bra and then lay her down so he could remove her pants. He removed his own shirt and jeans and lay gently on top of her so he could feel her breasts against his chest. He kissed her and then licked her lips with his tongue. His hand moved below her waist and down to her thighs, which became warm and inviting, as he softly kissed her nipple. They hadn't even touched upon the depth of foreplay when their sinful passion turned into hot lust and exploded between their legs and could no longer be contained. Their instincts quickly took over and within seconds he was inside her. It took only a short time there after for their bodies left trembling, for their desire for one another to again become reinstated.

* * *

It was fun being officially snowed in at Tristan's house, especially for Tristan now that Brooklyn and the Devils were literally his captive audience. He woke next to Brooklyn who remained asleep as he watched her in awe. When she began to stir, he just couldn't resist touching her hair and then running his finger down her naked back. She turned and opened her eyes to see Tristan smiling at her. "Good morning," she said.

"Good morning, love," he answered.

Brooklyn looked radiant in the morning, tangled up in her own blond hair. She jumped out of bed and ran into the bathroom to brush her teeth. While she was gone, Tristan dialed Dazzel and asked her to please bring some Keurig Starbucks coffee upstairs. Dazzel answered jokingly, "Yes, ma'am." Brooklyn ran back to Tristan and climbed up onto his lap and kissed him furiously. He returned her kiss and hugged her tightly. He asked himself out loud, "Is it possible to be this happy?"

The knock on the door did not cause Brooklyn to move from her position on top of Tristan. "Is it safe to enter?" Dazzel called out through the door, holding a tray of coffee and freshly baked corn muffins, still warm. Dazzel brought the tray to Tristan and curtsied. "Where should I place the tray for your princess, sir?"

Tristan pointed to the night tables and Dazzel put it down. "Thanks, Daz, you're the best," exclaimed Brooklyn.

"Oh, my pleasure, Your Majesty," Dazzel said as he looked at the two lovers and shook her head. "Ugh, I better leave now before I see something I know I will regret," Dazzel said as she closed the bedroom door behind her.

"What was that princess stuff about?"

"Oh, I called her while you were in the bathroom and ordered you coffee," Tristan said proudly.

According to the weather channel, fifteen inches of snow had already fallen. "What a lovely day to rehearse," remarked Tristan.

"What songs have you selected for us?" Brooklyn asked.

"Come here," Tristan asked. He held her in his arms and couldn't help but kiss her everywhere.

"I love when you change the subject this way," Brooklyn told him. "Hey, did you take your medication?" she asked.

"Yes, love, I did," he assured her. "Terence will be coming by later if it's possible with all this snow," he informed her.

"And if it's not?" she asked.

"I don't know," he said. "I try not to think about it too much, but it's always in the back of my mind. Just another thing for me to became frightened about," he said sadly. "I don't want to become paralyzed. Time passes quickly and eventually it will happen, and if I keep skipping physical therapy, it's more likely to happen sooner," he said.

Brooklyn leaned over and kissed him. "Don't you know what you do in physical therapy?" she asked.

"Of course I do." He laughed.

"Then improvise. Do what you can without Terence. Tell me what to do and I'll help, you," she offered.

"Really?" he asked. "Yep, it's better than doing nothing isn't it?" she asked. "I suppose so," he said.

"Hey, I don't want you to be paralyzed either. I don't want anything bad to happen to you, but be assured whatever you have to face, I'll face it with you," she promised as he bent over to him and kissed him. "I just hope that you're man enough to accept my help," she said.

"Wow," he said, "man enough? I'll show you man enough." And he kissed her long and hard and unleashed every sensitivity she had in her body.

"I just know that I love you so much, and my soul would die without you," she whispered.

"You will never have to be without me," he promised. He made love to her with a strength and power that she hadn't recognized but thoroughly enjoyed.

Shortly after, Terence phoned and assured Tristan he was on his way. He arrived three hours later and informed Tristan he would be staying. He invited Brooklyn to watch and learn, and she thankfully accepted, very relieved that Terence had guided him through two hours of physical therapy and taught Brooklyn how to massage his legs using the best method of stimulation. He now had to concentrate on providing the Devils with material and guidance for Monday's show. He would have plenty of opportunity since Stars was closed tonight due to weather and the Devils weren't going anywhere in the snow.

* * *

Week eight and nine came and went quickly. Both bands did remarkably well. However, the fact that Devin Liam was still twice as popular as Tristan couldn't be denied. Tristan would have to think of something crazy to even the odds. Week eleven was to be a surprise challenge to be aired the night of the grand finale. Week twelve would promise to be historical and epic since it would be the most viewed show in the entire history of television, as the fate of one group would be decided in one swift moment.

Chapter 8

The Light through My Darkness

On the Wednesday following the tenth week of the show Tristan lay sequestered inside his hotel room. He was expected to join the Devils at the original studio, where this all began, with the red door and the number 5 written in black upon it. The fact was, however, that he was in agony and had a raging headache as well, which was causing him to feel quite sick. He had sent Brooklyn ahead with the Devils making the excuse that he had to stop by the set to speak with Adonis. He hated lying to her, but he hated frightening her even more. Finally after injecting himself with a substantial amount of morphine, he decided to try and make it the distance to the studio to rehearse the Devils for next week's challenge.

An hour or so had passed and still no Tristan. Brooklyn hesitated to call him, not wanting to interrupt an important rendezvous between him and Adonis, but she was getting concerned. She lifted her phone to dial, when Colin reminded her that he was in a meeting. Just then Tristan made his entrance. He apologized for being late. He walked over to Brooklyn, took her hand and kissed it, then said, "I missed you," and walked over to the wheelchair that was positioned in front of the room. Brooklyn hadn't seen Tristan sitting in a wheelchair since the beginning and an uneasy fear came upon her. Before she could ask Tristan if he were okay, Garrett did it for her. "Hey, what's wrong with you? Are you all right?"

He answered, "I'm trying to be." Brooklyn ran to him and knelt down, putting her head on his legs gently. He stroked her hair and said, "I'm all right for now I think, but if you see me losing it, find Terence. See if he's at the hotel just as a precaution."

"But—" Brooklyn said.

Tristan interrupted her, "Please, baby, just see if you can find Terence."

"Okay," she said and stood up to find her phone in hopes of locating Terence.

Tristan grabbed her arm as she went to walk away and said, "Hey, I love you." Brooklyn squeezed his hand and returned to her phone to do as Tristan asked.

"Okay," Tristan said, "we need three songs from the 1980s. Call out your suggestions." Damian yelled out the name of one of Tristan's songs. He was surprised and touched, "You mean they don't suck anymore?" He directed the question solely at Brooklyn.

"I guess they kind of grew on me," she joked.

"I'm going to let you do that song," Tristan agreed proudly. "And thank you," he added. They also chose "Zombies" by the Cranberries, a choice Tristan was wild about. For the final selection Tristan had a brilliant idea. They would attempt to combine "Take on Me" by A-ha and "This Moment" by Pit bull and Christina Aguilera. If this could be made to work, they would certainly have a hit remix on their hands. After all the music was the same. Tristan was excited. He was feeling a little better and was exhilarated by the selections.

"Okay, perfect. Now three current songs, yell 'em out," demanded Tristan.

"'Danza Kuduro' by Don Omar," Damian suggested.

"Yes, but we'll do it in Spanish and English and Akon-ish. Good choice," Tristan said, full of enthusiasm.

"'Counting Stars' by One Republic," Dazzel suggested.

"Love it," Tristan said.

"'I Won't Give Up,'" Brooklyn whispered.

"Amazing, I was thinking of that one especially," Tristan declared. "These are all powerful songs, great choices, I'm proud of all your selections," Tristan said.

"And your brilliant idea," Damian reminded him.

Damian immediately began looking up the lyrics, while Colin found the music. Brooklyn just continued to watch Tristan carefully. He did seem better; however, he hadn't picked up a guitar all day, nor did he attempt to leave the wheelchair. What was even more unusual was he hadn't tried to kiss Brooklyn all day. Brooklyn knew he was a master of disguising the fact that he was hurting.

The Devils had accomplished much today and Tristan announced that they would continue tomorrow. "If I'm late tomorrow, keep going over the music," Tristan commanded as they all left the studio, except for Brooklyn. Tristan called to her, "Come here, love, did you locate Terence?" he asked.

"He's at the hotel," she claimed.

"Perfect," Tristan said. "Tell him to meet us at the hospital," Tristan announced. Brooklyn touched his face and he took her hand and kissed it. "Listen, love, I can't hold it together much longer," he whispered, barely able to speak.

"I'm calling an ambulance," she announced.

Wincing in pain, Tristan whispered, "No, no. I'm gonna take some morphine and we're going to take the limo to the hospital." She called Terence once again to find out exactly where he was. The hospital wasn't too far from the studio, and neither was Terence, so she persuaded him to stop at the studio. Tristan attempted to give himself a shot of morphine, but he was overcome with pain. Brooklyn took the syringe from him and gave him the injection instead. Several moments later Terence arrived.

"What's going on with you?" he asked Tristan, who's pain had eased because of the medicine.

He was at least able to speak. He looked at Terence and said calmly "I don't know, the pain is different, and I feel really sick. I've had a ravishing headache all day, making my life twice as annoying," he announced to Terence.

"Come on, let's get you to the hospital. Can you stand?" Terence asked.

"Yes, I'm okay for now. We'll take a cab or the limo and try to avoid press," Tristan said as he painfully stood up and limped to the door.

"You don't think the limo dropping you off at the hospital will alert anybody including the press?" Terence laughed.

"You have a good point, let's get a taxi." Tristan said as he was seemingly growing weaker.

Inside the taxi Brooklyn put her arms around Tristan, who was trembling. She kissed his forehead and realized he was awfully warm. "Hey, Trist, I think you have a fever."

"That might explain why I have this awful headache and I'm freezing to death!" he said. He then whispered in Brooklyn's ear. "Baby, I think I'm really sick."

Terence felt his head and agreed. "You are burning up, Tristan."

The taxi raced to the emergency room and let the three of them off quickly. Terence grabbed a wheelchair and Tristan sat down in it. They rushed into triage and Terence ran into the back to secure a space for Tristan. Once inside one of the small cubicles surrounded by curtains separating the patients, Tristan took Brooklyn's hand and pleaded with her not to leave him. His body temperature reached 102.7 and it was rising. The doctor started him on an IV drip and extracted blood from his arm. He also ordered a strong broad spectrum antibiotic in hopes it would begin to fight the infection that invaded his fragile body. The doctor also ordered x-rays and tests to help try and determine exactly what was causing the strange pain and fever.

After an hour they brought Tristan back to the cubicle. His fever had risen to over 103 degrees and he was out of his mind with pain. Tristan was really sick this time and frightened as well. "Put your arms around me," he begged Brooklyn. He was so warm and so weak. She held him for a minute, then uncovered him, opened his hospital gown. She found a washcloth, which she doused in cold water and began to wash his chest and forehead with it. She asked the nurse to bring him some Advil or else she was going to give it to him herself. Brooklyn saw her speaking to the doctor. She immediately came back with some fever-reducing medication and gave it to

Tristan. The morphine injection had long since worn off. His agony was reaching dangerous levels, so they added some pain-relieving meds to his IV. When his temperature was monitored again it had gone down to 100.4. The pain meds took effect swiftly and for a time Tristan felt relief. He rested his head up against her breast as she stroked his hair. He whispered to Brooklyn, "Stay with me, love. I'm . . . I'm scared," he admitted.

"Awww, Trist, shhh, it's gonna be okay," she promised, although petrified herself. He briefly fell asleep with his head still up against her.

Brooklyn tried to escape in hopes of finding Terence who had been gone a long time. She longed for answers as to Tristan's condition, but Tristan woke up. "Brooklyn, please, baby, don't leave," he begged. She sat back down on top of the bed and wrapped her arms back around him.

"I'm here, Tris, I'm not leaving, baby."

Terence finally returned to the cubicle. Brooklyn couldn't help notice that his eyes were full of worry and his expression impaled with concern for his friend. A tall female Chinese doctor entered the room and introduced herself as Dr. Cheng while Tristan clung to Brooklyn like a baby alone in a room full of strangers. Dr. Cheng announced that Tristan had an infection in his right leg and that his condition was quite serious. She went on to explain that they would admit him and start him on a large dose of penicillin. Brooklyn asked her candidly what would happen if the penicillin didn't work. Although the Chinese doctor spoke with a heavy Asian accent, they understood when she explained that, if the antibiotic failed, they would have to resort to more aggressive measure. None of them knew what she meant by "aggressive measure," and all of them were afraid to ask. Dr. Cheng prescribed some more pain medication for Tristan and had the first dose of penicillin was implanted into his IV drip.

As the hours passed, Tristan's fever began to climb once again. Terence suggested that the fever was fighting the infection and coaxed Brooklyn to stop trying to get rid of it. Sometime around 1:00 a.m. the fever caused Tristan to become delirious. Terence informed Brooklyn that it might now be a good time to reapply the cold compresses. Tristan was completely out of it, suffering from hallucinations, crying out into the darkness. Terence told Brooklyn to try and find the doctor and see if someone could come into the cubicle and just check on him. He felt that she needed to leave since high fevers could cause seizures and he didn't want Brooklyn to witness that.

Brooklyn peeked inside the waiting room and saw the Devils still there, waiting. They inquired about his condition, to which she answered, "He's really, really sick this time." Garrett asked if she were hungry. She shook her head. Damian asked if they could go in and see him, perhaps cheer him up. She explained that he wouldn't even know that they were there. Just then she spotted the Chinese doctor and told the boys she'd see them later.

She ran over to Dr. Cheng and asked, "Is he going to die?" The doctor saw the fear in her eyes and beckoned her to sit down inside her office. For the first time the doctor smiled. "We are not going to give up on him. Whether or not the medicine will work is in God's hands," she explained. "His condition is critical and if the fever doesn't break soon we might have to take him into surgery and be forced to amputate his leg, to save his life. However," she went on to say, "he should be showing signs of improvement within the next twelve hours, if the penicillin were to take effect. We're not going to let him die," the doctor reassured her. "But," she added, "he is gravely ill."

Brooklyn thanked her in a daze walked back to Tristan's room. Terence had been using cold compresses on him, which seemed to quiet him. As she entered the room, Terence asked her if she had seen a ghost. She started to cry until Terence grabbed her by the shoulders and told her she had to be stronger than she ever had been in her life for him. She wanted to explain to Terence how Tristan was in danger of losing his leg, but somehow she already suspected he knew. She sat down next to Tristan and whispered in his ear, "Fight this, baby, fight this if you love me." She took his hand and felt him weakly squeeze hers.

The Chinese doctor came into check on Tristan. She said nothing, but administered some more medication into his IV drip. When she left the room, Terence followed her. Brooklyn stroked Tristan's hair and whispered into Tristan's ear once again, begging him to keep fighting. For hours Tristan lay lifeless, occasionally squeezing Brooklyn's hand, just to make sure she was still there with him. Brooklyn silently prayed. The thought of Tristan losing his leg made her sick inside, but the thought of him dying was too overwhelming to even imagine.

Brooklyn lay her head upon his chest gently so she could monitor every breathe he took. At some point in the early morning hours, she dozed off from sheer exhaustion, still with her head resting upon his chest. She awoke to the feel of Tristan stroking her hair and calling to her. She looked up to see Tristan trying to smile. "It's okay," he whispered. "It's going to be okay," he repeated.

His fever had broken and it appeared the crisis had passed and the medicine was working. Tristan was lying in a pool of sweat. His hair was drenched, the sheets were soaked, and the sweat glistened upon his face. He wrapped his arms around her as she kissed his lips. "I'm a mess," he said to her.

"Yes, but you're my mess," she told him. "I love you," she told him.

"Yes, I think you really do," he answered back, trying to tease her.

Just then Dr. Cheng walked into the room. She had stayed way beyond her shift to see what the outcome would be. "You were very sick," she told Tristan. "You scared your poor wife," she added. She explained to Tristan in her Chinese accent, "You are not yet out of the woods. We will keep you on a large dose of penicillin for a few days until the infection has stabilized. You will experience pain for several days. We are going to get you a room and someone will change you and your bedding. You need to rest and to concentrate on getting better. It's a good thing you came to us when you did," she continued. She told them she was going home but would return to check on him later.

Terence, who had been asleep on the chair next to his bed, was elated to see him past his crisis. He shook his hand and informed him that he was going back to the hotel to get some real sleep and that he was taking Brooklyn with him. "No," she said, "I'm staying with Tristan!"

Tristan whispered to her, "I'll be okay, love, you need to get some rest. I need you to go back to the hotel and sleep. I'm going to need you to rehearse those Devils today for me."

"Oh no, the Devils, they're still here. I better tell them that you're okay," Brooklyn said.

"Please, love, get some rest. I'm okay. I promise!"

"I'm not leaving," she insisted.

"Yes, you are, princess, please," he asked again.

"I don't really think that you want me to go, but I will listen to you," she said. She kissed him and then kissed him again. "You up for saying hey to the Devils before I leave?" she asked.

"Of course, go fetch them." He laughed.

She exited the room to find the Devils. Terence looked at him and shook his head. "It's really hard for you to let her go even for a minute," said Terence.

"Yes, it is, but she's exhausted and she needs time to herself, time to navigate," Tristan explained.

"Navigate?' Terence asked.

"Never mind, it's from a song. I just know she makes me happy, all the time. Even when I'm in pain, she makes me happy," he explained to Terence.

"She was terrified last night. I saw it in her eyes, in her heart, in her soul. It's a really good thing you decided not to die," Terence added.

The Devils entered his room cautiously. They had all slept in the waiting room the entire night and were in need of a shower, and Dazzel a shave. "Hey, I'm gonna make a deal with all of you. You guys make sure Brooklyn gets some rest and then you bring her back to me later and I'll give you my credit card again," Tristan bargained.

"Deal," Dazzel jumped up and down as she went straight to his coat pocket, grabbed his wallet and his credit card right out of it. "Now go," he ordered Brooklyn.

She walked over and kissed him. "I'll miss you," she said.

Tristan took her face in his two hands and kissed her. He whispered, "This is really hard for me, to let you go, even for a few hours."

"I'll stay then," she volunteered.

"No, you won't, not with that queen in possession of my credit card. Now go before I lose the courage to let you go." She kissed him once again and then left with the Devils.

Terence stayed behind for a moment. "You should marry her, you know," Terence suggested.

"Oh, I'm trying, believe me, but she still has that little 'I'm a free spirit' attitude, and I don't want to rob her of that just yet. I asked her to live with me and she freaked. She finally agreed, but I think she did out of pity." Tristan laughed. "I'm going to marry her I'm just looking for the right time and place to ask her," he expressed to Terence.

"You should have asked her last night while you were dying. She would have done anything to keep you alive," Terence joked.

"I was pretty sick, huh?" Tristan asked.

"You were very sick, the closest to death I've ever seen you," Terence exclaimed.

"I know, I was so scared. I told her, but she told me to fight and that she loved me and couldn't live without me, so I fought. I'm sure that's why I survived," Tristan explained.

Terence shook his hand again and said, "See you later," and he left.

* * *

New York City had never experienced the likes of Dazzel Diamond as she led the Devils from store to store. The only reason that they finally returned to the hotel was because they could no longer hold their purchases. Their arms were breaking as they entered Dazzel and Brooklyn's room. "Let's have a delicious dinner on Tristan," suggested Dazzel.

"Forget it, Mary, you've done enough damage, and besides I'm going back there. I miss him and I know he really didn't' want me to leave. Besides we have to go to the studio and rehearse for a while," Brooklyn said.

Damian looked at his stuff and said, "I feel guilty spending all this money while he's lying there so sick in the hospital."

Brooklyn smiled and answer, "Tristan is so generous, he loved letting us use his card, once again, and I guarantee you he won't even ask how much we spent."

"Guurrlll, you are so lucky to have a man like that," Dazzel yelled. "Now go dress up pretty and surprise your man. He loves you so much.

Brooklyn took her advice. She became dressed to kill, wearing a hot-pink sleeveless dress and applied lipstick and shoes that matched the dress only laced in glitter. She topped the outfit with a white mink jacket. She wore her hair in an up do with long tendrils of blond hair flowing down. Brooklyn took the liberty of borrowing the limo since she knew Tristan would never allow her to return to the hotel at night in Manhattan alone.

Tristan had been brought to a room finally. On her way to the elevator she came across Dr. Cheng, who smiled when she saw her. "Tristan is doing much better," she exclaimed.

When Brooklyn walked through the door to Tristan's room, his face lit up. "My god, you look so beautiful," Tristan commented. "Like a delicious fantasy," he added. Brooklyn ran over and kissed him. He looked fragile and vulnerable, but she was glad to see him alive. She threw her fur on a chair and sat down on his bed. She couldn't seem to stop hugging him, and although still in quite a bit of pain, he did not protest. "Hey, love, it's okay, I'm okay," he finally said seeing that she was still emotional from the nights events.

"I know," she said, "I just missed you, that's all." Brooklyn took a breath and collected her thoughts. He asked, if she had fun with the Devils. She told him she had a blast but that Dazzel kept the credit card. He rolled his eyes and said "Jesus" but didn't even complain. "I'm only teasing," she said and handed him back the card. He handed it back to her and told her it was hers now. "No," she protested. I can't keep using your credit cards, I'm dangerous." Tristan laughed at her and insisted she use it whenever she wanted. He slipped it inside her dress and under her bra. She kissed him, became emotional again and reminded him how much she loved him.

"I should get sick more often," he joked, enjoying the fact that she suddenly became so attached and affectionate.

"Baby, how do you feel?" she finally remembered to ask.

"I've been better," he admitted. He was still in pain and was still running a low-grade temperature. She stayed for several hours. The two were just holding each other and planning for the future. He promised to take her to London to meet his family as soon as the show ended. They spoke about the tour if they were lucky enough to win the competition, and they even touched upon having babies together some day. She noticed Tristan getting especially exhausted, and she herself was running on borrowed sleep time. She told Tristan she had the limo, and he was relieved that she would get back to the hotel safely.

Before she left, she kissed him several times. He told her that he wanted to make love to her. She answered him by saying, if she thought he'd be able to, she would. They both laughed and kissed one last time before she left. He made sure to call her as she arrived at the hotel. He told her he missed her already and she expressed the same.

The Devils hit the studio early and practiced with a vengeance the next day. They were able to learn the songs, put a creative spin where they had to, and enhance Brooklyn's vocals with some electronic effects that they knew Tristan would love. However, they needed Tristan to help arrange the "Take Me On" / "This Moment" number. Brooklyn had Terence bring Tristan his guitar per Tristan's request to the hospital in case Tristan felt well enough to attempt an arrangement. She knew Tristan felt better today from the calls she received from him almost every hour on the hour. Tristan was trying to manage and mentor the Devils from inside the hospital bed. He asked Brooklyn to complete different tasks and commands but never failed to tell her he loved and missed her.

During one of those "call commands," Tristan asked her to enlighten Adonis as to what the situation was, leaving the drama of his near-death experience at home. Adonis was smart and intuitive. From Brooklyn's voice alone, he could somehow tell that the longitude of Tristan's plight was a lot more serious then she was displaying to him. "Poor guy," Adonis commented. "You know, Brooklyn, between you and me, and I'll deny I said this to the death, I have more respect for Tristan than any of the other coaches. He takes the concept of the show more seriously than the others, and despite the physical adversity he encounters, he manages to work twice as hard as the others. I feel like I want to visit him at the hospital because I actually care about him. However, I don't want him to think I'm going just to see that if he's going to be okay for Monday's show," Adonis confided.

"Then why don't you just tell him you're not?" Brooklyn laughed.

"True," Adonis said, laughing himself.

Tristan sat up, still weak and in pain, holding the guitar that Terence brought and trying to focus on an arrangement for the song in question when Adonis entered the room. Tristan was shocked to see his surprise guest. "Adonis?" Tristan exclaimed.

"How are you doing?" Adonis asked.

"I've been better, but I'll live," Tristan joked.

Adonis took the guitar from Tristan and asked, "What, may I ask, are you doing, when you clearly should be resting and healing? You look awful," Adonis remarked.

"Listen, Adonis, the Devils need an arrangement, and I need to give them one. They are doing this challenge ultimately alone, when I should be with them. I will be all right by Monday, I assure you that—"

Adonis interrupted him and said, "No, that's not why I'm here. I happened to be genuinely concerned about you . . . as a person. I know that you will make it to the show, even if you're dying," Adonis expressed.

"I'm touched," Tristan said, half-joking and half-authentically touched.

* * *

As the evening rolled around, Brooklyn began to feel the urgency and need to see Tristan. The last phone call he made to her, he sounded painfully weak. She had instructed him to get some rest and not to call anymore so that he'd be strong enough to hang out later when she came to see him. He knew she was right, so he tried to sleep despite the pain he was in.

Brooklyn ran from the studio directly to the hospital. She had brought a change of clothes and makeup along with her, knowing that rehearsal would run late. Once again she looked ravishing, adorned in a black and magenta dress, both short and tight, covered by a magenta-dyed rabbit jacket. The limo let her off in front of the hospital. She rushed inside out of the cold and walked to the elevators. She was excited to see Tristan and find out about his visit with Adonis, which he briefly described to her on the phone.

She was just about to enter his room when she caught a glimpse of the Chinese doctor heading toward her. She stepped into the doorway of his room, but Tristan was gone. A scare so horrible came over her between the doctor rushing toward her and Tristan being absent that she felt like she would pass out. She held onto the wall as Dr. Cheng approached. Paralyzed by fear she managed to ask the doctor where Tristan was. But the doctor was smiling. Surely if anything happened to Tristan she wouldn't be smiling. "I want you to see something," Dr. Cheng said in a whisper, still smiling. "Follow me," she demanded.

"Don't you ever leave the hospital?" Brooklyn asked her.

"I'm off this weekend," the doctor answered. Brooklyn followed her down the hall and to the elevator. They took it in silence to the fifth floor. "Shhh," the Chinese doctor insisted as she brought her to a large room. They stood in the doorway, and behold, there was Tristan singing songs to the children. He was playing his acoustic guitar and holding a sleeping baby on his lap at the same time. Brooklyn stood by the doorway, secretly spying on him as he sang lullabies to the small sick children, all sitting on tiny chairs in front of him. Brooklyn, so touched by this, fell in love with Tristan all over again. The Chinese doctor gave Brooklyn a small push toward the children, signaling her to join Tristan. He was singing a folk song "Puff the Magic Dragon." She silently walked over to him and began to sing the harmony to the song. When the song finished, the children clapped and yelled "More!" and "Another!"

Tristan looked up at her and whispered, "You look amazing . . . again."

"I missed you," she whispered back and bent down and kissed him quickly.

One of the children called out, "Is that your wife?"

He smiled and said, "Not yet, but I hope she will be soon. What do you think, guys? Should I marry her?"

The children applauded and one of the little girls yelled, "She's beautiful, like an angel."

"Yes, she is," Tristan agreed.

Dr. Cheng came in and announced to the children that it was really late and time to go to sleep. The children protested and asked for just one more song please. Tristan volunteered, "Tell you what, if you all return to your beds we'll sing one more very special song for all of you."

The children scattered, all scampering to their own beds. Tristan motioned for Brooklyn to grab a chair and he handed her the guitar. She looked at the sleeping baby resting up against him and asked, "What have you got there?"

"It's a baby," Tristan answered proudly.

"I can see that." Brooklyn smiled. Brooklyn then asked, "What are we singing?"

"You choose," he answered.

"Nope, this is your concert," she insisted.

"'Just Give Me a Reason,' Pink," he decided. They sang the song together and it was awesome. The doctor clapped when it was over as the children begged for still another. Tristan had to promise that he would return for another "concert" tomorrow.

Dr. Cheng reached over to Tristan and attempted to take the baby out of his arms. He looked at the small child he was holding and said, "How am I going to be able to give this one up?"

On the way back to Tristan's room, the doctor explained that the baby was taken away from its mother, who was on crack. She was just there for observation before being turned over to foster care. Shakira was approximately eighteen months old, Hispanic and beautiful. Dr. Cheng added as they entered Tristan's room, "She can be adopted, you know."

Brooklyn helped Tristan into bed and covered him with a blanket. She hopped up on the bed next to him. "How are you feeling?" she asked.

He answered, "Lucky to be alive and even luckier that you're here with me." Brooklyn turned and gave him a real kiss. "You taste delicious," he commented. "Have I thanked you yet for saving my life again?" he asked.

Brooklyn laughed. "I never saved your life"

He put his arms around her and began to whisper, "Every time you smile at me or touch me, when you kiss me, you save my life." He went on to say, "Before I met you, I existed in a life filled with pain and loneliness with nothing to look forward to but more of the same. When I was asked to do the show, it was as if God threw me a lifeline. Then we met, and I fell in love . . . hard. I thought it an impossibility for us to ever be together, but then a miracle happened. Somehow and I still don't know why you fell in love with me and saved my life. Now you are my life. I wake each day thinking about you, and as I fall asleep each night, you're the last thing I think about. I'm happy all the time. The pain seems an insignificant price to pay for this kind of happiness. I know that people search their entire lives for the love that we have." Tristan paused and kissed her on top of her head, and then continued, "The other night you were so strong for me. I know you were as scared as I was, but when you held me close, I felt your strength and your love and it made me fight harder. I remembered the first time we kissed, it was as if a whole new world opened up for me, a whole new life, and it made me want to go on living. You gave me back my life." The two kissed, both had tears in their eyes. Tristan held her face in his hands and asked, "Can you understand that?"

With pride Brooklyn replied, "I only understand that it's an honor to love you, Tristan, and that I will never stop. Tonight when I saw you singing to those babies, I fell in love with you all over again, and stuff like that keeps on happening. You have taught me more about love and romance, then I ever dreamed possible and I look forward with excitement and wonder to seeing what our future together holds." Tristan took her in his arms and kissed her with all the emotion and passion locked deep within his soul.

His kiss left Brooklyn trembling and breathless. If he never kissed her again, the passion in that kiss would have been enough to last her a lifetime. Tristan continued to hold her in his arms until she finally recovered from that kiss enough to tell him. "Besides, you're the sexiest man that ever lived."

Embarrassed, Tristan simply blushed and said, "Thank you."

It was becoming late and Brooklyn felt that Tristan should rest. He was still so very weak from fighting the infection that nearly took his life. "I think that it's time that I should go back to the hotel," Brooklyn suggested. "

You're not staying here with me tonight?" Tristan asked, truly believing that she would.

"You need to go to sleep, and if I stay here, you won't," she said firmly.

"But—" Tristan began.

"No buts," Brooklyn interrupted. "It's not an option," she added.

"Did you take the limo?' he asked her.

"Yes, it's waiting out front," she told him.

"You're pretty and smart," Tristan joked.

Brooklyn smiled to herself all the way back to the hotel. Just as she approached the main entrance, her phone began to sing the song signaling that Tristan would be on the other end. Smiling even more as she answered it, she listened to Tristan start the conversation by "I miss you already." She told him that she missed him back and that she was safely inside the lobby. She assured him that she'd be there tomorrow and that she loved him. After she hung up the phone, she stared at it with and even bigger smile as though it were Tristan she was looking at. She then took the elevator to her room.

She unlocked the door with the key card and found Dazzel still wide awake. "How's he doing?" she asked.

"He's better," Brooklyn said. "That poor tortured creature," Brooklyn added. "I feel like if I spend the rest of my entire life making him as happy as I'm capable of, it still wouldn't make up for the way he suffers," Brooklyn admitted. The thought of that brought tears to her eyes.

"Hey, did he yell about the credit card?" Dazzel inquired.

"He never even asked about it, and when I tried to return it to him, he told me to keep it."

"Gurrlll, you are so lucky. I'm so jealous," Dazzel shouted on the top of her lungs.

Brooklyn laughed and exclaimed, "I don't blame you, I'm even jealous of me."

* * *

Terence called Brooklyn early. "Hey, Brook, Tristan just called. They are releasing him this morning," Terence informed her and added, "He wants to surprise you and just show up at the studio, but I think we should surprise him instead. You should take the ride with me to pick him up."

"Do I have time to get ready?" she asked.

"You have an hour, I'll come down and get you on the way," Terence offered.

"Perfect," she said.

When the two arrived at Tristan's room, he was gone. He had a small bag packed on top of the bed, but his guitar and himself were missing. "Where do you think he could be?" asked Terence, seeming a little concerned.

"Follow me, I know exactly where he is. He promised those children a concert today, and there is no way in this world he would disappoint them," she said.

"Children? What are you talking about?" asked the bewildered Terence.

They found Tristan conducting a sing-along with twenty little children and one Asian doctor. Terence, shocked, looked at Brooklyn and asked, "What in the world is going on?"

As soon as the children caught a glimpse of Brooklyn, they all ran over to her and competed for a hug. Tristan wasn't surprised to see Brooklyn but happy just the same. "His" baby Shakira, whom he'd grown attached to, was perched upon his lap while the children who remained seated joined in the chorus of one of Tristan's songs that he taught them. Dr. Cheng explained that he was there all morning, since 6:00 a.m., singing to the children. Brooklyn walked over to Tristan who had just finished his song. Brooklyn kneeled down next to Tristan's chair to say hello to Shakira, who was awake and smiling. "This is Shakey. Shakey, meet Brooklyn," Tristan said as he handed the baby to Brooklyn. When Brooklyn held her, the baby no longer smiled; after all, Brooklyn was a stranger. She squirmed in her arms and turned back to Tristan with her arms out stretched, longing to return to him.

"Shakey, huh?" Brooklyn whispered.

"Yes, that's what I call her."

"I bet you didn't know that Tristan loved children so much," Terence commented.

"I didn't," Brooklyn replied.

Terence laughed. "Well, neither did I. As a matter of fact, neither did Tristan I bet," Terence said.

Tristan sadly said good-bye to all the children and reluctantly handed Shakey back to Dr. Cheng. Tristan whispered to the doctor, "Can you keep her around a few extra days until I talk to Brooklyn?"

The doctor winked at Tristan. "I am the only one who can release her," she said.

Tristan hugged the doctor and returned to his wheelchair. Terence took hold of it and proceeded to exit the room. Tristan was afraid to look back, and as they reached the elevator, he thought he heard the baby he'd grown so attached to cry.

Until they were all comfortably seated inside the limo, they were all silent. Finally Terence broke the ice, asking Tristan, "So what's with the baby?" Tristan smiled but said nothing. "I don't like that devilish look in your eyes," Terence commented.

"I liked that baby," Tristan finally said.

"Your lifestyle is not conducive to raising a baby, Tristan, especially as a single parent, especially since you can barely take care of yourself," Terence reminded him. Brooklyn sat in silence, almost afraid to comment. She knew that his heart was breaking leaving that baby behind in the hospital. The last thing she wanted was to break his heart. He had given her everything she ever could even imagine she wanted. Who was she to deny him something he wanted so desperately? Yet she wasn't going to get his hopes up either, so she continued to sit in silence.

Tristan turned to her and took her hand. Gently and calmly he asked, "What do you think of becoming a foster mum?" Before she could answer he continued, "There's a six-month trial period and then we can adopt her," he added. "Or they could choose to take her away from us."

Brooklyn said, playing devil's advocate, "I saw it in your eyes, your heart broke when you had to return that baby to the doctor. Just imagine really being attached to her, you would be devastated if that happened, beyond recovery."

Terence then chimed in, "It is so unfair for you to drag Brooklyn into this, and furthermore don't you have to concentrate on winning a contest?"

"Okay, I get it, you're both right. I just got caught up in the moment. I'm sorry, love, I didn't mean to—"

Brooklyn interrupted him, "Hey, Trist, I love you, and if you really want that little baby, then go for it. I'm with you 100 percent."

"Are you crazy, girl?" Terence yelled.

"Really?" Tristan asked.

"Really," Brooklyn echoed him.

Terence shook his head. "Brooklyn, have you lost it too?" he asked.

"Hey, Terence, Tristan has given me everything I've ever longed for. He's made every dream come true for me and has satisfied all my wildest fantasies. His heart is already broken. Besides that baby was adorable. I loved watching him love that little angel," Brooklyn admitted as she touched Tristan's face.

On the top of his lungs Terence yelled, "*He can't even take care of himself!*"

"I know," Brooklyn said, "that's why he has me." She turned to Tristan, who had tears running down his cheeks, and said, "I guess I'll have to learn to share you with another woman."

He grabbed her and hugged her, using all the strength he still possessed and said, "Thank you!"

Tristan insisted they stop at the studio. The Devils rejoiced at the sight of Tristan's return. His coaching and creativity was sorely missed. It became a very productive session. Tristan was pleased with the Devils' progress, the Devils were pleased with Tristan's arrangement of the combined songs, and Brooklyn was pleased with Tristan, who stayed off his feet and took his medication on time. As the day began to wind down, Tristan became exhausted. He suggested to Brooklyn that they return to the hotel and enjoy a lovely romantic dinner via room service, relax, and talk a little. "What do you think?" he asked.

"Sounds amazing. Just being near you is amazing," Brooklyn said. They both knew sex was out. Tristan was too weak still and still in a lot of pain, although he would never admit it. Each other's company was more than enough for the two anyway.

They took pleasure in having dinner by candlelight. They relished the warm shower they took together and adored lying in each other's arms afterward, just making small talk. Tristan's arms were wrapped around her tiny frame as she rubbed her hand up and down his chest. He kissed her ear and whispered, "Please let me make love to you." He practically begged.

"You're out of you mind," she whispered back. Tristan took her hand and kissed it. He moved his lips up her arm until his lips reached her neck. "You're making this so hard," Brooklyn whispered.

"Shhh, we'll take it real, real easy. Please, baby, don't say no," he pleaded.

She couldn't resist Tristan, like a junky couldn't resist a needle filled with heroine. As he kissed her lips so sensuously, every bit of willpower she might have had disintegrated. She whispered to Tristan, "I don't want to hurt you, please, baby . . . I . . ."

"Shh, you know you can't resist me," Tristan whispered, teasing her.

She looked at Tristan. He was so sexy and she was so addicted to him She could no longer protest. He took her slow and gently. She was careful not to hurt him, yet it was emotionally intense. They ended their lovemaking nose to nose. He kissed the tip of her nose and then her lips and thanked her for not denying him. She savored this time with him, especially after nearly losing him.

Brooklyn sat up feeling guilty. "Hey, hey what's the matter?"

She laughed and hit Tristan with a pillow. "I could have hurt you," she said.

"The only way you could have hurt me was for you to refuse me," he said. Then he kissed her over and over and over again. "So let's talk," Tristan suggested.

"Okay, let's talk," she agreed.

"Now that Terence isn't here to yell at us, what do you really feel about little Shakey?" Tristan asked. "You realize this could be a lifelong sentence. I don't want you to do it because you love me," Tristan announced.

"But I do love you," Brooklyn insisted.

He smiled and kissed her hand. "Do you love me enough to move your belongings to the Gatsby mansion? I know you said you would live with me, and we've been kind of busy, but I guess I just want to make sure you really meant it," Tristan confessed.

"Trist, we're together every day and night. In essence we've been living together," she said to him.

"It's not the same," he said gently. "I want to know that, when the madness is over, you'll come home to me. When I travel to London, I want to know you'll be at my side. I want you to take your key and unlock our door when you come home from shopping or being with friends. I want you to be home waiting for me when I come home from the studio. I just want that extra. Oh god, I'm gonna say it—I want that commitment. How can you commit to having a child when you can't even fully commit to me?" Tristan raged on. Brooklyn stared at him, wide-eyed and attentive. Then Tristan suddenly stopped his rant and touched her face. He threw his hands up in the air and said, "Who am I kidding. I'm an ass. We both know how much I love you. I'll take any part of you that you wish to give me, anyway you want me to have you."

Brooklyn, still cherishing the fact that he was still going on and on, finally burst out laughing. She touched Tristan's hair and proclaimed, "You're forgetting one thing and that is that I love you so much too. Of course I'll commit to you. I just assumed we were both pretty committed." Brooklyn laughed.

Tristan held her face in his two hands, "Baby, why did you allow me to act like such a jerk just now?" Tristan asked. "I am such a douche," Tristan proclaimed. Brooklyn sat there laughing at him.

"That was your punishment for inviting me to move in and then never doing anything about it," Brooklyn said, pretending to be angry.

"Brooklyn, I was scared to death. Do you know the courage it just took for me to rant like that? Baby, I don't do well with rejection, especially yours," he confessed.

"Who said anything about rejection?" she asked, laughing. "Now kiss me, jerk," she demanded. He bent over and kissed her.

* * *

Tristan's creative abilities helped the Devils to thrive during week ten. Still Devin Liam's popularity kept the groups neck n' neck when tallying America's votes. Devin had been appearing as a guest on various talk shows throughout the contest. He also appeared as a guest performer during certain concerts. These appearances elevated his popularity, and it was time Tristan fought back. When Tristan was offered an interview along with Brooklyn on a national talk show, he said yes. He knew the talk show host would insist that he did a number, but he would have Brooklyn do one instead. They only problem with that was that Brooklyn had never gone solo.

"Brooklyn," Tristan called to her, "listen to me, we've gotten an extra chance to win America's hearts. We've been asked to appear together on the *Johnny Michaels Show*." She looked at him waiting for him to say something more. "So what do you think? Are you up for it?" he asked.

"Just me and you?" she asked.

"I think they are hoping for 'the romantic angle,'" he commented.

"Will we need to do a song for the show?" she inquired.

"You will, love," he informed her.

"Alone?" she asked.

"Alone," he answered.

"I don't do alone, I never have," she reminded him.

"Well then, we have quite a dilemma here now, don't we?" teased Tristan, using his strongest cockney accent.

"Why haven't we ever been asked to appear on one of these type shows before now?" she wondered.

"We have, I just never accepted the invitations. I felt we needed to focus more on us than someone else's show. Somehow, I don't think it's ethical that Devin keeps showing up everywhere. His band isn't really winning the competition. He is, through his popularity. Now I just think that maybe we need to fight back a little. The Devils have already proved themselves in my book," Tristan explained. "Now let's prepare to help Adonis end this week's show. Break is nearly over."

Adonis came out on stage and made some announcements pertaining to the voting and the best show. He then announced Devin's up and coming concert this weekend. Proudly he told the audience to tune in to the *Johnny Michaels Show* live tonight. Adonis held the mic under Tristan's lips and asked, "So the couple of the century and all their romance appear live tonight. What will you be performing on the show?"

Tristan answered, "The couple of the century along with their romance are currently fighting about that, as we speak. Stay tuned."

The audience roared with laughter at Tristan's attempt at sarcastic comedy.

"Okay, America, voting for week ten starts *now*. Next week will be the very last time the contestants will be competing on this stage, and the last week America will have the opportunity to vote for the winner. The first challenge will entail both groups doing a twenty-minute medley of their favorite songs, together, as one, with one another. Now the second challenge—watch out, America, it's going to be a huge surprise. It will be announced next week right on this stage, and I promise you it will be a life changing experience. It will be epic and earth-shattering. Until next week!" Adonis yelled. They all waved good-bye and shook hands with the audience, and the set went dark.

"The show is tonight!" Brooklyn asked alarmed. "Tris, are you out of your mind? Tonight . . . tonight . . . what were you thinking?" Brooklyn yelled across the set.

"Look, I'll make a deal with you?" Tristan offered.

"Am I selling my soul to the devil?" she asked.

"No," Tristan said, "just to me."

Brooklyn sighed. "You already have my soul," she stated.

"Baby, this is going to be really hard for me to do, near impossible, but I will back you up on guitar." Brooklyn thought for a moment offering to play guitar in front of a live audience might be the first step in helping Tristan conquer his stage fright nightmare. It wasn't exactly a concert hall, but it was at least live television and an audience.

"How about you back me up on guitar and you sing backup harmony?" she suggested. She could see Tristan begin to squirm already and she could swear he was involuntarily beginning to hyperventilate at even the thought.

"I'll say yes for now. However, promise not to hate me if I'm unable to do it at the last moment," he said hesitantly.

"Deal," she agreed, fully knowing that Tristan wouldn't have the balls to disappoint her. "I'll make it easy on you," she promised. "'Total Eclipse of the Heart' by Bonnie Tyler," Brooklyn decided.

Tristan rolled his eyes. "Wow," he said. "That's not an easy song, love," he said, visibly trembling.

"Look, we'll do it acoustically, okay?" she insisted.

"Yes, ma'am," he answered.

Brooklyn ran into wardrobe to change. When she returned to the set, she found Tristan sitting on the darkened stage with his hands covering his face. Just the thought of performing for an audience was causing his heart to race and his anxiety level to heighten, making him feel utterly uncomfortable. He couldn't say no to Brooklyn, especially since it was he himself who accepted the offer to be on the show. She knew he was freaking out. Brooklyn calmly sat down next to him on the stage, coaxing his hands away from his face. She took her hands and half his face in her palms. Then she pressed her lips against his lips. Brooklyn easily overpowered him partially because he was still weak from the infection in his leg and partially because he let her. She gently forced him to lie down upon the stage and cautiously climbed on top of him, never removing her lips from his lips. Adonis walked by them and commented, "The *Johnny Michaels Show* is rated PG, not X," and continued to pass them without stopping.

A cameraman yelled to Adonis, "Is that next week's challenge?" pointing to the couple.

Dazzel walked over to the two, whose lips were still locked together and said, "I guess you agree on a song."

Finally Garrett stood directly over them, shook his head, and suggested loudly, "Get a room!" They were unaware, however, that the cameraman filmed the entire make-out session to be aired during next week's show.

Brooklyn finally pried her lips off his and stared into his amazing blue eyes and asked, "What are you thinking?"

"I'm thinking of how much I love you and how to prevent the stroke I'm going to have." She stood up, took Tristan by the hands and pulled him up as well.

Tristan suggested, "Let's go back to the hotel, rehearse, make love, and get dressed."

"So you're okay with this?" she asked.

"I don't know, love." He laughed. "We will find out tonight on live TV."

Instead of going directly to the hotel, Brooklyn had the limo driver make a quick detour to the hospital. She thought that seeing his baby Shakira would calm his frightened spirits, and it would give them a chance to rehearse the number in front of a live audience, the children. "You always know the right things to do," he told her as they entered the children's playroom inside the hospital. They sang "Total Eclipse" and then for fun did "Picture" by Kid Rock. Tristan secretly loved to sing country and western. He hugged Shakey, who had formed such a strange attachment to him. They were handed a stack of paperwork to review and be filled out by Dr. Cheng in order to start the foster parent process and then returned to the hotel.

* * *

The two were asked to dress upscale casual for the *Johnny Michaels Show* but decided to go over the top. They dressed in matching black, silver, and pink costumes with sparkling tailed jackets trimmed with pink sequins, silver shirts, and black pants. The silver and pink high-top sneakers also matched as well as their matching hot pink lipstick and silver eyeliner. Johnny Michaels announced them as "the lovers of the century," Punk Rock Rebel Tristan Bondage and the beautiful lead singer Brooklyn from Precious Little Devils, both from the new mega hit reality show *So You Wanna Be a Rock Star*.

They walked out hand in hand, with Tristan in the lead, as the audience applauded and the young fans screamed wildly. Tristan properly allowed Brooklyn to sit down first, then joined her. "My goodness," the host Johnny Michaels declared, "you two look like something out of Cirque du So-Gay. Who picked those outrageously magnificent getups?" the host asked Brooklyn.

"That would be Tristan. He selects all our costumes," she reported.

"Does he dress you too?"

He asked, trying to be funny. Brooklyn replied, "Every chance he gets," and winked at Johnny.

Johnny continued the interview. "So whether or not you win the competition, you two certainly have become America's newest sweethearts. Now, Tristan, there's a little bit of an age difference."

"Quite a bit," Tristan corrected him and smiled.

"How is that working out for you Brooklyn?" the host inquired.

"Tristan is the sexiest man alive," she said as the fans agreed and applauded. "Right, girls?" Brooklyn turned to the audience and asked. The audience roared wildly.

"I understand this wasn't always a paradise for the two of you," Johnny remarked.

Tristan answered, "We had a bit of a rough go at it at first. Totally may fault. I was madly in love with her but figured I didn't have a chance in hell, so I retaliated by being harsh with her and the Devils. I guess I thought, if I couldn't get her to love me, she might as well hate me. It wasn't logical, but then often the mind isn't always logical, is it? She finally had enough of my bad behavior and quit the show. I panicked, begged for forgiveness, and changed my evil ways." He laughed.

The host asked Brooklyn, "What made you fall in love with him?"

"I was in love with him the entire time," she answered.

"Well then, how did the two of you work it out?" asked Johnny.

"He asked for another chance, I gave it to him, and he turned that second chance into something out of a fantasy," she explained. Brooklyn turned to Tristan and touched his face affectionately, while he took her hand and kissed it. The audience cheered once again.

"Do you live together?" asked Johnny.

Tristan answered, "Were still trying to figure that out. Last night Brooklyn agreed to transport her belongings to my house, but we're together 24/7 anyway." The audience clapped in support of Tristan's statements.

"Do you ever fight?" Tristan replied.

"Not very often, and when we do it's simply devastating to me."

"Brooklyn, does he win any of those arguments?" Johnny wondered.

She answered, "We both win, especially when we make up." Brooklyn winked. That answer brought the audience to their feet as they broke for a commercial. Johnny told them they were doing a fantastic job.

As the commercial ended, Johnny Michaels reintroduced the two and went on to say to Brooklyn, "I've been noticing that you can't seem to keep your hands off one another. Are you sitting too far apart? Would you like to sit on his lap?"

Brooklyn answered, "Yes please," and left her chair to sit on Tristan's lap. Again the audience rose to their feet in admiration.

"All right." The host stood up now in an attempt to tame the crowd. "Here's the question of the night," Johnny threatened. "Brooklyn, how is Tristan in bed?"

Without even flinching, Brooklyn very matter-of-factly answered, "Epic," and continued to say, "I am addicted to sex with Tristan. I just can't ever seem to get enough of him." Tristan buried his beet-red face in her breast.

"So," Johnny asked, "you'd say he rocks your world."

Brooklyn calmly answered, "He rocks a lot more than my world." With that the audience became chaotic.

Johnny yelled above the noise, "We have an audience uprising, let's break."

During the break Johnny ran backstage and apologized to his other scheduled guests and explained that there wouldn't be enough time to have them on the show tonight and that he would reschedule them as soon as possible. He then ran back and asked Tristan if he and Brooklyn would be up for some questions from the audience. Still beet red, Tristan looked at Brooklyn, who nodded yes. "Questions from the audience would be fine," Tristan agreed. Tristan then turned to Brooklyn and told her that he loved her. He lifted her chin with one finger and kissed her, just as they returned from commercial break. Johnny chimed in as the audience continued to go wild.

"Busted, everyone. This was an unrehearsed, unexpected kiss. Is this really happening?" The host shook his head and laughed. "Okay, ladies and gentlemen," Johnny yelled, "I'm going to pass the mic around for our audience. It's question and answer time. Feel free to ask either Brooklyn or Tristan anything you want. Now who's first?" asked Johnny.

A small woman stood first. Johnny asked for her name and then instructed her to ask her question. "This question is for Tristan. It's all well and good to live together, but do you have any future plans to marry Brooklyn?"

"Yes I do," Tristan exclaimed. "I would marry her this very minute, live on this show."

The girl then addressed Brooklyn, "And you?" she asked.

"I would do anything Tristan asked. I love him and I plan to be with him forever."

The audience applauded and the mic was passed to a young teenage girl. "What's Tristan like alone, and I don't mean in bed?" she asked Brooklyn.

"I might be ruining his rebellious reputation, but he's very gentle and sweet, almost kind of shy, and extremely romantic," Brooklyn admitted, and the mic was once again passed.

This time a man in his fifties stood and asked Brooklyn. "I bet he buys you beautiful gifts, what's your favorite?"

Brooklyn blushed. "He buys me the most beautiful gifts imaginable, but the best gift of all, my favorite, he gives me every single day and that's the gift of love," she confessed. The audience strongly approved.

Next a group of girls all stood. Their spokesperson addressed Tristan, "How disappointed will you be if you don't win the competition?"

"Well, you can't always win, but it's all about the journey. In my heart I've already won, and the prize is more than I ever thought possible," Tristan said as he hugged Brooklyn.

"We're going to break for commercial, and when we return we will hear a song from the beautiful little Devil and I think Tristan Bondage," Johnny announced. "Don't' go away."

During the break, Brooklyn was led to the stage. Tristan accompanied her, but he was in a cold sweat and paler then she'd ever seen him. "Hey," she said, "are you all right?"

"Please, love, don't be angry, but I'm not sure I can do this," Tristan said.

Brooklyn looked at him. She could see that he had worked himself into a frenzy and she was frightened something might happen to him on live television. "Hey," she said. "I can do it alone, I'm not nervous at all."

"I don't want to do that to you," he expressed.

Brooklyn took his hand. He was trembling so much so, Brooklyn didn't even think he would be able to play the guitar. As a matter of fact he looked as though he was going to pass out. Brooklyn just didn't have the heart to put him through this. "It's fine," she told him. "I can do this. Why don't you just announce me?"

"Are you sure?" he asked her, still pale and frightened.

"I'm sure," she said.

"God, you must really love me," Tristan whispered.

"Yes, I do," she said as she smiled.

As the commercial ended, Tristan stood in front of the stage and announced, "I give you the love of my life, who I'm so very proud of." The audience applauded. Tristan eyed the guitar resting against the chair he was supposed to sit in while he accompanied her. At the very last second he moved slowly to the chair, picked up the guitar, took a breath, and somehow began to play "Total Eclipse of the Heart." After all, he was an entertainer and possessed a very special and unique artistry of his own. Smiling outside and in Brooklyn began the song. By the time she arrived at the second chorus, Tristan was able to sing the harmony with her. Once again the magic of their voices together won the hearts of all. The applause and the ovation was amazing. The audience begged for an encore. Johnny came onto the stage, applauding himself. "Any last words before we close with yet another number form the lovers of the century?"

Tristan took the mic and turned to Brooklyn, "Love, I can't thank you enough for being the light through my darkness and the person who could believe in me, when I couldn't believe in myself." Brooklyn took his hand. She was near tears, touched by his last statement. He looked at her strongly and mouthed the work "Pink" to her. They ended the show performing "Just Give Me a Reason" by Pink. The audience applauded so long that the show ran a minute over its limit.

The two rode back in the limo hand in hand. They began receiving texts from everywhere, offering interviews on shows, spots on commercials, recording contracts, and concert tours. They also received congratulations from many, including people they never saw in their entire lives. Brooklyn just kept kissing Tristan over and over again and telling him how proud she was to have performed with him. He smiled at her, obviously embarrassed by her overabundance of praise, and pulled her onto his lap right in the limo and said, "Jesus, just come her and kiss me." She willingly obeyed.

When they collapsed on top of the king-sized bed in Tristan's hotel suite, Brooklyn told Tristan how much fun she had. He told her she was amazing and stole the show. "Liar," she exclaimed. "You were the show. I'm so jealous of all those screaming beautiful girls, still so in love with punk rock idol Tristan Bondage. They were all so in love with you," she teased.

"You never need to be jealous. There will never be anyone else in my life as long as I have you, and I pray that its forever," Tristan said as he mischievously began to tickle her. She laughed like a child and begged him to stop as she tried to catch her breath from the laughter.

When Tristan finally stopped tickling her and changed to kissing her instead, she asked him, in between kisses, which text was he planning to answer first and which offer was he going to accept. "None," he answered.

"Why?" she asked, sitting up while he still attempted to kiss her. He saw the look of puzzlement upon Brooklyn's face and explained, "If you make yourself too available, you become less special, less in demand. Besides we have a contest to concentrate on winning, and the way Devin is putting himself out there, we have a lot of work still to do. It's going to take all our efforts to combat his popularity."

"Then why did you agree to the *Johnny Michaels Show* so all of a sudden?" she inquired.

"I did because with Devin's popularity being so high right now, I wanted us to do something different. He was never asked to appear as a guest on that show. They only chose us because we portrayed a romantic twist. Michaels has a huge national audience and I knew, if we did that guest spot, it would wind up exactly the way it did—fabulous." Tristan added, "If we win the contest, there will be plenty of shows, but right now I think we have something way more important to concentrate on. Come here." Brooklyn moved closer. Tristan whispered, "Let's feed that addiction of yours that all of America now knows about," he said, teasing her.

The moment he touched her nothing else mattered. Her body became warm and receptive to whatever he was offering. She thought him so incredibly handsome and sexy, especially tonight. He kissed her neck, her breasts, and then her thighs as he prepared her body for what was to come next.

Chapter 9

Demons and Love in London

Week eleven seemed more terrifying than any week prior. There would only be one more chance to win the hearts of America and their votes. There would be only one more chance to wow the judges, and there was no way to prepare for the surprise challenge that was yet to be announced.

Although spirits were high, nerves were raw. The two finalists rehearsed all week together in unison and their performance promised to make television history. Their medley of favorites ran precisely seventeen point four minutes. The bands would implement the medleys by taking turns executing one of their selections, trading songs back and forth until the finale, where they would perform one unified song together in harmony.

When Adonis stepped onto the stage to unveil the mysterious challenge, Brooklyn gripped Tristan's hand in anticipation of their plight. He held her hand to his lips and kissed it and then put his arm around her as though he was attempting to protect her from danger. Dazzel gazed at the two and stated, "You know this isn't the *Johnny Michaels Show.*" The Devils laughed as Tristan blushed.

He defended his actions and said, "Brooklyn is a bit nervous."

"Well then, in that case," Dazzel said.

The audience began to applaud as Adonis welcomed America to the show. "It is finally time to present our final challenge. Tonight we will find out just what kind of chemistry our mentors have developed with their groups. We will ask each group and coach to decide on a song—a song that they will perform together, live. This song shall be well thought as it will constitute the very last song America and the judges will hear from our competitors." Adonis paused for the audience to cheer.

"During the time the bands and mentors will have for preparation, we invite you to view a recap of the high points of both groups from week one until now. But first when we come back from break, Blood Red Orange and Precious Little Devils will impress you with the first portion of the challenge." Adonis added, "Stay tuned, we'll be right back."

As the set dimmed for commercial break, Adonis instructed the groups to get into their assigned positions for the medley. "As soon as we're back, you sing, no announcements, just sing!" Adonis commanded. Brooklyn quickly took a detour over to Tristan to make sure he wasn't freaking out over the challenge. It was a good thing Tristan sang on the *Johnny Michael's Show* or he really would have an issue. Still he was nervous, and Brooklyn saw it in his eyes and his smile. Brooklyn touched his face. He mouthed the words "I love you" and pointed to the stage where she was supposed to have been and urged her to return.

When the commercial ended, the bands began their first challenge of the night. It became a historic performance that was more amazing than anyone expected. Applause was heavy, the judges super impressed, while the mentors were very proud.

It was now time for both bands and their mentors to become sequestered inside their own private sound proof studios, where they would pick a song, learn it, rehearse it, and perform it like they have never performed in their lives. Adonis walked up to the two bands on stage applauding furiously. "Both Blood Red and Precious Devils are neck and neck in this competition America. I just cannot believe weeks and weeks of trials and tribulations and it's all going to come down to this one final performance—the entire competition! So coaches don't let your band down," Adonis said as both Devin and Tristan appeared worried and very apprehensive. Tristan shook his head and Devin covered his mouth with his hand, both afraid to own up the fact that their bands might win or lose because of them. "Coaches are you ready, as Ru Paul would say, to sing for your lives? You have exactly one hour . . . starting now!"

Blood Red and Devin Liam ran backstage, while Tristan grabbed Brooklyn and took her to the side to compliment her on her performance. "I was very proud of you just now, it was a superior display, and I enjoyed it very much. Now," Tristan continued, "before I freak, and cry to you that I can't do this, do you have a particular song in mind?" he asked.

"Yes, I do," she answered.

"Do I know it?" Tristan wondered with anticipation.

The Devils then joined the two, reminding them that time was of the essence and the clock was ticking. Garret in his devilish wisdom, teased Tristan by asking him if he remembered how to sing with a band. Damian added, "He's been too busy doing other things," implying his sexual involvement with Brooklyn.

Dazzel simply said to the two of them sarcastically, "Just pretend that you're both shining stars!"

"Hey, Devils, let's have a huddle," Tristan insisted. The Devils gathered round to listen to the wisdom of their fearless rebel leader. "Until the *Johnny Michaels Show*, I hadn't sang or played for a public audience in over fifteen years. Karaoke that night at Stars was the closest I'd come. I want you to know that I'm scared. I don't want to be the cause of us losing," Tristan admitted as he bowed his head.

Brooklyn lifted his chin and said, "Then be the cause of us winning." The Devils applauded Brooklyn.

Tristan smiled and said, "Let's do it!"

"Oh, and speaking of karaoke . . ." Brooklyn smiled and off into the studio they went.

When the hour had ended, Adonis summoned both bands and their mentors to the stage. Adonis took a quarter from inside his pocket and asked the lead singer of Blood Red to choose heads or tails. She yelled out "Heads." Adonis threw the quarter up in the air, and when it landed, heads it was. "Okay, Blood Red, do you wish to go first or second?" Adonis asked. The singer looked at her band who voted to go first. Strange choice, Tristan thought to himself. He was elated by their decision since he figured being last would be remembered longer. The Devils were dismissed from the stage while Adonis announced, "Doing their final number in the competition, let's hear it for Blood Red Orange and the newest member of their group, Devin Liam!" The audience welcomed them through their wild applause and excited cheering.

Blood Red chose an older 1980s song by Dead or Alive entitled "You Spin Me Round." It was an upbeat number, full of life and excitement. Devin and Joy (the lead singer) choreographed it and sang it flawlessly together. They performed it as though they had practiced it for months. It was tight and void of mistakes. The judges' remarks were also flawless and the audience gave them a standing ovation. They couldn't have hoped for a better outcome. The Devils watched them in awe, and when it was their turn to come out to the stage, they were nervous. Even Adonis wondered how the Devils would top what he had just witnessed from Blood Red.

Adonis announced a sponsor intermission. During the break he congratulated Devin and told the Devils to become ready. Tristan had the group gather round one last time in hopes of boosting their confidence, which was difficult since his own faith was dwindling. Brooklyn whispered to him, "Tris, this is a powerful song with so much meaning . . . just sing it to me." He knew exactly what she meant.

"And I will sing it to you." The words were written for Tristan to sing to Brooklyn. Tristan took a breath and instructed Brooklyn to watch him carefully and follow his lead.

"You're scaring me," she whispered.

"I'm trying to," he whispered and winked.

Adonis stood in the center of the stage, with the Devils and Tristan ready behind him. "I give you for the very last time performing on this stage for the competition, Tristan Bondage and his Precious Little Devils!" Adonis walked off the stage, the lights dimmed except for an eerie spotlight on Tristan and Brooklyn. They softly began to sing a capella, "Demons" by Imagine Dragons. And the band started to play behind them after the first eight bars, which translated into after the first two lines of the song. Their voices once again reigned from the heavens and although they began softly, this song was made to build and build . . . and that it did.

Tristan soloed for the lines "I wanna hide the truth, I wanna shelter you, but with the beast inside . . ." and Brooklyn took the line "There's no where we can hide." They both sang the chorus using their unique harmony and angelic tones that came naturally to the two, especially when they sang together. Then the drama began. The two portrayed the rest of the song as though they were on Broadway in *Phantom of the Opera.*

"Don't wanna let you down."

"But I am hell bound."

"Though this is all for you."

"Don't wanna hide the truth."

As they sang that portion of the song Tristan fell to his knees and took Brooklyn's hands in his. This song was filled with emotion for both of them. It took them back in time when they nearly lost each other to Tristan's demons. Tristan sang it as though it was draining his soul, and Brooklyn sang it as if she were saving his soul.

For the second chorus he viciously grabbed Brooklyn by her hair.

"When you feel my heat."

"Look into my eyes."

And then he released his grip and they sang, "It's where my demons hide, it's where my demons hide."

They faced each other, palm to palm.

By the time the third and last verse began the audience sat on the edge of their chairs all tightly gripping the arms of their chairs in suspense. There were tears streaming down the faces of the audience and the judges as if they knew their story in the beginning.

Brooklyn went on to sing, "They say it's what you make."

"I say it's up to fate."

"It's woven in my soul."

And finally Tristan sang, "I need to let you go." With that he fell to his knees once again. Tears streamed down his cheeks as he actually cried, remembering and feeling the sadness that night on his patio when he almost let her go.

Brooklyn followed his lead and kneeled down next to him. She lifted his face and his tears flowed as she sang, "Your eyes they shine so bright."

"I wanna save that light."

Tristan stood, helping Brooklyn to her feet and sang through his tears, "I can't escape this now."

"Unless you show me how."

The band stopped playing and there was silence everywhere for a moment. Then suddenly as though an exorcism had been done, the band began to play the last chorus, and Tristan and Brooklyn sang the remainder of the song, hugging each other until the last two lines, at which point they raised their arms to the heavens as though they repented and were praying for forgiveness.

When they song ended Tristan took Brooklyn in his arms and he kissed her using all his emotion and passion that he managed to have left. Tristan was literally still wiping his tears off his cheeks. The band left their instruments and came up front to Brooklyn and Tristan and they all held hands and bowed. Then Brooklyn and Tristan, as if they were the leads in the Broadway play, held hands and bowed again. Instead of enjoying the ovation they were receiving, the two chose to hug again. Out of the corner of her eye she caught the image of Devin Liam behind stage shaking his head in disgust as if he already admitted defeat.

Adonis reached the stage holding a tissue box and removed a single tissue from the box, dried his own eyes, and then gave the remainder of the box of tissues to the judges. He then actually put his arms around Tristan and hugged him and then turned to the audience. "What a way to end this competition!" Adonis addressed the judges and America. The audience was crazed and still standing. Adonis announced a commercial break, still in tears.

When the commercial was over, Adonis asked the judges to weigh in. The first judge simply said, "What do you expect from two star-crossed lovers. This was probably the grandest display of entertainment that I have ever witnessed."

The MTV VJ stood up, holding a tissue. Filled with tears the judge said, "This says it all," and held up the tissue.

Judge number three sat there stunned. "If it were up to me alone, you guys just clinched the win," claimed the 1980s icon.

"America, we've heard from the judges and it's all up to you now. We shall return next week with the winner of *So You Wanna Be a Rock Star*. Good luck!" Adonis wished to say more about next week; however, the show was running late, so the set went black.

"I have to sit down for a minute," Tristan requested. "Come with me," Tristan said as he took Brooklyn's hand and ran with her into Adonis's private office. He shut the door, sat down, and pulled her onto his lap.

"Hey, are you okay?" Brooklyn asked him, concerned.

"Yes, I'm fine, I just wanted to be alone with you for a moment, to tell you that I love you and to let you know how proud I am of you," Tristan said, smiling. "I just wanted to tell you that . . . oh, and this", Tristan whispered and kissed her.

"Well, I think that you need to be proud of yourself, you have probably singlehandedly won this thing for us with that dramatic work of art you just did," she said in between kisses.

"I just keep on lovin' you more and more and more," Brooklyn exclaimed.

"I've never witnessed anyone perform like that, and if you don't start doing concerts again, I will be so mad at you," she finished.

"Firstly I didn't do it alone, we are a team. Anything that happened on that stage was inspired by my love for you, not to mention you were awesome. Baby, we are a team, both professionally, musically, and personally . . ." Tristan didn't get to finish that thought as Brooklyn interrupted him with a romantic kiss.

"I knew I'd find the two of you slobbering over each other," Dazzel yelled as she barged into the office in the middle of one of their kisses. "Everyone's looking for you two. The set is buzzing with that performance. I have to say, I never knew you had it in you, Tristan," Dazzel admitted. Dazzel stuck her head out of the door and yelled to the others, "I found them, they're in here having sex!"

Garrett yelled back as he made his way to the office, followed by the rest, "Then why are you watching them?"

"Ugh," Damian commented and then congratulated Tristan on his magnificent display.

Colin came in and shook his hand. "I have never seen anything like that," he told Tristan. "Can I have your autograph?" Colin added.

Adonis pushed through the Devils into his office and told Tristan that he was amazing. "I could build an entire show around you and Brooklyn, and I think I just might," Adonis exclaimed. "I never knew you could perform like that," he added.

"Neither did I," Tristan said, teasing Adonis.

"Well, you guys have a well-deserved week off. Take advantage of it. Tristan, can I have a word . . . privately for a second?" Adonis requested. The Devils sauntered out of the room, taking Brooklyn with them, but not before Tristan kissed her one last time.

* * *

With an entire week of leisure ahead of them, the Devils decided to cancel their gig at Stars this week and take advantage of a whole week of vacation, uninterrupted. However, with week twelve approaching and the performance of a lifetime last night on the show, offers started to pour in for interviews, talk show appearances, and invitations to open for concert tours. Tristan was exhausted. He hadn't yet fully recovered from near-death experience and was still heavily medicated with antibiotics and pain medication. Brooklyn decided to allow the Devils some interviews and TV exposure (as long as Tristan agreed to it) while she looked upon this short hiatus as a chance for Tristan to rest and get stronger. Tristan, however, looked upon this opportunity quite differently. He viewed it as a marvelous chance to return to London with Brooklyn and introduce her to his friends and family.

Since the show was aired in England, he knew that publically they would be well received, and besides he couldn't wait to show off his beloved.

"Brooklyn, do you have a passport?" Tristan asked.

"Somewhere," she claimed. "Why?" she asked.

"Well, I was contemplating several different adventures we can indulge in."

"How about you rest this week and try and get healthy? We can stay in bed and make love all night, and I could take care of you for a change. Then maybe I could start transporting some of my belongings to the Gatsby mansion if you'd like," she suggested.

"Making love all night and you officially moving in sounds lovely, like a dream come true. However, the resting part sounds annoying." Tristan laughed and kissed her. "Listen to me for a moment," he asked of her.

"I'm listening," she said as she finished packing up her hotel room and bid a silent good-bye to her home away from home for the past eleven weeks.

"Come here," Tristan said and coaxed her onto the bed he was sitting on. "How does this sound to you—somewhere warm and beautiful, with shining blue waters, white sandy beaches, where we could lie on a blanket in the sun, sip margaritas, and listen to the sound of the waves crashing upon the shore. Or we can go somewhere cold and damp, like London for instance?" he conveyed to Brooklyn.

Feeling that Tristan only tempted her by the first option, to test how well she really knew him, knowing how he longed to return to London for a visit with his family, she said, "I've always wanted to go to London." He kissed her passionately and thanked her. "Thank you for what?" she said. "You know I'd go to the ends of the earth as long as you were there," she teased. Brooklyn's theory about Tristan's testing her might have been somewhat correct, but there was certainly no need to determine how well he knew her as he had already purchased the tickets to London. He took the tickets out of his coat and held them up. Brooklyn jumped on top of him and told him that she just loved him. She knew this trip would be anything but restful, but she also knew it meant so much to Tristan to go. She decided that she would try and take care of him as best as she could.

They spent the night at the cottage since Tristan had to pack only a couple of items, all of which he was able to gather from his hotel suite. He had all his personal items and a wardrobe of costumes already at his flat in Camden. Although they could have taken a limo to Kennedy, Dazzel and Damian insisted upon driving them to the airport, simply to bid them an emotional good-bye. American Airlines flight 100 left promptly at 5:45 p.m. and touched down at Heathrow 6:45 a.m. London Time. Both had been quite comfortable in their first-class seats and relaxed about the flight in general. They took a taxi directly to Tristan's flat, where they made love, showered, and became ready for their London journey.

Tristan's flat was surprisingly small. It was filled with Victorian decor and reminded Brooklyn of a museum. The kitchen was tiny, filled with only the necessities that would allow one to prepare a meal. The living room was decent-sized and contained historic Victorian furniture. Off the living room was a second bedroom, which Tristan had decorated in early guitars and punk rock posters all tastefully hung on the walls. It had a desk, a computer, and television. His master bedroom contained a Victorian king-sized bed, with a master bathroom. He had a walk-in closet, two night tables, and not much of anything else. Tristan had not seen his flat in nearly a year but felt comfortable and truly at home the moment he entered it.

"What would you like to do first?" Tristan asked.

Brooklyn shrugged her shoulders. "This is your town, you lead, I'll follow," she answered. Brooklyn was excited to be in London and Tristan was even more excited to show her London.

"Come on," he said and they left the flat, ran outside, and caught a red double-decker bus. They had purchased a metro card at the airport and as they entered the bus Brooklyn watched as the other people used the card to gain entrance onto the vehicle. Brooklyn ran to the top deck of the bus and Tristan followed. He put his arm around her and his head on her shoulder as a proper British female voice announced each stop before the bus arrived at it. After a few stops Tristan left his seat and took Brooklyn's hand to exit the bus. He had decided to take her shopping and Camden was a good place to do so. Brooklyn noticed that, each time they crossed a street, there were arrows in the crosswalk directing people which way to look for oncoming cars. "If you get hit by a car here, it's your fault," he teased and remarked, "The London drivers are crazy!"

They visited several upscale stores and Tristan showered her with gifts from the streets of London while he treated himself as well. They returned to his flat, both somewhat tired but still full of excitement. "We are invited to have dinner at my mum's house tonight. She can't wait to meet you," he told her.

"I'm nervous, what if she doesn't like me?" Brooklyn asked.

"She will love you, she loves anything I love," he joked.

"Can you choose an outfit for me please?" Brooklyn asked.

"Of course, dear," he teased. Tristan looked tired, although they both slept on the plane for several hours. It was a seven-hour flight. "We have some time before we go, love, so what's next? Do you want to sight see a little?" he asked.

"No, I want to lie in your arms while you rest for a while," she insisted. They did just that, for the next couple of hours, although it wasn't a completely restful venture, once in each other's arms.

They hailed a taxi to Kensington, where Tristan's mom lived. "What should I call her?" Brooklyn asked, realizing for the first time that Tristan Bondage probably wasn't his real name. "Hey what is your real name?" she asked, laughing at the fact that she didn't even know the love of her life's real name.

He had to laugh too. "It's Tristan, but it's not Bondage," he admitted.

"Well, what is it then?"

"Tristan William Davis," he announced.

"Well, it's a pleasure meeting you Mr. Davis," she joked and extended her hand.

"You can just call her Joan or mum," he suggested to Brooklyn. "She'll answer to either," he added.

"I'm more nervous to meet your family than doing all eleven weeks together," she said quietly.

"When they all see how much we love each other, I promise, they will love you too," he told her.

"They?" she thought to herself.

Tristan was right. He absolutely kept his promise, he introduced her to his mother, his sister and brother-in-law, as well as several family friends, and an aunt and uncle. "She's quite lovely," his mum said to Tristan as though Brooklyn wasn't standing next to him. By the end of dinner, his entire family was fighting over who would take Brooklyn where and when, without even as much as inviting Tristan along. "Hey, what about me?" Tristan asked. "I'd like to spend a little bit of time with her in London," he insisted.

"You can spend time with her anytime. While she's here, we'd like to get to know her," his sister, Meredith, insisted.

"You don't seem to take your eyes off her for a second," his mom commented.

"Or your hands," Meredith said.

"But I love her," Tristan expressed and took her hand and kissed it.

"Yes, we've all noticed," his aunt Jeanette added.

Tristan's mom, Joan, was beautiful. She had the same blue eyes as Tristan and the same contagious smile. She was only about five feet and thin, with curly black hair, which of course in reality must have been naturally white by now since she was eighty-three years old. She was spunky and energetic for her age and very much in love with her son. Meredith was blonde with green eyes and also slightly built. She didn't resemble Tristan as did his mum, but she was pleasant looking and probably quite pretty some twenty years prior.

Before they left, Joan hugged her son and told him that it was so good to see him, especially so happy. She then hugged Brooklyn as if she were a long lost daughter and whispered in her ear, "Thank you for loving my son so much. You've made him happier than I ever remember seeing him."

"I do love him," Brooklyn admitted.

Brooklyn hugged Meredith, who reminded her that she would pick her up in Camden tomorrow for lunch near the London Bridge. Tristan helped Brooklyn on with her new coat he had bought for her today, and they left.

"I told you they would be all over you," he reminded her.

"I love them, Tristan," she admitted.

"They were a bit much." He laughed. "But I'm glad it worked out so well," he said happily. "Are you up for going out with my mum and Meredith tomorrow, because if not, I'll make an excuse," he offered.

"Nope, I want to go," she said confidently. "I'm sure your mom will let you come if you wanted to."

"No, I have things to do, and you will have fun with them alone. Besides they can't talk about me, behind my back?" he laughed.

Tristan lay in bed, smiling from ear to ear. Although their schedule thus far had been relatively rigorous, he seemed more relaxed than Brooklyn had never seen him. "Come here," he demanded, still smiling.

"You seem so happy here," Brooklyn remarked.

"I'm here with you, in my hometown, you love my family and they love you, and I'm about to make love with you. You're right, I'm very happy," he whispered. He turned to Brooklyn and kissed her lips. He ran his finger gently up and down her naked body, tracing her breasts and down passed her thighs. He kissed her breasts and nipples and then licked her stomach with his tongue. When he could no longer control his own passion, he climbed on top of her and slipped inside her.

"My god, you feel so good," she whispered.

"Easy, baby, let it last," Tristan whispered.

Only he couldn't last. He exploded inside her as she trembled, filled with his love.

* * *

Joan and Meredith picked Brooklyn up at Tristan's flat at eleven. She was ready, equipped with Tristan's credit card as he insisted on paying for the girls' day out. Tristan put them into a cab, first Meredith, then his mum, and finally Brooklyn. He whispered in her ear, "I'm going to miss you." He kissed her and gave her an extra key to the flat just in case. "Have fun," he yelled as the taxi sped away. They showed her the London Bridge, which was quite disappointing. It looked like a regular bridge, less impressive than any in New York. The London Towers were magnificent, however. They could be seen from the bridge and looked just as she expected from pictures she'd seen.

They picked a restaurant in a mall-type setting in between the bridge and the towers. It was filled with cafes, including a Starbucks. In the center of the mall was an abstract vision of a ship. They sat outside at one of the cafes, and once again Joan thanked Brooklyn for taking such good care of her son. She told stories of when Tristan was a baby and a small boy. Brooklyn listened intensely and laughed at her stories. She couldn't learn enough about him. The time went by quickly and all too soon it grew dark. They hailed a taxi and returned to the flat, where Tristan ran to the door to greet them. "I was about to call the police on you ladies," he scolded as he hugged both Brooklyn and his mum simultaneously and declared, "I will always remember this moment as one of my happiest, with my three favorite women. Are any of you hungry?" Tristan asked. They all declined but agreed to a glass of wine. "Did Brooklyn eat lunch?" Tristan asked. "She hates British food and I'm worried that she'll starve," he added.

"I won't starve. I'm taking advantage of the food issue as a fabulous way to diet," Brooklyn admitted.

Tristan led his favorite girls into the living room, along with their glasses of wine. Tristan inquired about the health and whereabouts of various friends and family, while his mum questioned her son about his health and his other life in the US. Finally exhausting all small talk, Meredith asked Tristan point blank, "Does the vast difference in your ages get in your way at all?"

Tristan smiled and answered, "Well, sometimes I don't know whether to make love with her or take her out for an ice cream soda and date at the playground." They all laughed as Brooklyn blushed.

"I have an announcement to make," Tristan exclaimed.

"You're pregnant! Meredith joked.

"Kind of," Tristan said, thinking about Shakey, "but that's a whole other story. This one is for Brooklyn," he explained. "Tristan Bondage, back from the depths of hell, debuts Friday night at the Hammersmith Apollo Concert Hall." Brooklyn gasped and covered her mouth in surprise. "I arranged that today, especially for you," he told Brooklyn, who was actually shocked. Tristan stood up and noticed the tears in Brooklyn's eyes. He took her hand and pulled her off her seat. "Hey, hey, no tears, love," he whispered. She hugged him as though she were never planning to let go of him. Tristan explained to the other two, who thought her reaction a bit strange (but had no idea of the meaning behind his surprise), "She tends to get emotional sometimes, but that's one of the reasons I love her so much." Tristan lifted her chin, which was still buried in his chest, and kissed her. She kissed him back and mouthed the words "I love you" silently.

Meredith rose from the couch and said jokingly, "I think this might be an opportune time to leave." She helped Joan out of her chair.

The two escorted Joan and Meredith down to the street, making sure they safely found a taxi. Brooklyn hugged them both and thanked them for an awesome day. Meredith reminded Brooklyn of the plans they had made for the following days ahead. She then hugged her brother and whispered in his ear, "You did well, Tristan, make sure you hold onto her."

"I will," he promised as they entered the cab and drove away.

"Did you have a nice time today?" Tristan inquired as they walked back inside his flat.

"I did," Brooklyn said enthusiastically. "I learned a lot about baby Tristan." She laughed.

Tristan rolled his eyes and said, "Jesus, I bet you did." This time it was Tristan's turn to blush. "Are you tired?" he asked.

"Not at all," she said.

"Good, then go ahead and change into something crazy. I want to take you somewhere.

"Where?" she asked with excitement in her voice.

"Down to Soho. Trust me, it will make you feel like you're at home." He laughed, knowing that she'd absolutely love what he had in store for her.

Brooklyn did as she was told. Before they ventured out to Soho, she hugged Tristan once again. "I'm so proud of you and so excited to see you in concert. I know that had to be really hard for you."

"It was," he admitted, "but I love you that much." He laughed. "It's a huge venue, I'm nervous," he admitted.

"Tristan, I just love you so much," she exclaimed.

"Then it's all worth it," he said filled with emotion.

"Now let's go before we change our minds," he pretended to demand.

A short time later they appeared in the streets of Soho. She thought Soho resembled New York City and figured that was what Tristan meant by his statement "It will make you feel at home." Suddenly they turned the corner and there on almost every storefront and bar loomed the colorful rainbow flag that she had grown to love and respect. "Oh my god," Brooklyn exclaimed as the excitement she felt earlier began to multiply. Immensely. Her heart was racing as they entered the first bar, entitled She. She wondered if British gays would be different than those in the States. Within seconds she felt totally at home. As in New York, the young gay men seemed to flock to Brooklyn as though she were a gay magnet. They had one drink there and then went down the block to Ku bar, bringing with them an entourage following Brooklyn from She bar. After Ku they entered a large two-story club called G-A-Y. Once again Brooklyn was bombarded by gays, both British and European. Tristan was astounded to see them fighting for her attention, kissing her as though they knew her for years, dancing with her to the sounds of the DJs and throwing their contact information at her as though she were the queen of England. When it came time to say good-bye, her new entourage became tearful.

As a rule Tristan barely drank, but tonight shots were being thrown at both of them—to Brooklyn just because and Tristan because he was with her. Brooklyn took notice of two facts that she found hilarious. One was that every bartender in London it seemed measure their drinks using a shot glass and the other was that at ten o'clock at night, the entire bar was already bombed and having a party, while in New York the gay clubs barely opened by ten. Tristan explained, already half-drunk himself, that the clubs closed early in London, some by 2:00 a.m., others as early as 12:00 a.m.; therefore, the partying began at 3:00 p.m. or 4:00 p.m. in the afternoon, especially on what Tristan referred to as a bank holiday.

It was suggested that they all visit another bar called Heaven, which was only a block or two from Trafalgar Square, so off they went, not even sure how to get there. Not to worry though, the even newer entourage went along with them. There they met several people from the first and second bar and it became a long-lost reunion. By 12:00 a.m., Tristan was wasted, and Brooklyn was buzzed but not drunk enough to worry about him drinking and the effect it might have on the medication he was taking. She lied and told him that it had been a long day and that she was getting tired.

"Okay," he said, "let's go home," and he kissed her in the gates of Heaven. She retained a slew of British cell phone numbers and promises of getting together before she left for the states.

Tristan seemed to be fun when he was wasted. He laughed a lot and caused Brooklyn to laugh as well. He told her funny stories of his concert experience and how bad he was as a teenager. She enjoyed him. It also seemed she noticed that since the plane touched down in London his British accent became more pronounced and so much more British. However, being drunk he sounded three times as British as she had a difficult time understanding all that he said, and being so drunk he said a lot. They laughed the entire ride back to Camden, and when they arrived at the flat, Brooklyn had to use her key to open the door as Tristan couldn't even focus on the lock. Brooklyn helped him inside and into the bedroom, where he collapsed, still laughing on top of the bed.

Brooklyn ran into the bathroom to get ready for bed, but by the time she returned, Tristan was fast asleep and snoring. She gently removed his shoes and his pants. Luckily he had already thrown his jacket onto the floor. She unbuttoned his shirt but didn't remove it as she didn't wish to wake him. She cuddled on top of his chest and kissed his lips. He managed in his semiconscious state to give her a half smile and to put one of his arms around her.

Brooklyn woke up early as she was used to doing. She showered and dressed quietly so she wouldn't disturb the still sleeping Tristan. He awoke not long after with a headache and a hangover but happy about the memory of last night. That is, whatever he managed to remember. Without needing to ask, Brooklyn brought him some Advil and water. "How did you know?" he asked.

"From the look of pain in your eyes in the sunlight." She laughed.

"Is it that apparent? Did I act like an ass last night?" he asked.

"You were more fun than ever before," she teased him.

"Don't get used to it, I don't tend to drink." He carefully picked his head up, and after adjusting to the room spinning around him, he walked into the shower. As he brushed his teeth, he called to Brooklyn and informed her that he would have to rehearse today all day with his band that he had been able to form in one day. He had played with them all before, but not in over fifteen years, however.

"Can I come?" she asked.

"Nope," he said.

"Really?"

He said, "I want to surprise you, and besides don't you have plans with my sister already?" he reminded her.

"We're going sightseeing," she confessed.

"Say hello to the queen for me." He laughed.

"Do you have a band opening for you?" she asked.

"Oh, I meant to talk to you about that," Tristan, still brushing his teeth, yelled through the closed bathroom door. "How about you open for me?" he yelled. He received no answer, only silence. He opened the door to the bathroom to see Brooklyn staring at him, her eyes wide with surprise. "Well?" he asked. Still he received only silence. "You're not getting stage fright are you?" he teased. "I figured on the three songs you did for the concert during the show. Then I would go on at some point during my show call you back onto the stage so *we* can do a couple of songs together," he suggested. Now she didn't know if he were serious or not. "You didn't think I was going to do my first concert in fifteen-plus years without you, did you?" he asked.

All of a sudden Brooklyn became nervous but managed to say through her shock and dismay, "I'd be honored to open for you!"

"Perfect, then it's set," he said, happy that she finally agreed, although hesitantly. "I'll do your sound check and you can rehearse Friday morning, okay?" he inquired.

"Okay," she concurred.

Tristan glanced outside form the window and noticed Meredith getting out of a cab. "My sister is here already. I wanted to take you out to breakfast first," he insisted.

"No," Brooklyn said, horrified at the thought of having to eat another meal in London.

"Do you want McDonald's?" he asked. "It's almost American."

"No, thank you, I don't even eat MAC Donald's (she corrected him) in America, why would I try it here?" She laughed.

"Come on then, we'll have a cappuccino at the local cafe" he insisted, "and then we'll leave from there."

"Tristan," she called to him, "thank you for last night. That was very special."

Tristan kissed her and told her that she was very special and added, "Don't tell my sister you're going on stage, I want them to be surprised." He bent down and kissed her again; this time it was a deep, endless kiss just as Meredith walked into Tristan's flat.

"Now tear yourself away, she's mine today," Meredith joked. He ignored his sister's funny remark and continued kissing her until both of them nearly stopped breathing.

Tristan left the two girls at the coffee shop, kissing them both on the cheek and then returning to Brooklyn for a real kiss on the lips, and then he was gone. "Where is your mom?" Brooklyn asked.

"We're going to get her, but I figured we'd have some sister time together first for a little while. I love my older brother, and he's been through a lot and I can't even tell you how it feels to see him so happy and so much in love," Meredith began. "I suppose I want to thank you for that personally. I can see it in your eyes when you talk about him, and when you're with him, it's your heart that speaks. Well, what I'm trying to say is that I know that you love him very much. I guess I just want to make sure that he doesn't blow it. I've already warned him." Meredith laughed. "I want to welcome you into our family and make you promise to stay," she finished.

Brooklyn smiled and gave Meredith an awkward hug. "You have nothing to worry about. Tristan's got my heart, my soul. He's my life," Brooklyn said.

"Yes, I can tell, but things happen in life. He's so much older than you and he has so many health problems," Meredith said.

"Oh my, now you sound like Tristan when we first fell in love. He actually attempted to dump me because of everything you've just mentioned. I know how old he is, but really, he's very childlike. He's sweet and gentle and romantic. He's generous to a fault. He has so much love inside him to give, and he gives it all to me. Not to mention the fact that he's so handsome. I look at him sometimes and I'm amazed at how sexy he is and I wonder sometimes why he chose me," Brooklyn went on to say.

"Well, you are quite beautiful yourself," Meredith commented.

"Thank you, but beautiful girls are a dime a dozen. He could have anyone he wants. I see the way woman look at him and young girls scream on top of their lungs for him, and, Meredith, if I can be candid with you for a moment," Brooklyn said cautiously.

"Go on, please," Meredith permitted.

"He's amazing in bed," Brooklyn whispered.

Meredith clapped her hands together in excitement. "Oh good, that really helps," Meredith exclaimed, excited that Brooklyn shared that fact with her.

"Look, I know his medical condition and it makes me sad that he suffers so much still, but whether I'm with him or not he's still going to be in pain. He tries to hide it from me, but I'm getting better at noticing when he's in trouble. I think if I can just give him his medication when he can't or just hold him in my arms when he needs me to, massage his legs . . . I don't know . . . I just feel better watching over him," Brooklyn said sadly.

"How much of his situation do you know?" asked Meredith.

"I think I know it all now," Brooklyn said.

"Do you know his prognosis? I mean, do you know he will eventually be . . . paralyzed?"

Brooklyn interrupted her. "Yes, of course," Brooklyn admitted.

"My mum doesn't know, we've decided not to tell her just yet. She'd only worry every day then."

"You know what, Meredith, if it happens in ten years, that's amazing. If it happens in five years, it's still amazing, because of the precious time we have together and will have together while he can walk. When it happens it will still be amazing, because he's amazing," Brooklyn said, holding back her tears just thinking about it.

"But you're so young," Meredith pointed out.

"Meredith, I am the luckiest girl that has ever lived. As long as I can hold his hand, talk to him, listen to him speak, see him smile at me, I'll be all right. Oh, and one thing I forgot . . . as long as he still loves me the way he does, I'll be better than all right," Brooklyn said. "You know, I think I can pinpoint the day he found out that news. He sent me and the Devils on a shopping spree with his credit card, and while we were all having fun at his expense literally, he was alone finding out that horrible news, all by himself, and then keeping that locked inside himself for days. He's very brave, you know. But I just keep on falling in love with him again and again," Brooklyn concluded.

Meredith, now holding a tissue, declared, "How beautiful that was said. We must be going now, Joan will be concerned," Meredith announced. "Thank you, Brooklyn," Meredith said as they got up to leave.

After picking Joan up at her home, they traveled to the Eye, then to Big Ben, Trafalgar Square, and finally to the Palace. They took pictures and sent them to Tristan, who called Brooklyn each time he received one, and added his own commentary to their sightseeing tour.

"Why would he be working when he should be spending time with you?" Joan wondered.

"He's doing this for me," Brooklyn defended Tristan. "I told him that my biggest fantasy was to see him in concert. He hasn't done a concert in over fifteen years. I'm so excited to see Tristan do a concert. He wasn't sure he would be able to, but he is, and I'm so proud of him," Brooklyn claimed with pride.

"Well, dear, if you don't mind, I guess I'll forgive him." Joan laughed.

"Mum, don't be so critical, they are entertainers, that's what they live for, besides each other," Meredith said.

"I suppose," Joan agreed.

When they had run out of sights to see, the women returned to Joan's house where she prepared dinner. Tristan met them just in time to eat. He was exhilarated form the rehearsal, but he looked so tired. They left after dinner giving each other the appropriate hugs and thank-yous. The two rode home exchanging the days' stories and both refusing to let each other's hand go.

Tristan was so tired, he could barely make it into the shower. Once the water fell upon his face, he woke up enough to call Brooklyn in with him, just to hold her in his arms. Brooklyn took the shampoo and washed his hair, massaging his head with her nails and afterward dried his hair with a towel. He lay back upon the pillows and called Brooklyn to lie with him. It was only 8:30 p.m., but within moments Tristan fell fast asleep.

* * *

Both Tristan and Brooklyn were pacing in different directions behind the huge stage of the Hammersmith Apollo Theater. They would be performing for a sold out crowd. Tristan had to laugh. He grabbed Brooklyn and said, "Why do we do this to ourselves?" He answered his own question as he whispered into Brooklyn's ear, "Because it's in our blood," and he kissed her. The roadies set the instruments and the stage. The other band members sat smoking butts and joking with one another. "Ten minutes, love." Tristan's mom, sister, aunts and uncles, and friends, some of which Brooklyn hadn't yet met, all huddled on the other side of the stage.

Then it was time for Brooklyn. Tristan came out on stage, surprising the audience and Brooklyn. He announced his prodigy and returned backstage. She was nothing short of amazing. The audience cheered. Flashes went off. Tristan was proud. She did the three songs that she had done on the show, with the same special effects including the burning dress, the falling stars, and one hundred dancing men with white umbrellas descending from the heavens. Tristan's family was astounded. They marveled at her talent. When her last song ended, she ran backstage and was greeted by Tristan, who said, "That was amazing. Are you trying to make me look bad?" he joked.

"Trist, how are you doing?" she asked.

"I'm a fucking wreck! But I love you!" he answered. The audience continued to cheer and the stage went dark.

Tristan was a mess. His palms were sweating profusely. He felt sick to his stomach and numb with fear as he sat quietly waiting for the roadies to switch the stage for his band. He had only moments before he was to go on. He silently prayed that he wouldn't freeze as he did each and every time during his horrifying nightmare that plagued his sanity. Brooklyn stood behind him soundlessly and touched his shoulder. He grabbed her hand from behind and kissed it. She bent down and whispered in his ear, "I love you." He suddenly realized that she was the only thing that really mattered. He was doing this for her, and no matter what, he wasn't going to disappoint her. His band was signaled to take the stage. "Kiss me for luck," he asked.

She kissed him deeply and said, "For luck and for love," as he ran onto the stage.

The moment the once ruler of the punk rock world, Tristan Bondage, hit the stage and began to sing, an unexplainable magic came to pass. He had a stage persona that ignited the room. The sound of his voice, clear and perfect, echoed through the huge venue as the sound of screams from women, old and young, filled the arena. It was as though it were thirty years ago during the height of his fame. Tristan felt strong and confident.

Brooklyn watched from behind the stage, awed by his wizardry. She was astonished by his performance and at the same time filled with pride as continued to wow the audience. She felt as though her heart would burst with love for him. She had never loved him more than she did now, and that love kept on growing with each song that he executed. This was so much more than she had ever imagined. He captured the audience, he owned the stage, he owned the venue, and he owned the world. Most importantly, he owned her heart.

He remained on stage for over two hours. He sang his hit songs from the 1980s. He implemented new songs that he'd never had the opportunity to do on stage. He joked with the audience and eventually summoned Brooklyn to the stage. She stood at his side and he took her hand and proclaimed his love for her for his following to witness. Tristan kissed her hand, causing the congregation to cheer, and they began to sing their dramatic version of "Demons," just as it had been done on the show. They followed it by covering Chris Brown's song "With You," a romantic rendition of the beautiful love song, "With Hearts All Over the World," causing security to have to enter the mosh pit in an attempt to calm the assembly. The two bowed and walked off the stage hand in hand as the stage grew dark.

Once behind stage, Tristan and Brooklyn kissed passionately, and Tristan ran to do a costume change. On his way back to the stage Brooklyn whispered, "I'm so proud of you. He mouthed the words "Thank you," winked, and returned to his screaming admirers as they chanted his name over and over again.

Tristan sang another song and then dimmed the stage lights and prepared to address the onlookers on a more serious and personal level. He possessed the ability and gift of making each and everyone in the audience feel as though he were personally and separately speaking only to them. "I want to thank you for coming out tonight. It's been a long time since I've done this, but it feels good to be back. It just feels right." Tristan paused, allowing the crowd to voice their admiration. "Just letting you know, I'm here to stay." The fans cheered wildly. Tristan then introduced his band, performed one last song, threw kisses to the crowd, and left the stage.

Brooklyn, still dazed by Tristan's charisma, applauded for him as he greeted her and the press backstage. The lights in the venue were turned up high as the fans leisurely left the auditorium. Both Tristan and Brooklyn were congratulated by family, friends, staff, and each other. The press and the critics spoke briefly to Tristan as photographers snapped pictures and shot videos. It wasn't exactly a worldwide event, but it was certainly a start, a new beginning. Bottles of champagne began to pop as a celebration party began. The first opportunity Tristan saw he grabbed Brooklyn's hand and dragged her to privacy where he took her in his arms and thanked for her encouragement and belief in him. "Thank you, love," he exclaimed, "for saving my life once again." He kissed her over and over again while trying desperately to control the erection her return kisses were causing him to get.

When they returned to the celebration, Tristan unmistakably and accidentally wore her lipstick upon his lips. He introduced Brooklyn to his friends and to acquaintances he pretended to know well. Tristan's mum and sister said their farewells and insisted upon taking the ride to the airport with them the following day. Tristan agreed but made Meredith promise there would be no tears. The party would last until dawn, but Tristan and Brooklyn secretly left around 2:00 a.m., returning to their limo for their journey back to Camden.

Tristan leaned his head back and closed his eyes. Brooklyn could tell he was hurting. She took his hand and said, "Tris, you're in pain, I should have forced you to leave earlier."

"No, no, no," Tristan said, smiling. "There is no time for guilt tonight. I had the most remarkable night and I wouldn't trade it for all the morphine in the world," he joked. She felt him trembling and watched him grow pale. He pulled a syringe from his pocket and a clear vial and handed it to Brooklyn, who promptly gave him a dose of medication. He continued to lie back with his eyes still closed and waited for the pain to ease. Still attempting to joke, he asked her, "So was my concert as good as you'd hoped it would be?"

"No," she said, trying to tease him back.

He opened his eyes and sat upright. "Really?" he asked, perplexed, having thought that he put on a pretty good show.

Smiling she said, "It was a million times better than I could ever have imagined. I was astonished and overwhelmed by you tonight and I never loved you more than I did tonight."

"Well then, come here and kiss me!" he demanded.

Noticing his pain had dissipated, Brooklyn settled up against him and put her head on his chest. "I never respected anyone more in my life, I'm so proud to be your . . ." She paused, not knowing what to call her role in this relationship.

"My wife," he said, finishing the sentence for her. "Maybe now you won't run for the hills when I mention the word *commitment*," he teased.

"Driver," Tristan said suddenly. "Can you please stop at Carlton Vale in Kensington?"

"Where are you taking us at nearly 3:00 a.m.?" Brooklyn asked.

Tristan took her hand and kissed it, "There's something I have to do before we leave London," he explained. "I wasn't sure I would be able to do this, but I feel strong when you're with me." Brooklyn looked at him confused. "I have to put some kind of closure on this," he said, almost speaking in riddles. Finally he said, "I need to go back to where it happened. I think I can if you're by my side. Are you up for that?" he asked. Now knowing he was talking about the alleyway where he was mercilessly attacked, she kissed him on his forehead and he knew it was okay with her.

He left the car alone, telling Brooklyn to stay inside the limo. He walked a few steps and stared at the place where his brutal attack took place. He began to recall the terrible pain he felt that night when they kicked him so viciously, it caused his ribs to shatter. Then he saw in his memory the attackers as they took a steel pipe and broke his legs. He fell to his knees on the cold, damp ground as he vividly evoked the memories, one by one. Finally he clutched his chest with the recollection of the pain he felt as they cut his chest with the beer bottle. He turned and looked at Brooklyn and mouthed her name. He put his hand out to her. She saw the pain in his soul and ran to his side where he began to sob violently. She kneeled down next to him and held him tightly as he continued to feel the pain and the horror of the night. Then he thought of the repercussions the attack brought to his life. Realizing his chance to live a normal life was now limited because of this evil attack, he grew silent. His tears stopped as he considered the fact that eventually he would be paralyzed, sentenced to a wheelchair for the rest of his life, while Brooklyn, the woman he loved so much, would have to care for him forever. There would be no more concerts, no more walks along the beach, no more walking hand in hand. He turned and looked at Brooklyn, and said tearfully, "You did nothing to deserve this, except fall in love with me."

She wished she could say something to take the pain away from his eyes. She whispered to him softly, touching his face, "Let it go, Tristan! I'm sorry they hurt you, but no matter what happens, no matter what you're thinking in your precious little mind, we will deal with it together, as one." Tristan grabbed her and hugged her and began to sob uncontrollably once again on her shoulder. "Tell me what I can do to make it better, baby?" she whispered in his ear. It wasn't until now that Brooklyn realized the true gravity of his attack, both physically and emotionally.

Tristan seemed to grow calm. He lifted his head and with his hands held Brooklyn's shoulders and asked angrily, "Do you want to spend the rest of our lives together pushing me in a wheelchair and taking care of me? You're a free spirit sentenced to a life with the man you love imprisoned in a wheelchair. Is that what you want?" he yelled as he shook her.

Realizing that his anger was certainly not directed toward her, she took his face in her hands so that he would be forced to look in her eyes and focus upon what she had to say. "Baby, it's not my first choice to see you in a wheelchair for the rest of your life. But it is my first choice to love you and stay with you for the rest of our lives no matter what the future holds. What if the roles were reversed, would you choose to leave me?" she asked.

"You know the answer to that. I would never want to be with-out you," he admitted.

"Well, the only way you're going to get rid of me is if you can tell me, and make me believe that you don't love me anymore. Well?" she asked.

"I love you more than I love my own life," he said to her.

"I don't know how to make those awful memories go away, nor do I know how to ease your pain, but one thing I do know is how to love you. I also know that my life would mean nothing without you in it. Loving you is the best thing that's ever happened to me," she said as she released her hands from his face and began to softly cry. Through her tears, she said, "Let's just enjoy one another in every way possible for the rest of our lives. I don't want to be without you ever, under any circumstances," she stated.

Tristan stood up and helped Brooklyn to her feet. In that one instant all the pain, the fear, the uncertainty seemed to fade. He kissed her lips gently, then touched her hair and then her face. He took her hand and led her back to the limo and helped her inside. He took a last look and got into the limo. "Driver, please take us to

Camden," Tristan announced. Brooklyn touched his face. He took her hand and held it to his lips. As he closed his eyes, he felt her heart. "I'm okay now," he told her. "I'm over it." He apologized for being such a drama queen and kissed her.

It was a serious kiss, full of emotion, full of love. Then he whispered to her, "We'll be okay, I promise." Finally he smiled at her. It was the sweetest smile she'd ever seen.

They returned home after 4:00 a.m. Tristan sat on the bed while Brooklyn gently began to undress him, carefully unbuttoning each button. "It was like being beat up all over again," he said quietly as she unzipped his pants. Brooklyn laid him back onto a pillow. He was dazed and beyond exhaustion. "Come here, love," he said. "I just want to hold you in my arms for a minute baby, please." She lay back in his arms. Within seconds they were asleep and would wake up in exactly the same position.

* * *

Before they were to leave for the airport, Tristan took Brooklyn for a ride in the infamous Tube. She had never been so excited to ride the subway in her life. Now she felt as though she'd been in London. Tristan laughed as they ran to get a train to nowhere that really mattered. When they returned, it was time to meet Meredith and Joan so they could escort the two back to Heathrow. As they walked back to the flat, Brooklyn noticed a group of girls pointing at Tristan and giggling. Although Tristan noticed as well, he pretended to ignore it. "Hey, Tris, make their lives, wave to them."

"Come on, let's go say hello," Tristan suggested.

The girls were all young and pretty. They saw him heading their way and began fixing their clothes and hair. "Good morning, ladies," Tristan said. Still giggling, they asked for autographs and pictures, all of which Tristan happily agreed to.

"We saw you last night at Hammersmith. We thought you were awesome!" one of the braver girls admitted.

"Thank, you ladies. Come, love, we better walk back. Bye," he said to the group of girls, who were still giggling.

"I'm jealous," Brooklyn admitted. "So many women and young girls love you. What if you fall in love with one of them?" she said, half-teasing.

"Hey, listen, I love you. Do you hear me?" Tristan yelled. He then began to yell it throughout the streets of Camden. "I love you, Brooklyn!" he yelled to anyone that would listen. They laughed until they couldn't breathe and then kissed in the street as Joan and Meredith got out of their cab. Meredith tapped Tristan on the shoulder, "Don't you two have a plane to catch?" He ignored Meredith while he stared into Brooklyn's eyes and told her he loved her and only her.

The limo driver loaded the car with their luggage and all the various gifts for the Devils and presents they had bought, then helped the ladies into the limo. When they arrived at the airport, the tears began to flow. Meredith hugged her brother and Brooklyn. They promised each other that they would keep in touch. Meredith also asked that they please let her know that they returned safely. "If you don't hear of a plane crashing, you can assume we made it home okay," Tristan sarcastically told his sister.

Joan took out a little box from her purse and gave it to Brooklyn. "Thank you for giving me my son back," she said as she handed the box to Brooklyn. If that wasn't enough to make Brooklyn cry, the box contained a locket with a picture of Tristan when he was a baby. Brooklyn hugged Joan and the two stood there crying. Tristan shook his head, smiling as they completed their good-byes and thank-yous.

"Look, when the show ends, we will come back, I promise," Tristan announced.

"Well that would be lovely, but in the meanwhile, you take care of each other, and, Tristan, don't blow it," Meredith demanded.

Tristan shook his head again and gave his mum one last hug.

By the time they reached customs and security, Brooklyn had finally stopped crying. Tristan put his arm around her tenderly as they walked toward the waiting area, where their plane sat waiting to be boarded. He thanked her for putting up with his dramatic family and for being so sweet to his mum. Brooklyn told him that she loved his family, and that made him happy.

Tristan was happier than he ever remembered being. He felt as though a huge weight had been lifted. With Brooklyn's help and encouragement, he had managed to conquer his personal demons and he knew in his heart there would be no more of those horrible nightmares. Tristan was leaving London with a confidence he hadn't ever felt before, even at the height of his fame and popularity.

As they reached the boarding area, Tristan took her hand and held it as they sat down to wait until first class was called. Brooklyn noticed her shoe lace untied and attempted to let go of Tristan's hand to tie it. He refused to allow their grip to be broken. Brooklyn laughed and told him she had to tie her high-top pink sneaker. "No," he said. "I don't want to let you of you."

Brooklyn laughed even harder. "Just for a second, my laces are opened," she insisted.

"No," he insisted back. "I feel like I'm having a marvelous dream, and if I let go of you, I might wake up," Tristan explained.

A British woman sitting next to them overheard their conversation and felt compelled to comment, "If you don't allow her to tie her shoe, your dream will turn into a nightmare when she gets up to board and trips over her laces and falls."

"You're right," Tristan agreed. Tristan released her hand and kneeled in front of her and tied her shoe. He looked up and smiled at her. She noticed that as she looked into his eyes that pain and torture that she saw in them last night had disappeared.

She bent down and kissed him and told him, "You look so beautiful to me today."

The same British woman smiled and said, "I love the magic of young love!"

"Thank you," Tristan said as he returned to his seat, secretly happy that she hadn't commented on their difference in age.

Before the plane boarded Tristan decided to go into the bathroom and give himself a dose of morphine for the ride. He had been feeling the potential for pain and figured he would just avoid it before it actually happened. When he returned, it became time to board. He escorted Brooklyn to her seat and held her hand as the plane ascended into the clouds. As soon as the plane had leveled, Tristan released her hand and told her how happy she made him. Brooklyn told him that she loved London and had the most magical time in her life. They talked to each other nonstop for seven hours. Tristan brought up their future and the fact that he missed little Shakey as well as the Devils. He told her stories from his past, and most importantly they laughed a lot.

It was raining when they touched down. Tristan had put his arms around her as if to protect her from the bumpy landing they had experienced. As they deplaned, Tristan told her once again how thankful he was for her and that she saved his life again in so many ways. She stopped in the middle of the aisle and kissed him as the people behind them hid their annoyance. "And thank you for that too," Tristan said. They walked hand in hand through American customs and then headed for the baggage claim where the Devils would be waiting to take them back to the island. Brooklyn made a quick call to London, letting Meredith know they were safe.

Dazzel screamed as she spotted Brooklyn, who ran toward her. Damian picked Brooklyn off the floor and spun her around. She hugged Colin and finally Garrett. Dazzel ran to Tristan and connected with him with such force that her tiny frame nearly knocked him off balance. They hugged as if they were long-lost lovers. All eyes were on the group while they waited for their suitcases to appear. "You're making a scene," Dazzel teased Tristan. Tristan just rolled his eyes and wiped Dazzel's kiss off his face. The Devils grabbed their luggage and headed outside to the white van that they borrowed for their trip to the airport.

"Did you buy us presents?" Dazzel boldly asked.

"For everyone but you," Tristan teased.

"So tell us about your concert. Were you any good, did anyone come?" Garrett teased.

"There will be plenty of time to tell you all about London and the concert on the ride home," Tristan insisted as they entered the van.

Chapter 10

The Win

Sunday night found the Devils and Tristan back at the cottage. It was the night before *So You Wanna Be a Rock Star* would unveil the winner, America's new rock superstar, the voting would close at midnight. Tristan insisted they all chill together. He wisely chose the cottage because to him that's where it all began. The vibrations were happy there for all the Devils and Brooklyn as well.

Tristan lay sprawled out on the couch, head on a pillow, while Brooklyn sat Indian style positioned in between his legs. Colin had a spot on the love seat, sipping a bright red cosmo. Both Dazzel and Garrett sat on the floor, drinking wine from a bottle and playing video games, while Damian pranced about the room, visiting and annoying each of the band members while happily sucking down a cocktail.

"Look how quiet we all are," Brooklyn announced breaking the silence.

"Well, it is do or die tomorrow," Colin reminded the room, as Damian added, "We're all scared to death."

"True," admitted Colin. With that Tristan sat upright. The band all knew there was a speech coming attached to the change of position.

"Listen. I've said it before it's not only about the win but about the journey as well. This journey has been amazing for all of us, especially for me, and whether we win or lose, I just want to say how much I love all of you. I could not have chosen a better band or a closer bunch of friends. It's been an honor flying with you."

Damian couldn't help but laugh at Tristan. "Hey, Trist, you're not going all girly on us, are you?" he asked.

"No, really, guys, I've never regretted my selection for a second," Tristan continued as Dazzel interrupted, "Someone care to remind him of the first three weeks please."

"Please don't." Tristan laughed and rolled his eyes.

"So what's your prediction, fearless leader?" Damian asked.

Tristan pulled Brooklyn closer to him until her back was leaning up against his chest and his arms found their place around her. He rested his chin upon her shoulder and took a deep breath before choosing his answer. "I honestly can't be sure. The Devils are better than Blood Red, but America loves Devin. They barely remember me, and that's not your fault. If the judge's decision weighs heavy, we will win. If America's vote counts more . . ."

"Are you kidding?" Colin interrupted. "After that last performance of 'Demons' as well as the *Johnny Michaels Show*, I think America has fallen in love with you all over again."

"They already love, Brooklyn," Dazzel commented.

"Not as much as I do," Tristan remarked, smiling that contagious smile of his as he kissed the back of her neck.

"What if we lose?" Dazzel suggested sadly.

Tristan, still smiling, took his chin off Brooklyn's shoulder and said, "Then I'll miss you all very, very much."

Brooklyn pretended to be angry and said, "What's that supposed to mean?"

He replied, "Well, all of you will return from whence you came and I will return to London."

"Oh really?" exclaimed Brooklyn. "Let's see, where was Billy Blaze's number?" she teased.

Tristan grabbed Brooklyn even tighter and said, "And then I'll kill myself," as he laughed and continued on, "You, young lady, are going nowhere without me!"

Brooklyn turned her head upside down and kissed Tristan. "Promise?" she asked.

He kissed her shoulder and said, "I promise."

Garrett looked up from his video game and said to Brooklyn. "Girl, you got it going, we're gonna win."

Tristan scolded him, "Mary, don't be arrogant!"

Brooklyn laughed and said to Tristan, "Did you really say that?"

Tristan blushed and he and the Devils laughed until their stomachs hurt. Still laughing Colin remarked, "None of us are going to be able to sleep tonight."

Dazzel retorted, "Speak for yourself, I need my beauty sleep."

"Well then, you should have started hours ago," Damian jokingly suggested and received a pillow in his face, courtesy of Dazzel.

Garrett stood up and grabbed the guitar that lived by the fireplace and brought it over to Tristan. "Daddy, can you sing us a lullaby?"

Damian also chimed in, "Yes, Daddy, sing us a lullaby."

"Really? Daddy?' Tristan said and shook his head. He sat up all the way as Brooklyn changed her position from the inside of Tristan's legs. "Okay, bad children, how about a love song?" Tristan asked. They all gathered around him and Tristan began to strum the acoustic guitar and began to sing "Gotta Be a Sin" by Adam Ant.

It's burning holes into my heart . . . To leave that face so tenderly
I know that I can't stop the pain . . . but oh the pain cannot stop me
Into a heart so lost and broken . . . an angel seized the pain
Swallow her breath, hold it to my chest . . . and feel so warm in love again
Right from the first time I made love with you
I had nothing in life to compare that moment to
But it's gotta be a sin, gotta be a sin, gotta be a sin . . .
Gotta be a sin, gotta be a sin
I want to wake up really early . . . want the first thing that I see
To see your eyes still softly closed . . . and your lips waiting patiently

By midsong Brooklyn became extremely turned on by the sexy words emanating from Tristan's melodious voice. Tristan was such a sexy man and he was singing such a sexy song.

I know the saddest sight in this world
Is you climbing out of bed
Vision you are clipping on that bra
Maybe we'll stay in bed instead . . .

When the song was completed, they all applauded except for Brooklyn, who took the guitar out of his hands, gave it to Damian, and slithered beside Tristan, pushing him back down on the pillow. She climbed on top of him and began seductively kissing him. Tristan felt strong and pain-free and up to taking full advantage of that and the fact that Brooklyn was being so aggressively sexy. He scooped her up into his arms and said, "Good night, ladies," to the Devils and carried her into the bedroom and locked the door behind them.

Brooklyn laughed and whispered, "Put me down, Hercules, before you get hurt." Tristan walked over to the bed and kissed her hard and passionately then gently laid her down upon the soft bed. He lay next to her, searching her face and her eyes as if he were seeing her for the very first time. "God, I love you!" he said and began kissing her lips ever so softly and gently. He barely touched her but found her trembling already. He began rubbing her back through the tiny tee she was wearing. Then he positioned both of his hands under the tee and touched her everywhere. He unfastened her bra and pulled her T-shirt off and then her panties. He gently and purposefully maneuvered his hands upon her soft skin, causing chills throughout her body. He began to massage her thighs and then gently kiss them, moving his lips up above them. Brooklyn touched him gently. He was so hard and ready for her. She slipped underneath him and he slipped inside her.

When they were finished, he stayed inside and put his head between her breasts, still panting from the magic that had just taken place. She ran her fingers through his hair and whispered, "Colin's correct, no one's sleeping tonight."

"Whatever happens has already been decided, there's nothing to prove anymore. We did our best, above and beyond our best, win or lose. No more pressure, love," Tristan whispered to her.

"I just don't wanna let you down," she said quietly.

"No, baby" he whispered. "Don't you see? I've already won something more precious than anything else in the world—you. I have everything I've ever wanted or needed in you," he confessed.

Brooklyn began kissing him again and felt him grow hard inside her once again. "I feel you, baby," she whispered.

Pushing inside her, he whispered, "You see, I've won again."

* * *

The set was filled with anticipation and raw nerves. The two bands hugged each other and wished each other luck. They all walked into the green room in silence and sat down. It was as if they all were in a hospital, anticipating a life-or-death surgery.

In another part of the set, Adonis and the two remaining mentors sat behind closed doors in a private meeting for what seemed to the bands like a lifetime.

The Devils all wore matching costumes for the introduction of the last show. Brooklyn wore a flaming-red mermaid gown, which pointed out every single curve in her body. She was adorned with Tristan's beautiful gift of radiant, sparkling diamonds. The Devils all wore flaming-red tailed jackets with matching red bowties, flamboyant red suspenders, and bright red Converse high-top sneakers. Even Johnny left Dazzel in the closet and dressed as the others had. Perhaps later he would invite her out of the closet.

Both bands reluctantly prepared a "losers' song," a last number to be performed by the band that would be saying farewell. The Devils decided that, if they lost, it might make Tristan feel a little better if they surprised him and did one of his songs for their good-bye. Blood Red was so sure they had won that they practiced an original half assed song, not expecting to have to sing it. In any case both bands hoped that it would be the other band doing the last dance.

At last Tristan, Devin, and Adonis emerged from their secret meeting and headed to the green room, where the two bands sat nervously in silence. "Well, this is it," commented Devin. "Good luck, dude," Devin said to Tristan. Tristan immediately hugged Devin and wished him good luck.

"Good luck to all of you," Adonis said as he cleared his throat signaling that he was about to address the room. "First, I want to thank all of you for making this show a success beyond my wildest imagination. All your hard work and that of your coaches have made this show the best rated in the history of television." Adonis went on to tell them that he had some amazing surprises in store for them before the night was over.

"We love surprises," Garrett said happily.

"Well, in fact, the first surprise is about to happen," said Adonis. "By popular demand I'm going to open the show very unconventionally. Last week's performance by the Devils and Tristan will be repeated via video. Tonight that's how we're going to start the show. We received an influx of demands to play it again in its entirety. As a matter of fact we received as many requests for the performance as almost all the voting put together . . . So here goes . . ."

The darkened stage awaited some life. It longed to be filled with lights, song, and applause, and it became so, as the set was transformed into a giant video screen. There were the Devils once again playing behind Brooklyn and Tristan as they performed their heartfelt, dramatic, and emotional "Demons." Tristan felt uneasy at the fact that "Demons" was revisited. Perhaps Adonis already knew they lost. Otherwise why would he begin the show with such a strong recap? Devin felt the same way, only he felt excited instead of uneasy.

Tristan summoned the Devils into a huddle. "Remember, it's not always about the win, it's the journey that's most important," and then Tristan kissed each of the Devils on the cheek.

"Oops, do you know something that we don't?" Dazzel asked as Johnny.

"No, not at all. I just wanted all of you to know that I love you, no matter what the outcome," Tristan said. His eyes filled with water as he turned to Brooklyn and looked at her proudly. "Princess, may I escort you to the stage when the time is right?" he asked nobly.

"I'd be honored," Brooklyn answered.

When the video ended, the audience repeated their performance of last week and then the lights on the stage grew dark once more. The random voice bellowed through the auditorium as he welcomed America and introduced the host, Adonis Hartly, this season.

Lights began to bounce off the stage and one another as Adonis walked slowly to center stage. Applause was high. Adonis's eyes sparkled as he presented his opening welcome. "Finally week twelve has approached! America, before the night is over we will unveil the winner—America's newest super group, the group that will go on tour, get a record contract, and be introduced to the world on a special television concert. Their mentor will gain the honor of the win and will tour with the group." While the audience applauded, Adonis reintroduced the judges for the last time. They took their places at the judges' table.

"Judges," Adonis called, "let's see what's on your mind and in your hearts."

The 1980s icon began. "This is by far, the most difficult decision I've had to make in my entire life. I'm just so thankful that we had help from America."

The promoter spoke next. "Both bands and both mentors are incredible. I want to especially mention Tristan and Devin, the most amazing coaches. Whatever the bands have both become since the beginning, they owe to these two musical geniuses." He pointed to the mentors. "Blood Red, Devils, applaud your teachers, they deserve it!" The last judge from MTV stood and waited for the arena to silence.

"This is a bittersweet evening. I'm so thrilled for whoever the winner will be and I'm so ecstatic for the mentor who becomes victorious. However, both coaches and both bands worked so very hard. I just feel the runner-up deserves something as well, something beyond a pat on the back." The audience rose from their seats in agreement.

"Devin Liam, please chaperone Blood Red to the stage," Adonis ordered. When they entered the set, the audience shrieked loudly. "Next, here come the Precious Little Devils." Brooklyn was gracefully escorted by the sexy and rebellious Tristan Bondage. As the two walked out together, with Brooklyn draped on his arm, the audience suddenly gave them an unexpected ovation. The two looked so eloquent and regal, like a prince and princess in a modern fairytale. Tristan was so handsome, dressed in a white business suit with a red tie and red high-tops matching Brooklyn's persuasive red gown. Tristan's beautiful blue eyes twinkled every time he smiled that contagious smile and looked at Brooklyn as they stood together awaiting their fate.

Adonis summoned both Tristan and Devin to his side. Devin took the right side, while Tristan stepped to Adonis's left, however not before he bowed to Brooklyn and kissed her hand as a prince would. Adonis put his arm around Devin and then his other arm around Tristan and began to speak. "I wanted to personally congratulate both of you for your hard work and efforts. I am overwhelmed with gratitude to both of you as well as the two finalists, Blood Red and Precious Devils. You are both winners in my book, but unfortunately there can only be one champion." Adonis faced the audience and asked, "Who will it be? Stay tuned."

When the show broke for the sponsors, Tristan walked back over to Brooklyn and took both her tiny hands in his. Brooklyn smiled at him shyly and apprehensively. He kissed both her hands and then released them. Then Tristan lifted her chin with one single finger and reminded her, "Remember, I've already won the greatest prize imaginable."

She hugged him gently and said, "No, I have."

Tristan's eyes filled with tears for a second. "Hey, I have a surprise for you later. I'm just praying that you love it," he said.

Odd, thought Brooklyn; why wouldn't she like any surprise he offered?

Just before the commercial ended, Tristan took his place once again to the left of Adonis. The show reopened to a video of the third judge's remark: "Both coaches and both bands worked so very hard. I just feel that the runner-up deserves something as well." The audience once again rose and clapped in agreement.

"I promised both bands that tonight would be filled with magic and surprise," Adonis said proudly. Well, the sponsors and producers of *So You Wanna Be a Rock Star* have decided, because of the closeness of the voting, to invite the runner-up along on the concert tour!" The bands gasped and hugged each other. The two mentors hugged as well. This was a joyous and unexpected event and the audience went totally ballistic.

Adonis feebly attempted to calm the audience but that proved impossible. Finally he made the microphone squeak loudly as chalk on a blackboard. The shrill sound made the audience jump to attention as he announced, "I have another fantastic surprise. Coaches, Blood Red, Devils, there are several people who would love to wish you well." From behind the stage out paraded Delilah Carnes and Citi Girls, followed by Jamison Brown and Sin-cerely Yours. Finally the Rising Tides entered the stage with coach Billy Blaze. The congregation cheered violently and relentlessly. The joyous reunion brought about chaos both on and off the set. The members of each band hugged each other as did all the mentors, even Billy and Tristan.

The love continued through the commercial break until the finalists were ordered to wardrobe to change for the second half of the show, and then Billy, Delilah, Jamison, and their groups were treated to a seat in the front row of the auditorium. Johnny hurried to dress Dazzel and bring her back to life. Win or lose, Dazzel needed to make her presence known. Brooklyn changed into a gold-sequin sleeveless top with black leather pants and high gold boots, while the Devils wore short gold shirts up to their belly buttons with tight black pants and high gold boots as well. They all had on gold-fringed leather jackets embraced with rhinestones, while Dazzel chose a gold-sequin gown and black seven-inch high heels.

While the Devils played in wardrobe, Tristan sat in the green room alone and prayed that his phenomenon would be well received. His surprise was risky. Although Adonis and the sponsors supported and encouraged his intention, it could very well end in disaster.

Both the Devils and Blood Red stood backstage as the theme song of the show played and Adonis walked to the front of the stage. The bands, the mentors, and America held their breath as Adonis, in low voice (so that the audience would be forced to listen in silence), announced, "Ladies and gentlemen, judges, and all of America, the time has come to divulge the winner. Will both bands and their coaches please join me." The two groups congregated on either side of Adonis, standing nervously together, all holding hands. "Here we go," spoke Adonis. "Please dim the lights. Drum roll please." Adonis continued, "The grand champions of *So You Wanna Be a Rock Star*, the newest rock star idol, is . . ." The pause and the drum roll continued for forty-five seconds before the winner was unveiled. The forty-five seconds seemed longer than the entire twelve weeks of the show. Finally Adonis raised the microphone to his mouth. "Congratulations . . . *Precious Little Devils!*"

There was a huge audience uproar, confetti, and streamers fell from the heavens as fireworks exploded from the stage. The Devils hugged and kissed and cried. They picked Brooklyn up into the air while spotlights bounced upon her face. They finally passed her over to Tristan, who seemed to be in shock. He held her in his arms as tears of ecstasy rolled down both their cheeks. The other bands rushed to the stage to congratulate the winners as well as the judges and anyone else that could fit on the New York set.

As the fireworks ceased and the confetti stopped raining from above, Adonis spoke into the mic, "Tristan . . . Tristan . . . you've done it . . ." He handed the microphone to Tristan. "What have you got to say for yourself?" Adonis asked as he passed the mic to the proud and shocked mentor.

Tristan took the microphone from Adonis. He was out of breath, filled with emotion and struggling to compose himself. He took Brooklyn's hand and wiped his own tears of joy from his face with the hand that held the mic. The arena grew silent as he began to speak. "I am so thankful to you Americans and of course to you judges, and, Adonis, I thank you with my heart and soul. First, I want to recognize the others who have worked so very hard on this journey along with us—Delilah and Citi Girls, Jamison and Sincerely, Billy, my good friend, and Rising Tides, and of course Devin and Blood Red. Guys, you deserved to win as much as we did." The audience cheered as Tristan continued, "My Precious Little Devils, and my precious little love," he added as he kissed Brooklyn on the forehead, "in all my centuries in the music industry and the entertainment field, I have never worked with a more talented, creative, and driven bunch of performers. I've had the most memorable time of my life with you, Garrett, Colin, Damian, and my devilish Dazzel, my friends . . . my family. These past weeks have been filled with fun, laughter, and a lot of love. And, Brooklyn . . . you are what dreams are made of."

Tristan handed the mic back to Adonis and bent down and kissed Brooklyn. The fans continued to roar as Adonis handed the mic over to the overwhelmed, emotional Brooklyn.

Brooklyn barley recovering, through tears of her own, began speaking. "America, judges, Devils, Adonis, thank you! I am very grateful to all of you. Tris, you continue to fill my world with fireworks and fantasies that dare to come true. I know that this is just the beginning of a never-ending story, the beginning of the greatest adventure of our lives. I love you, Tristan." And with that Brooklyn could no longer hold back her tears. She buried herself in Tristan while Damian rescued her and took the microphone.

Damian, the spokesman, proudly began to speak. "On behalf of myself and my extremely emotional Devils and my extremely emotional mentor and dear friend, I want to reiterate the thank you and appreciation we feel toward you America, to our judges, and to Adonis as well as the sponsors. This clearly is an amazing time for music. Tristan, you are an extreme musical genius. The Devils would be absolutely nothing without your mentoring, your patience, your motivation, and especially your trust, tolerance, and love! We are all honored to have worked with you, and we all feel privileged to call you our friend. We couldn't be more excited by the fact that we get to tour with you together. That to me is the best part of winning.

The spectators rose to their feet in admiration of Damian's speech. Garrett whispered to Damian, "Great speech," and then to Brooklyn, "You sucked!"

Adonis recouped the mic and began to address the wild onlookers as well as the Devils. "America, it's been magical night for the Devils, filled with glory and surprises. However, I have one of the biggest surprises left for the Devils yet to come. I promise you this, when we return the Devils, America, the universe will be astounded. This promises to be the grandest finale ever . . . when we come back."

Backstage was swarming with photographers and press. Brooklyn ran to makeup, past the reporters, past the interviewers, and within moments, she was again ready to face anyone.

She tried to find Tristan, but with all the confusion, he was nowhere in sight. Little did she know he was hiding in a private dressing room, preparing to give her a surprise of a lifetime—at least he hoped it would be!

The Devils were bombarded by the press. A reporter yelled over to Brooklyn, "How does it feel to be America's brightest star?" she asked.

"Amazing!" Brooklyn answered.

"What was it like working with the sexy Tristan Bondage?" asked another reporter.

Dazzel yelled out "Hot!" while Brooklyn answered, "The best experience of my life!"

Yet another reporter put her arm around Brooklyn and asked quietly, "You seem to have a very special relationship, you and Tristan. Did that make it more difficult to work together?" she asked.

"Not at all, we grew closer with each moment that we spent together," Brooklyn answered.

"Especially in the bedroom," volunteered Dazzel.

Adonis yelled out, "Devils, sixty seconds!"

Brooklyn excused herself and looked for Tristan once again before she went back onto the stage. "Guys, anyone see Tristan?" she asked.

"Can't you do without him for one minute?" Damian asked, annoyed.

Brooklyn answered, "I can but I don't want to."

Blood Red had just completed their farewell song. The spectators screamed in admiration of the band that had come so close. The favorites from day one, they were hugged by the judges and saluted by their followers. Devin took the mic and announced. "It is a privilege and an honor to be able to join the Precious Little Devils on tour. We want to thank the judges and the sponsors for an overwhelming experience, and of course Adonis for inviting us to partake in this amazing journey. One last thing, Tristan, my friend, good job!"

"Give them some love!" Adonis screamed through the mic. "Now," Adonis began, "America, as promised I have one last astonishing revelation this evening. Devils, please come join me." The Devils entered the stage and stood behind Adonis as the admirers continued to applaud. "I have a special guest star who would like to perform in your honor, Devils. Come stand by me, Brooklyn, and help me announce your surprise guest," Adonis offered. Brooklyn walked over to Adonis, who took her hand and held it. He leaned over so that his face would be directly in front of hers and asked, "Are you ready?"

"Ready," she replied.

Adonis spoke clearly into the microphone, "It is my extreme pleasure to present to you, going solo on this stage for the very first time, the man who has helped shape the fate of Devils and who is now about to pave the road to his own destiny, accompanied by the Precious Little Devil boy. The one, the only . . . the rebellious Tristan Bondage. Live!"

Brooklyn's mouth fell opened and her eyes grew wide in astonishment as she covered her mouth with her hand. Tristan walked onto the stage wearing an overly impressive gold Swarovski-crystal-inlaid jacket bordered with black crystals. His pants were made of black leather, fitting him tightly and adorned with gold high-top sneakers. He was in full makeup including but not limited to mascara, eye liner, and red lipstick. His Fender guitar was draped upon his waist as he made his way to the golden pedestal, which awaited his arrival in the center of the stage. He raised his guitar into the air. The onlookers rose to their feet before he even began his performance and chanted his name: "Tristan, Tristan, Tristan." Brooklyn looked on in amazement. He commanded the stage as the spotlight shined upon him.

When he approached the golden pedestal, he turned to Brooklyn and motioned to her with his index finger to join him and said, "Come her, little girl." He sat down and patted the small pedestal next to him, beckoning her to sit beside him. When she was seated, he turned to her and kissed her and the crowd screamed.

Tristan turned to the audience and said, "I'm a little bit nervous, but let's see what happens. Brooklyn this is for you." Tristan began to play his guitar and sing "I Need You" by Marc Anthony. Brooklyn considered the fact that Tristan was performing especially for her or even the fact that he was performing at all the greatest and most precious surprise of the evening. However, she would soon find out just how treasured the performance was and that in fact the performance wasn't even the true epiphany.

From the day that I met you, girl
I knew that our love would be
Everything that I ever wanted in my life
The moment you spoke my name
I knew everything had changed
Because of you I felt my life would be complete
Oh, baby, I need you
For the rest of my life
I need you, to make everything right
I love you and I'll never deny . . . I love you
Nothing matters but you my love
And only God above would be the one
To know exactly how I feel
I could die in your arms right now
Knowing that you somehow
Would take my soul and keep it deep within your heart . . .

Tristan sang those verses softly, but when he reached the bridge in the song, he stood and handed Dazzel his guitar. He then reached down and captured Brooklyn's two hands and coaxed her to a standing position as well. Then he got down on one knee (still holding her hands) and sang,

I need you, for the rest of my life
I need you, say that you'll be my wife
Oh, I love you

Won't you, marry me, marry me
I need you . . .

Brooklyn realized that Tristan had just proposed to her in the most romantic, tender, and loving way possible, through a song, and at that moment everyone seemed to disappear except Tristan. When the song ended, still on one knee, he professed, "I love you, Brooklyn, you are my universe. Would you do me the greatest honor of becoming my wife?"

Her eyes shined through her tears as she answered, "I love you, Tristan. I would feel privileged to become your wife."

Tristan stood and pulled a huge diamond ring from his tight pocket and placed it on her finger, Tristan turned to the audience and yelled, "She said yes, everyone! She said yes!" and then turned to her and deeply and dramatically kissed her.

The fans silent until now, half holding tissues to wipe their own tears of joy away, suddenly became alive and once again chaos broke lose in the arena. Just then Dazzel dragged a large prop from the back of the stage, a life-size, five-foot diamond on wheels over to Brooklyn. The audience howled and Adonis, yelled, "What a way to end the show of the century, with the engagement of the century! Only it's not over yet. Tristan, the Devils insisted on a fabulous prewedding gift for you, so together they made arrangements to get you a little something from our home in London." With that Meredith and Joan walked out on stage, tear-stained yet overjoyed and congratulated the two with an overabundance of hugs and kisses for both.

"You didn't think we'd miss this event, did you?" exclaimed Joan as she clung to her son, who was so choked up he couldn't even respond.

The confetti poured down upon the stage once more as Adonis closed the season. "I promised you the grandest finale in history and so it was. America, please watch for the concert dates as they unfold. Until next season! Good night."

Tristan grabbed Brooklyn and held her tight as the set went dark and the colorful rain ceased. He whispered in her ear, "You've made me the happiest man in the world, love, thank you." Brooklyn buried her face in Tristan's chest while he put both his arms around her.

Dazzel came up behind them to wish them well. "Look at the two of you, I don't know whose mascara is running more," Dazzel commented.

"I'm just so happy," Brooklyn told her drag sister.

"And so emotional," Dazzel added as he looked at Tristan and began to address hm. "What if she would have said no?" Dazzel asked.

Tristan, now smiling, replied, "I would have followed that song with 'I Won't Give Up.' I was prepared to do it just in case."

Brooklyn started laughing. "Did you really think I would have said no?" she inquired.

"I thought there might be a chance," he replied, half-joking with her.

"Nothing like once again stealing an intimate moment with millions," Damian said as he too wished them congratulations.

Lastly Adonis hugged Tristan and gave Brooklyn a giant kiss. He then reminded the Devils and Tristan that they had to be at the victory party set up for them at the hotel with guests and the press in an hour. Tristan suggested that Brooklyn go to makeup and wardrobe here so they could make a proper entrance. She touched Tristan's face, took Meredith by the hand, and was gone.

* * *

The Devils rode to the ball in a pink limousine. Tristan helped Brooklyn, his mom, his sister, and Dazzel out of the car and walked inside arm in arm with his bride-to-be while Garrett escorted his mom and Damian his sister. Dazzel and Colin walked in arm and arm as well. The entrance to the victory party was embellished with a red carpet and filled with press and photographers. When they entered the room, they were immediately congratulated by all for both the win and the engagement.

Terence finally greeted them as the crowd around them thinned. He picked Brooklyn way up into the air and hugged Tristan tightly. "I'd like to formally ask you to be my best man," Tristan announced to Terence.

"I'd be honored," replied Terence and added, "Does that mean I get to escort Brooklyn's maid of honor, Dazzel?"

"I promise you this," Tristan said, "this will be quite an unconventional affair."

Terence nodded in agreement and asked, "Any idea where the wedding will be, or at least what country it will take place?"

Tristan replied, "I haven't thought that far ahead. I was concentrating on her saying yes first, but if it were up to me alone, it would be here and now. Only Brooklyn deserves the gayest, most marvelous wedding in the world, and I'm not about to rob her of that."

"So maybe you just ought to marry her at Madison Square Garden in front of millions during a concert. The two of you seem to be good at that," Damian joked sarcastically.

Tristan stopped dead in his tracks. The Devils all noticed the gleam in his eyes, that look of "I can make that happen."

"No, no, Tristan, that was a joke," Damian insisted.

Dazzel, wide-eyed and in disbelief, threatened, "You wouldn't dare."

"Why not?" asked Tristan.

"I love that idea."

"She's gonna kill us," said Damian right in front of Brooklyn as though she weren't present.

"No, Damian, she's just going to kill you," Dazzel remarked.

"It's not like I'm not standing here listening to this conversation." Brooklyn laughed. "I love the idea too, but I would marry Tristan anywhere—on the top of Mount Everest, in outer space, at the Garden."

"That's my girl," Tristan said proudly.

The grand ballroom had a huge stage that was mysteriously set up for a band to play on. Adonis approached Tristan and asked if he and Brooklyn might consider doing a number. "We'd love to," volunteered Tristan. Even if he had refused to cooperate, *So You Wanna Be a Rock Star* contractually owned Tristan and the Devils for the next three years. The Devils took the grand ballroom stage and began to play "Marry Me" by Bruno Mars. Tristan sang the first verse and Brooklyn came in on the second.

"It's a beautiful night, we're looking for something dumb to do."

"Hey, baby, I think I wanna marry you."

They did "I Won't Give Up" for their second song and finally "Demons" for their final act. Afterward Tristan and Brooklyn were whisked away by a local TV station and the press for a long-awaited conference. One reporter who seemed to be directing the press conference congratulated the couple for winning and then for both choosing the perfect mate. Then the questions began. "Tristan, do you think by asking Brooklyn to marry you took away from the glory of the win?"

Tristan thought for a second and then replied, "When I told the producers of my intention, we carefully considered that very question. It was discussed and decided that the winner would be announced first. If it were us, my engagement to my lovely bride to be would just enhance the win. The win was already celebrated in a very majestic way. If Blood Red had won, we would both have left the season victorious. Rumors of our romance were prevalent from day one, perhaps even before it actually existed, so what better way to end the show?"

"Brooklyn," another reporter asked, "were you surprised?"

"At which, the win or the proposal?" she replied.

The reporters in the room laughed. "Both," another one volunteered.

"Blood Red seemed to be the favorites all along. I was surprised that we won, but when Tristan asked me to marry him, the win seemed insignificant. And yes, I was shocked. He told me he loved me, he asked me to live with him, but he never asked me to marry him," Brooklyn stated.

"I needed the right place and the right time as well as the courage. I wasn't nervous to ask her. I was nervous she'd say no. I figured she wouldn't have the nerve to refuse in front of the nation." Tristan laughed. Jokingly Tristan turned to Brooklyn and took her hand. "You still want to marry me, right? You haven't changed your mind, have you?"

"Never," she answered.

As dawn approached Tristan's medical issues were threatening to become a problem. It was a long day and night, both joyous and stressful, filled with emotion. When the pain in his legs became apparent to Brooklyn, she insisted that they leave. Once again the Devils and Tristan found themselves sleeping back at the hotel along with Joan, Meredith, Blood Red, and Devin.

The night had been overwhelming. Back in Tristan's suite Brooklyn quickly undressed while Tristan sat upon the bed just smiling. Once in her tee and panties she jumped on the bed next to Tristan and began to help him undress. "Are you so exhausted?" he asked.

"Nope," she replied. "Wide awake, and so in love." She looked at Tristan tenderly and fell into his arms. "Baby, are you okay?"

"I am amazing," Tristan told her. "I took some pain meds, so I'm flying." Brooklyn put her hands on Tristan's cheeks, cradling them in her palms and kissed him. "Umm, you taste delicious," he exclaimed. "Come here and give me some more," he gently demanded. She moved closer to him and he began to kiss her as though he were actually tasting her.

"You better not start something that you can't finish," Brooklyn warned.

Tristan turned to put his arms around her but was suddenly surprised by a sharp, electrifying pain up and down his right leg. It happened so abruptly that he hadn't the time to hide it from Brooklyn as he winced. "Awww, you're still hurting," she said compassionately.

"I'm all right," he argued. "It just hurt for a second," he insisted. "Now where were we?" Tristan whispered as he resumed his prior position.

"I don't know where we were, but I know where we are going and that's to sleep," Brooklyn said insistently. Brooklyn hated to refuse any type of sex Tristan offered but he was still intermittently in pain and she didn't want to risk him being hurt more.

"Really?" he whispered disappointedly. "Come on, love," he attempted one last time.

"Later," she whispered and laid her head on his chest. He instinctively wrapped his arms around her and within minutes both were asleep.

* * *

With love comes sacrifice. Tristan was about to make one of the most difficult, painful, and heart-wrenching decisions of his life. His belief that he was doing the right thing for all those concerned might perhaps ease the emotional agony he was already feeling. He sat by the window and stared blankly as the morning brought about a surrealistic reality he would be forced to face.

Tristan watched as the snow began to fall upon the city streets and thought they had won the contest, and he was going to marry the love of his life. Life couldn't get any better. So why then was Tristan so sad? He had to try and push that sorrow somewhere else in his universe and deal with it at a later time.

A newspaper lay in front of him with a large impressive spread covering last night's events. He looked at Brooklyn, who was still peacefully asleep. He loved watching her sleep, especially knowing that, as soon as she awoke, he would be her first thought as she opened her eyes. It had been a struggle for Tristan to finally believe in her love. London had convinced him that marrying her was going to be all right. He began to believe that their lives together would be amazing despite his affliction. He gained the confidence to believe that their love would guide them through whatever life had to offer.

Brooklyn began to stir, putting his thoughts temporarily on hold. He walked over to the bed and brushed her hair away from her face. He sat down next to her and showed her the centerspread inside the newspaper and offered her the rest of his coffee that he had barely tasted. She loved the newspaper and was grateful for the coffee. Tristan was just grateful for her. Brooklyn thought that Tristan was very unanimated considering the huge news article but just figured him to still be tired. She looked into his piercing blue eyes and thought that she noticed a hint of sadness and asked him if he was all right. He nodded and told her she was beautiful. She smiled at him and mouthed the words "I love you," then ran into the bathroom to brush her teeth and shower.

As soon as Tristan heard the sound of the shower running, he picked up his phone and dialed Dr. Cheng. His hands were trembling and his heart was breaking as he informed the Chinese doctor of his change of heart. He searched for the right words to tell her that he no longer thought that the adoption of little Shakey would be wise. There was no response from the doctor, only silence. Tristan perceived uneasiness in the pit of his stomach as he listened to the awkward silence on the other end of the phone. He felt compelled to continue his explanation despite the doctor's lack of words. He told her how he thought it selfish and unfair to adopt a child in the midst of beginning a new life with his wife-to-be. He explained that he didn't want to overwhelm Brooklyn in the light of the fact she would be touring the country and abroad. He imagined that touring would not be a stable or valid lifestyle for a tiny child. The doctor finally spoke and said coldly, "I understand," and she hung up the phone abruptly. Tristan stared at the phone in disbelief. He noticed his own tears falling from his eyes and wiped them away. He felt as if he had just relinquished a piece of his heart, and no matter how hard he rationalized the fact that he made the responsible choice for all involved, he felt no relief from the sorrow he was feeling.

Brooklyn was still a free spirit and it had never been his intention of taking the "free" away from the "spirit." He also did believe that touring would be detrimental to a baby. Besides Brooklyn needed to focus on her career now, not a baby that *he* so desperately wanted. Tristan never realized that Brooklyn was as excited as he was to welcome that little miracle, "Shakey," into their lives as well.

Tristan knew that Brooklyn would certainly suspect something when she came out of the shower and saw the agonizing state he was in. He could hide physical pain from her at times, but this emotional torture would prove to be more difficult to disguise. Tristan wrote her a note informing her that he was going to show Joan and Meredith the newspaper and then spend some time some time with Terence. He suggested that she invite his family to go shopping and see the sights while he prepared for tonight's press conference and mini concert in the grand ballroom of the hotel once again. He ended it by saying he would miss her terribly and of course that he loved her.

When Brooklyn emerged from the bathroom, she spotted the note he left on the door for her and smiled. She was content that he left because this gave her some time alone to reenact the events of last night in her mind as she leisurely dressed. However, her thoughts of last night were suddenly interrupted as he singing cell signaled a phone call. She grabbed the phone and answered "Good morning" as she thought it might be the Devils calling to tell her about the newspaper.

"Brooklyn?" Dr. Cheng asked.

Surprised at the voice on the other end, Brooklyn answered, "Yes, Dr. Cheng. How are you?"

"I've been better," she said with her thick Asian accent. Brooklyn asked her first if the baby was all right and without waiting for her answer she inquired as to what was wrong.

Dr. Cheng knew from the sound of Tristan's voice earlier that his decision to give up that baby was killing him. She was intuitive enough to realize that Tristan was basing his conclusion upon an illusion that it was best for Brooklyn and that was trying to be what he considered responsible and unselfish towards Brooklyn rather than from his heart for the child. The doctor explained to Brooklyn what transpired just a short time before, knowing that Brooklyn had no clue as to what Tristan tried to do. "Oh my god," Brooklyn exclaimed, "what was he thinking?" she said, referring to Tristan.

"He was thinking of you. He did not wish to overwhelm or inundate you with extra responsibilities," Dr. Cheng replied. The doctor went on to tell Brooklyn that he sounded devastated by his own resolution and that, although she tried to comprehend his concerns, she needed to call her before she could rest.

Brooklyn felt awful knowing how badly Tristan wanted that baby. It would have been annihilating to him to have abandoned his dream of adopting Shakey. Brooklyn was determined not to allow that to happen and asked Dr. Cheng if it were possible to get the papers in order and the baby ready for her to be released into her custody. She announced that she would be able to come for her shortly. Dr. Cheng was overjoyed.

Brooklyn rushed to get dressed and leave before Tristan returned to the room. She called Dazzel and demanded that she meet her in the lobby in fifteen minutes and that she would explain later. She then called over to Joan and Meredith's room, hoping Tristan had already visited them and left. Meredith and Joan were alone. Tristan had been there, confessed his devastating plight to Meredith, and left to see Terence. Hearing the disappointment in Meredith's voice at Tristan's decision, she said, "Meredith, would you and Joan care to secretly accompany me to the hospital to pick up the baby? I'm going to surprise that dumb brother of yours tonight during the concert," Brooklyn explained.

"I knew there was a reason I loved you so much," the excited Meredith replied.

Brooklyn went on to say, "I just can't allow Tristan to hurt any more than he's already been hurt."

"I told Tristan that it was not a proper decision to make without consulting the other half of him," Meredith exclaimed. "Joan will be so excited to become a grandmother," she added.

"I'll meet you in the lobby in fifteen minutes," Brooklyn said, and Meredith agreed.

Brooklyn left the room leaving Tristan no note. She decided to let him worry just a little in hopes that it might teach him a lesson not to make such rash decisions without her ever again. He deserved a little something to think about. Dazzel was already waiting in the lobby for Brooklyn, and Joan and Meredith joined them on the decent of the next elevator.

* * *

Meanwhile Tristan took refuge in Terence's hotel room, crying his heart out while Terence scolded him. "How could you ever think to get away with making such a foolish choice and not consulting your wife to be about something so important?" he asked. Tristan tried to explain to Terence that, if he would have told Brooklyn first, she would never have allowed him to make that phone call. He went on to say that Brooklyn was a lot less selfish than himself and would have accepted that baby just to make him happy. Terence replied, "Did you ever consider the fact that she might love and want that baby too?"

Tristan answered, "We're going on tour. That means somewhere different every couple of nights, traveling, packing, late hours, plus she agreed to marry me. Her entire free lifestyle will be disrupted. I don't want to risk totally overwhelming her. She's liable to leave us all!" Tristan finished.

Terence glared at him angrily. "Do you even know her?" he asked Tristan, referring to Brooklyn. "If someone made that kind of decision for me, affecting the rest of my life, without talking to me, I would be pissed. That alone would motivate me to leave them," Terence yelled. He walked over to Tristan's phone, picked it up, and handed it to him. "You better fix this now, you better call that Asian doctor and tell her you were temporally insane and need some time to talk it over with Brooklyn. If someone made that decision for me, I'd be gone!" Terence reiterated.

Tristan required not a second more of Terence's coaxing to dial Dr. Cheng. "Dr. Cheng, it's Tristan. I made a grave mistake this morning," Tristan admitted.

"Yes, I believe you did," said the doctor. "Please hold on for a moment while I get to my desk," she requested. Tristan's timing could not have been better—or worse, for in front of the doctor stood Brooklyn, Dazzel, Joan, and Meredith. The doctor put Tristan on hold and told the others with a motion of her finger in front of her lips. "Shhh, Tristan is on the line, as you've no doubt heard. I'm going to put him on speaker phone. Perhaps it will shed some light upon what he is truly feeling. . . . Tristan, I'm here now," the doctor said, once again coldly.

"My phone call to you this morning was quite impulsive. I made a decision based on what I thought was the responsible thing to do. I was not trying to be selfish, when in fact by not discussing it with Brooklyn was probably one of the most selfish acts I've committed. I didn't consider the fact that Brooklyn might love that baby too. Most importantly I forgot to feel what was in my heart. You see, I love

Brooklyn very much and for a second I became frightened that, with all that was happening, she might be too overwhelmed to the point of leaving me. I always felt that it was difficult for her to commit to anything past the fact that she loved me, and now she was being forced to commit to everything at once," Tristan tearfully confessed. The doctor knew that it must have been difficult for Tristan to make either of those calls. Finally no longer able to compose himself, he paused and then, barely being able to speak, he added, "I want you to know that I love that baby with my entire heart." The secret audience could hear him holding back his tears.

Brooklyn felt guilty for not telling him her intentions, but she wanted him to realize that he couldn't make such decisions of importance alone, and also, she desperately wanted to surprise him. Dr. Cheng intuitively told him that since he had so easily changed his mind, she'd have to think about his stability. She asked that he meet her in her office tomorrow at 11:00 a.m. to discuss the matter. She explained that this would give him the time he needed to discuss the adoption with Brooklyn. Cruel as the doctor sounded toward Tristan, he was still happy to have the chance to prove himself and his true intentions.

Tristan, having some glimmer of hope for retrieving Shakey, concentrated on reaching Brooklyn. He had been with Terence for hours and thought it strange that Brooklyn hadn't tried to reach him. He dialed her, but she didn't answer. She felt terrible that he felt so sad and longed to comfort him. She knew his decision was made for honorable reasons and because he loved her so much. She also knew he was suffering and feared it might affect his health as stress caused his body to generate pain. Brooklyn sent a text to Terence, asking him to please stay with Tristan. She quickly explained what she was planning and that she didn't wish Tristan to be affected physically by the torture he was apparently going through, even though it was partially self-inflicted.

Tristan decided to return to his hotel suite in the hopes that Brooklyn left him a note as to her whereabouts. The uninvited Terence followed him in an effort to show some respect for Brooklyn's text. He could see Tristan was indeed stressed and held some concern that the pressure might weigh heavily upon Tristan's condition. Terence texted Brooklyn, agreeing with her own concern, and suggested that she call him. There was no point in letting him worry about her on top of worrying about how to construct his redemption for the meeting with the doctor. She excused herself and went into the hallway to dial Tristan.

"Hey, baby, I just saw that you called," she told him, pretending that nothing at all transpired.

"Where are you, love?" he inquired.

"We're all out shopping, your sister, your mom, myself, and Dazzel," she replied.

"Are you having fun?" he asked.

"Yes, I am but I miss you," she told him.

"Not as much as I miss you." He laughed.

Brooklyn went on to explain that she didn't leave him a note because they were all waiting for her in the lobby and she was late. He in turn apologized for leaving this morning while she was in the shower without saying good-bye. He told her that he expected to come back to the room before she had left. "No worries," Brooklyn said and added, "besides I love when you spend time with Terence. It gives me more time to shop," she said, teasing him. He smiled at the phone and told Brooklyn he loved her while she reiterated the same sentiment to him.

When they ended the call Tristan said to Terence jokingly, "See, it's happening already. She's glad that I spent time with you so she could have some freedom from me while she shops!" Terence laughed and slapped Tristan in the back of his head. "Hey, instead of worrying about Brooklyn choosing to shop over spending time with you, why don't you concentrate on reality and think about what you plan to say to her about that baby? By the way what are you going to say to her?" Terence asked.

"I have no idea," Tristan admitted, but it would be all he could think about for the next couple of hours.

* * *

The ladies finally left the hospital with Shakey and began their quest. They had a lot of ground to cover and little time with which to do it. They stopped for a quick bite and then proceeded to the Toys R Us on Broadway to secure bottles, binkies, toys, clothes, and nappies, as Meredith called them, which translated into diapers. Joan requested that a crib be placed in her hotel room tonight so that she could bond with her new granddaughter. Brooklyn was thankful for her offer since it would give her time to spend alone with Tristan, and she wouldn't have to worry about leaving the press conference early. From there they found a specialty shop in the village where Brooklyn purchased a matching costume for her and the baby to wear tonight. Aunt Dazzel wheeled Shakey in the pink stroller she herself selected while Shakey napped. It seemed as though the timing was perfect. It was approaching five o'clock and they had finished their purchases. They had dinner at a cafe, while getting to know Shakey. Brooklyn seemed a natural. Her maternal instincts proved to be spot on while Dazzel and Meredith were totally enjoying the roll of Aunt Joan seemed to be in heaven. Shakey had stolen her heart just as she had stolen Tristan's.

Six o'clock arrived quickly. Tristan, now getting nervous that the women in his life were still out gallivanting, called Brooklyn in somewhat of a panic. "Love, you do remember that we have a little concert tonight?" Tristan said, teasing her.

"Tris, we're running a little late," Brooklyn announced.

"Really?" he announced sarcastically.

"Tris, can you please do the sound check for us?" she begged.

"Done." He laughed. "You know, love, this is kind of a big deal. It's only invited guests, but I believe they've invited all of New York and half of LA," he joked. "It's not like it's going to be all over TV, the eleven o'clock news, and a probable documentary. No worries, just take your time," he again said sarcastically.

"Please, Tristan, don't be mad. I'll tell you what if you cover the opening song, I'll join you for the second in a giant grand entrance that will make you so proud and happy. Please, please," Brooklyn begged.

"And the worst part of this is I miss you and I wanted to hold you for a minute before the conference, but you're lucky, I love you. Grand entrance, second song," Tristan said.

"Thank you, I love you," Brooklyn said, relieved as she pressed the End button. This gave her a little extra time to dress herself and the baby. Dazzel rushed to repaint as she needed to be there when the Devils were introduced. After all she was the guitarist, and her job was to escort Meredith and Joan down to the festivities.

Brooklyn dressed herself and Shakey in matching hot pink jackets with tails of course and hot pink leggings. The jacket was trimmed with black crystals that matched their tees underneath and dazzling black high-tops. Both of them wore two pigtails with hot pink rubber bands. Brooklyn intended to immediately give Tristan the feeling that they belonged together, the three of them.

Brooklyn carried Shakey down the elevator and through the lobby to the grand ballroom. As they approached, she heard Tristan singing one of his more prestigious hit songs and thought to herself, *He's so talented.* She traveled with Shakey to the back of the grand ballroom, where security led her through to the backstage entrance, where Meredith and Joan were watching the show. She handed the baby to Meredith and became ready to make a grand entrance and surprise Tristan.

And a grand entrance, as promised, was made. The Devils began to play a child's rendition of "London Bridge Is Falling Down." Tristan thought to himself, *She's lost it.* He had to laugh at her conception of a grand entrance. Above the stage was a video screen depicting little British children acting out the song "London Bridge" as Brooklyn sang it right on stage. The audience was amused at her childlike interpretation of the song. However, Tristan was confused. She watched him standing in the wings of the stage with his hand over his face, shaking his head in disbelief. When Brooklyn hit the verse "Take the key and lock her up, lock her up, lock her up. Take the key and lock her up, my fair lady," She stopped suddenly. Tristan lifted his hand off his face and looked up frightened of what was to come next. "Tristan, can you come here please?" Brooklyn called out.

Almost embarrassed he arrived back on stage. He whispered, "Okay, you have everyone's attention, even mine. What the hell are you doing?" he finished in a whispered frenzy.

"I need someone else British to complete 'London Bridge,'" Brooklyn said as she looked around.

All of a sudden Meredith came from behind the stage for her five minutes of fame. Tristan turned pale as Brooklyn positioned her in front of Tristan. Meredith took Tristan's hands and raised them along with hers and said, "Tristan, you know the way the game goes."

By this time Tristan had no choice but to go with it as the Devils started the song again where Brooklyn left off. Brooklyn darted behind stage and grabbed the baby from Joan's arms and ran under Meredith and Tristan's bridge. The Devils ran behind him to cover him in case he passed out from the shock of what had just happened. Facing Tristan's side of the bridge, Shakey reached her tiny arms out to Tristan, who stood there dumbfounded, astounded, and full of emotional tears as he took the baby from Brooklyn's arms. "What did you do?" was all he could manage to say to Brooklyn through his tears.

"I saved you from a life of regret," she whispered back. Tristan stood in front of the stage and introduced Shakey to the audience. "This is our daughter, Shakey. We just adopted her." And the entire ballroom rose to their feet and applauded. "And the other half of the London bridge is my sister, Meredith," he added.

While the crowd applauded, Brooklyn took Tristan's hand and whispered, "And the next time you make a decision like that without me, I'll cut your dick off!"

He looked at her and squeezed her hand lovingly, "If I ever make a decision without you again, I'll let you," he whispered back. "I tried to fix it," he added.

She whispered back, "I know, that's why I'm allowing you to live. And besides my daughter needs a daddy. Now go sing something wonderful," she ordered. That's exactly what Tristan did. He sang "Wonderful" by Adam Ant to his baby while holding her and then let Brooklyn and the Devils finish the concert as he held his baby backstage along with Joan and cried his eyes out once again.

The Devils with Brooklyn performed for the next hour. When they had finished, Tristan joined them on stage still holding Shakey. They took a bow and then the press consumed them. The reporters and photographers stayed long and delve deep into their personal lives, their plans for the future, and the fact that yesterday they got engaged and today they had a child.

At midnight Tristan finally stood up and announced that their baby, who had long since fallen asleep in an adorable pair of pajamas that Aunt Meredith bought for her to change into and had to be literally put to bed. He reached for Brooklyn's hand, kissed it, and asked her if she were ready. Brooklyn thanked them, allowed Dazzel to kiss Shakey on the top of her head, and said good night.

The little exhausted family was ultimately alone with one another. "Come with me to your mom's room. We put the crib in their room," Brooklyn explained.

"She can't have a babysitter on her first night with us," Tristan commented.

"Tris, it's her grandmother, not a babysitter. Besides we will have her for the rest of our lives. Give your mom and sister a chance to get to know her." Tristan agreed that she was right. They left their baby with Joan and Meredith, who were excited to have temporary custody of the child. Tristan gently put the baby in the crib and stared at her for a moment. "Now take good care of her," Tristan insisted. He turned to his mom and said, "We have the day off, we can all spend a lovely day together tomorrow." Brooklyn watched his family interaction with a smile on her face. Tristan turned to her and took her hand. They all said their good nights and Tristan left with Brooklyn at his side.

The two walked hand in hand to Tristan's suite. The room was dark and silent. The only light was an eerie glow shining through the window from the city lights, which made the room seem sexy and mysterious. Tristan pulled his fiancée close to him, caressing her tenderly. He whispered directly in her ear, "How can I ever begin to thank you."

She whispered back, "You can start with a kiss." He touched her face and traced her lips with one finger in the darkness. He bent over and pressed his lips against her, breaking the silence of the room by the sound of their kisses magnified by the darkness. With each kiss Tristan grew more aroused. Their jackets fell to the floor. He lifted her tee over her head and unfastened her bra. She slowly unbuttoned his shirt while he softly ran his finger up and down the lines of her breasts, sending chills throughout her body. He lifted her off the ground into his arms and carried her onto the bed. He took her with and urgency and a passion she had never felt before his sweet kisses heighted her climax. His own climax left him trembling and drained.

Tristan sat against the headboard, leaning against a soft fluffy pillow. Brooklyn joined him, still weak and glowing from Tristan's passion. She sat up against him and pulled his arms around her. He kissed the back of her neck and asked the question he had been dreading all day. "Don't you want to yell at me?" Tristan blurted out.

"I think that you probably beat yourself up enough for the two of us today. I was in Dr. Cheng's office when you called today. She put you on speaker phone and we heard everything you had to say to her," Brooklyn confessed.

"Oh lord," he said.

"I know that you did what you did because of me. You volunteered to surrender that baby that you love so much for me, and I couldn't let you do that. I will never allow you to give up anything you love on my account. You've been through too much pain and suffering and you never deserved any of it. Besides, I wanted Shakey also," she announced. Tristan was flawed at her forgiveness. It was something he would never forget as he fell in love with her all over again.

Tristan embraced her compassionately, which made every vessel in her body want him all over again. "I can't get enough of you," Tristan said as though he were reading Brooklyn's thoughts. Tristan moved gently on top of her leaving her trapped underneath the strength of his body. Their hearts danced inside their chests as their passions burned inside the lower portions of their bodies. Their lovemaking grew more intense and reached a euphoric height incomparable to anything either of them had ever felt before.

Tristan rolled over on his back and took her hand. He kissed it and laid it on his chest placing his own hand over hers. Brooklyn stared up into the ceiling and whispered, "I never dreamed that anything could feel so good."

"You have taken a part of my soul that had been gone for a long time and given it back to me," Tristan said as he turned to Brooklyn and kissed her.

Chapter 11

I Choose You

The element of excitement had been deleted with the finale of the television show. A let down comparable to the feeling one experiences the day after Christmas was felt by all. However, New Year's Eve, so to speak of was imminent, as Tristan and the Devils began to prepare for their up and coming world tour, which was scheduled to commence only a short month away. The bulk of the preparation and development for the tour would fall upon Tristan. He would have to produce and plan the performances, the special effects, the costumes, the dance, and the encore numbers. There was also the small task of planning and executing the wedding of the century to take place in Madison Square Garden so that Tristan could invite the world to attend.

The rehearsals would become intense, as well as the offers to appear on every show imaginable. Invitations from talk shows, variety shows, tabloids, radio stations, and venues were pouring in, most of which Tristan would contractually be forced to accept.

The tension and stress would cause anyone to wind up in an insane asylum. However, Tristan was driven. Fortunately the Devils deep connection with their mentor caused them to be able to anticipate nearly every move he made and allowed them to act accordingly. Brooklyn, concerned with the fact that the pressure might affect Tristan's health, became his self-appointed assistant. She began to focus upon doing anything that might make his job and his life easier.

Their top priority began with making sure Shakey became settled in her tiny new life and developed some kind of routine. Along with a "proper English nanny," whom Tristan hired and whom lovingly became known as Mary Poppins, as well as Aunt Dazzel and her uncles, the Devils, the baby was well taken care of and very much loved. When their busy day ended or during an empty moment in their schedule, both Brooklyn and Tristan made sure to spend some special time with their daughter either separately or together. Shakey was a blessing for the two of them as they both needed something besides each other to love and obsess over.

Because their day began at 6:00 a.m. and didn't end sometimes until after midnight, the Devils made their new home inside Tristan's mansion. They left only to rehearse the special effects and make appearances around town. Tristan worked closely with Adonis, who made himself available to travel to the mansion. This proved to be a godsend to Tristan, who was lucky enough to get four or five hours of sleep a night. Brooklyn mastered the technical aspect of the concert production and was able to help with sound and light direction. Still Tristan's schedule or lack of schedule, as well as the pressure he felt to complete the project on time, began to take a toll on his health. By the time the second week of production ended, Tristan was suffering from severe exhaustion, which caused the pain he already lived with to worsen. He began to delve heavily into his pain medication, secretly, so Brooklyn wouldn't be alarmed.

It was not unusual for Brooklyn to find Tristan fast asleep on the floor of the nursery, next to Shakey's crib, since he insisted upon singing his daughter to sleep each night. It grew common for Brooklyn to visit the nursery and find him, gently wake him and then watch him limp into their bedroom, shower, and continue working with the Devils. She would tease him about spending all his free time, sleeping with the other woman in his life, and he would kiss her and insist that she not be jealous. He would then continually reassure her that he was fine. Brooklyn did her best to believe him because she had no other choice, but she still worried about his health and emotional state.

Somewhere in the midst of the third week of madness, something inside Tristan snapped. Brooklyn had been massaging his legs, which she so often did to relieve his pain, when on this particular night they hurt him so badly that even her gentle touch greatly enhanced his agony. "Brooklyn," he uttered softly.

"Am I hurting you?" she asked.

"Come here please," he vocalized.

She stopped massaging him and kissed his shoulder. Tristan sat up and turned to her. Tears were streaming down his face as he declared, "Baby, I don't think I can do this . . . I'm so tired, my legs hurt unbelievably, I'm taking way too much pain medication than I can handle just to be able to function, and worst of all I feel as though I'm letting you down. We haven't spent any quality time together, nor have we made love in forever. I'm so emotionally weak it frightens me."

Brooklyn took his hand and held it to her own heart. She brushed the tears off his face with her other hand and began to speak compassionately to him. "Trist, I'm so proud of you. I love you more each day that passes if even possible. I'm so thankful for your strength, but I'm strong too, so if you're running low on yours, come and borrow some of mine. Baby, you need to sleep a little more and delegate. You're so spot on, so on schedule. I'm flawed by your talent and I get off on your wisdom. You've got my heart, baby. I don't care what kind of time we spend together as long as we're together."

Tristan laid his head down on Brooklyn's lap as she stroked his hair. He listened to her and took comfort in what she had to say to him. He knew she was right, and somehow his body seemed to relax and the pain in his legs grew dull. It was Brooklyn's motivation that caused him to be able to continue. Tristan started to speak of the wedding plans, which made Brooklyn unbelievably happy. They shared their thoughts about the wedding party and the colors they would choose and the vows they had decided to sing to one another. In the back of his mind Tristan knew he could not afford a hospital stay, even a brief one, he decided to start delegating per her suggestion.

Tristan resolved he would sleep in the next morning and he also decided it was time for him and Brooklyn to make love. He kissed her gently and caressed her caringly, and when he awoke next to Brooklyn at 11:00 a.m., he felt like a new person. "You saved my life again," he whispered.

"It's the magic of sleep," she teased. "Now stay here and don't move, I'll be right back," she demanded as she ran into the bathroom.

Tristan openly and defiantly disobeyed her orders and ran in the bathroom after her. She hadn't even finished brushing her teeth when he turned the shower on and dragged her into it along with himself, both still wearing T-shirts and underwear. He trapped her against the corner of the shower and began to kiss her wildly as the water soaked their clothes and ran down their bodies. He undressed and let her clothes fall to the shower floor while his followed. As the warm water poured down upon them, the steamy shower hid their bodies as their strong and barely controllable emotions were unleashed upon one other.

By some miracle of fate disguised as Tristan, everything for the tour was completed with three days to spare. Tristan wanted the Devils to use these days wisely and insisted they spend the time with their families and away from each other. Tristan wanted Brooklyn to see her family as well, but he didn't want to be away from her for even a second. "I think you should see your family too, love," he voiced. "It's a long tour," he added.

"Don't you like my family?" Brooklyn inquired.

"Of course, I love your family," he said, laughing."

"So then why don't we invite them here for dinner? They haven't even seen where I live now and they've only met Shakey once," she reminded him.

"I was hoping you'd suggest that," he admitted.

Brooklyn's mom and dad came alone. They were anxious to bond with the baby but even more interested in talking to Tristan just to ensure their daughter wasn't making a mistake. Brooklyn's mom was a great fan of Tristan Bondage and still felt awed by him each time they met. Tristan greeted Dawn and Greg as they entered the Gatsby mansion. He took their coats and offered them a seat and a drink while Brooklyn brought the baby downstairs. Dawn was beautiful, just as her daughter was and Greg still extremely handsome. Both her parents were younger than Tristan by several years, which was awkward to begin with knowing that Brooklyn loved and respected her family made Tristan slightly nervous having a one-on-one with them. However, confident that she loved him the way she did, Tristan knew in his heart that Brooklyn was her own person and couldn't be influenced by anybody, not even him.

Dinner was cordial and civilized. Dawn loved Shakey and spent a great deal of time laughing and playing with her during and after dinner. After a time Brooklyn decided to bath Shakey and get her ready for bed. Greg invited himself to accompany her, leaving Tristan and Dawn alone. "So," Tristan volunteered as he fidgeted in his seat.

"This is extremely weird for me," Dawn admitted. "You already know I was one of your biggest fans. I went to all your New York concerts and even brought Brooklyn to some. You know, when Brooklyn was less than a year I took her to one of your concerts. Some very tall boy with liberty spikes offered to hold her on his shoulders so that she'd be able to see. He was so nice, and I figured she would be safer six feet higher than in my arms in a mosh pit, so I let him. We were only steps from your stage and you reached out and touched Brooklyn's hand. I vowed never to wash my baby again," Dawn recollected.

"I didn't know that, but I kind of remember a baby was it at St. John's University?" Tristan asked.

"Yes, I think it was." Dawn laughed. "Just so you know, I'm still a fan, although if I were sitting here thirty-some-odd years ago, I would have passed out or at least asked you for your autograph," Dawn admitted.

"I don't suppose you still want it?" asked Tristan jokingly.

"I might," Dawn said, "but there's something I want more," she indicated.

"And what's that?" Tristan wondered out loud.

"I want you to love my daughter, treat her with respect, and give her a good life."

Shortly after, Brooklyn arrived back on the scene with Greg and the clean and pajama-clad Shakey.

Dawn took her granddaughter while Brooklyn knelt down between Tristan's legs where he sat. He smiled at her and pushed her hair away from her face. She stretched her lips up to his and kissed him. This caused Tristan to blush. He looked at his bride to be and mouthed the words "I love you." Tristan stood up and helped Brooklyn to her feet. He looked into her eyes and smiled as he caressed her face. Dawn observed the unconditional love for one another in both their eyes. Greg walked over and put his arm around Tristan and bluntly asked, "So how old are you anyway!"

"Daddy!" Brooklyn yelled, horrified. "This is the man I love and it wouldn't matter if he were ninety."

Tristan put his hand over his face and then on Brooklyn's shoulders. He whispered in her ear, "It's all right, love." Tristan then turned to Greg, "I love your daughter from the depths of my soul, and I can promise you this, she will never cry anything but tears of joy as long as she's with me. I have long ago decided to dedicate the rest of my life to making her happy. I thank God each day for her love. I live only to make each and every one of her dreams come true," Tristan declared.

"My daughter said she loves you, and after that Shakespearian speech, I have to believe you love her too. So welcome to our family," Greg exclaimed and hugged Tristan.

"We would like to take Shakey home with us for a few days and get to know our grandchild," Dawn asked.

Tristan looked at Brooklyn, who nodded. "I think it would be okay then," Tristan said and volunteered to pack a suitcase.

Ultimately alone Brooklyn sat on the couch laughing hysterically. "What's so funny?" Tristan asked.

"With that accent you did sound like a Shakespearian actor."

"Maybe, love, but I meant every word of it," he said tenderly.

"I know you did, you were amazing . . . you are amazing." Brooklyn sighed.

Tristan walked into the kitchen to get some white wine from the fridge, while Brooklyn undressed until she lay naked on the couch in anticipation of his return. Holding the wine, Tristan stopped in his tracks. He quickly put wine down and rushed over to Brooklyn, kneeling beside her and kissing her hand in the most seductive manner. "God, you're so beautiful," he murmured. With his lips he kissed her between her legs as he gently caressed her thighs. He touched her where his lips had just been. She became paralyzed, unable and unwilling to move from his touch and his kisses that followed. His tongue became a vessel of pure pleasure as it danced between her legs and maneuvered itself in such a way it left her entire body trembling, longing for him to find his way inside her. She had never remembered feeling such physical glory before, not even with Tristan. She was near delirious with pleasure. She begged Tristan to take her. "Not yet, my love," he whispered inside her ear while he nibbled gently on her ear. He placed his erection outside its destination.

"Please," she pleaded.

He gently thrust himself inside her but refused to move, driving her beyond the limit of passion and lust. Once he began to make love to her ever so slowly, he drove her into a hallucinatory fantasy that ended in a climax that nearly made her heart stop. Tristan fell on top of her carefully so as not to hurt her. She put her arms around him tightly and begged him not to move. "I want to remember this forever," she divulged.

"Baby, this is just the beginning of our lives together. There will be so much more to come." He promised.

* * *

They had three days alone to enjoy every moment together, and every moment was precious. Their closeness caused them to become closer. Their love drove them deeper in love and their kisses led to more kisses. They made love over and over again as though they had never been with anyone else. They spent their time engaged in moving conversations, including wedding plans and their future. They sang songs to one another, they laughed, and then they laughed some more. They celebrated their honeymoon before they were even married. Instead of being star-crossed lovers, like Romeo and Juliet, they were lovers who were stars.

"Would you ever want to give up this lifestyle?" Brooklyn questioned.

Tristan touched her cheek with his two fingers and answered, "It's what we do, love. It's what we know and it's what we love."

She looked at Tristan, knowing he was right, and smiled. "But," he added, "if you want me to give it up, I will . . . for you."

She laughed and said, "I would never allow you to give it up just as you wouldn't allow me to either. It's just that these past three days alone with you have been so amazing, and I try and picture what it would be like to live that way always."

"You would grow tired of it and me," he expressed.

"Never," she said.

He replied, "Because of our lifestyle, these last three days were so very precious. Tomorrow we embark on a brand-new journey, together. And what could be better than doing something we both love together?

* * *

Tristan arrived at the coliseum early to do a sound check. The television cameras had not arrived yet, but the press and several fans had greeted him as he tried to sneak into the auditorium secretly and quietly. The Devils were getting ready together. They were nervous. This was no longer a reality show but actual reality. Brooklyn prepared the four costume changes she would need for the concert. She would paint inside the concert hall backstage and arrive in jeans and a sweatshirt as suggested by Tristan. It was early in the day, but as each second passed, the more nervous and apprehensive the Devils became.

The Devils spent the rest of the morning practicing Brooklyn's surprise for Tristan. She had selected a very special song for him. One that she had considered using for her wedding vows but reconsidered and decided her vows should be written by her. She chose this song because it best fit her and Tristan and she knew he would be touched by it. When Tristan finally walked through the door, she ran into his arms. He laughed and recalled the first day of *So You Wanna Be a Rock Star* and muttered, "Here we go again." The team arrived via limo approximately two hours before show time. Blood Red Orange was first. They would be performing eight songs, after which Devin Liam would be singing three of his own. Next Adonis would be announcing Billy Blaze who agreed to do this one concert as a guest performer. Adonis would then proudly introduce the Precious Little Devils to the world. They would do a set of twelve songs, Brooklyn having to do one costume change in between. The songs were hand-picked by Tristan as were her clothes and the special effects. Tristan agreed to go on after the Devils and do five of his own songs and then "Demons" with Brooklyn. They would be using Tristan's own band from 1980s for his numbers.

The Devils would then take the stage once again and Tristan and Brooklyn would perform three more songs together along with the Devils. Brooklyn would then change quickly and do her encore number—Tristan's surprise. She would call him onto the stage and let him introduce the Devils person by person. She then would announce the dedication. She knew he'd be flawed by her choice but hoped he wouldn't become too emotional.

Five minutes before the beginning of the show, Brooklyn peeked into the audience from behind the stage. The coliseum was filled with a sold out crowd filled with adoring fans. *What a rush*, she thought to herself.

Tristan came up behind her and whispered in her ear, "I'm so proud of you."

She turned and hugged him and said, "Did I ever thank you, for saving my life?"

He mouthed the words "I love you" and she whispered "I love you" right back to him.

After Billy's songs, the Devils nervously awaited the roadies to ready the stage for their debut. Adonis enjoyed his usual place, center stage, and proudly announced the winners of *So You Wanna Be a Rock Star*. Tristan watched from the wings of the stage proudly.

The Devils were awesome. Their special effects were over the top. Tristan applauded after each of their songs, and when they had completed song number twelve, he greeted Brooklyn with hugs and kisses. He was elated at their performance as he became ready for his.

Brooklyn thought Tristan amazingly calm and looked upon that as a personal victory.

All at once Adonis took the stage again. "And now I have the pleasure of presenting the man responsible for the win. I give you the man you've all been waiting for, the rebellious Mr. Tristan Bondage." The audience rose to their feet as Tristan took the stage. Once again Brooklyn fell in love with Tristan all over again. He was electrifying. He began "Demons" by himself and Brooklyn walked on stage to sing the following portion of the verse he began. Their drama filled performance affected the crowd greatly as it had in the past. The two performed three other songs together to an audience uproar, and then they left the stage with the fans begging for more and chanting both Tristan's and Brooklyn's names, one after the other—"Tristan, Brooklyn, Tristan, Brooklyn . . ."

Brooklyn returned to the stage alone as the audience screamed. She thanked the audience and then called Tristan back to join her. Not knowing what she was up to, he went with it and kissed her as soon as he was close enough. On the mic she asked Tristan if he minded introducing the Devils. He shrugged his shoulders as Brooklyn ran behind stage to make one last costume change. She wore a simple white flowing dress almost resembling a wedding dress. "And lastly, my girl, Dazzel Diamonds, on guitar," Tristan said, wondering where the hell Brooklyn was. Tristan then improvised. "The love of his life and what dreams are made of . . . Brooklyn."

Brooklyn caught Tristan's hand as he began to exit the stage. "Tristan, can you hang out for a minute," she asked him using the mic.

"You know I can't deny you anything," he expressed as the congregation laughed.

Brooklyn walked out to the very end of the stage. The lights were dimmed and she began to speak. "I am the luckiest woman in the entire world, especially tonight in front of an amazing, welcoming audience, being the winner of the most spectacular reality show that ever hit the history of television. I'm a part of the most talented band who are not only my colleagues but my true friends as well. I'm blessed with my new, beautiful baby. Where's Shakey?"

Brooklyn demanded. "Can we bring her out to her daddy, please?" Brooklyn insisted. Mary Poppins brought the baby out on stage and handed her to Tristan. The "awwwws" from the fans filled the room as Brooklyn continued to speak. "And then there's Tristan . . . Tristan's had my heart from the very beginning of this journey. He's shown me more love than I ever thought could exist within one person. Trist, I love you so much. This is for you, my love . . . my life," Brooklyn confessed to the world and began to sing "I Choose You" by Sara Bareilles.

> Let the bow break
> Let it come down crashing
> Let the sun fade out to a dark sky
> Can't say I would even notice it was absent
> I could live by the light in your eyes
> I'll unfold before you, what I've strung together
> The very first words of a life-long love letter
> Tell the world that we've finally got it all right
> I choose you . . . I choose you
> I'll become yours and you'll become
> I choose you . . . I choose you

As the clarity of Brooklyn's voice rang through the coliseum, Tristan Buried his head, using Shakey as a shield to hide his tears that came flowing down from his eyes.

> There was a time when
> I would have believed them
> If they told me you could not come true
> Just loves illusion
> But then you found me and everything changed
> And I believe in something again.
> My whole hear, will be yours forever
> This is a beautiful start to a life-long love letter

The only thing that allowed Tristan to hold it together was the fact that he was holding his baby. If not for the baby, the emotional Tristan would have lost it beyond the point of being consoled.

We are not perfect
We'll learn from our mistakes
As it as it takes
I will prove my love to you
I am not scared of the elements
I'm under prepared but I am willing
And even better, I get to be the other
half of you

Brooklyn walked over to Tristan and Shakey and touched his face as she completed the finale.

Tell the world that we finally got it all right
I choose you . . . I choose you
I'll become yours and you'll become mine
I choose you . . . I choose you . . .

As she sang the last "I choose you," Tristan handed Shakey to Dazzel, lifted Brooklyn's face, ignoring the world around him, and kissed his bride through tears of joy and emotion, in a celebration of life.

And the stage grew dark.

About the Author

I was born in Brooklyn, am the messiah to my mother, and wrote a best-selling book, *The Star Trek Medical Reference Manual*, at age twenty. More recently I write for *Get Out!* magazine, a gay weekly tabloid, where I do all the features and covers and celebrity interviews. I also write for *Louder Than War*, a music magazine based in the UK, as well as the *Huffington Post* blogs.

I run and produce a drag pageant, now celebrating its fortieth-year anniversary, something inherited by me when I bought a flamboyant gay nightclub on Long Island, where I live now, with my three children and my nine baby grandchildren, as well as my gay soul mate, Colin.